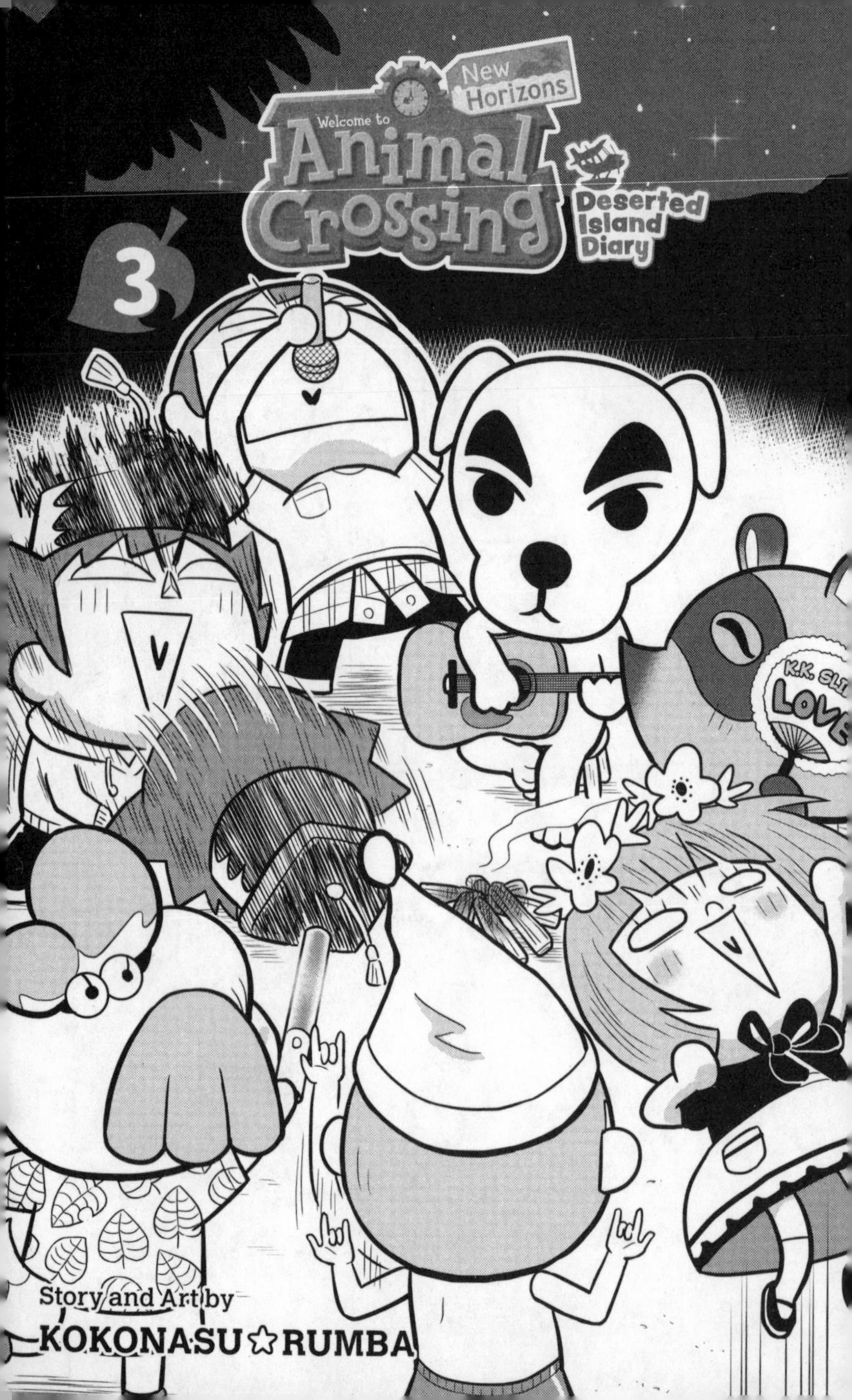
New Horizons
Welcome to
Animal Crossing
Deserted Island Diary
3
Story and Art by
KOKONASU☆RUMBA

DESERTED ISLAND PALS

Himepoyo
One of Coroyuki's friends. This strong-willed princess is richer than rich!

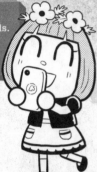

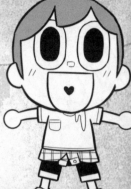

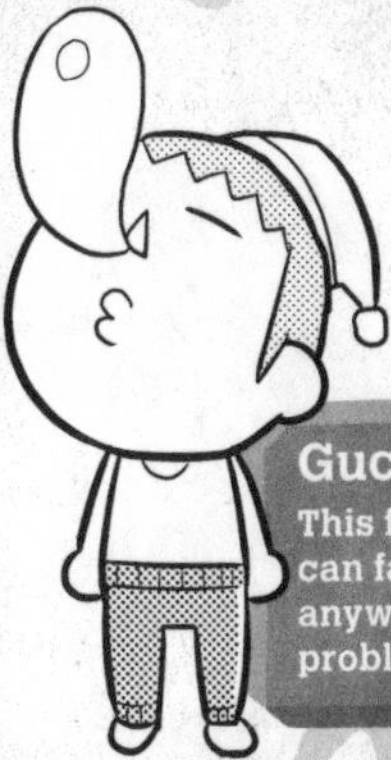

Guchan
This friend of Coroyuki's can fall asleep anytime, anywhere, with no problem!

Coroyuki
The leader of this group is a glutton with endless curiosity!

Tom Nook
As the head of Nook Inc., he's here to support everyone's island lifestyle!

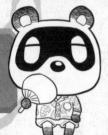

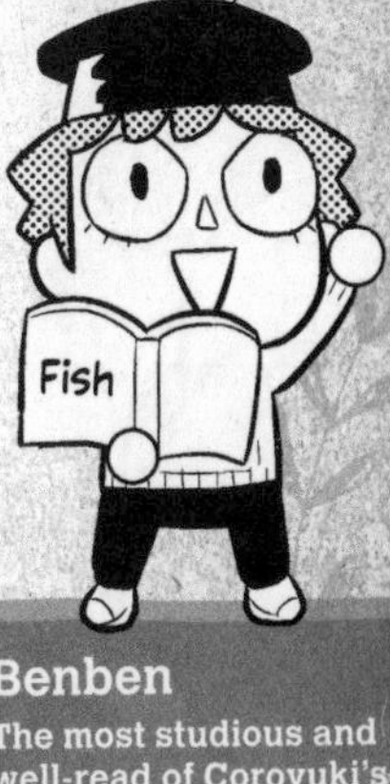

Fish

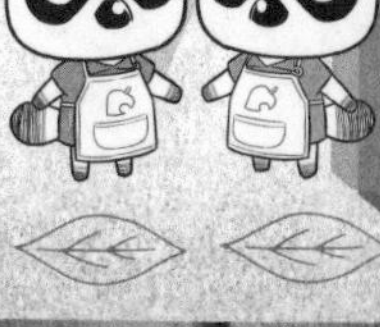

Timmy & Tommy
The twins who run Nook's Cranny. Timmy is technically older.

Benben
The most studious and well-read of Coroyuki's friends!

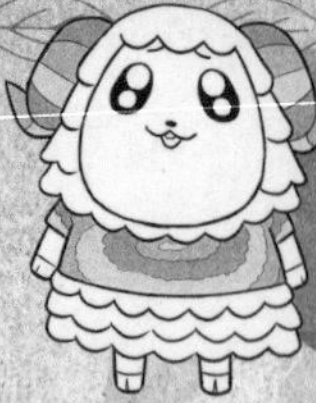

Dom
An excitable sheep resident with adorably round eyes. Fun fact: He's into bodybuilding.

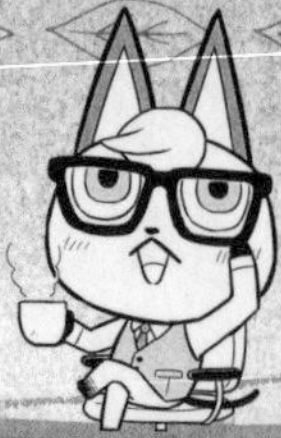

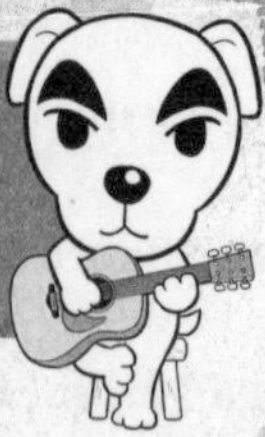

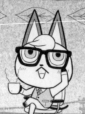

K.K. Slider
This roaming musician is as hip as they come.

Raymond
This stylish narcissist resides on the island. His catchphrase is "crisp"!

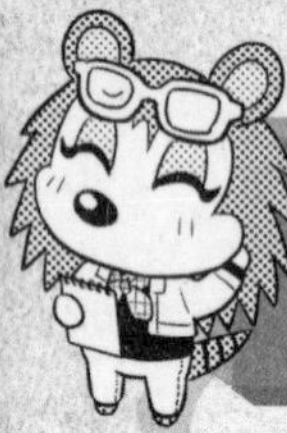

Label
A fashion designer always in search of cutting-edge styles.

Isabelle
Reliable and kind, she's the consultant who works at Resident Services.

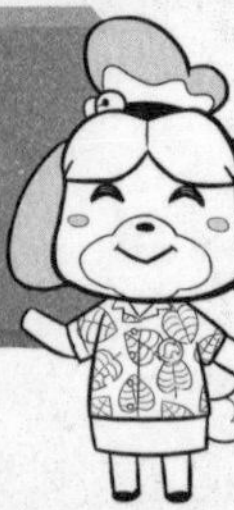

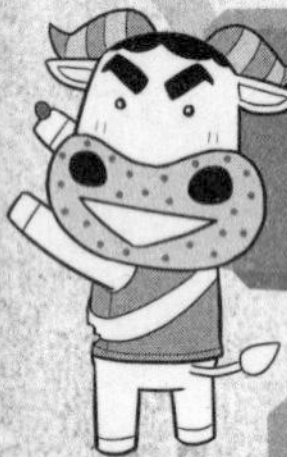

Coach
A new island resident known for his ever-present stubble.

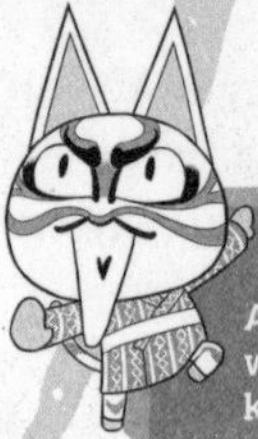

Kabuki
A new island resident who resembles a kabuki theater actor.

Harvey
Owner of the Photopia photo studio. Very easygoing.

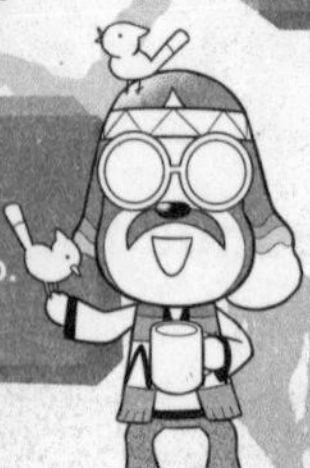

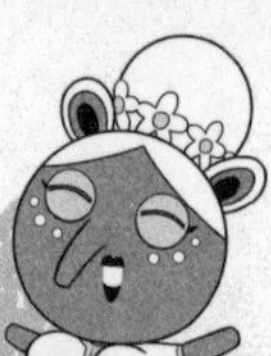

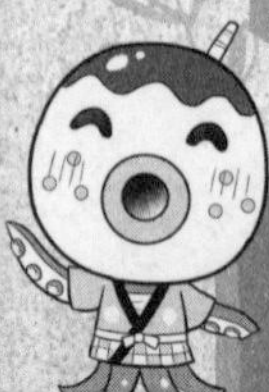

Zucker
A new island resident who makes a splash on his very first day!

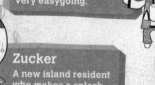

Luna
A dream therapist who guides you to islands you never could have imagined.

CONTENTS

Fall Is for Letting Your Fashion Flag Fly 5

Feel Our Passion, K.K. Slider! 21

So You Want to Build a Perfect Snowboy 37

100 Secret Tips to Having a Happy New Year . . 50

The Ultimate Photoshoot! 62

Need Some Action? Try Dream Islands 77

Make Anything at All with DIYs! 94

At Last, Time to Name the Island! 101

Bonus Diary

• • • • • • • • • • • • •

Rumba-Style Animal Breakdown . . . 118

Rumba's ACNH Game Diary 120

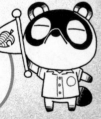

FALL IS FOR LETTING YOUR FASHION FLAG FLY

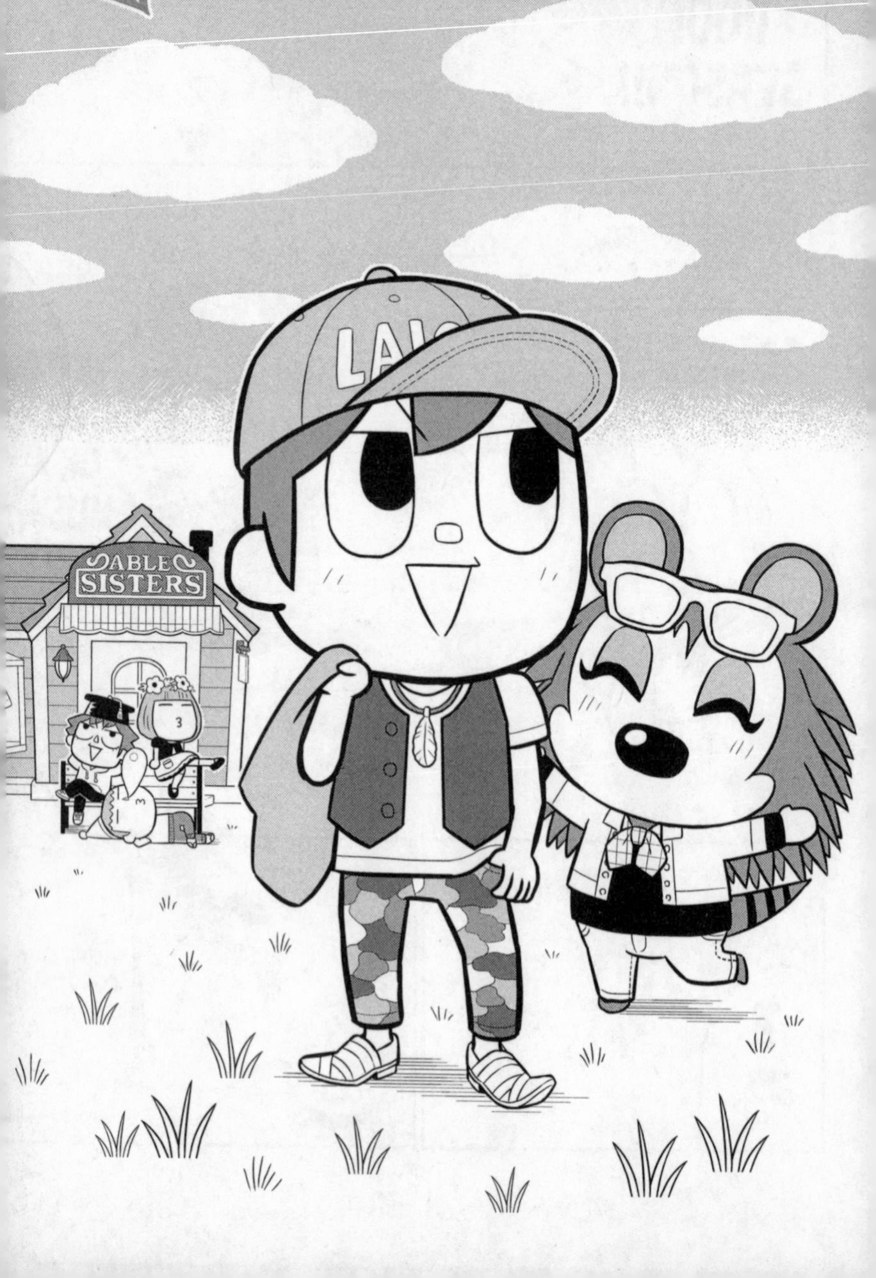
ABLE SISTERS
LA

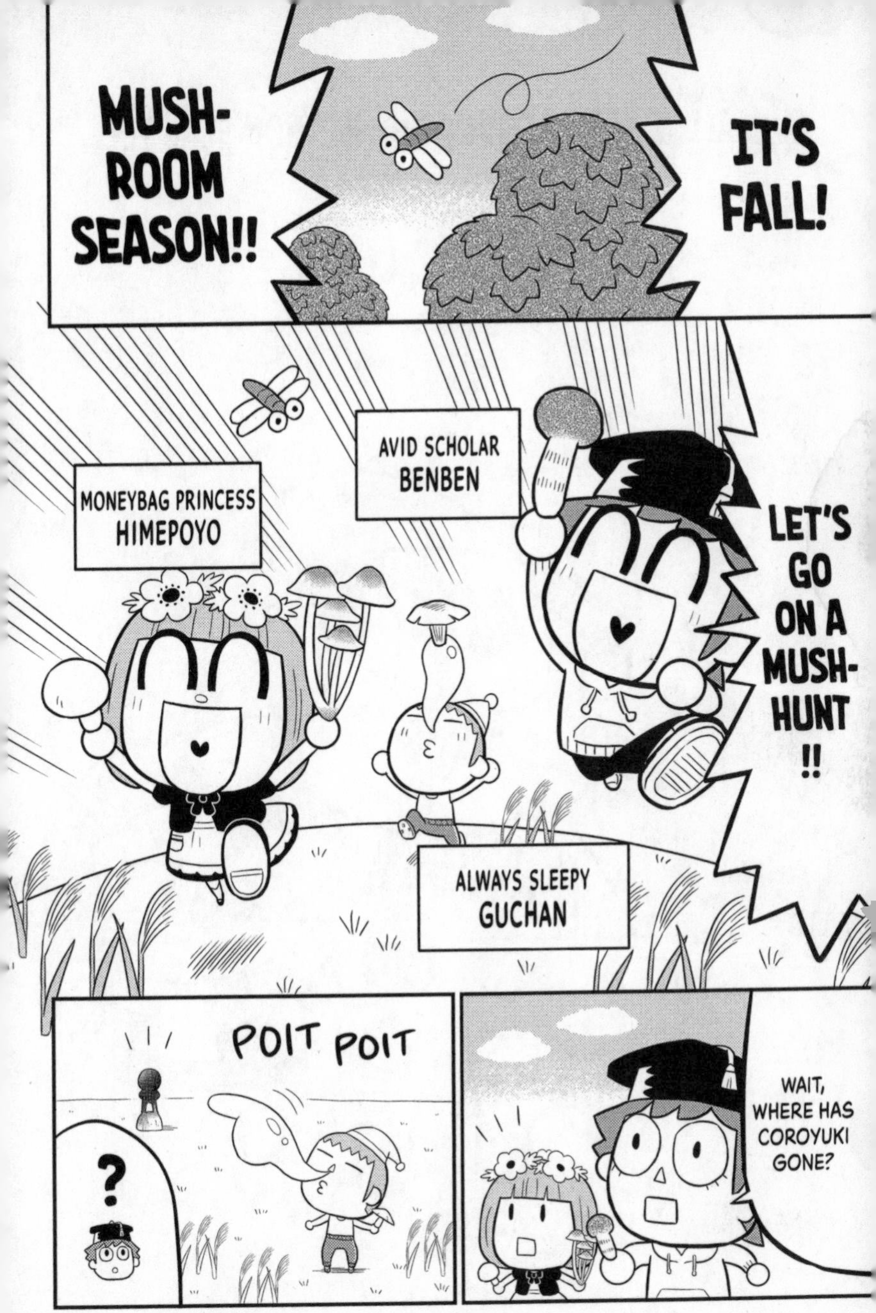
IT'S FALL!
MUSH-ROOM SEASON!!
LET'S GO ON A MUSH-HUNT!!
AVID SCHOLAR BENBEN
MONEYBAG PRINCESS HIMEPOYO
ALWAYS SLEEPY GUCHAN
WAIT, WHERE HAS COROYUKI GONE?
POIT POIT
?

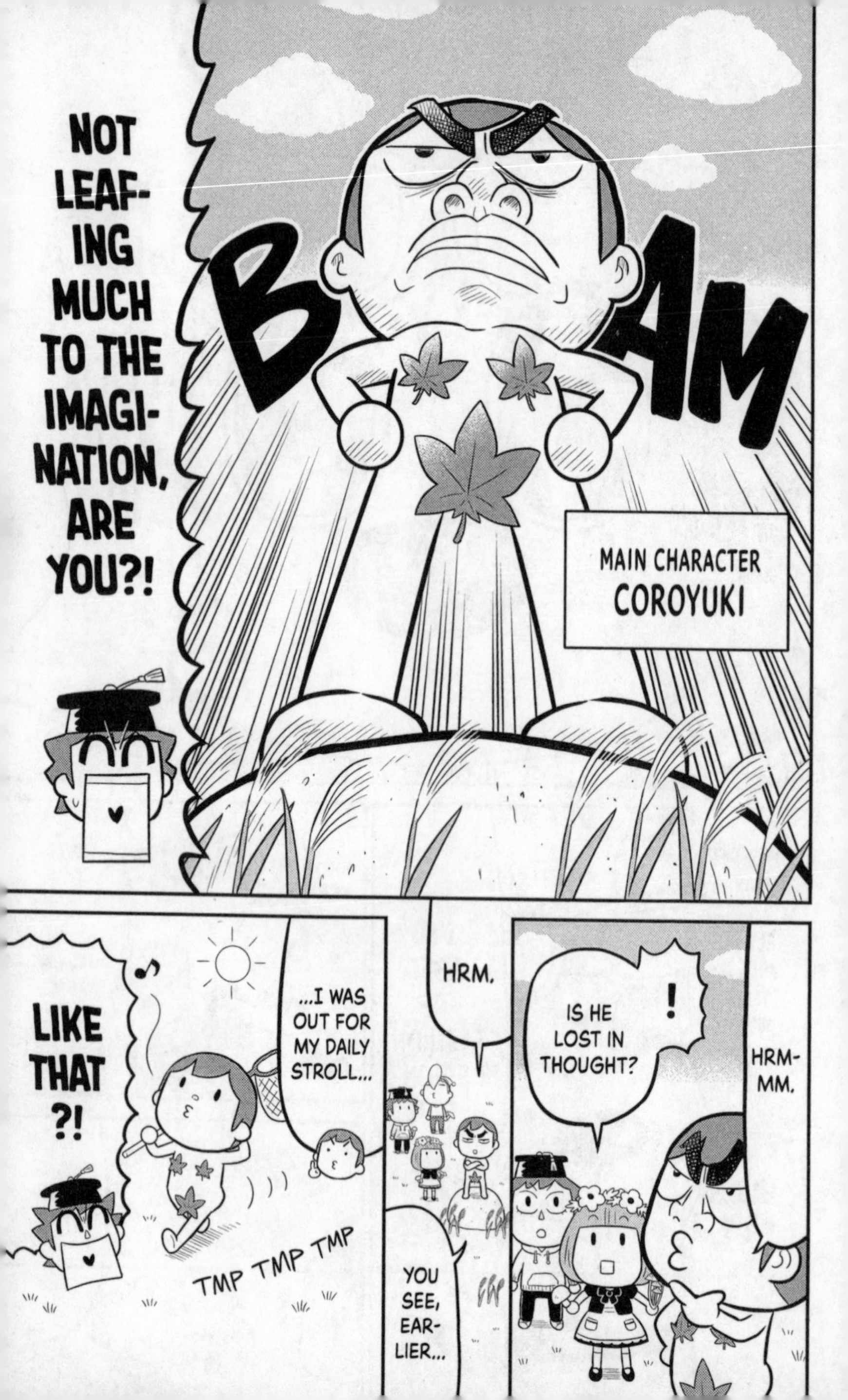
BAM
MAIN CHARACTER COROYUKI
NOT LEAFING MUCH TO THE IMAGINATION, ARE YOU?!
HRM-MM.
!
IS HE LOST IN THOUGHT?
HRM.
YOU SEE, EARLIER...
...I WAS OUT FOR MY DAILY STROLL...
LIKE THAT?!
TMP TMP TMP

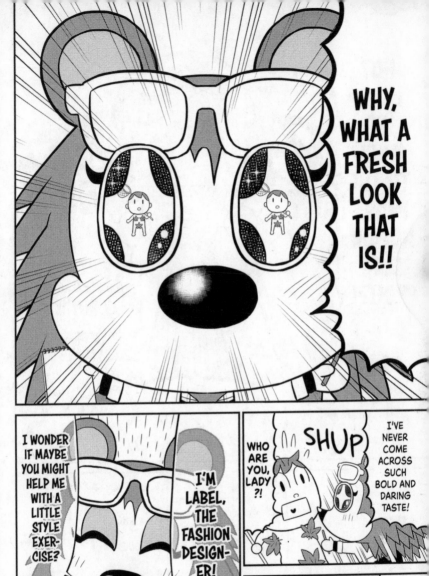

WHY, WHAT A FRESH LOOK THAT IS!!

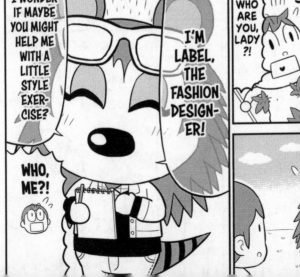

I WONDER IF MAYBE YOU MIGHT HELP ME WITH A LITTLE STYLE EXERCISE?

I'M LABEL, THE FASHION DESIGNER!

WHO, ME?!

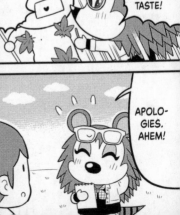

WHO ARE YOU, LADY?!

SHUP

I'VE NEVER COME ACROSS SUCH BOLD AND DARING TASTE!

APOLOGIES, AHEM!

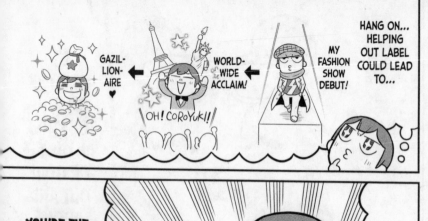

HANG ON... HELPING OUT LABEL COULD LEAD TO...

MY FASHION SHOW DEBUT!

WORLD-WIDE ACCLAIM!

GAZIL-LION-AIRE ♥

OH! COROYUKI!!

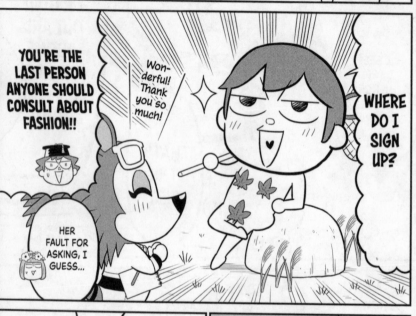

YOU'RE THE LAST PERSON ANYONE SHOULD CONSULT ABOUT FASHION!!

Wonderful! Thank you so much!

WHERE DO I SIGN UP?

HER FAULT FOR ASKING, I GUESS...

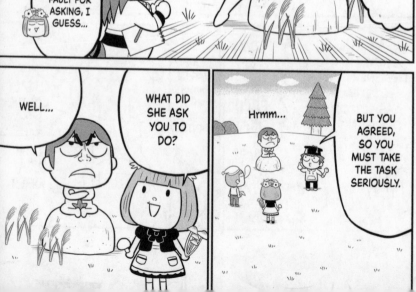

WELL...

WHAT DID SHE ASK YOU TO DO?

Hrmm...

BUT YOU AGREED, SO YOU MUST TAKE THE TASK SERIOUSLY.

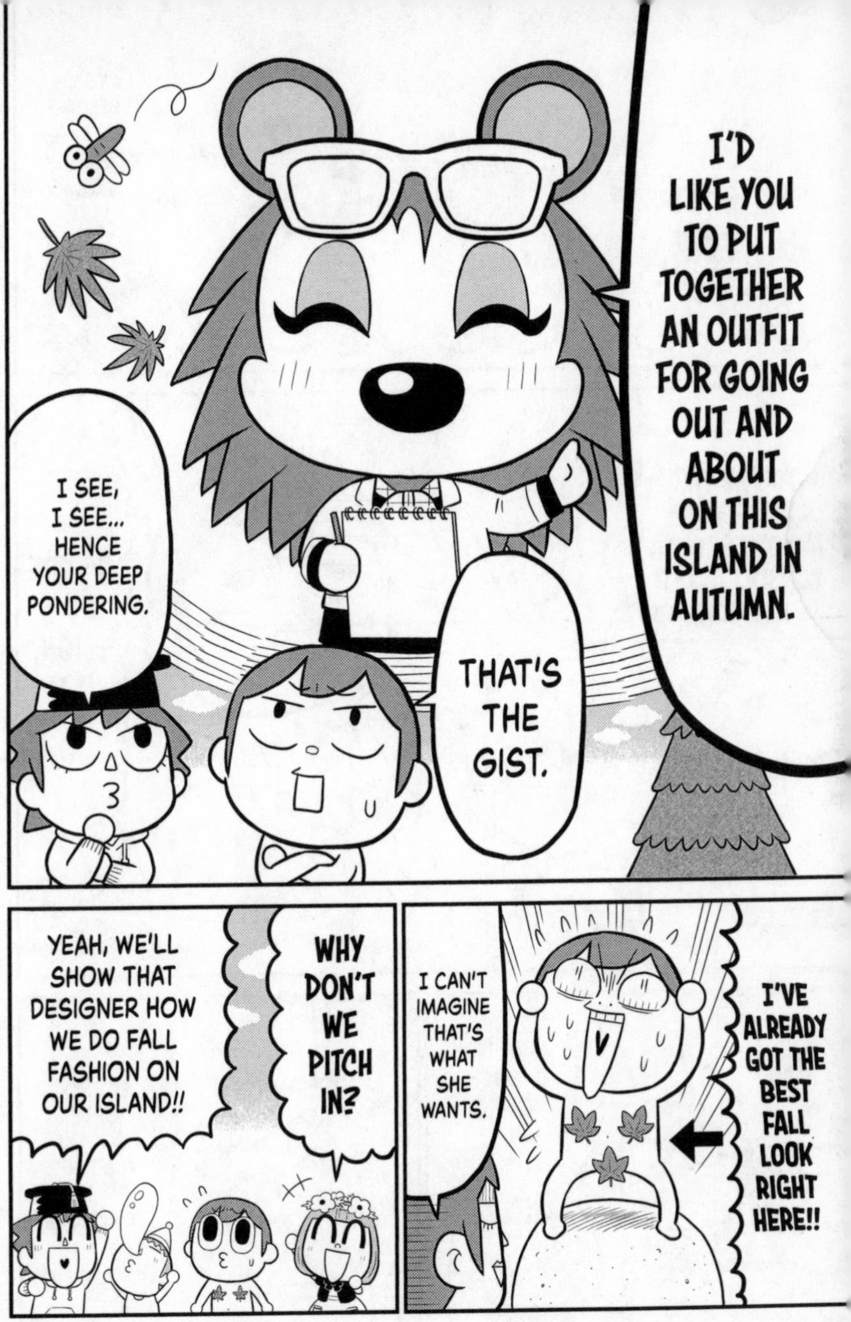
I'D LIKE YOU TO PUT TOGETHER AN OUTFIT FOR GOING OUT AND ABOUT ON THIS ISLAND IN AUTUMN.
THAT'S THE GIST.
I SEE, I SEE... HENCE YOUR DEEP PONDERING.
I'VE ALREADY GOT THE BEST FALL LOOK RIGHT HERE!!
I CAN'T IMAGINE THAT'S WHAT SHE WANTS.
WHY DON'T WE PITCH IN?
YEAH, WE'LL SHOW THAT DESIGNER HOW WE DO FALL FASHION ON OUR ISLAND!!

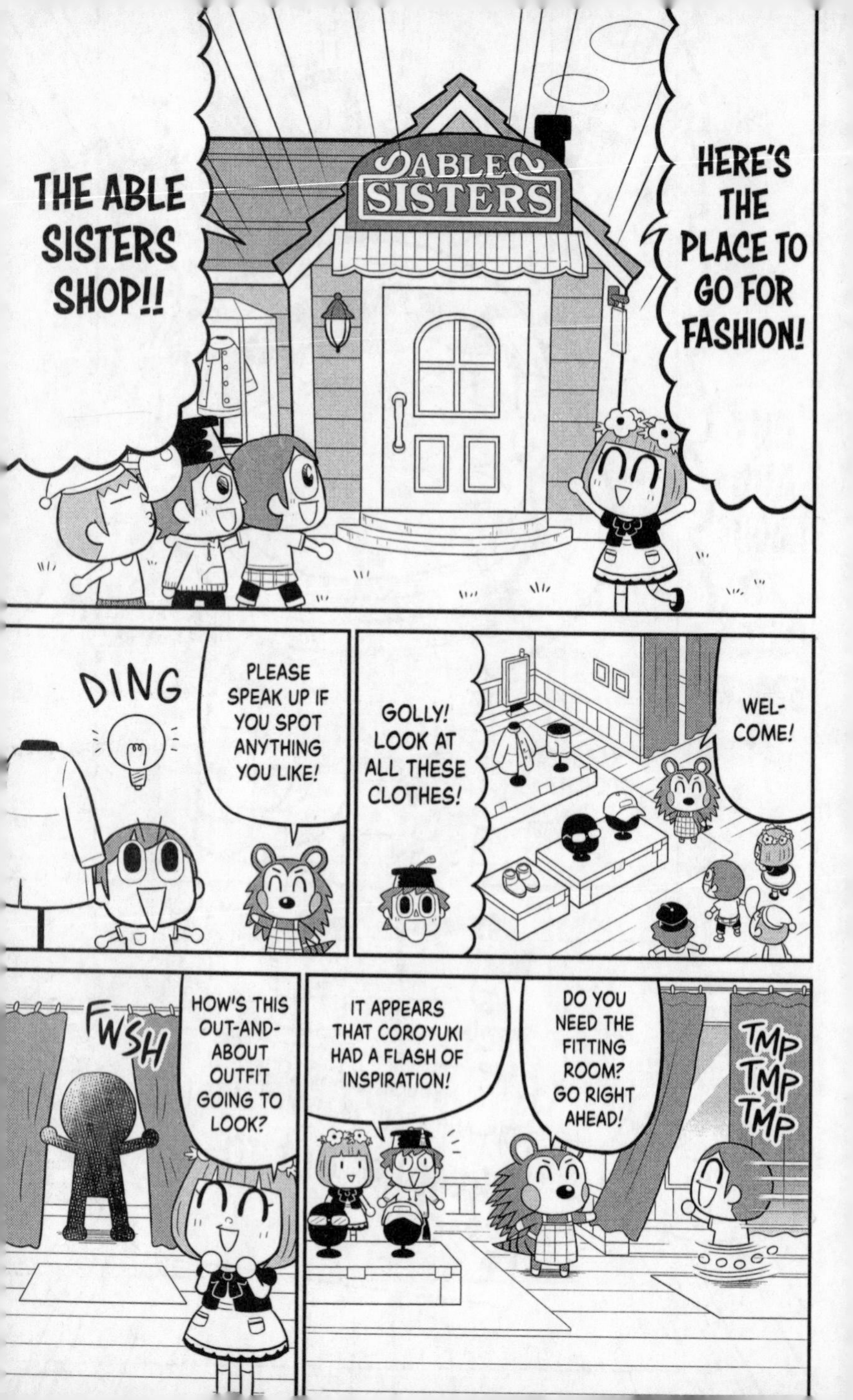
HERE'S THE PLACE TO GO FOR FASHION!
ABLE SISTERS
THE ABLE SISTERS SHOP!!
WEL-COME!
GOLLY! LOOK AT ALL THESE CLOTHES!
PLEASE SPEAK UP IF YOU SPOT ANYTHING YOU LIKE!
DING
TMP TMP TMP
DO YOU NEED THE FITTING ROOM? GO RIGHT AHEAD!
IT APPEARS THAT COROYUKI HAD A FLASH OF INSPIRATION!
HOW'S THIS OUT-AND-ABOUT OUTFIT GOING TO LOOK?
FWSH

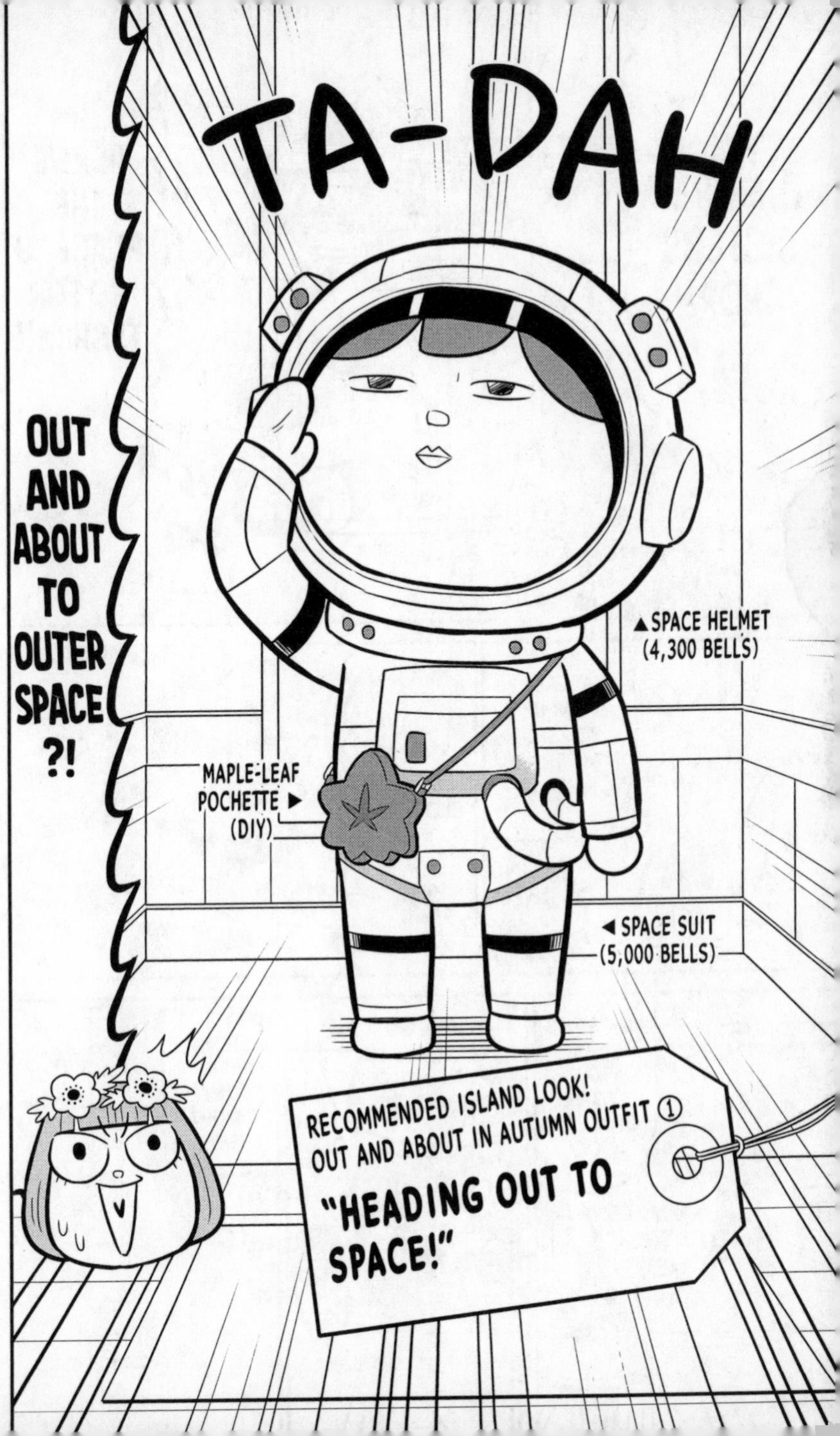
TA-DAH
OUT AND ABOUT TO OUTER SPACE ?!
▲SPACE HELMET (4,300 BELLS)
MAPLE-LEAF POCHETTE ▶ (DIY)
◀SPACE SUIT (5,000 BELLS)
RECOMMENDED ISLAND LOOK!
OUT AND ABOUT IN AUTUMN OUTFIT ①
"HEADING OUT TO SPACE!"

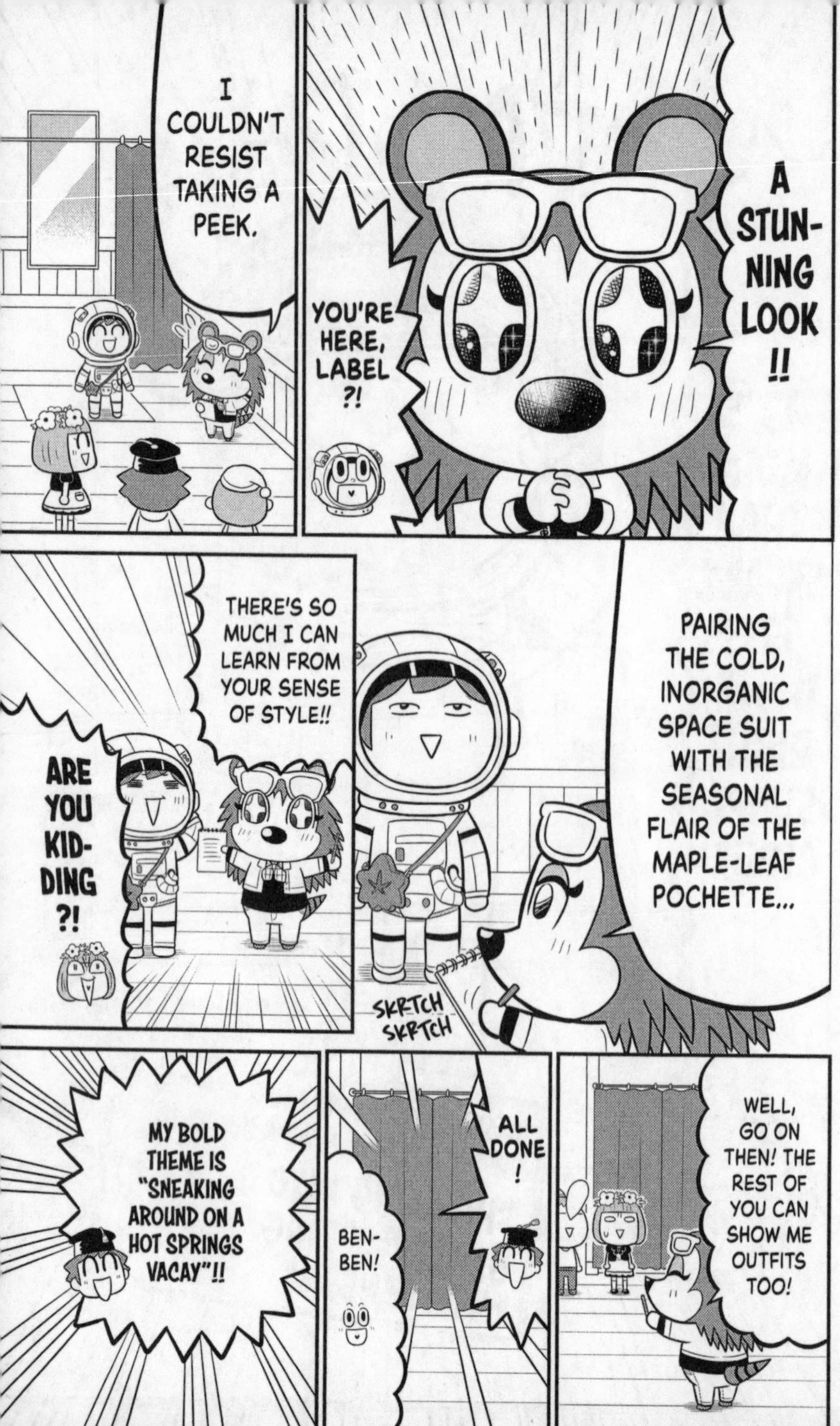
A STUNNING LOOK!!
YOU'RE HERE, LABEL?!
I COULDN'T RESIST TAKING A PEEK.
PAIRING THE COLD, INORGANIC SPACE SUIT WITH THE SEASONAL FLAIR OF THE MAPLE-LEAF POCHETTE...
SKRTCH SKRTCH
THERE'S SO MUCH I CAN LEARN FROM YOUR SENSE OF STYLE!!
ARE YOU KIDDING?!
WELL, GO ON THEN! THE REST OF YOU CAN SHOW ME OUTFITS TOO!
ALL DONE!
BEN-BEN!
MY BOLD THEME IS "SNEAKING AROUND ON A HOT SPRINGS VACAY"!!

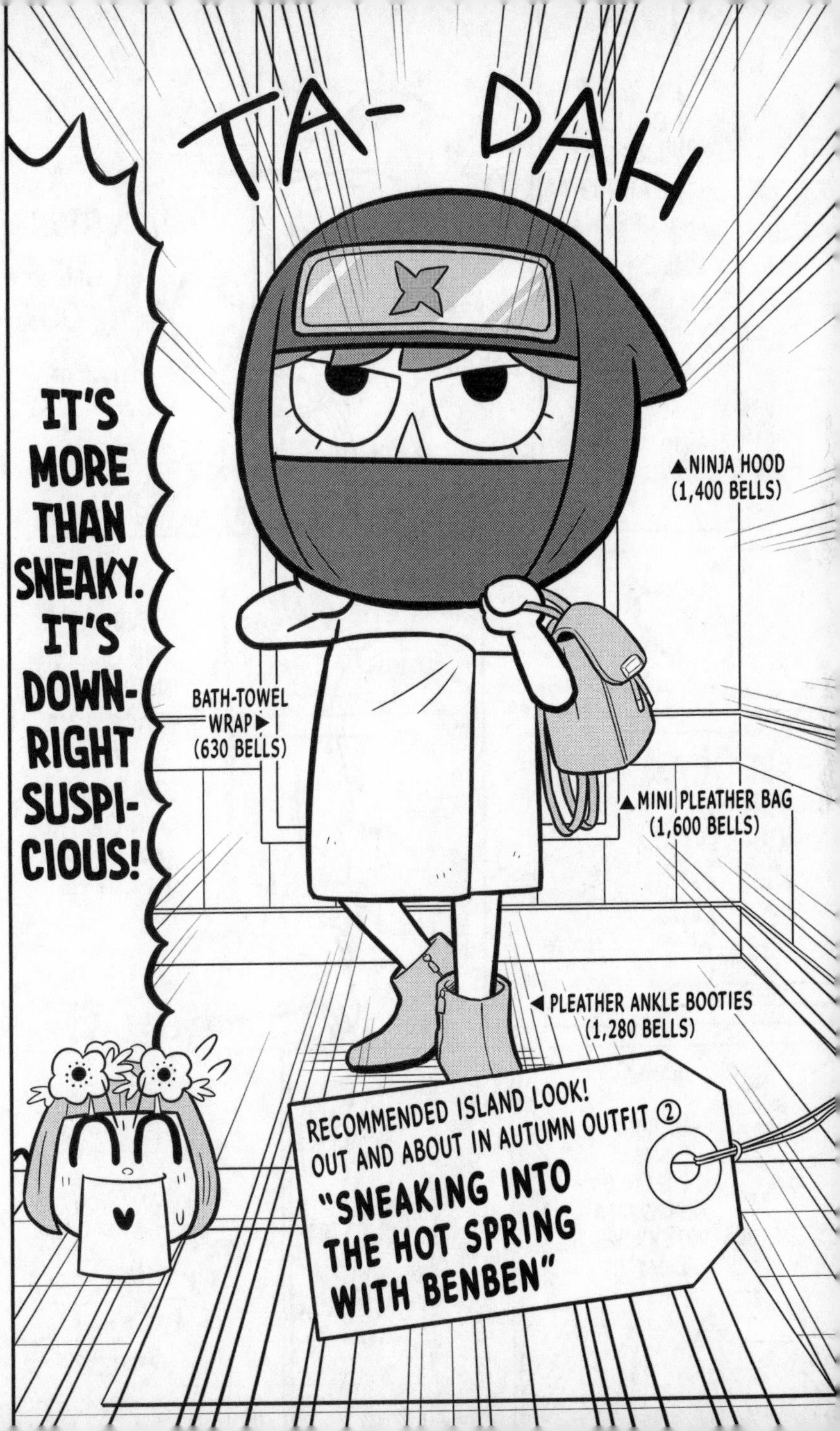
TA-DAH
▲NINJA HOOD (1,400 BELLS)
IT'S MORE THAN SNEAKY. IT'S DOWN-RIGHT SUSPI-CIOUS!
BATH-TOWEL WRAP▶ (630 BELLS)
▲MINI PLEATHER BAG (1,600 BELLS)
◀PLEATHER ANKLE BOOTIES (1,280 BELLS)
RECOMMENDED ISLAND LOOK! OUT AND ABOUT IN AUTUMN OUTFIT ②
"SNEAKING INTO THE HOT SPRING WITH BENBEN"

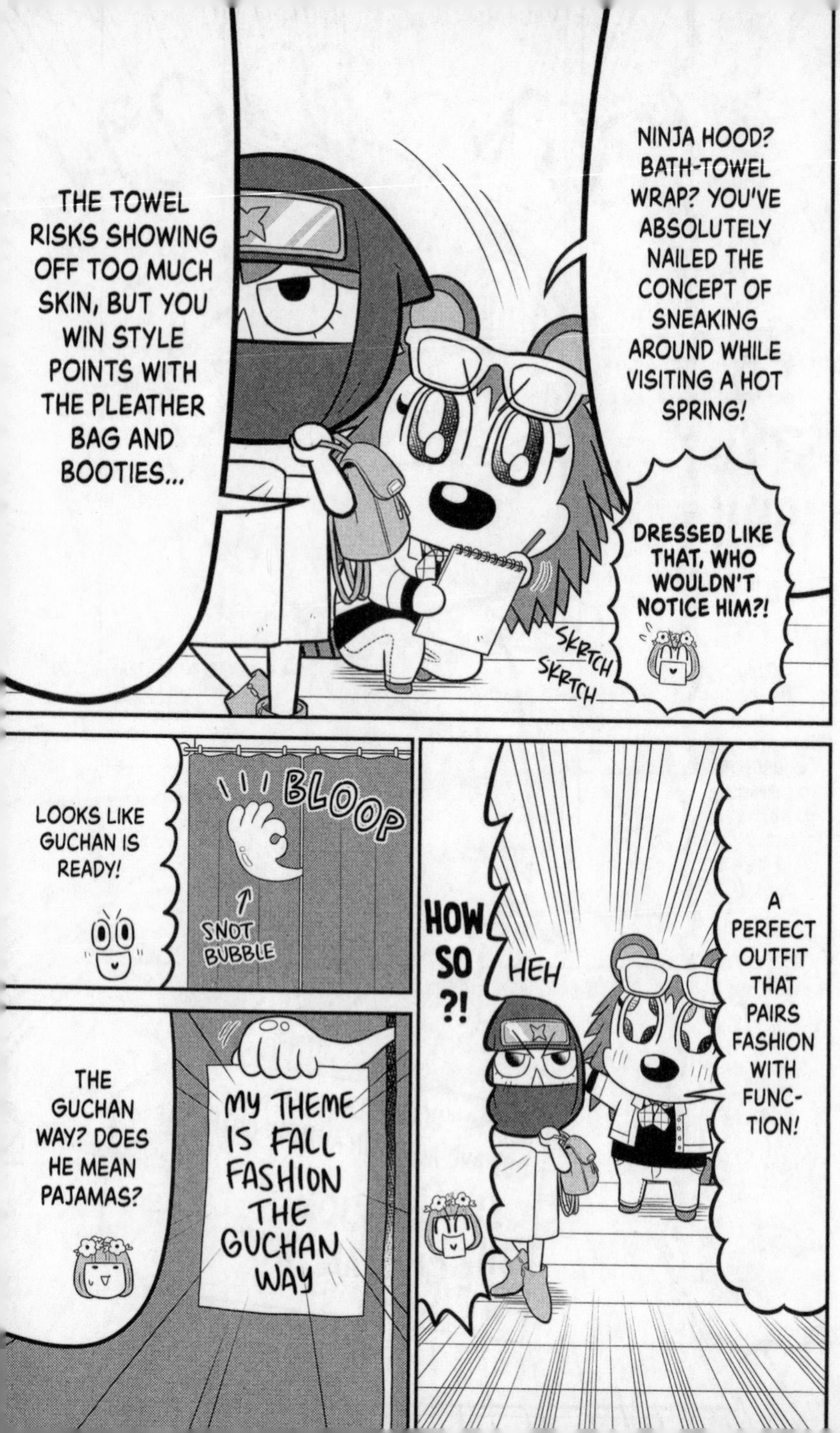
NINJA HOOD? BATH-TOWEL WRAP? YOU'VE ABSOLUTELY NAILED THE CONCEPT OF SNEAKING AROUND WHILE VISITING A HOT SPRING!
THE TOWEL RISKS SHOWING OFF TOO MUCH SKIN, BUT YOU WIN STYLE POINTS WITH THE PLEATHER BAG AND BOOTIES...
DRESSED LIKE THAT, WHO WOULDN'T NOTICE HIM?!
SKRTCH SKRTCH
A PERFECT OUTFIT THAT PAIRS FASHION WITH FUNC-TION!
HOW SO?!
HEH
BLOOP
LOOKS LIKE GUCHAN IS READY!
SNOT BUBBLE
MY THEME IS FALL FASHION THE GUCHAN WAY
THE GUCHAN WAY? DOES HE MEAN PAJAMAS?

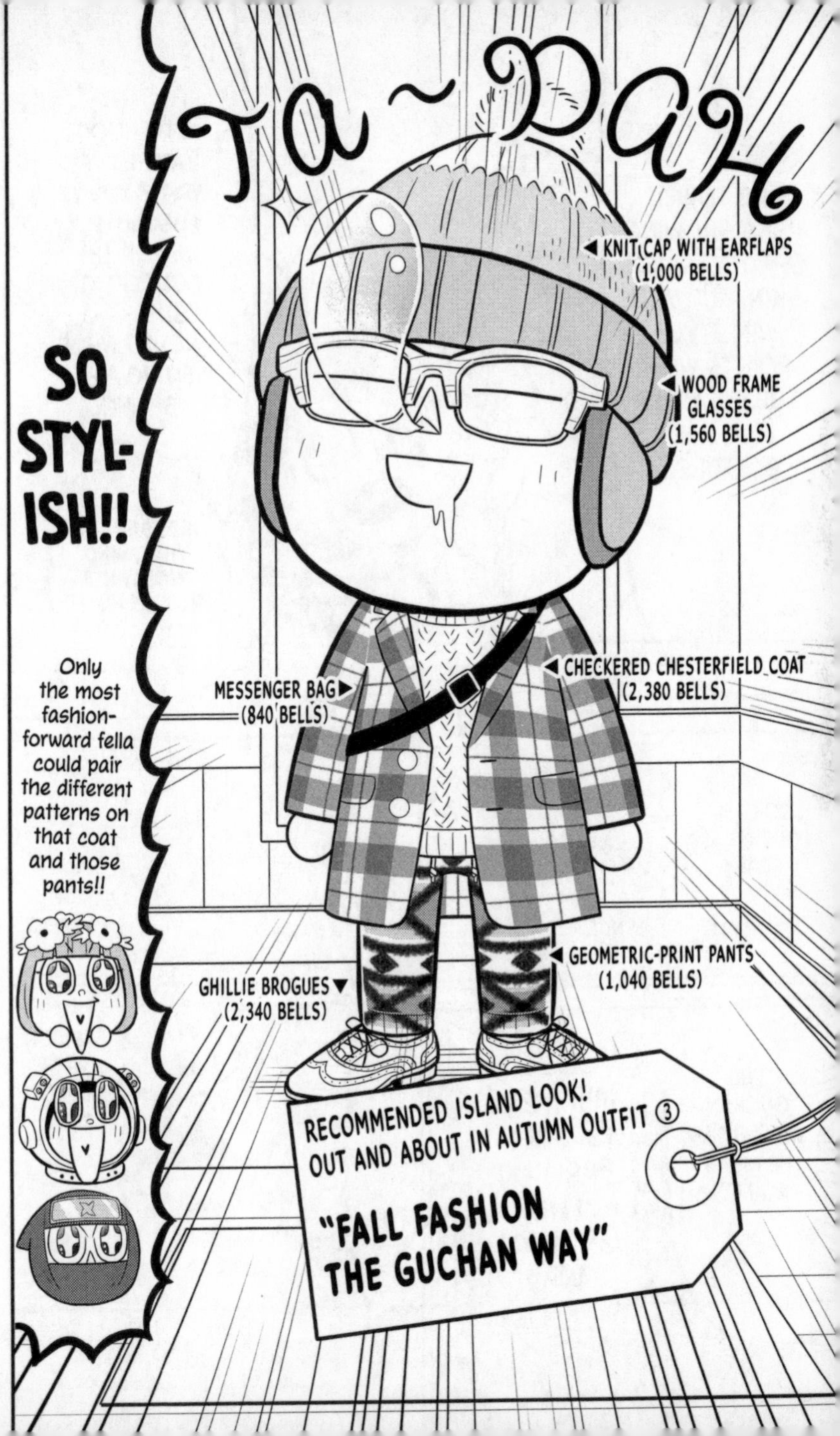

TA~DAH
KNIT CAP WITH EARFLAPS (1,000 BELLS)
WOOD FRAME GLASSES (1,560 BELLS)
CHECKERED CHESTERFIELD COAT (2,380 BELLS)
MESSENGER BAG (840 BELLS)
GEOMETRIC-PRINT PANTS (1,040 BELLS)
GHILLIE BROGUES (2,340 BELLS)
RECOMMENDED ISLAND LOOK! OUT AND ABOUT IN AUTUMN OUTFIT ③
"FALL FASHION THE GUCHAN WAY"
SO STYLISH!!
Only the most fashion-forward fella could pair the different patterns on that coat and those pants!!

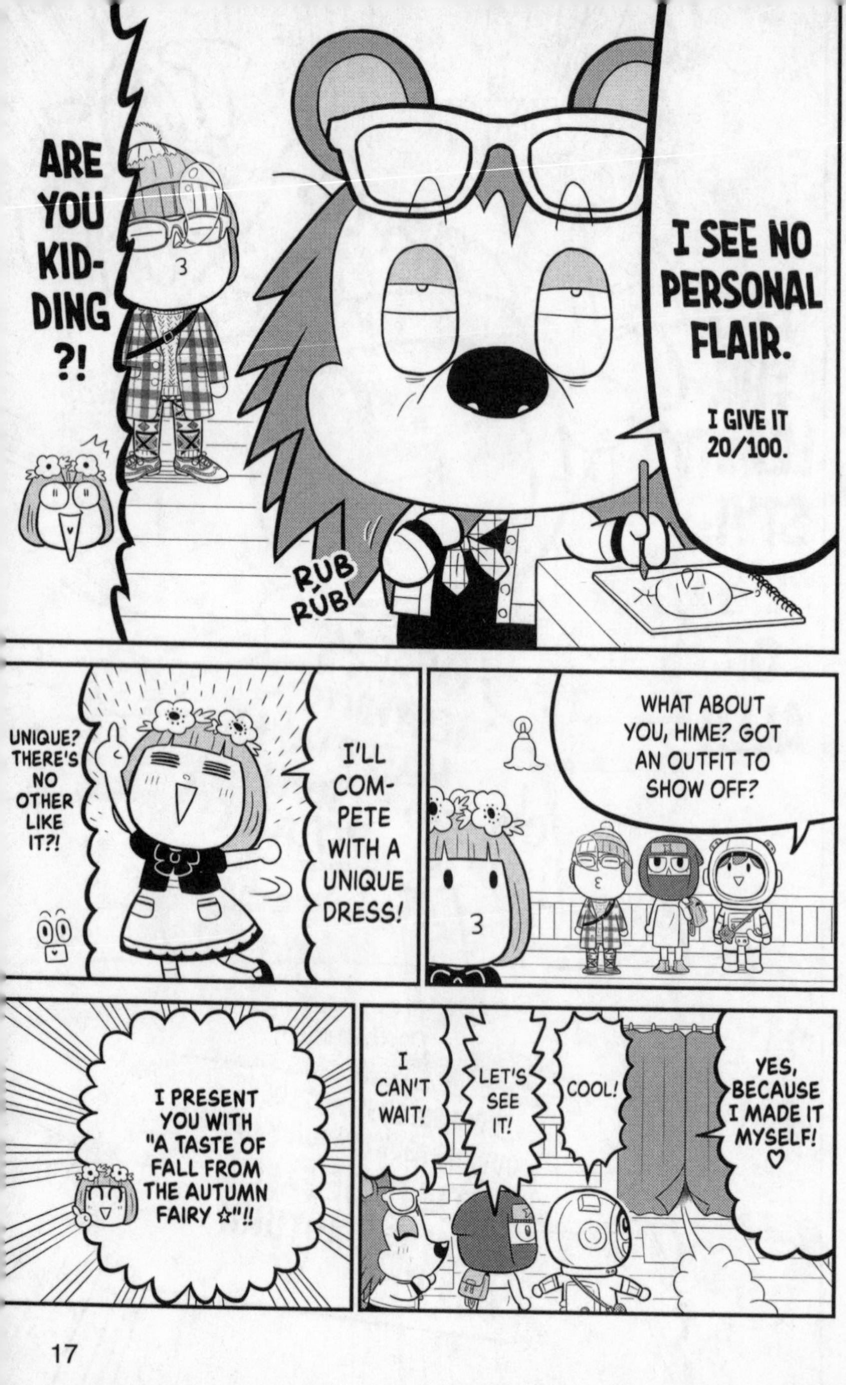
I SEE NO PERSONAL FLAIR.
I GIVE IT 20/100.
ARE YOU KID-DING?!
RUB RUB
WHAT ABOUT YOU, HIME? GOT AN OUTFIT TO SHOW OFF?
I'LL COM-PETE WITH A UNIQUE DRESS!
UNIQUE? THERE'S NO OTHER LIKE IT?!
YES, BECAUSE I MADE IT MYSELF! ♡
COOL!
LET'S SEE IT!
I CAN'T WAIT!
I PRESENT YOU WITH "A TASTE OF FALL FROM THE AUTUMN FAIRY ☆"!!

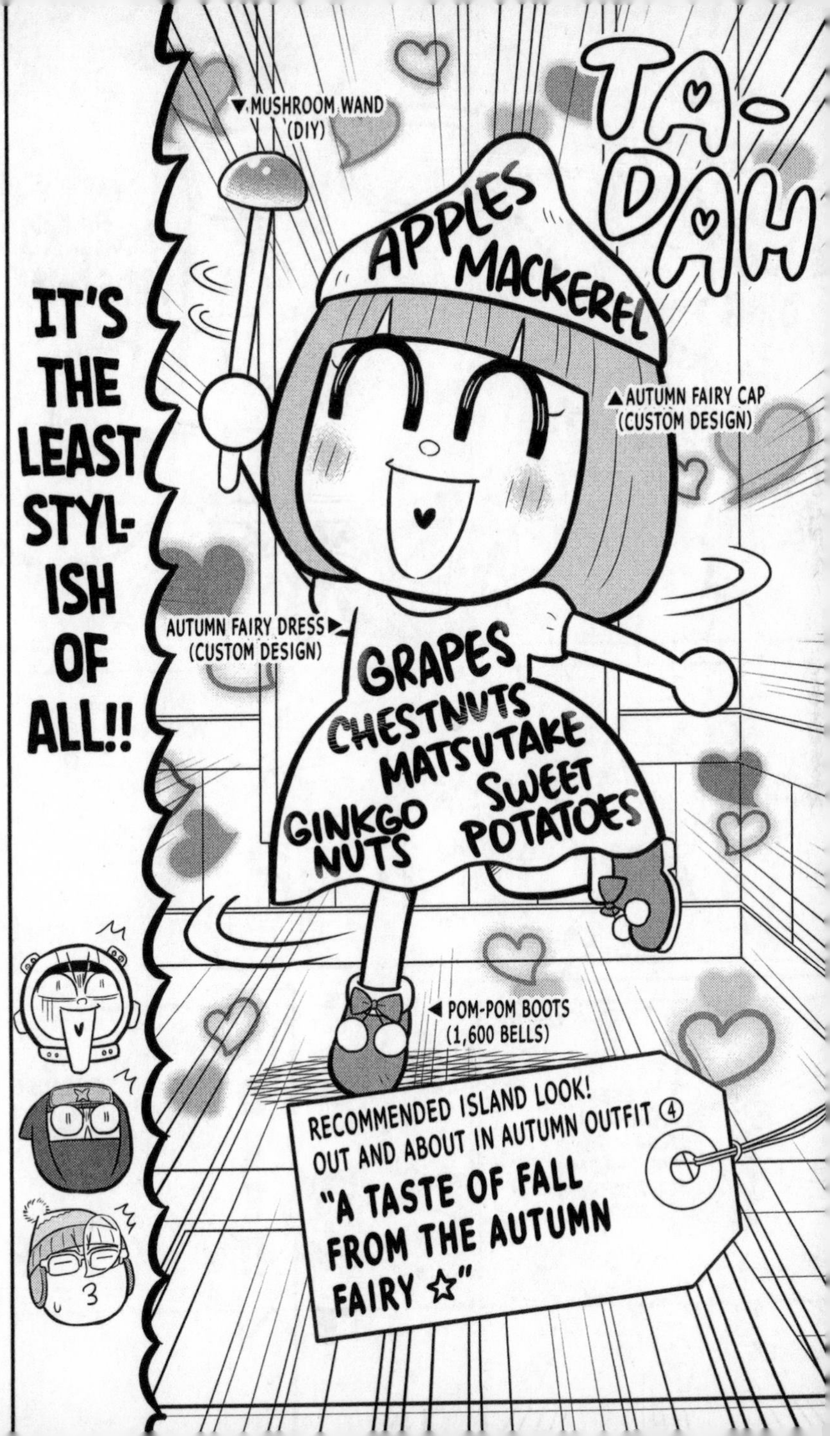
TA-DAH
▼MUSHROOM WAND (DIY)
APPLES MACKEREL
▲AUTUMN FAIRY CAP (CUSTOM DESIGN)
AUTUMN FAIRY DRESS► (CUSTOM DESIGN)
GRAPES CHESTNUTS MATSUTAKE SWEET POTATOES GINKGO NUTS
◄POM-POM BOOTS (1,600 BELLS)
RECOMMENDED ISLAND LOOK! OUT AND ABOUT IN AUTUMN OUTFIT ④
"A TASTE OF FALL FROM THE AUTUMN FAIRY ☆"
IT'S THE LEAST STYLISH OF ALL!!

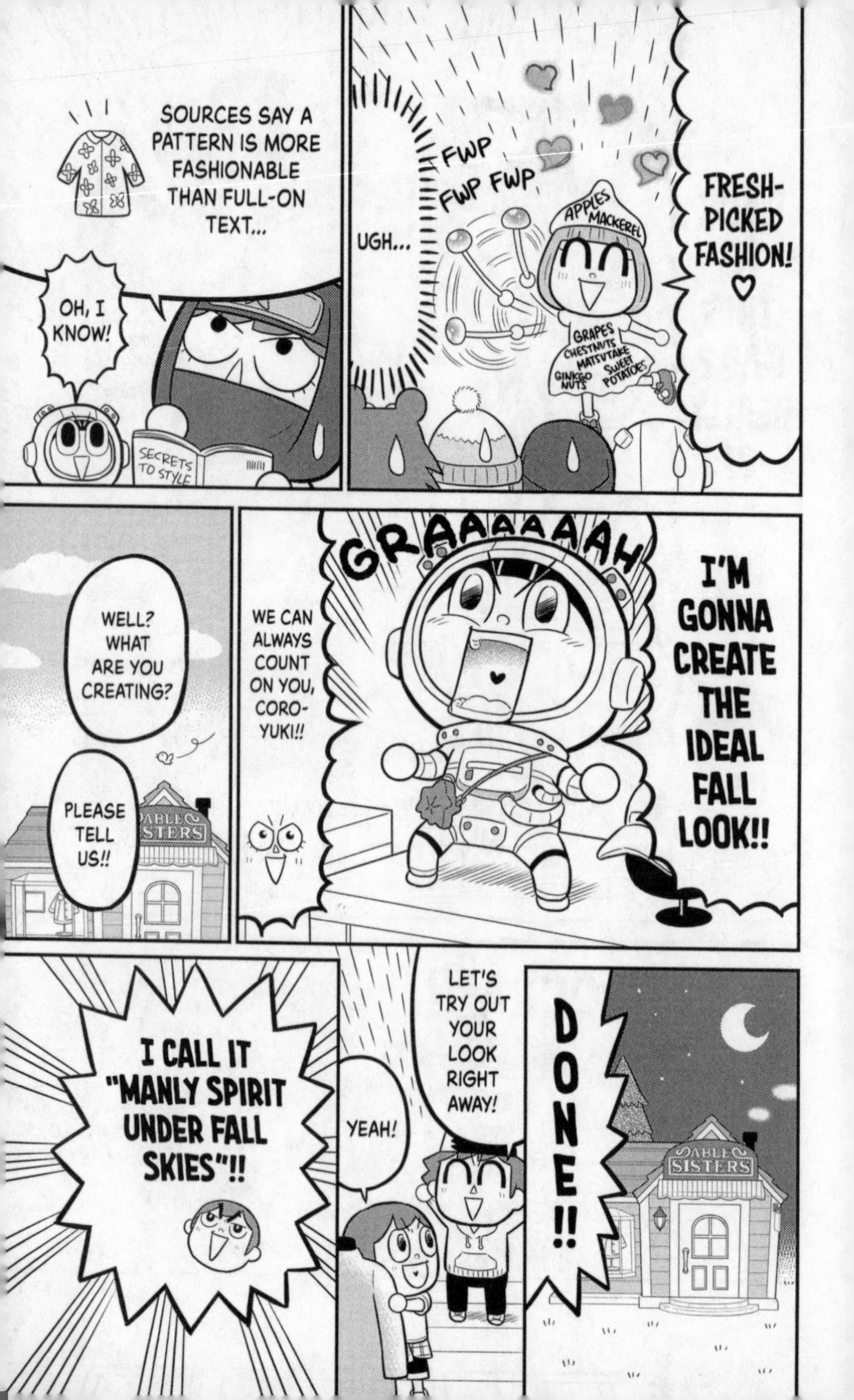
FRESH-PICKED FASHION! ♡
APPLES MACKEREL
GRAPES CHESTNUTS MATSUTAKE GINKGO NUTS SWEET POTATOES
FWP FWP FWP
UGH...
SOURCES SAY A PATTERN IS MORE FASHIONABLE THAN FULL-ON TEXT...
OH, I KNOW!
SECRETS TO STYLE
GRAAAAAAH
I'M GONNA CREATE THE IDEAL FALL LOOK!!
WE CAN ALWAYS COUNT ON YOU, CORO-YUKI!!
WELL? WHAT ARE YOU CREATING?
PLEASE TELL US!!
ABLE SISTERS
DONE!!
ABLE SISTERS
LET'S TRY OUT YOUR LOOK RIGHT AWAY!
YEAH!
I CALL IT "MANLY SPIRIT UNDER FALL SKIES"!!

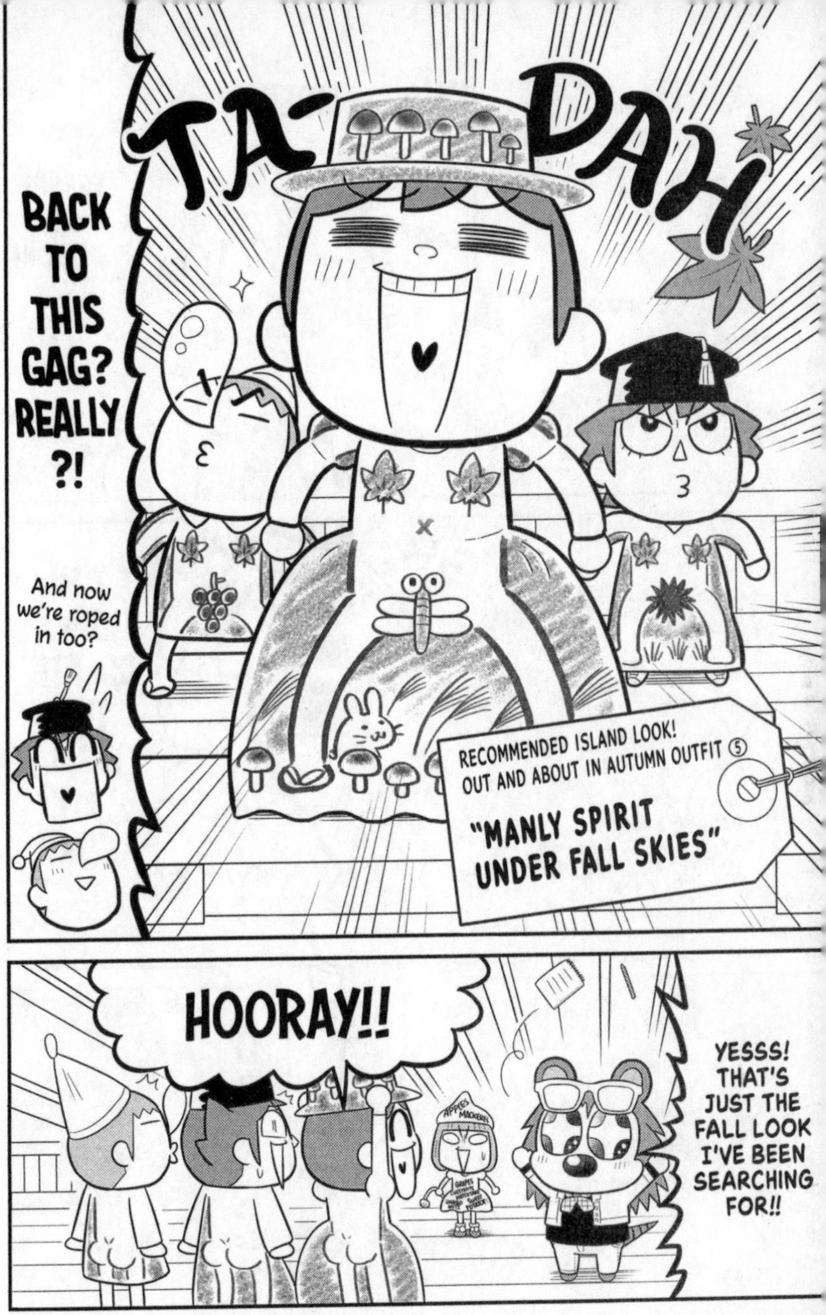
TA-DAH
RECOMMENDED ISLAND LOOK!
OUT AND ABOUT IN AUTUMN OUTFIT ⑤
"MANLY SPIRIT UNDER FALL SKIES"
BACK TO THIS GAG? REALLY?!
And now we're roped in too?
YESSS! THAT'S JUST THE FALL LOOK I'VE BEEN SEARCHING FOR!!
HOORAY!!

FEEL OUR PASSION, K.K. SLIDER!

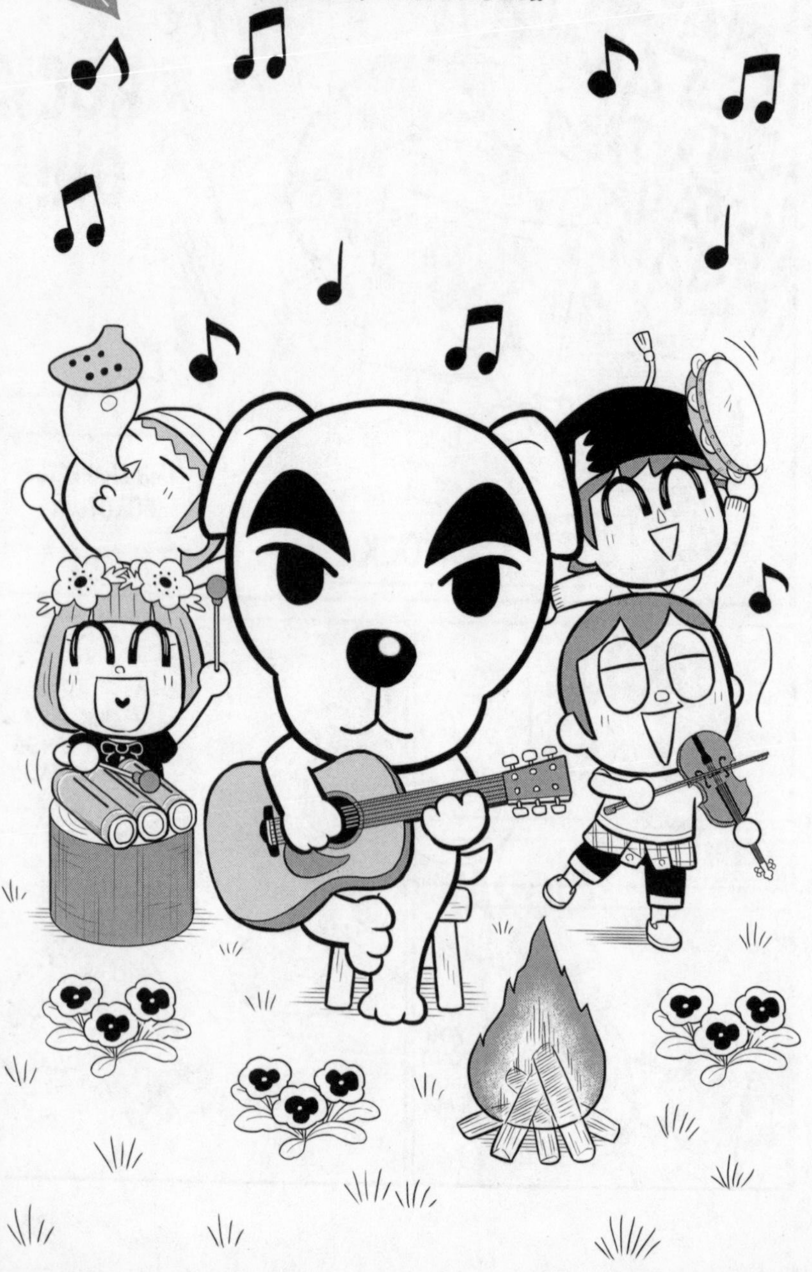

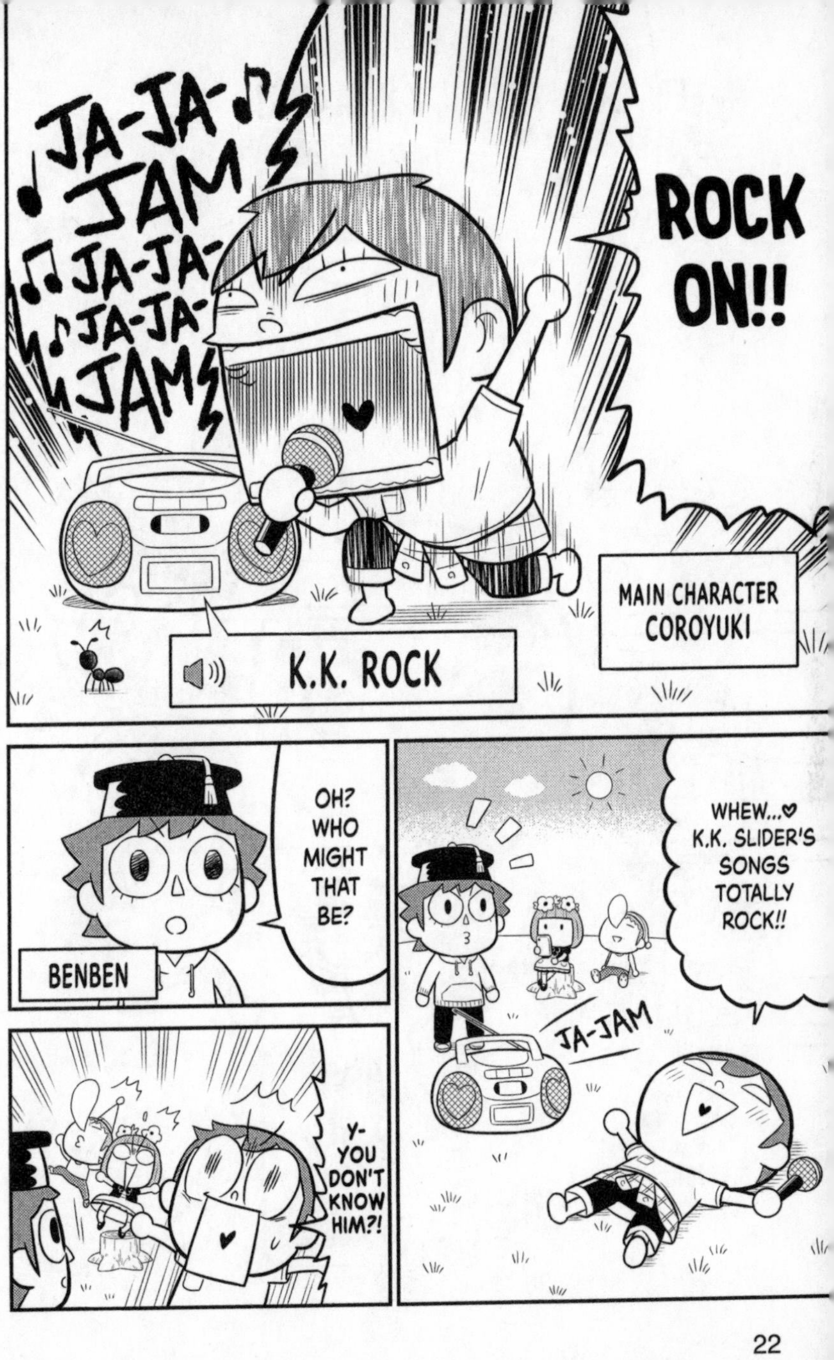
ROCK ON!!
JA-JA-JAM JA-JA-JA-JA-JAM
MAIN CHARACTER COROYUKI
K.K. ROCK
WHEW...♡ K.K. SLIDER'S SONGS TOTALLY ROCK!!
JA-JAM
OH? WHO MIGHT THAT BE?
BENBEN
Y-YOU DON'T KNOW HIM?!

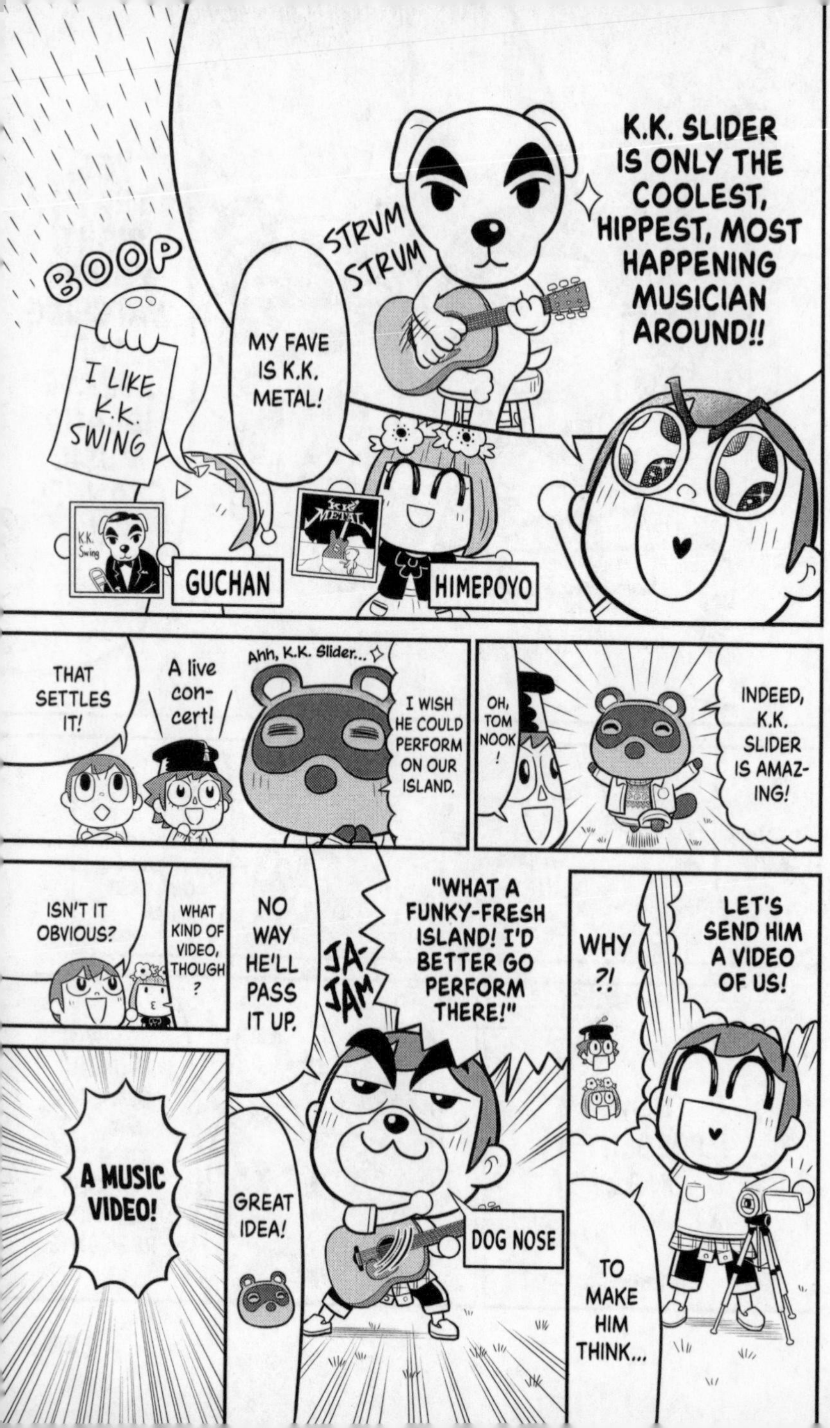
K.K. SLIDER IS ONLY THE COOLEST, HIPPEST, MOST HAPPENING MUSICIAN AROUND!!
STRUM STRUM
MY FAVE IS K.K. METAL!
K.K. METAL
HIMEPOYO
BOOP
I LIKE K.K. SWING
K.K. Swing
GUCHAN
INDEED, K.K. SLIDER IS AMAZING!
OH, TOM NOOK!
Ahh, K.K. Slider...
I WISH HE COULD PERFORM ON OUR ISLAND.
A live concert!
THAT SETTLES IT!
LET'S SEND HIM A VIDEO OF US!
WHY ?!
TO MAKE HIM THINK...
"WHAT A FUNKY-FRESH ISLAND! I'D BETTER GO PERFORM THERE!"
JA-JAM
DOG NOSE
NO WAY HE'LL PASS IT UP.
GREAT IDEA!
WHAT KIND OF VIDEO, THOUGH?
ISN'T IT OBVIOUS?
A MUSIC VIDEO!

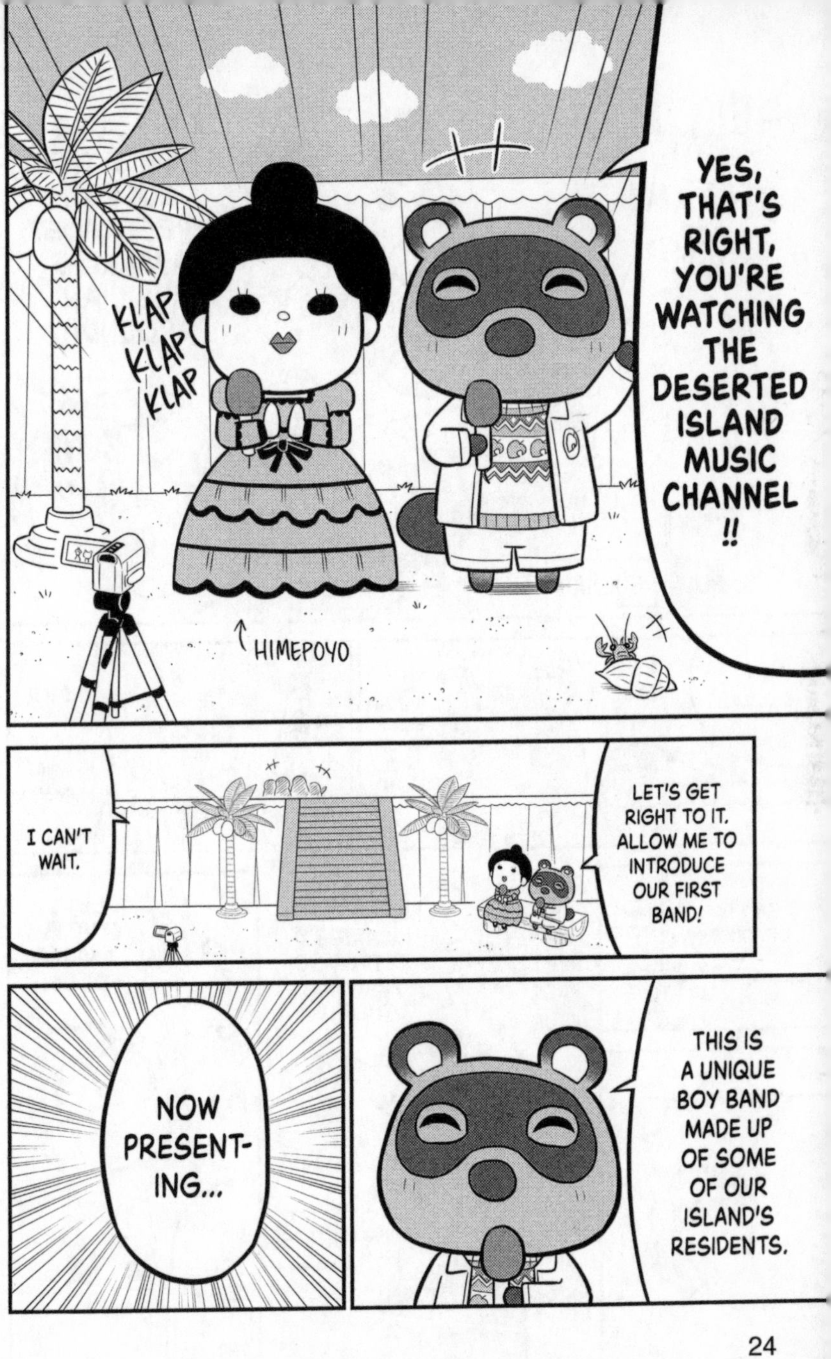
YES, THAT'S RIGHT, YOU'RE WATCHING THE DESERTED ISLAND MUSIC CHANNEL!!
KLAP KLAP KLAP
HIMEPOYO
LET'S GET RIGHT TO IT. ALLOW ME TO INTRODUCE OUR FIRST BAND!
I CAN'T WAIT.
THIS IS A UNIQUE BOY BAND MADE UP OF SOME OF OUR ISLAND'S RESIDENTS.
NOW PRESENT-ING...

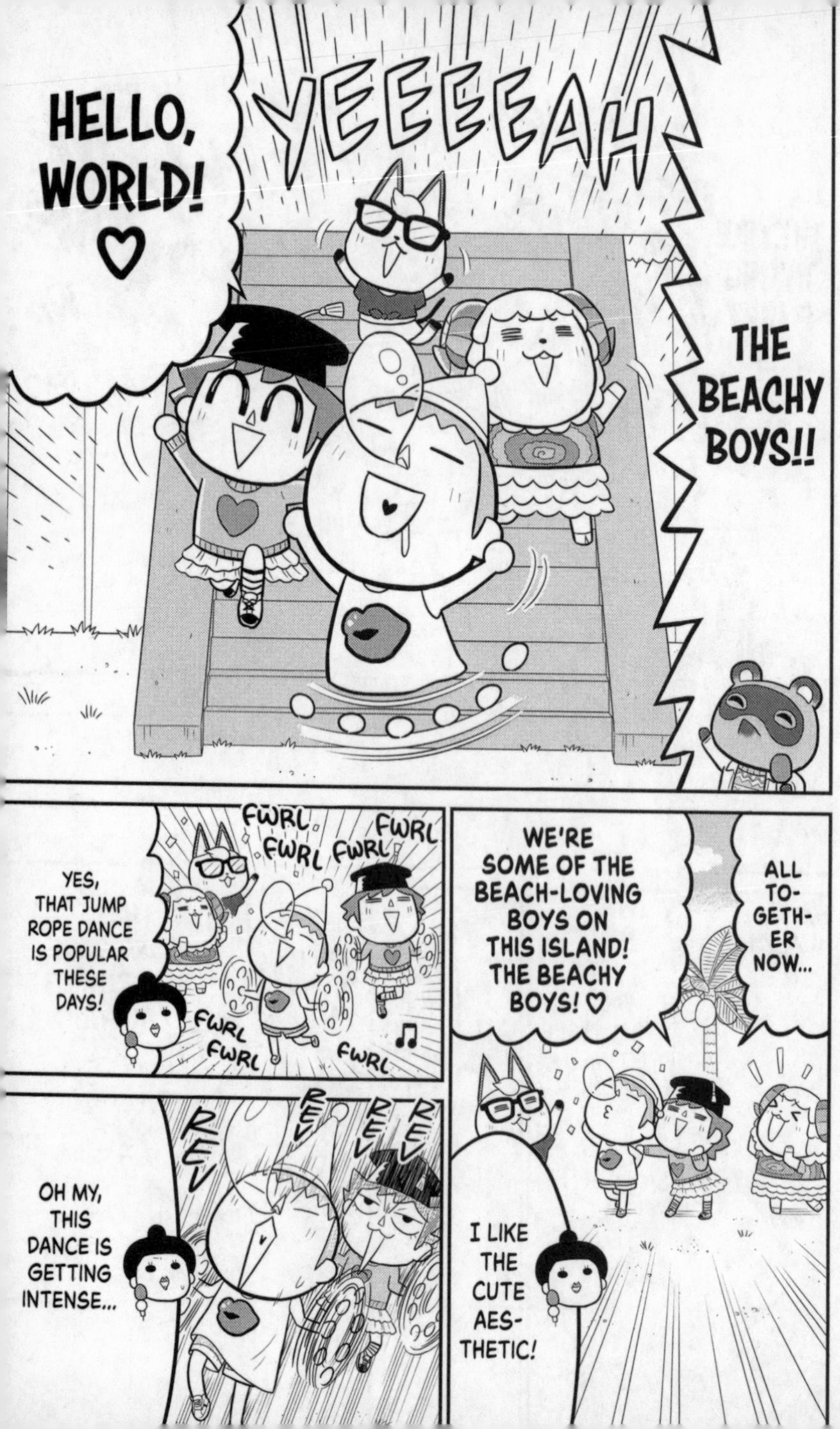
YEEEEAH
HELLO, WORLD! ♡
THE BEACHY BOYS!!
ALL TO-GETH-ER NOW...
WE'RE SOME OF THE BEACH-LOVING BOYS ON THIS ISLAND! THE BEACHY BOYS! ♡
I LIKE THE CUTE AES-THETIC!
FWRL FWRL FWRL FWRL
YES, THAT JUMP ROPE DANCE IS POPULAR THESE DAYS!
FWRL FWRL FWRL
REV REV REV REV
OH MY, THIS DANCE IS GETTING INTENSE...

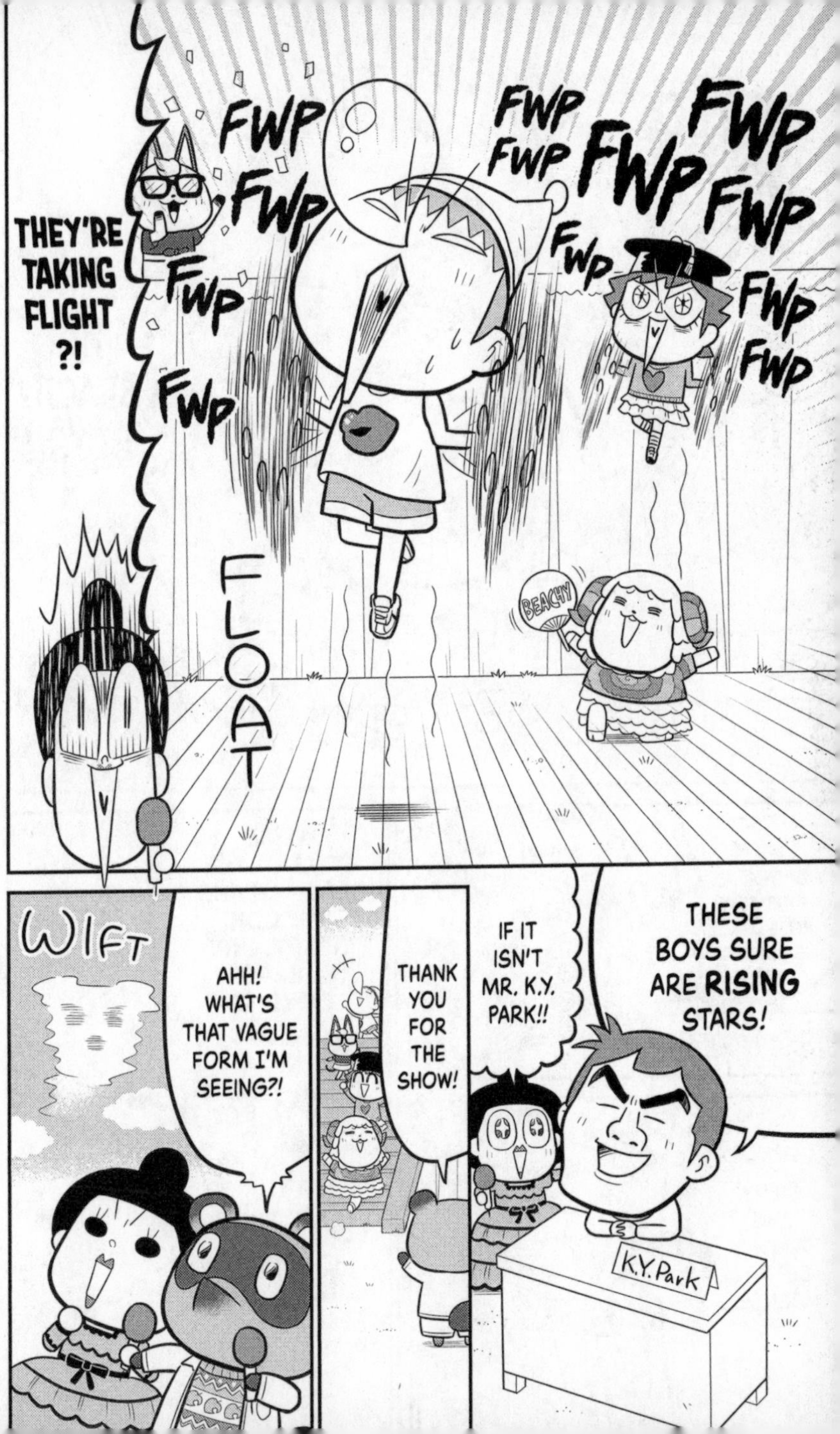
FWP FWP FWP FWP FWP
FWP FWP FWP FWP
FWP FWP FWP FWP
THEY'RE TAKING FLIGHT ?!
FLOAT
BEACHY
THESE BOYS SURE ARE RISING STARS!
IF IT ISN'T MR. K.Y. PARK!!
K.Y.Park
THANK YOU FOR THE SHOW!
WIFT
AHH! WHAT'S THAT VAGUE FORM I'M SEEING?!

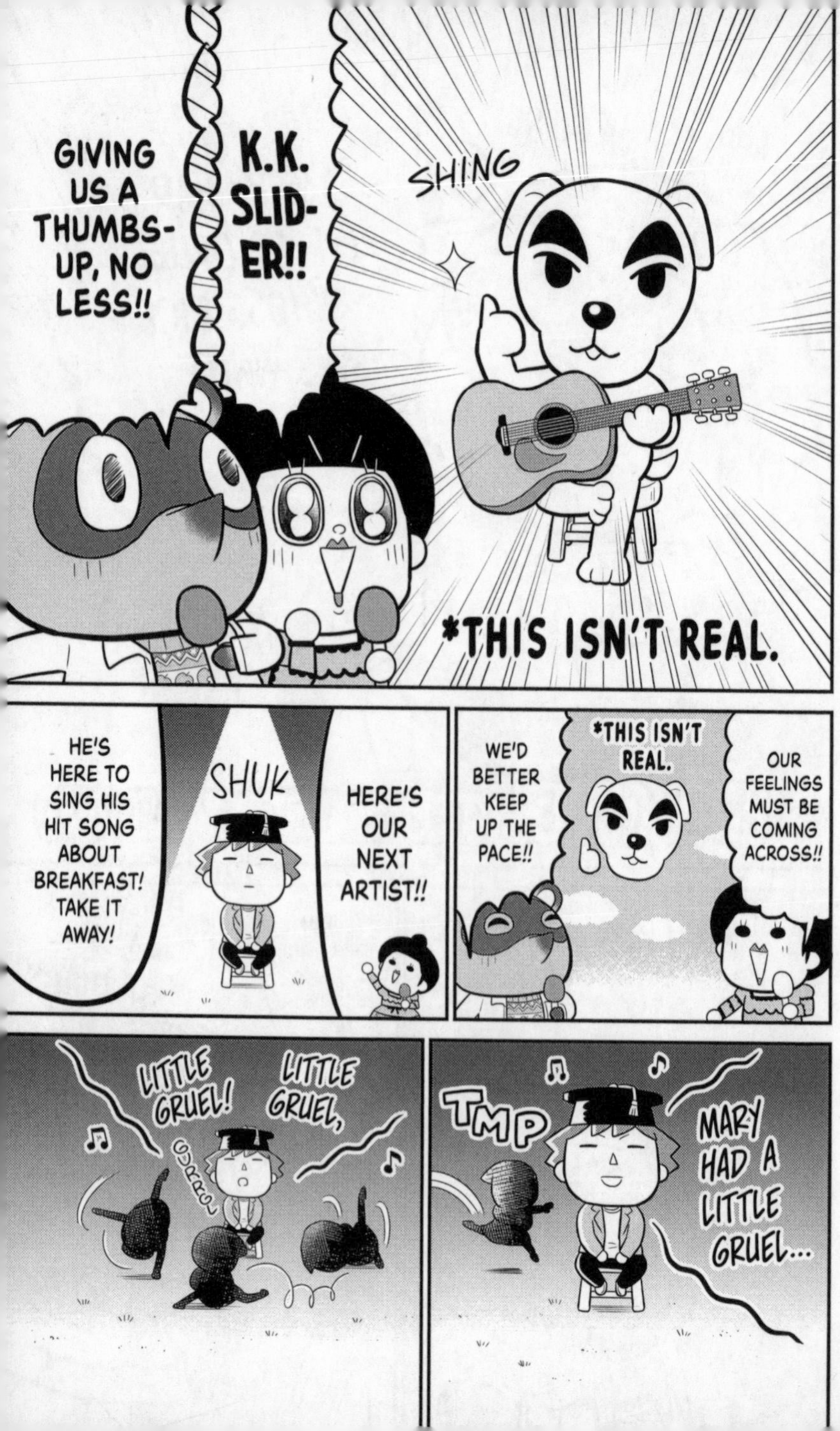
SHING
K.K. SLIDER!!
GIVING US A THUMBS-UP, NO LESS!!
*THIS ISN'T REAL.
OUR FEELINGS MUST BE COMING ACROSS!!
*THIS ISN'T REAL.
WE'D BETTER KEEP UP THE PACE!!
HERE'S OUR NEXT ARTIST!!
SHUK
HE'S HERE TO SING HIS HIT SONG ABOUT BREAKFAST! TAKE IT AWAY!
TMP
MARY HAD A LITTLE GRUEL...
LITTLE GRUEL,
LITTLE GRUEL!
GURRGL

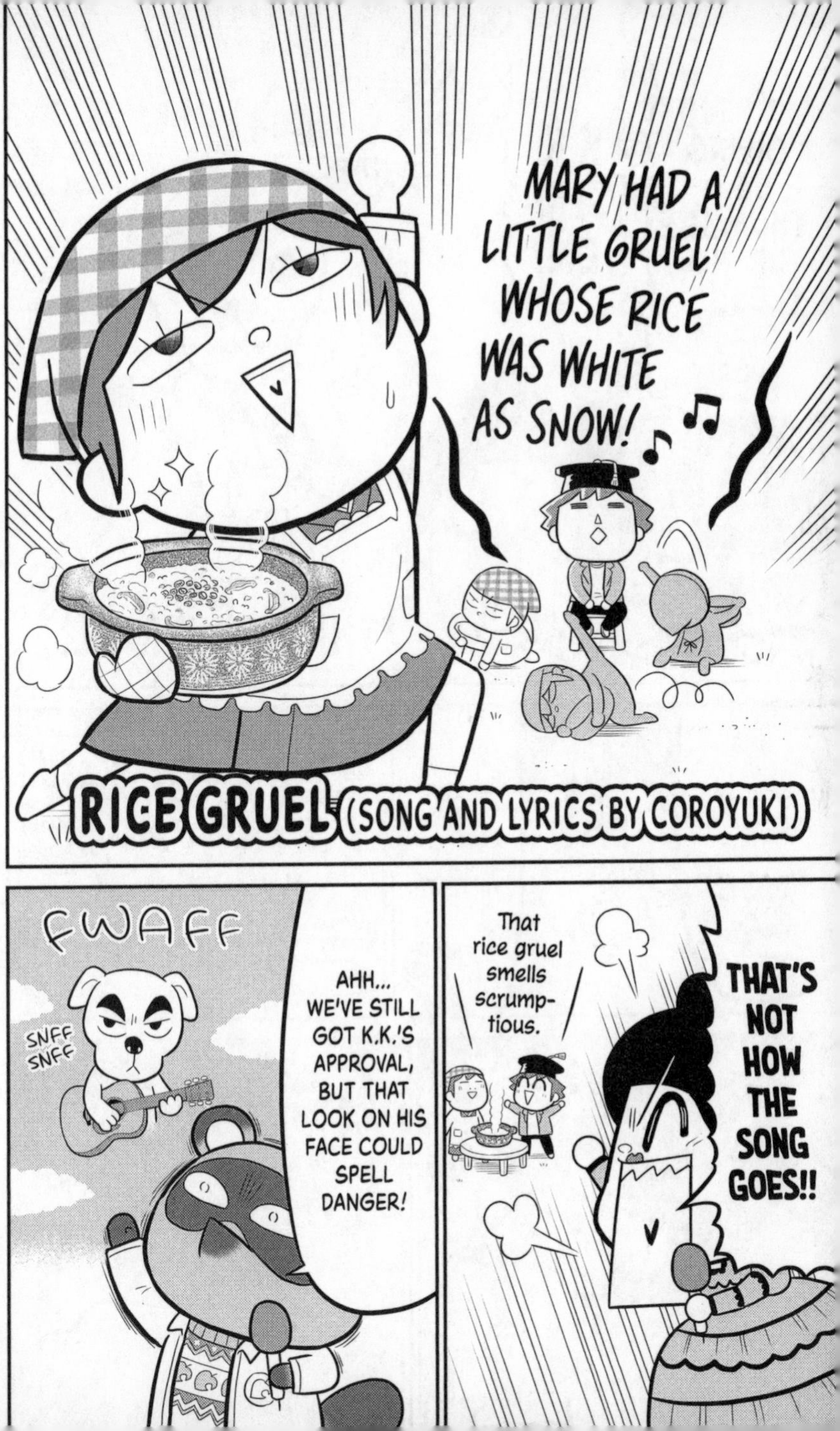
MARY HAD A LITTLE GRUEL WHOSE RICE WAS WHITE AS SNOW!
RICE GRUEL (SONG AND LYRICS BY COROYUKI)
THAT'S NOT HOW THE SONG GOES!!
That rice gruel smells scrump-tious.
FWAFF
SNFF SNFF
AHH... WE'VE STILL GOT K.K.'S APPROVAL, BUT THAT LOOK ON HIS FACE COULD SPELL DANGER!

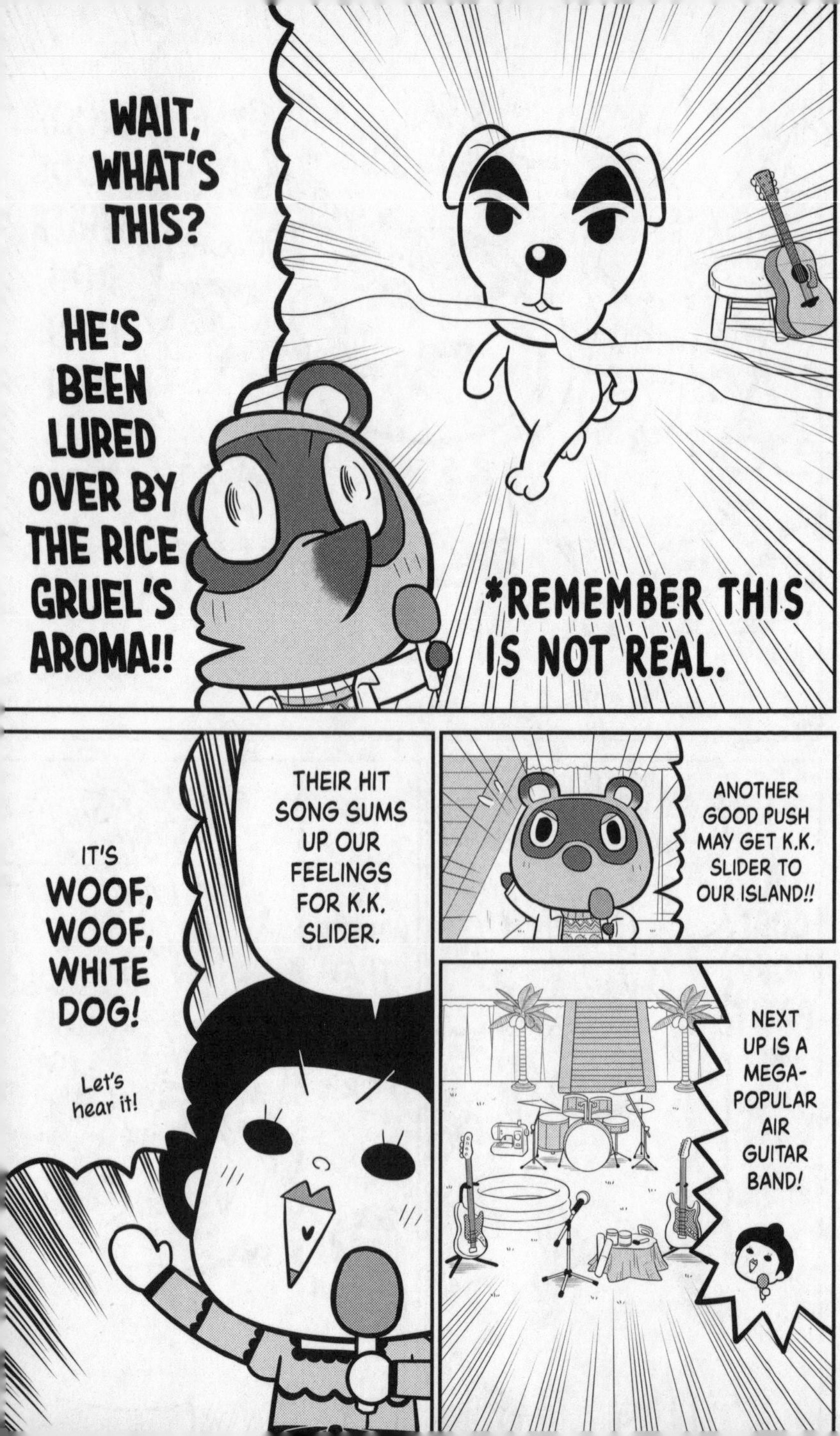
WAIT, WHAT'S THIS?
HE'S BEEN LURED OVER BY THE RICE GRUEL'S AROMA!!
*REMEMBER THIS IS NOT REAL.
ANOTHER GOOD PUSH MAY GET K.K. SLIDER TO OUR ISLAND!!
NEXT UP IS A MEGA-POPULAR AIR GUITAR BAND!
THEIR HIT SONG SUMS UP OUR FEELINGS FOR K.K. SLIDER.
IT'S WOOF, WOOF, WHITE DOG!
Let's hear it!

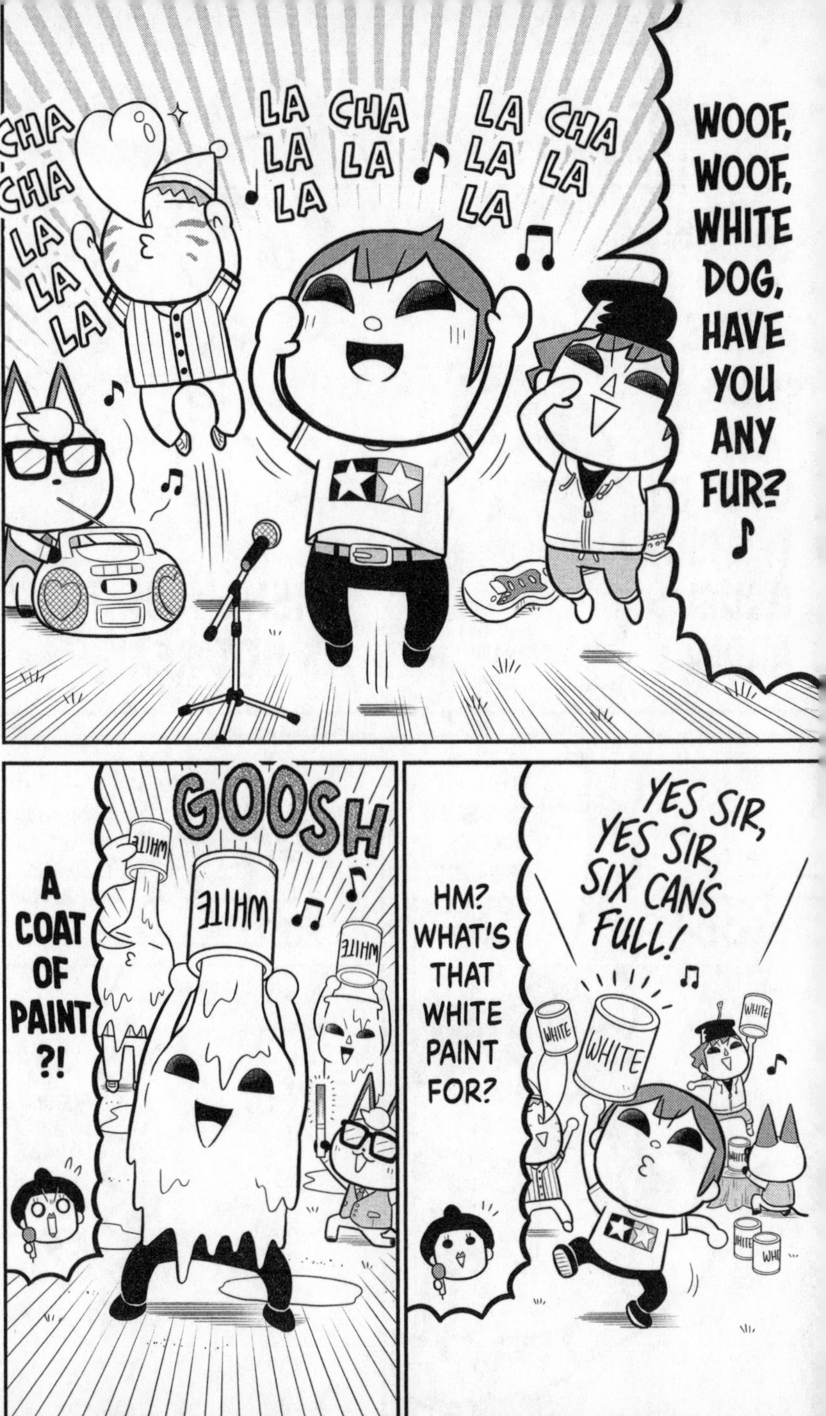
WOOF, WOOF, WHITE DOG, HAVE YOU ANY FUR? ♪
LA CHA LA LA LA
LA CHA LA LA LA
CHA CHA LA LA LA
YES SIR, YES SIR, SIX CANS FULL!
HM? WHAT'S THAT WHITE PAINT FOR?
GOOSH
A COAT OF PAINT ?!

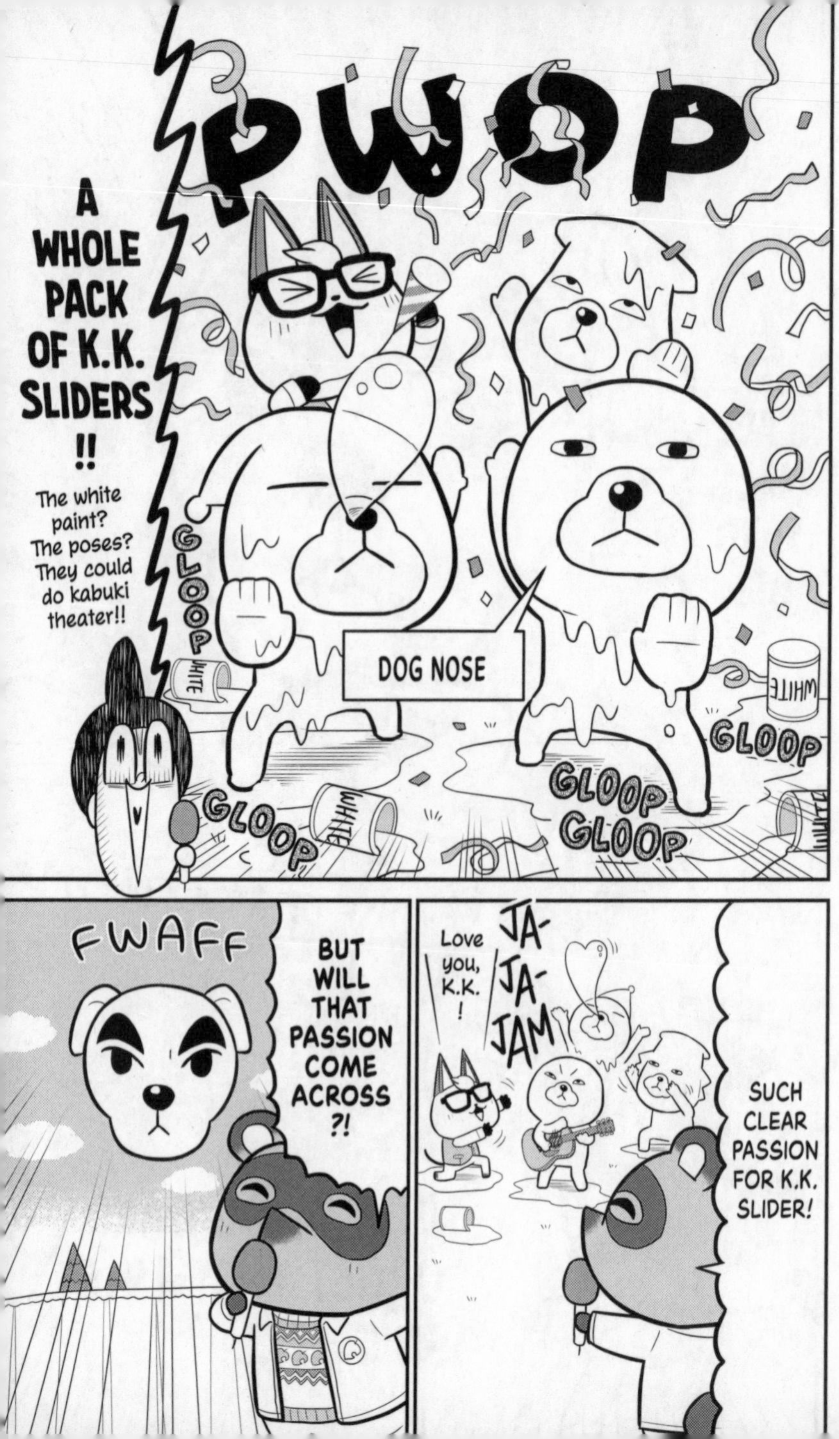
PWOP
A WHOLE PACK OF K.K. SLIDERS!!
The white paint? The poses? They could do kabuki theater!!
GLOOP
DOG NOSE
WHITE
WHITE
GLOOP
GLOOP GLOOP
GLOOP
WHITE
Love you, K.K.!
JA-JA-JAM
SUCH CLEAR PASSION FOR K.K. SLIDER!
FWAFF
BUT WILL THAT PASSION COME ACROSS?!

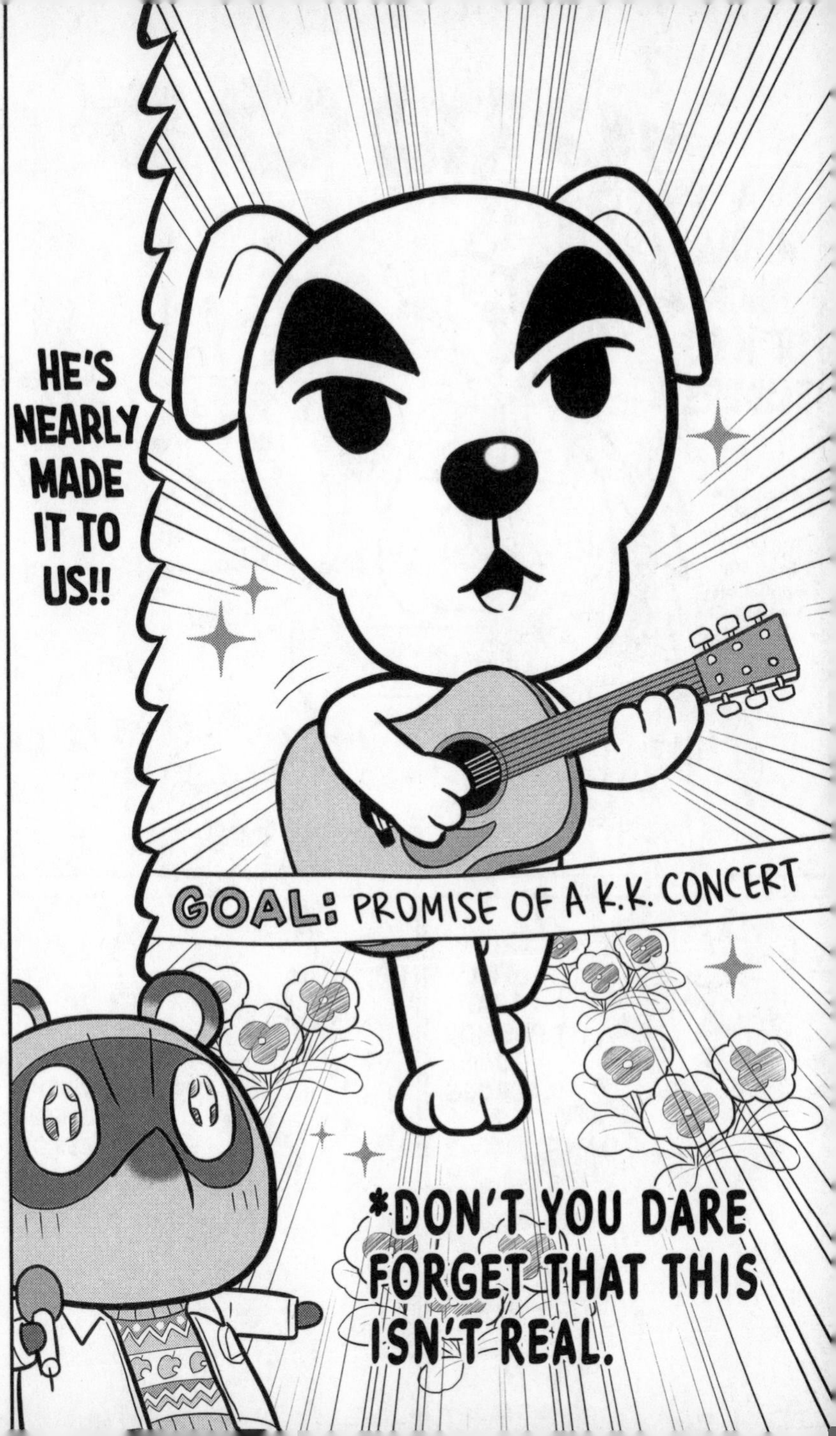
HE'S NEARLY MADE IT TO US!!
GOAL: PROMISE OF A K.K. CONCERT
*DON'T YOU DARE FORGET THAT THIS ISN'T REAL.

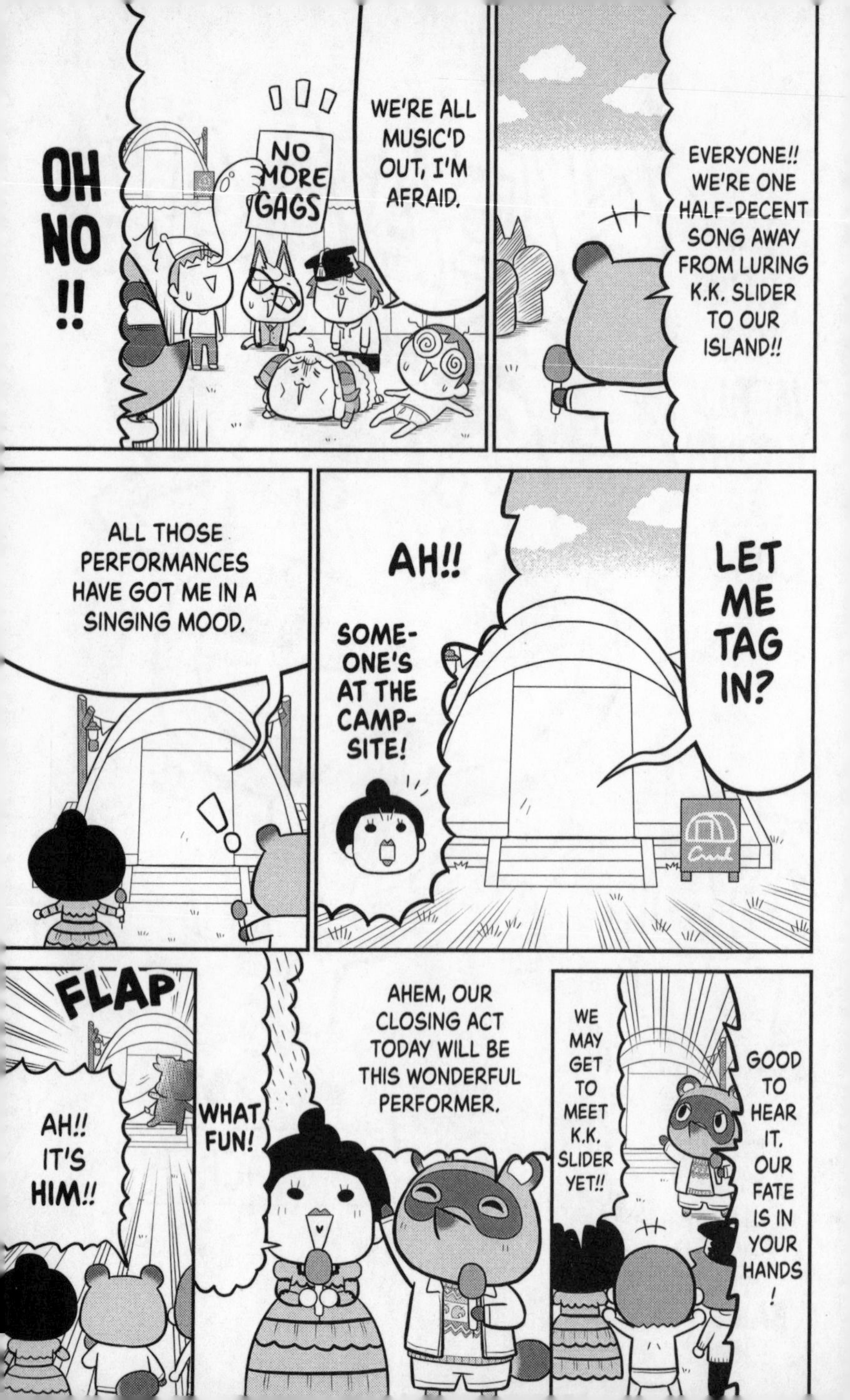
EVERYONE!! WE'RE ONE HALF-DECENT SONG AWAY FROM LURING K.K. SLIDER TO OUR ISLAND!!
WE'RE ALL MUSIC'D OUT, I'M AFRAID.
NO MORE GAGS
OH NO!!
LET ME TAG IN?
AH!!
SOME-ONE'S AT THE CAMP-SITE!
ALL THOSE PERFORMANCES HAVE GOT ME IN A SINGING MOOD.
GOOD TO HEAR IT. OUR FATE IS IN YOUR HANDS!
WE MAY GET TO MEET K.K. SLIDER YET!!
AHEM, OUR CLOSING ACT TODAY WILL BE THIS WONDERFUL PERFORMER.
WHAT FUN!
FLAP
AH!! IT'S HIM!!

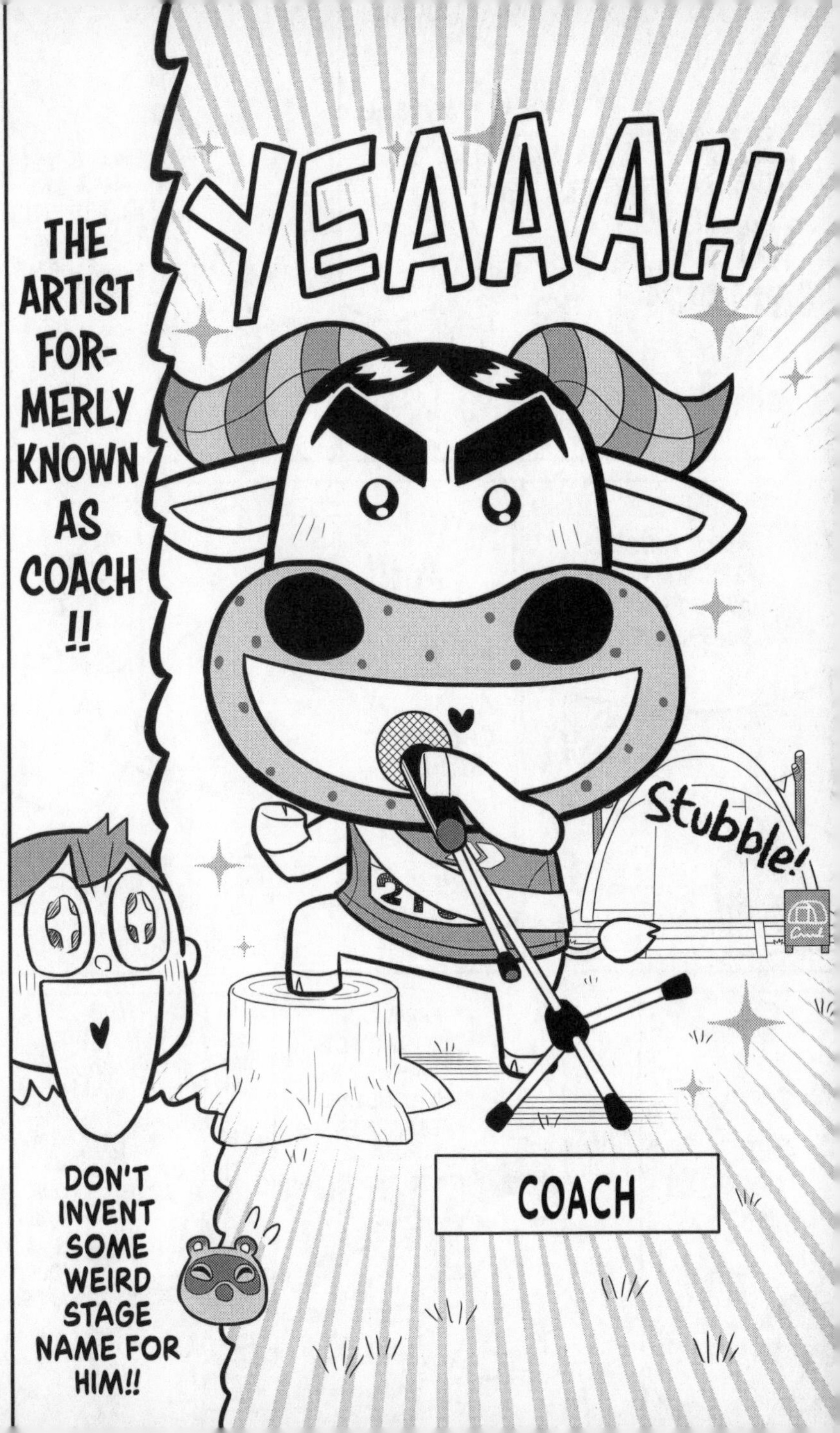
YEAAAH
THE ARTIST FOR-MERLY KNOWN AS COACH !!
Stubble!
COACH
DON'T INVENT SOME WEIRD STAGE NAME FOR HIM!!

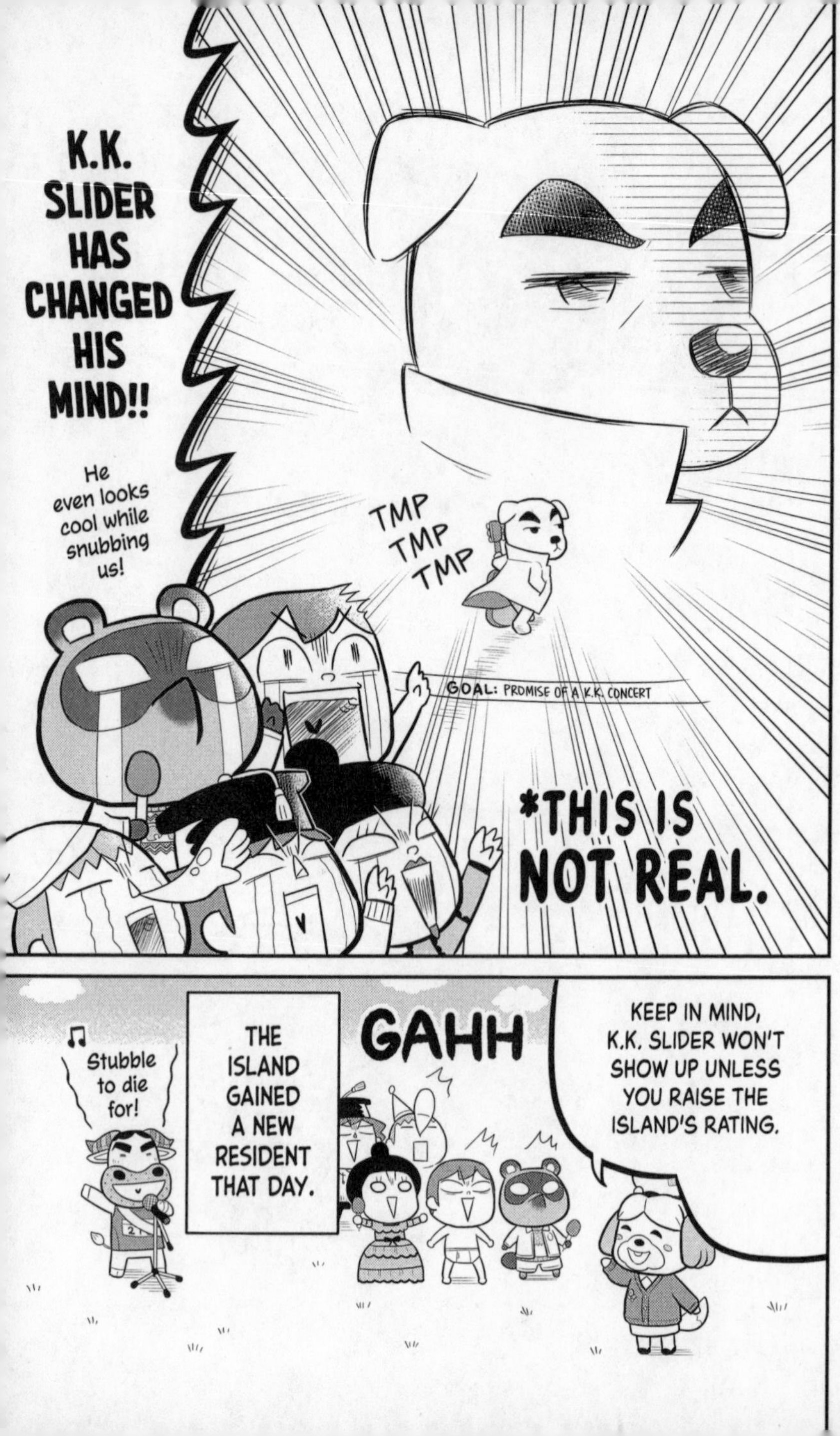
K.K. SLIDER HAS CHANGED HIS MIND!!
He even looks cool while snubbing us!
TMP TMP TMP
GOAL: PROMISE OF A K.K. CONCERT
*THIS IS NOT REAL.
KEEP IN MIND, K.K. SLIDER WON'T SHOW UP UNLESS YOU RAISE THE ISLAND'S RATING.
GAHH
THE ISLAND GAINED A NEW RESIDENT THAT DAY.
♫ Stubble to die for!

Animal Crossing: New Horizons

Welcome to Animal Crossing New Horizons

Deserted Island Diary

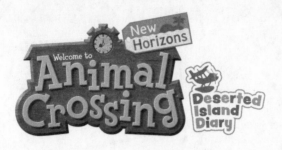

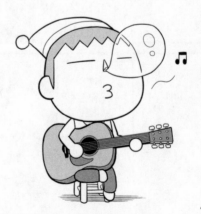

SO YOU WANT TO BUILD A PERFECT SNOWBOY

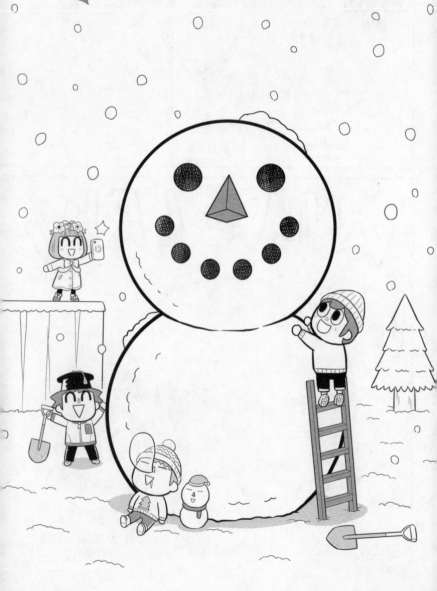

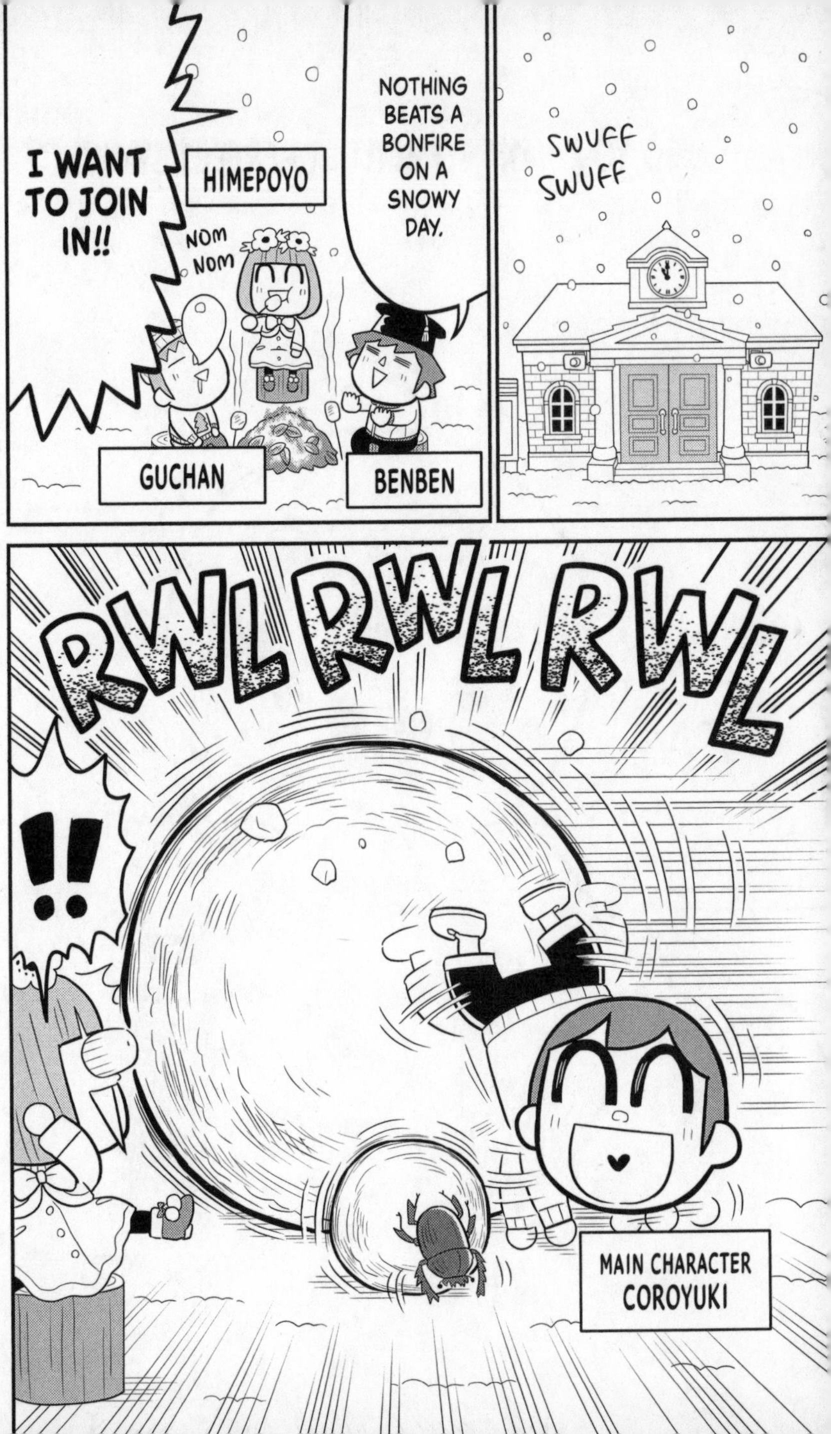
SWUFF
SWUFF
NOTHING BEATS A BONFIRE ON A SNOWY DAY.
BENBEN
HIMEPOYO
NOM NOM
GUCHAN
I WANT TO JOIN IN!!
RWL RWL RWL
!!
MAIN CHARACTER
COROYUKI

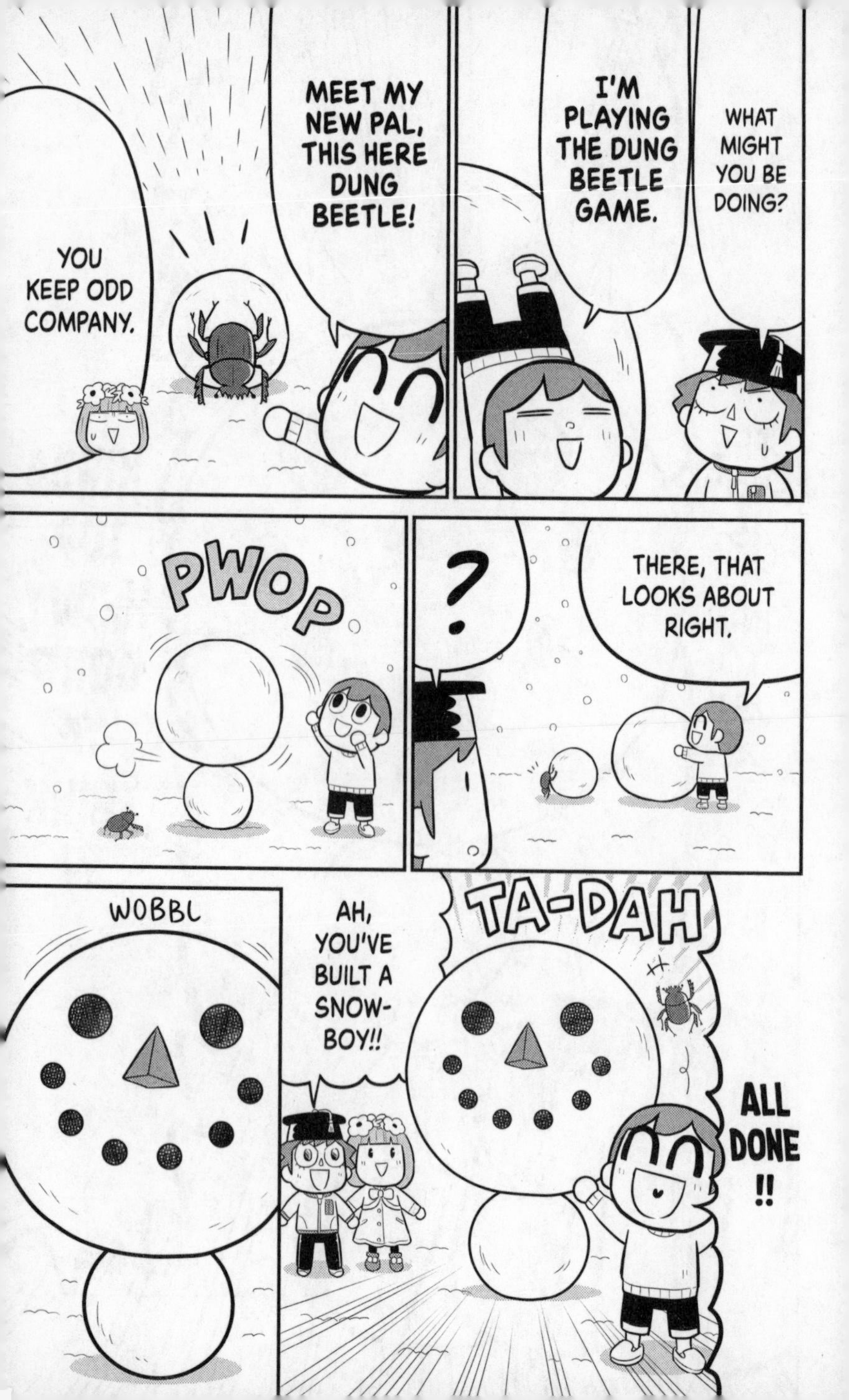
WHAT MIGHT YOU BE DOING?
I'M PLAYING THE DUNG BEETLE GAME.
MEET MY NEW PAL, THIS HERE DUNG BEETLE!
YOU KEEP ODD COMPANY.
THERE, THAT LOOKS ABOUT RIGHT.
?
PWOP
TA-DAH
ALL DONE!!
AH, YOU'VE BUILT A SNOW-BOY!!
WOBBL

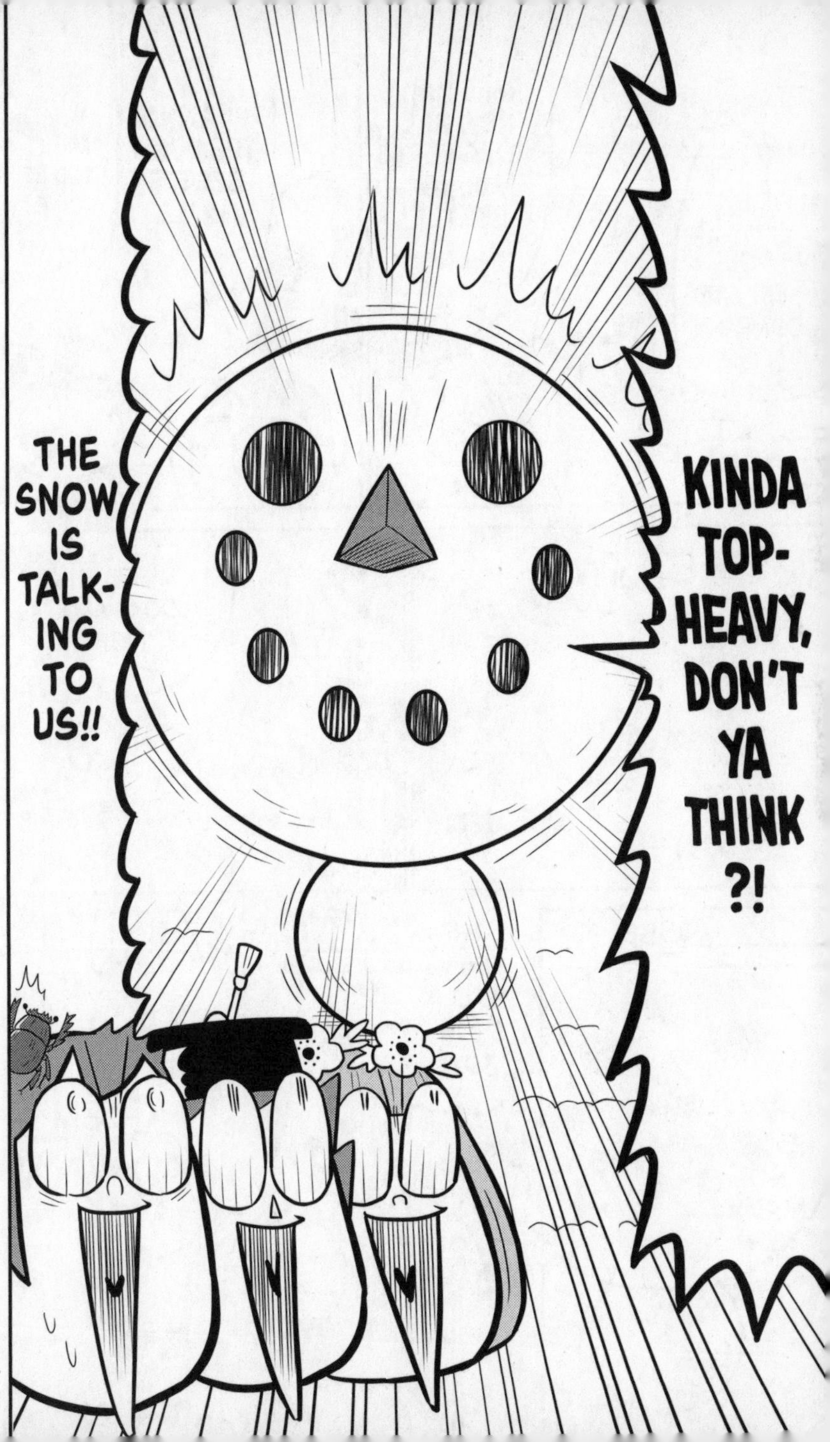
KINDA TOP-HEAVY, DON'T YA THINK?!
THE SNOW IS TALK-ING TO US!!

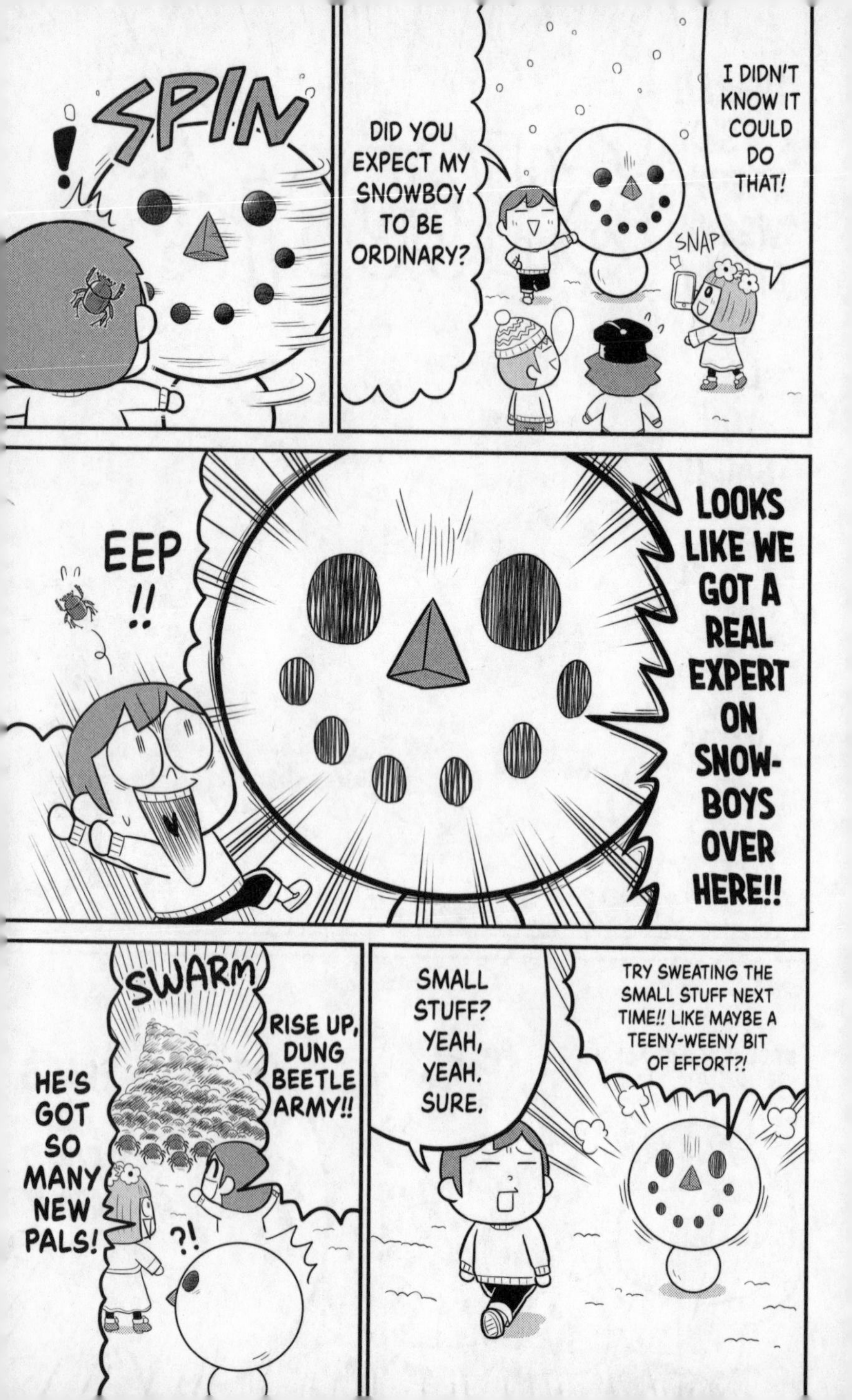
I DIDN'T KNOW IT COULD DO THAT!
SNAP
DID YOU EXPECT MY SNOWBOY TO BE ORDINARY?
SPIN
!
LOOKS LIKE WE GOT A REAL EXPERT ON SNOW-BOYS OVER HERE!!
EEP!!
TRY SWEATING THE SMALL STUFF NEXT TIME!! LIKE MAYBE A TEENY-WEENY BIT OF EFFORT?!
SMALL STUFF? YEAH, YEAH. SURE.
SWARM
RISE UP, DUNG BEETLE ARMY!!
HE'S GOT SO MANY NEW PALS!
?!

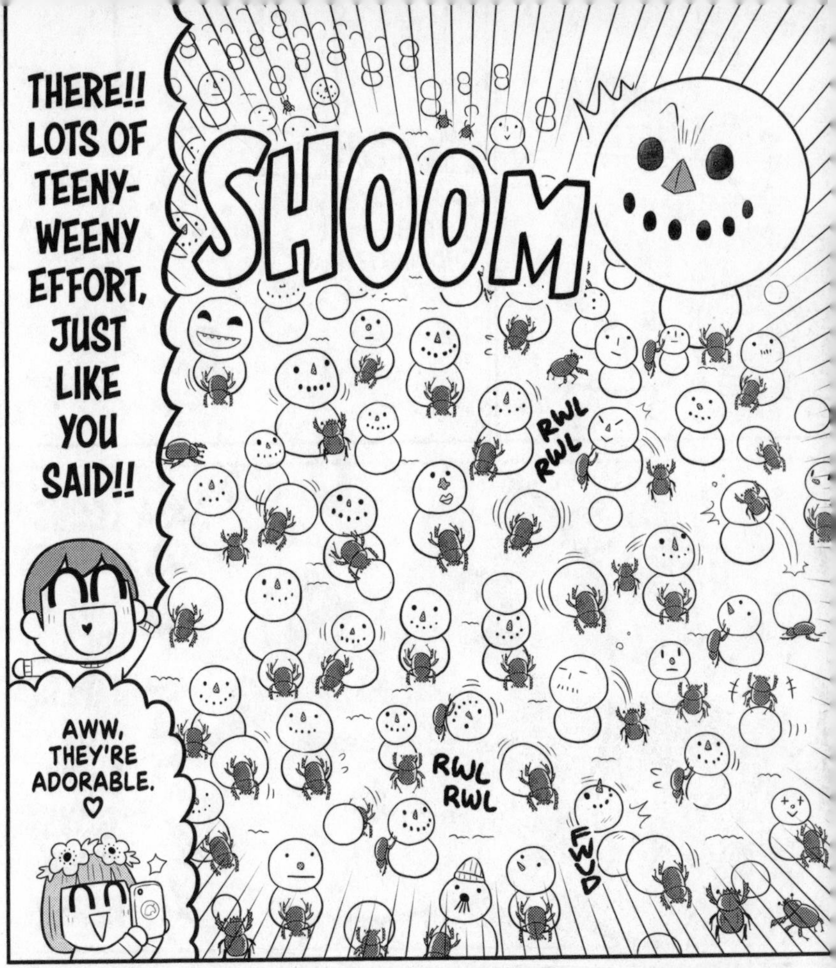
SHOOM
THERE!! LOTS OF TEENY-WEENY EFFORT, JUST LIKE YOU SAID!!
RWL RWL
RWL RWL
FWUD
AWW, THEY'RE ADORABLE. ♡
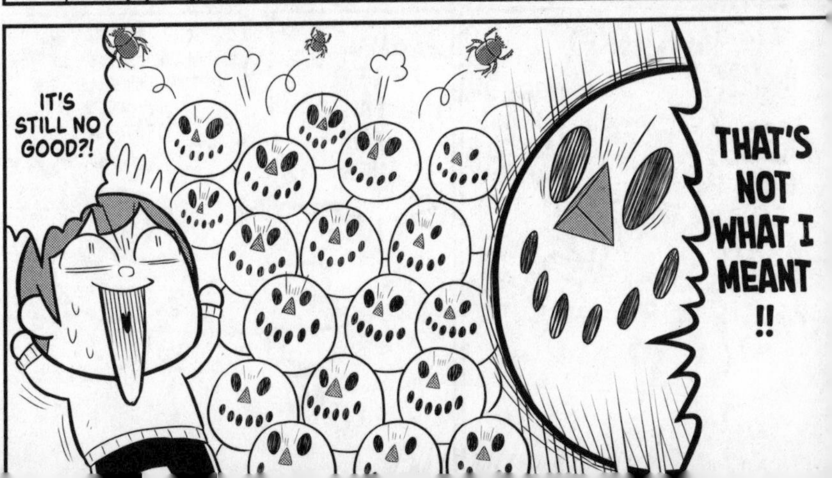
THAT'S NOT WHAT I MEANT!!
IT'S STILL NO GOOD?!

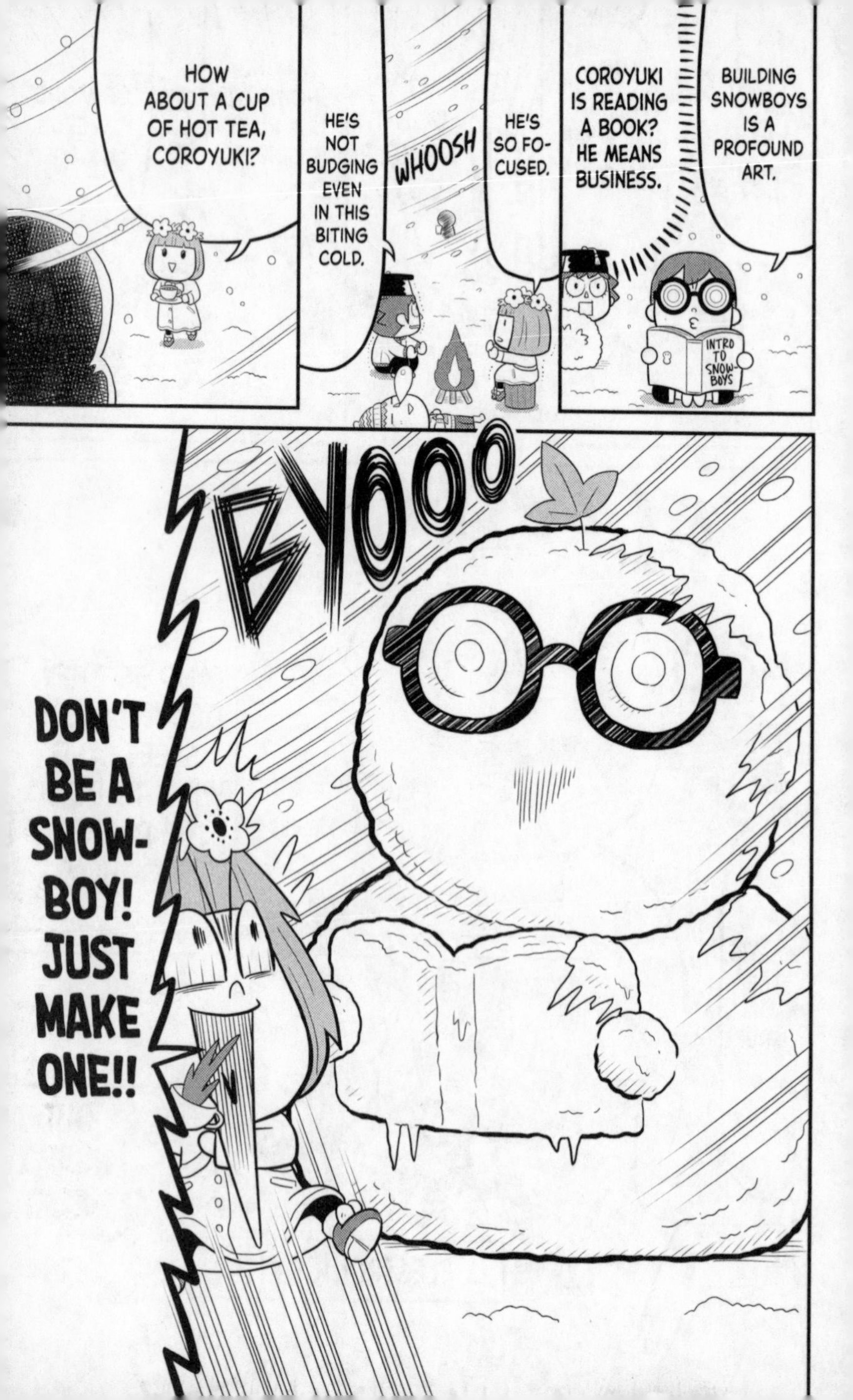
BUILDING SNOWBOYS IS A PROFOUND ART.
COROYUKI IS READING A BOOK? HE MEANS BUSINESS.
INTRO TO SNOW-BOYS
HE'S SO FO-CUSED.
WHOOSH
HE'S NOT BUDGING EVEN IN THIS BITING COLD.
HOW ABOUT A CUP OF HOT TEA, COROYUKI?
BYOOO
DON'T BE A SNOW-BOY! JUST MAKE ONE!!

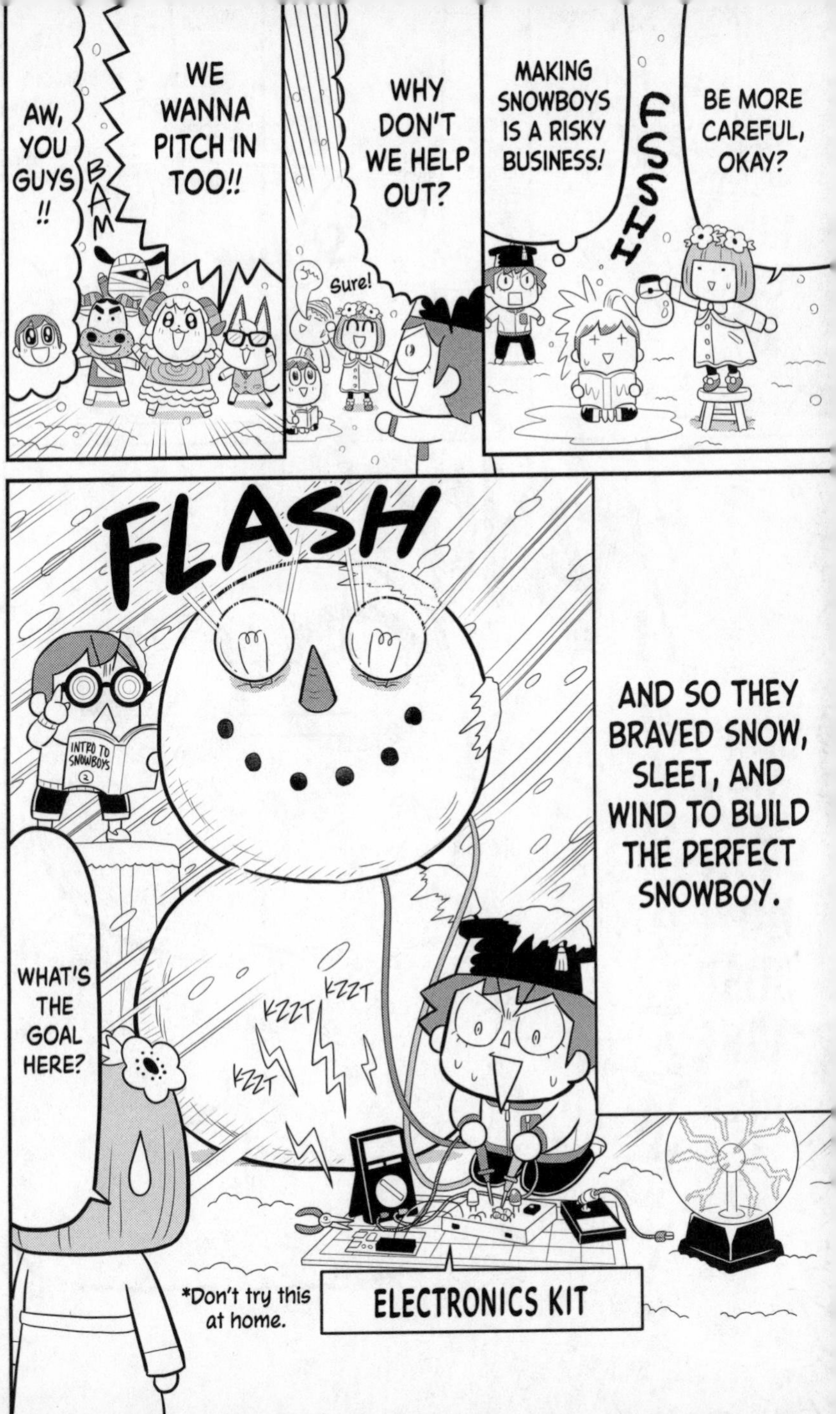
BE MORE CAREFUL, OKAY?
FSSH
MAKING SNOWBOYS IS A RISKY BUSINESS!
WHY DON'T WE HELP OUT?
Sure!
WE WANNA PITCH IN TOO!!
BAM
AW, YOU GUYS!!
AND SO THEY BRAVED SNOW, SLEET, AND WIND TO BUILD THE PERFECT SNOWBOY.
FLASH
INTRO TO SNOWBOYS 2
KZZT
KZZT
KZZT
WHAT'S THE GOAL HERE?
ELECTRONICS KIT
*Don't try this at home.

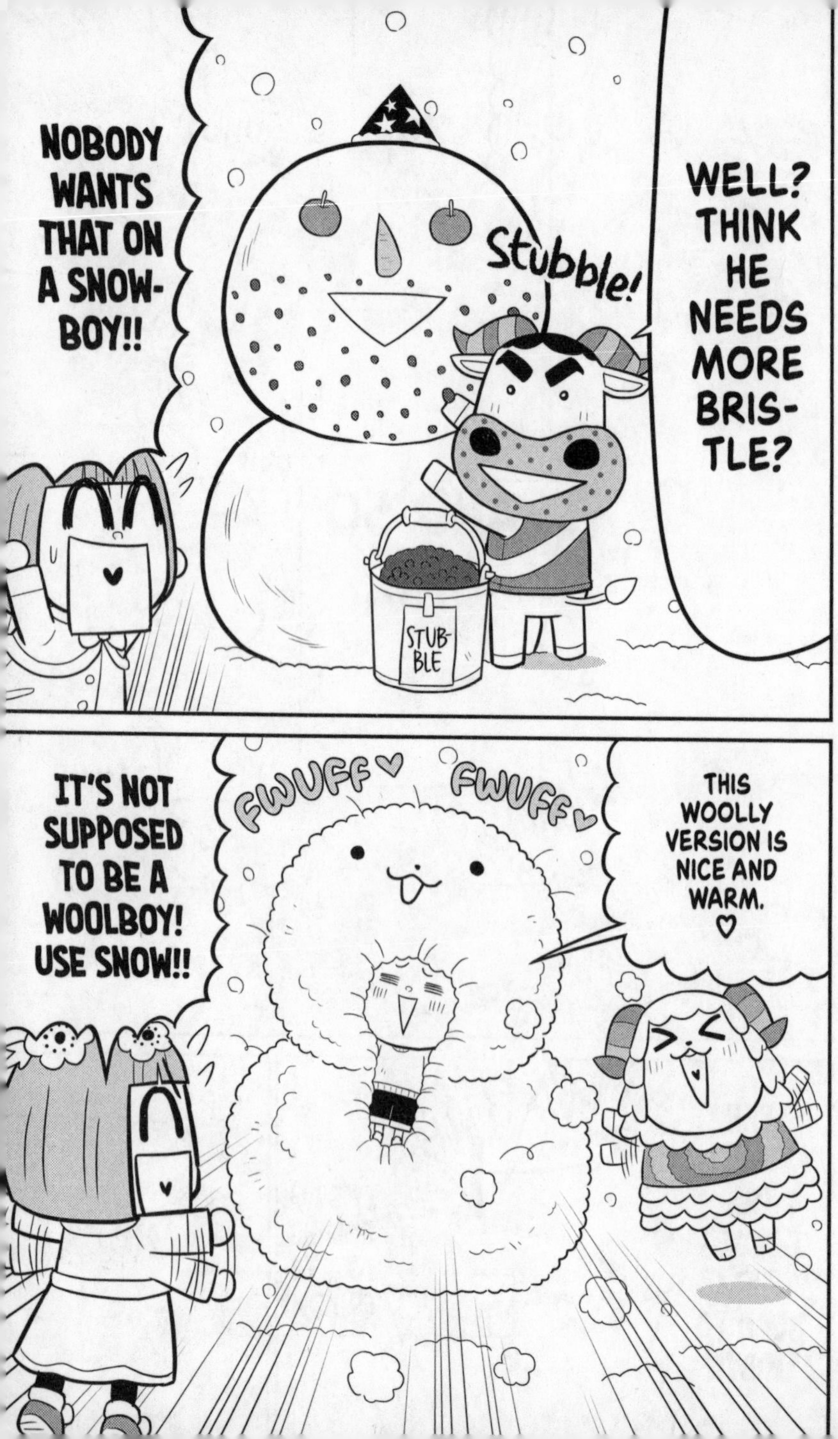
WELL? THINK HE NEEDS MORE BRIS-TLE?
Stubble!
STUB-BLE
NOBODY WANTS THAT ON A SNOW-BOY!!
THIS WOOLLY VERSION IS NICE AND WARM. ♡
FWUFF♡
FWUFF♡
IT'S NOT SUPPOSED TO BE A WOOLBOY! USE SNOW!!

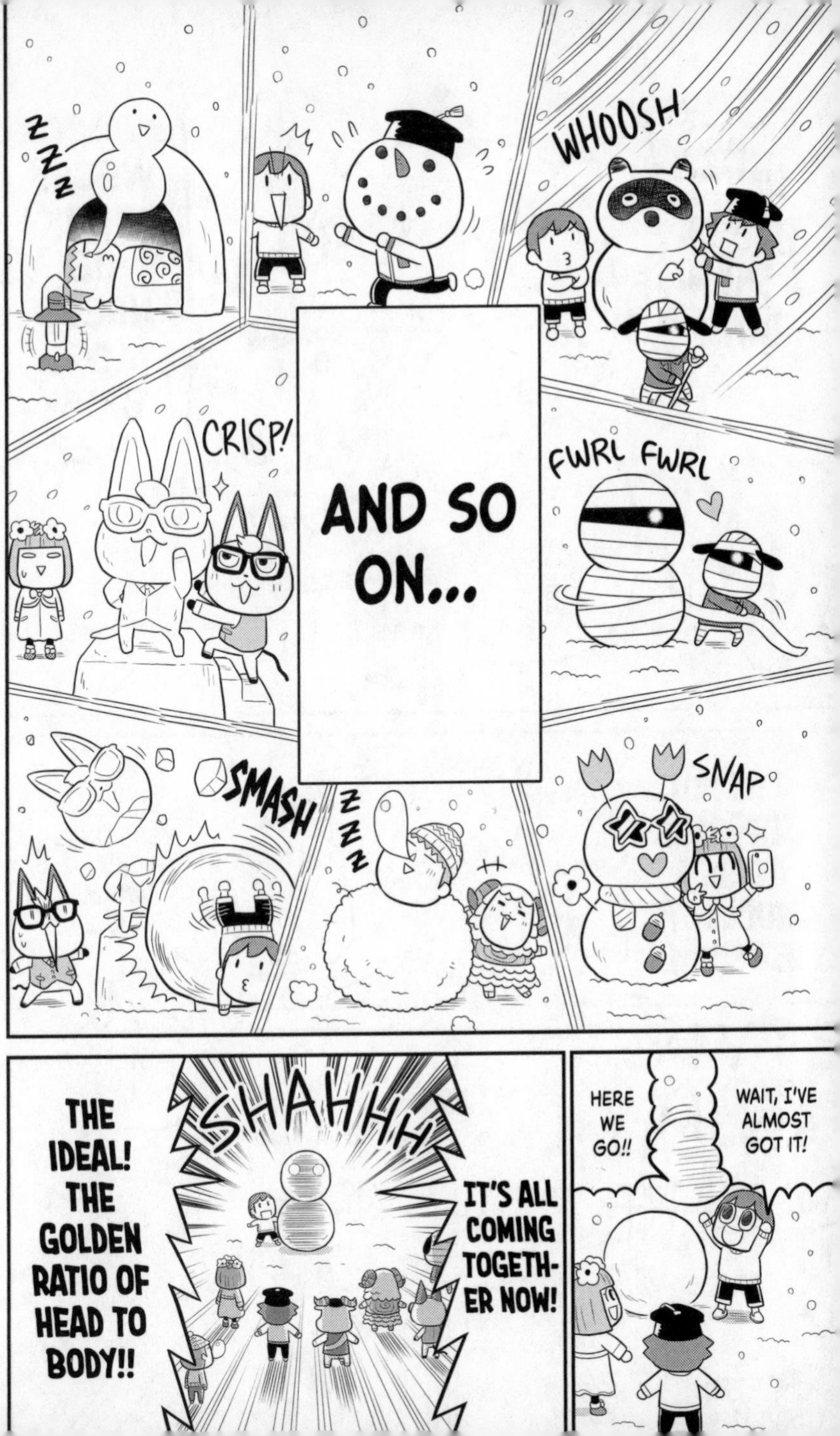
WHOOSH
Z Z Z
AND SO ON...
FWRL FWRL
CRISP!
SNAP
Z Z Z
SMASH
WAIT, I'VE ALMOST GOT IT!
HERE WE GO!!
SHAHHH
IT'S ALL COMING TOGETH-ER NOW!
THE IDEAL! THE GOLDEN RATIO OF HEAD TO BODY!!

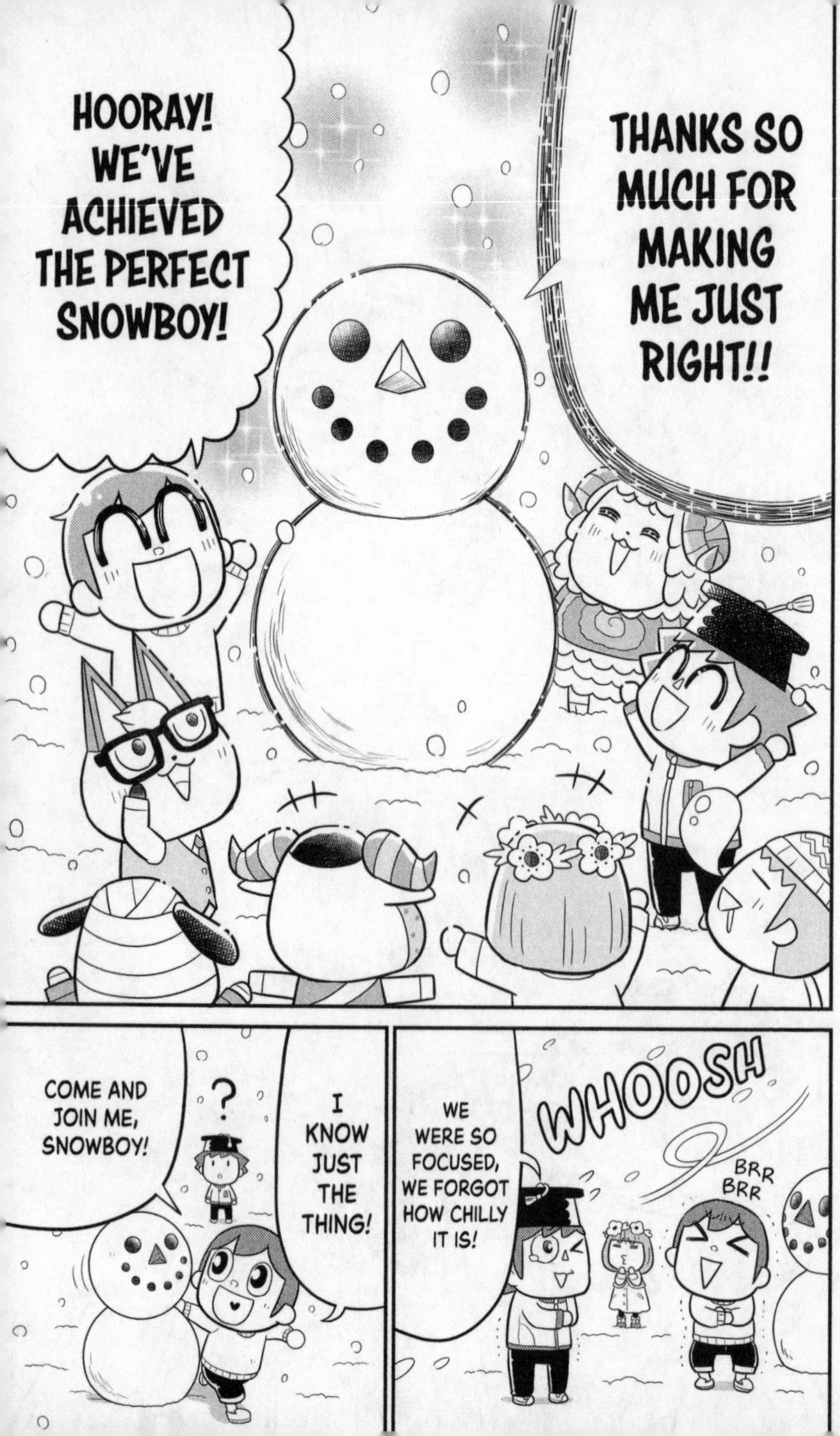
THANKS SO MUCH FOR MAKING ME JUST RIGHT!!
HOORAY! WE'VE ACHIEVED THE PERFECT SNOWBOY!
WHOOSH
BRR BRR
WE WERE SO FOCUSED, WE FORGOT HOW CHILLY IT IS!
I KNOW JUST THE THING!
?
COME AND JOIN ME, SNOWBOY!

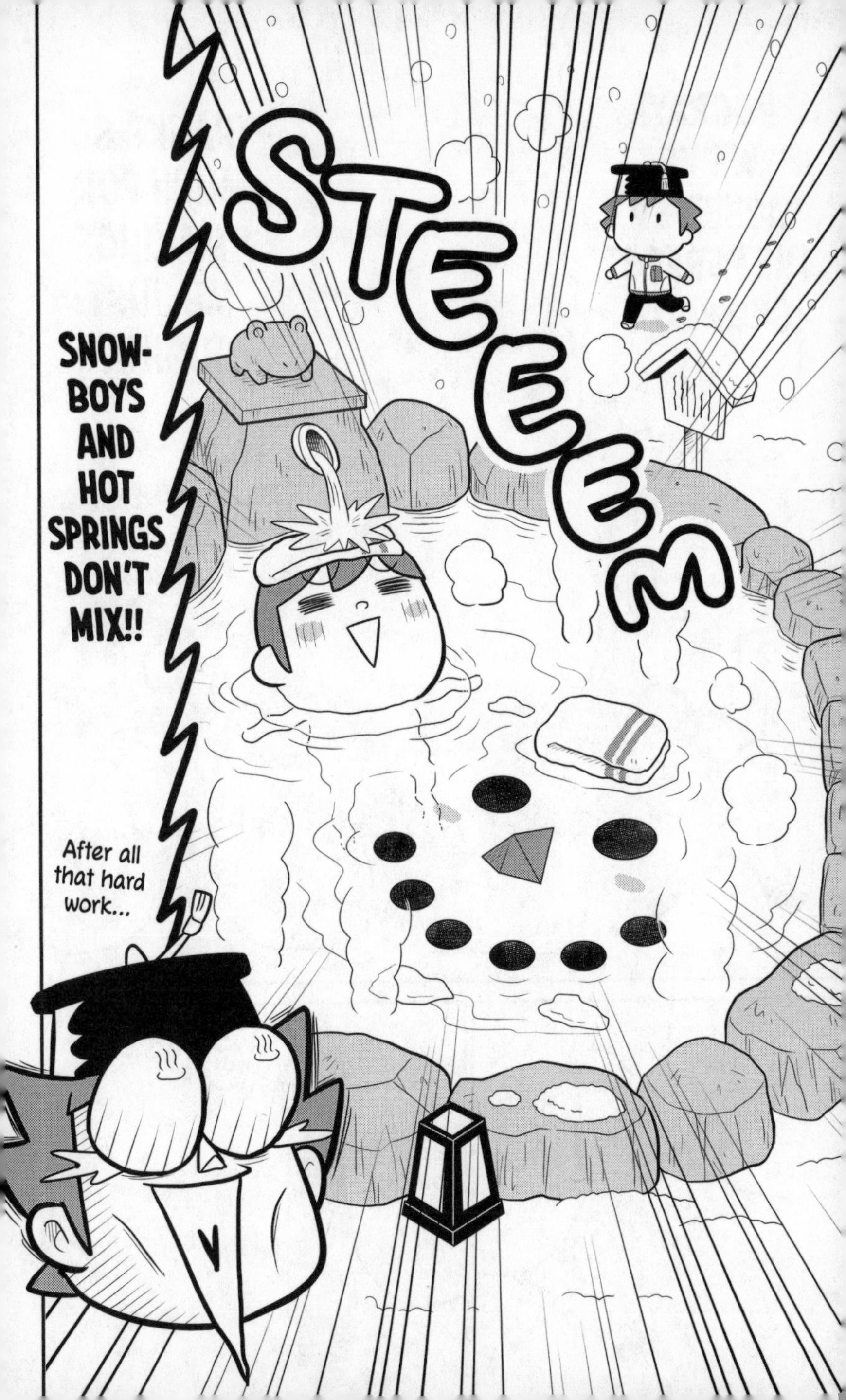
STEEEEM
SNOW-BOYS AND HOT SPRINGS DON'T MIX!!
After all that hard work...

Welcome to Animal Crossing New Horizons

Deserted Island Diary

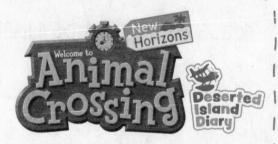

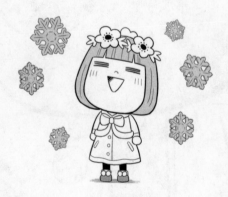

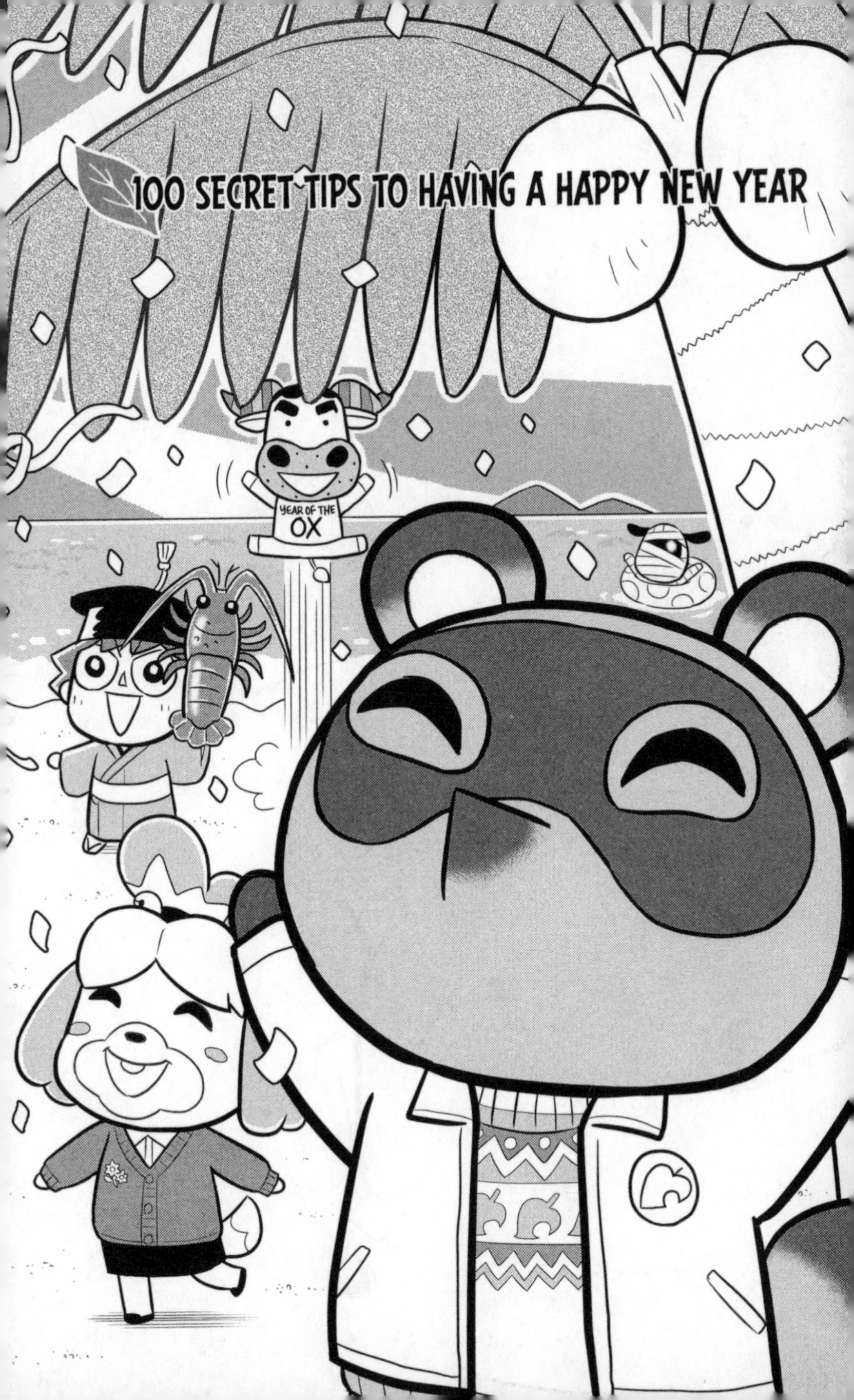

100 SECRET TIPS TO HAVING A HAPPY NEW YEAR
YEAR OF THE OX

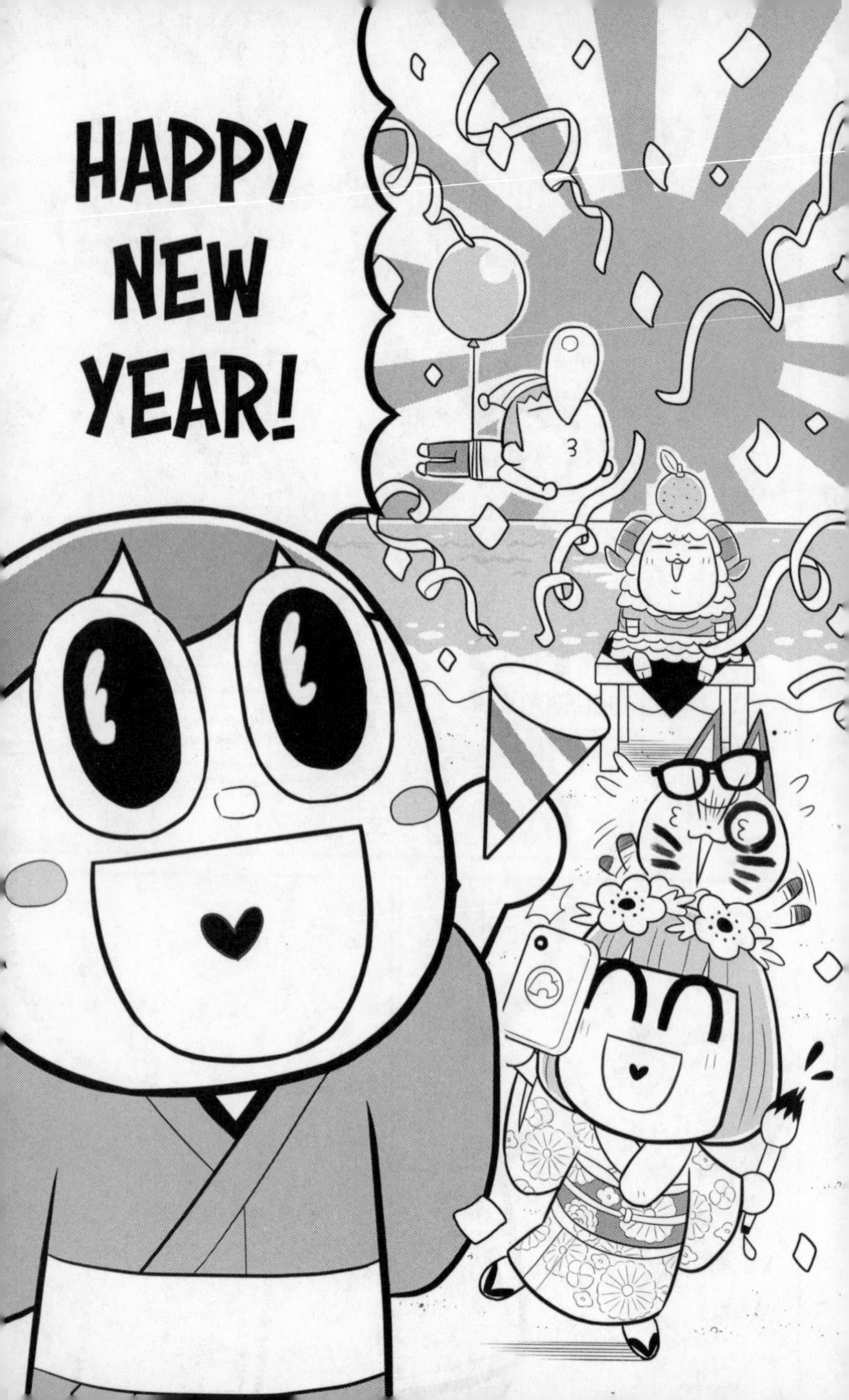
HAPPY
NEW
YEAR!

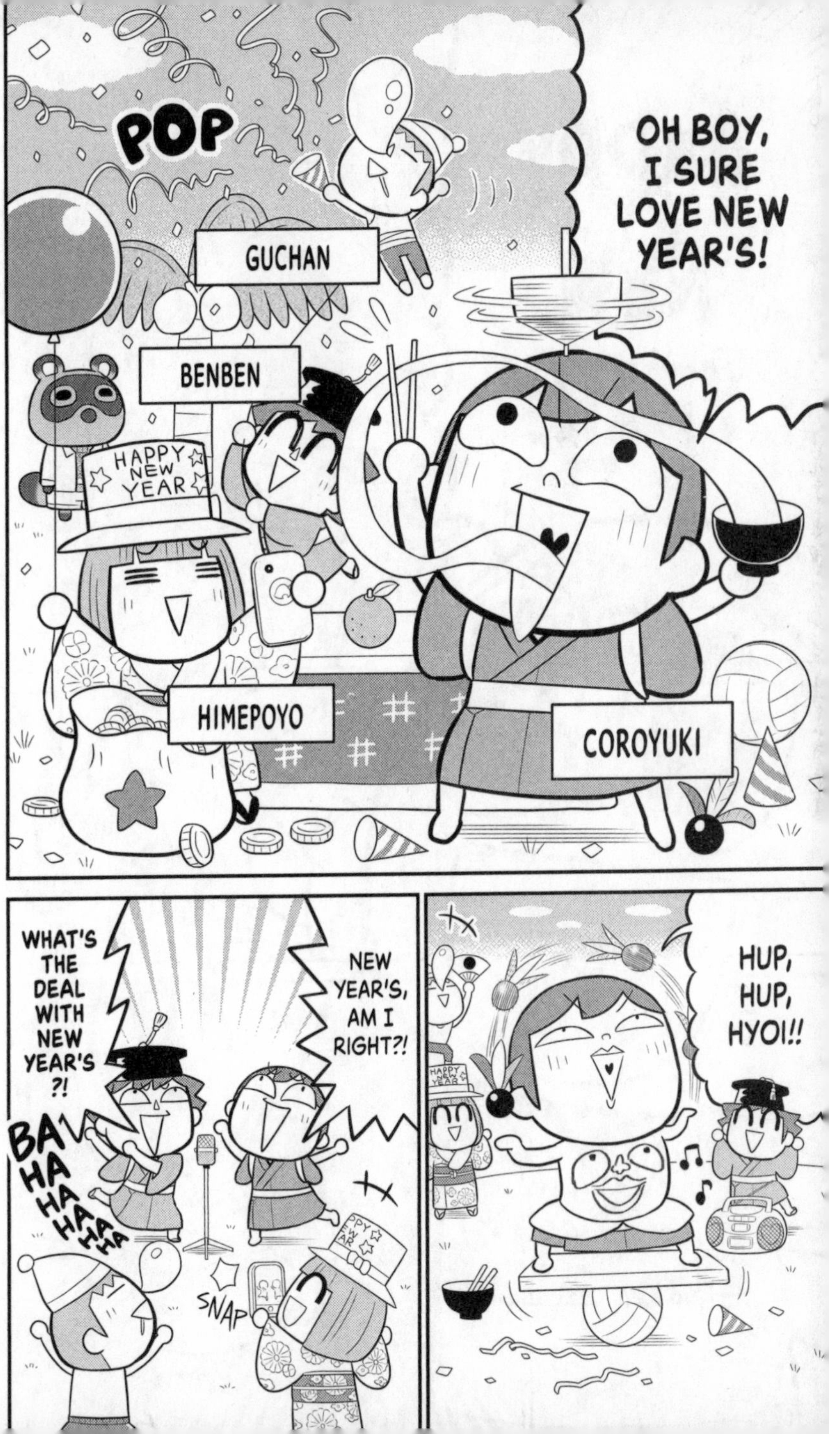
OH BOY, I SURE LOVE NEW YEAR'S!
POP
GUCHAN
BENBEN
HAPPY NEW YEAR
HIMEPOYO
COROYUKI
HUP, HUP, HYOI!!
HAPPY NEW YEAR
NEW YEAR'S, AM I RIGHT?!
WHAT'S THE DEAL WITH NEW YEAR'S?!
BAHAHAHAHAHA
SNAP

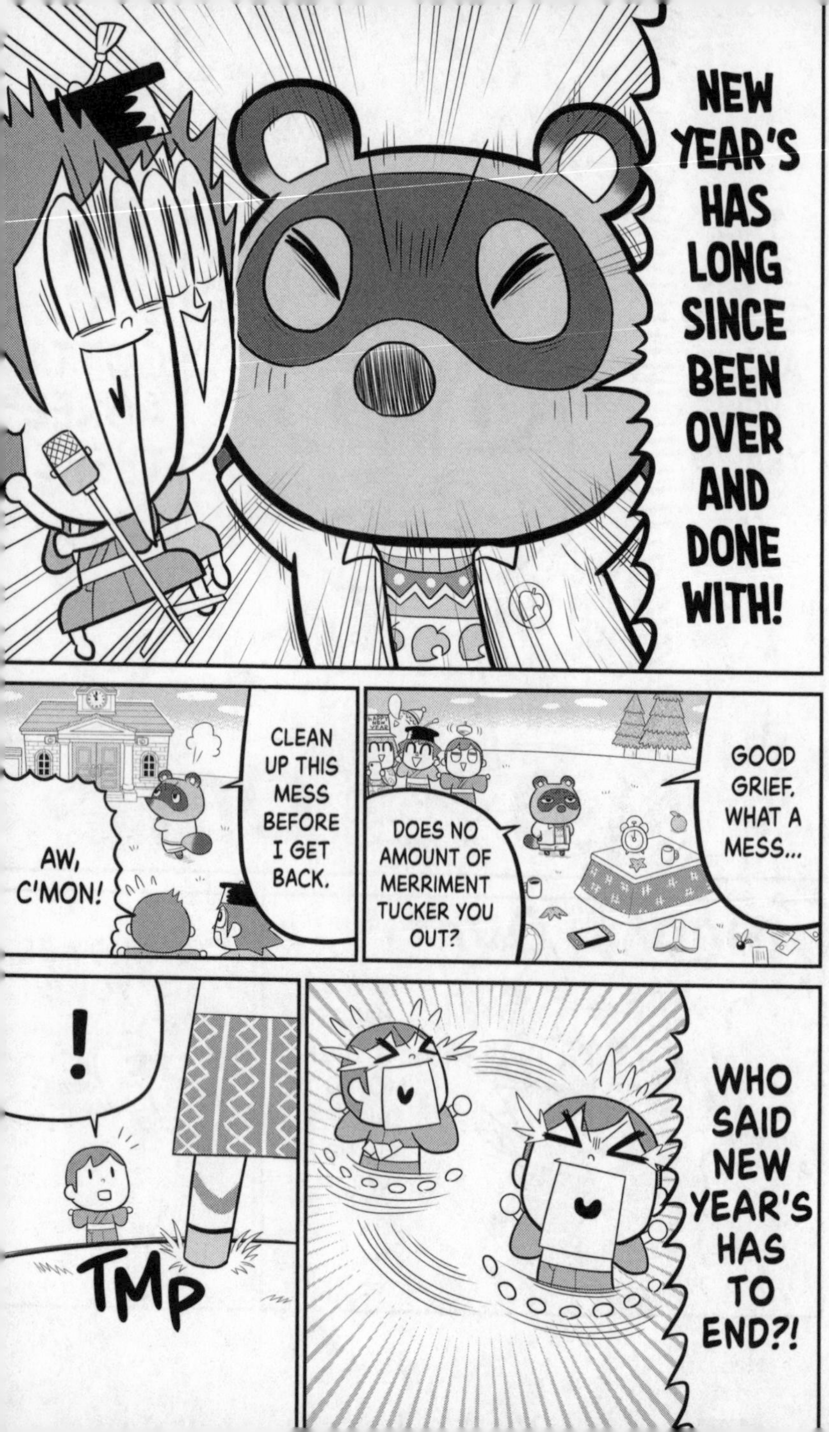
NEW YEAR'S HAS LONG SINCE BEEN OVER AND DONE WITH!
GOOD GRIEF. WHAT A MESS...
DOES NO AMOUNT OF MERRIMENT TUCKER YOU OUT?
CLEAN UP THIS MESS BEFORE I GET BACK.
AW, C'MON!
WHO SAID NEW YEAR'S HAS TO END?!
!
TMP

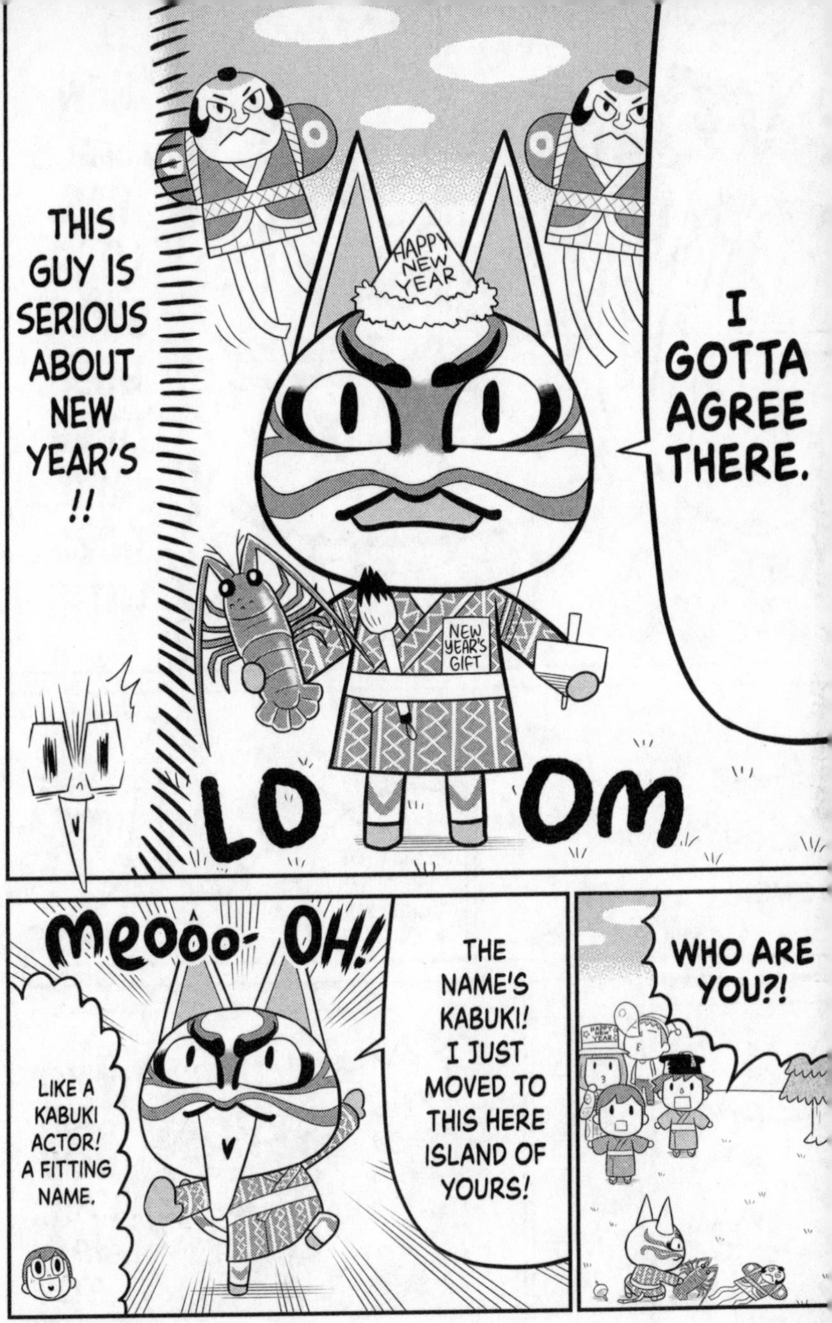
I GOTTA AGREE THERE.
HAPPY NEW YEAR
THIS GUY IS SERIOUS ABOUT NEW YEAR'S!!
NEW YEAR'S GIFT
LO OM
WHO ARE YOU?!
MEOÔO-OH!
THE NAME'S KABUKI! I JUST MOVED TO THIS HERE ISLAND OF YOURS!
LIKE A KABUKI ACTOR! A FITTING NAME.

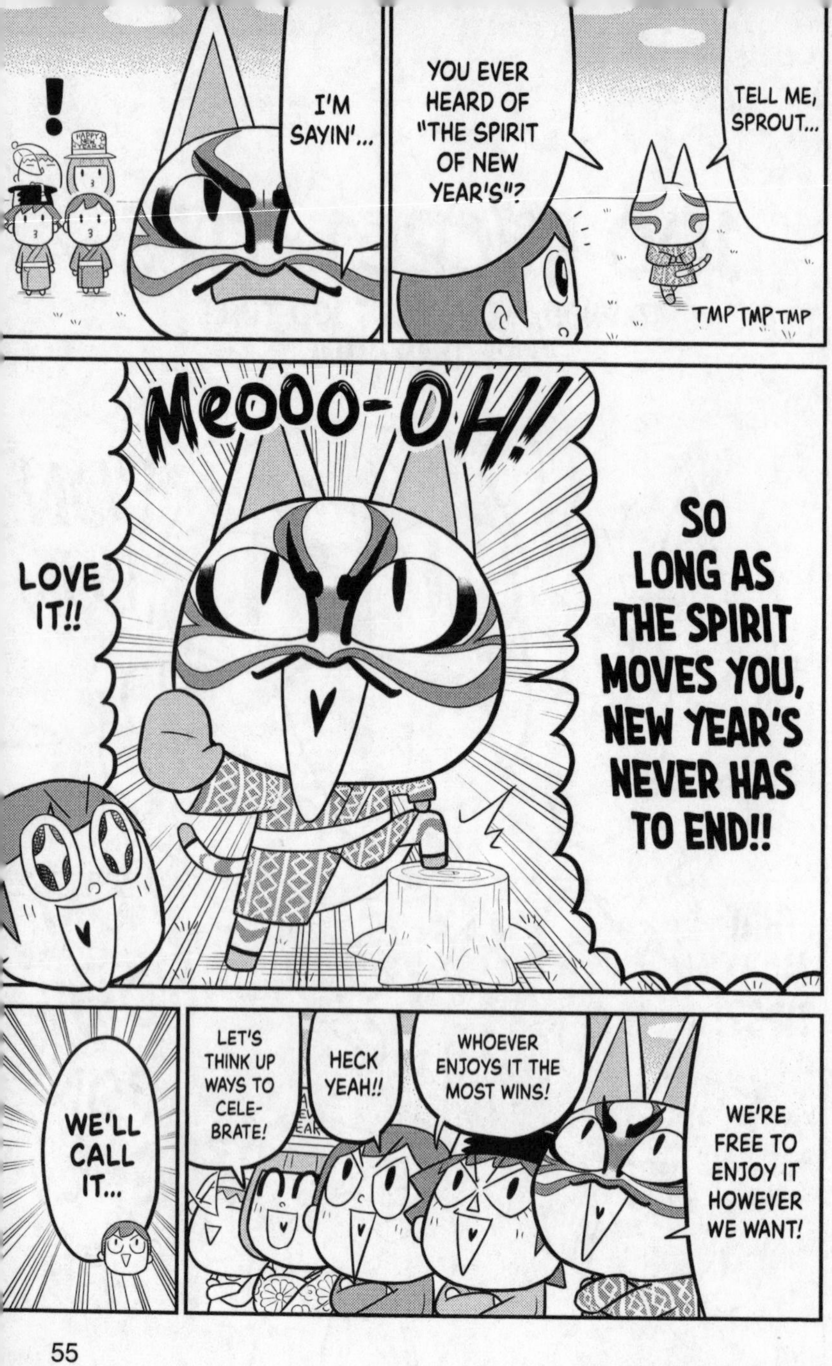
TELL ME, SPROUT...
TMP TMP TMP
YOU EVER HEARD OF "THE SPIRIT OF NEW YEAR'S"?
I'M SAYIN'...
!
SO LONG AS THE SPIRIT MOVES YOU, NEW YEAR'S NEVER HAS TO END!!
Meooo-OH!!
LOVE IT!!
WE'RE FREE TO ENJOY IT HOWEVER WE WANT!
WHOEVER ENJOYS IT THE MOST WINS!
HECK YEAH!!
LET'S THINK UP WAYS TO CELE-BRATE!
WE'LL CALL IT...

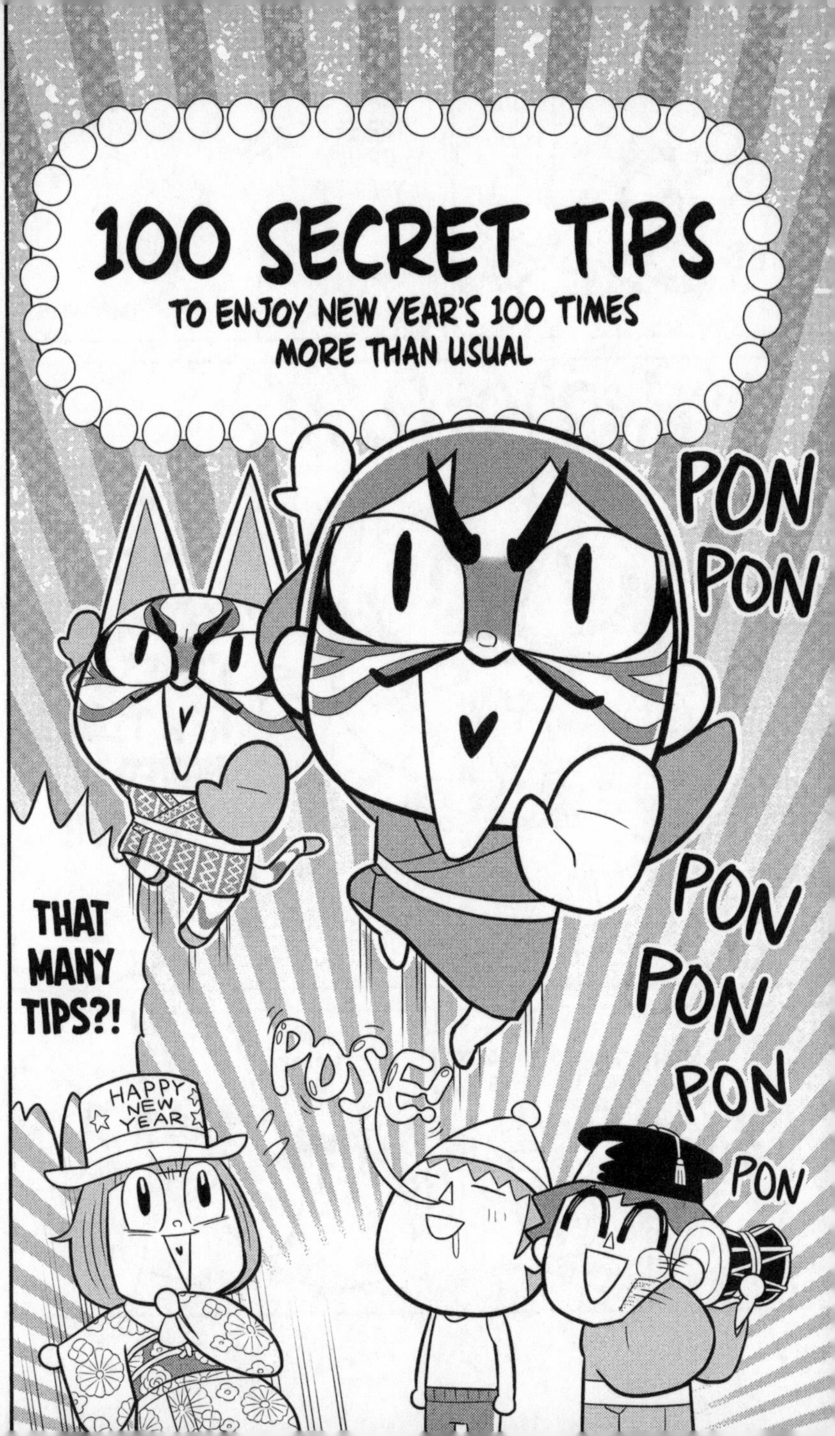
100 SECRET TIPS
TO ENJOY NEW YEAR'S 100 TIMES MORE THAN USUAL
PON PON
PON PON PON
PON
POSE!
THAT MANY TIPS?!
HAPPY NEW YEAR

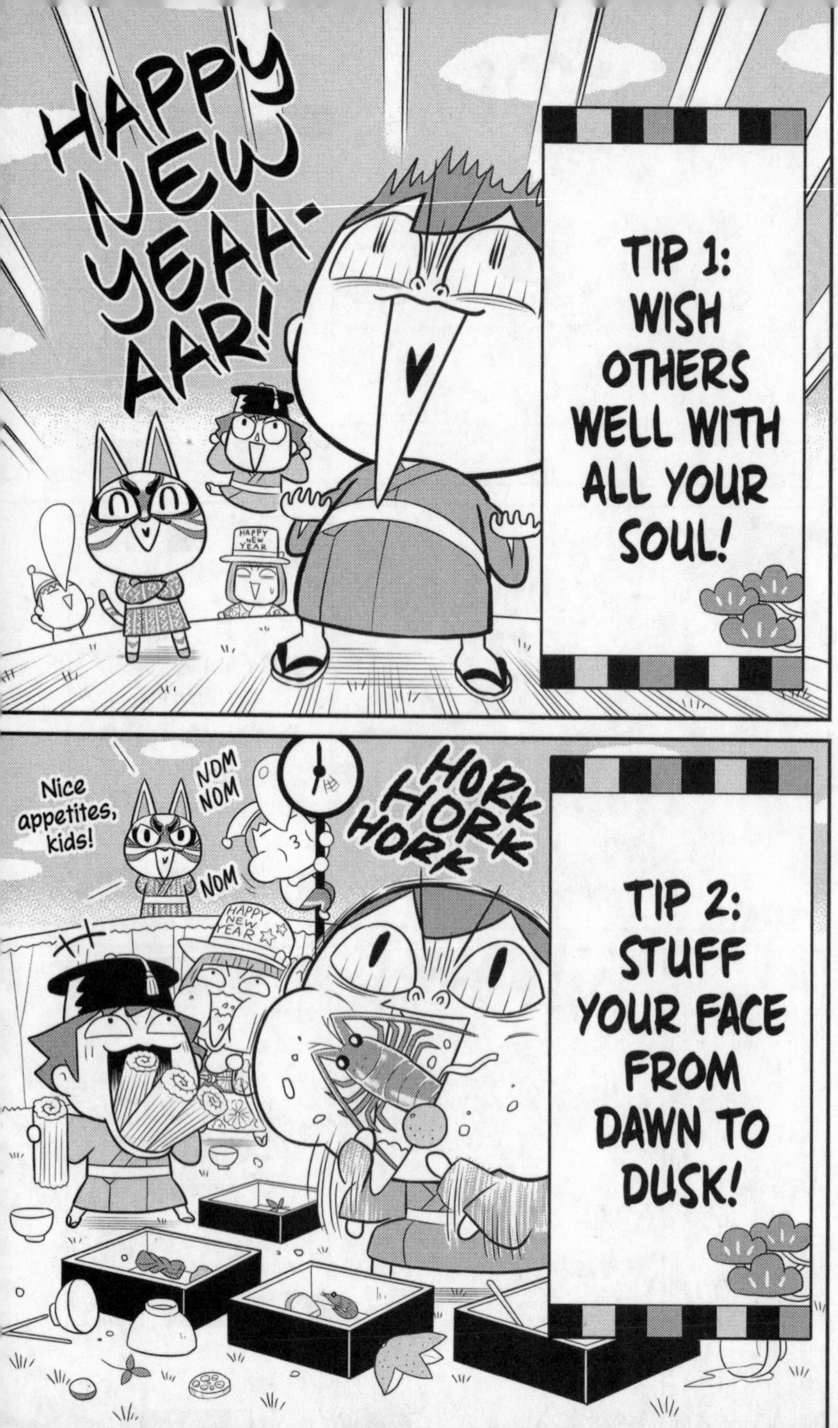
TIP 1: WISH OTHERS WELL WITH ALL YOUR SOUL!
HAPPY NEW YEAA-AAR!
HAPPY NEW YEAR
TIP 2: STUFF YOUR FACE FROM DAWN TO DUSK!
HORK HORK HORK
NOM NOM
Nice appetites, kids!
NOM
HAPPY NEW YEAR

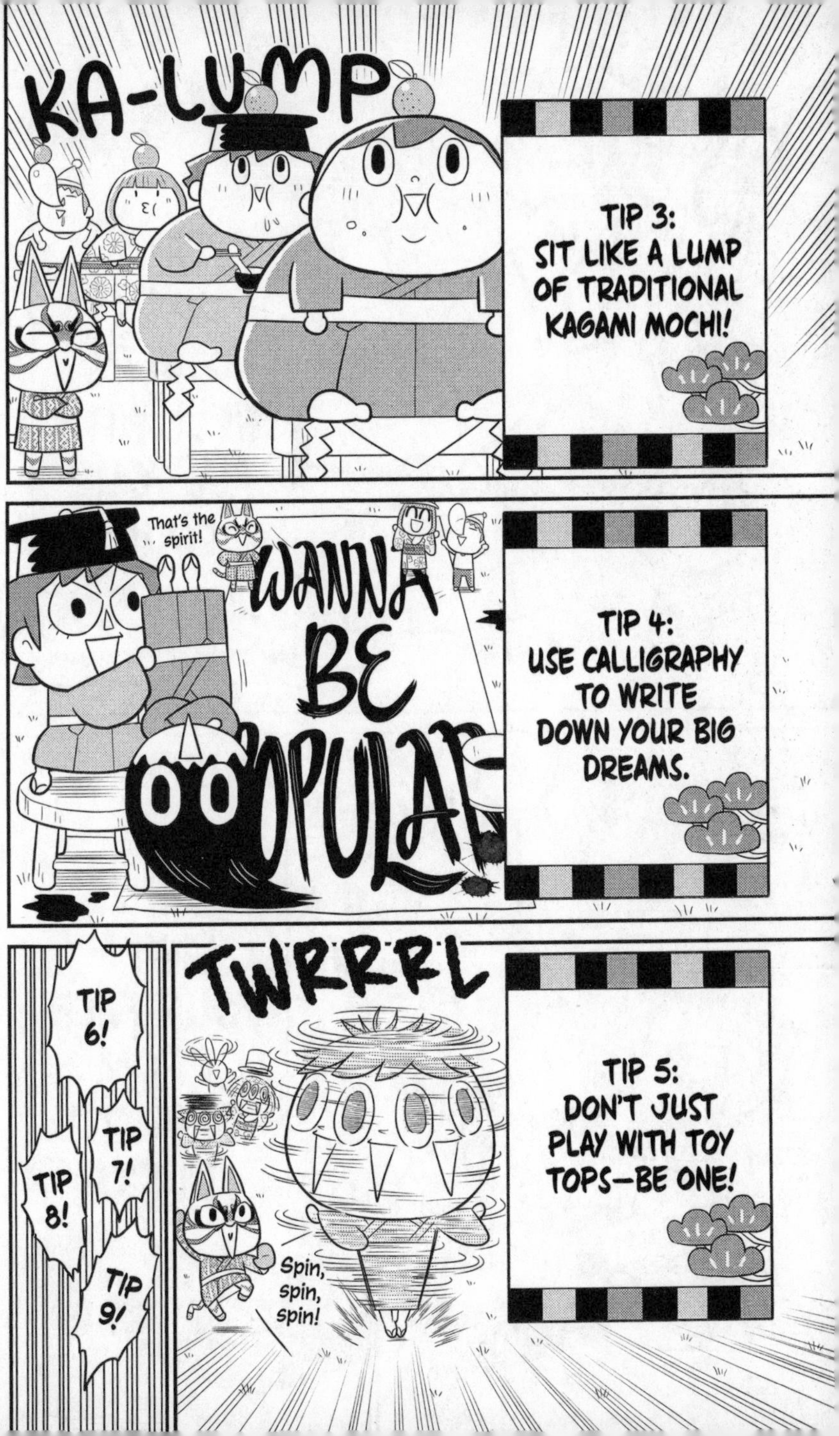
TIP 3:
SIT LIKE A LUMP OF TRADITIONAL KAGAMI MOCHI!
KA-LUMP
TIP 4:
USE CALLIGRAPHY TO WRITE DOWN YOUR BIG DREAMS.
WANNA BE POPULAR
That's the spirit!
TIP 5:
DON'T JUST PLAY WITH TOY TOPS—BE ONE!
TWRRRL
Spin, spin, spin!
TIP 6!
TIP 7!
TIP 8!
TIP 9!

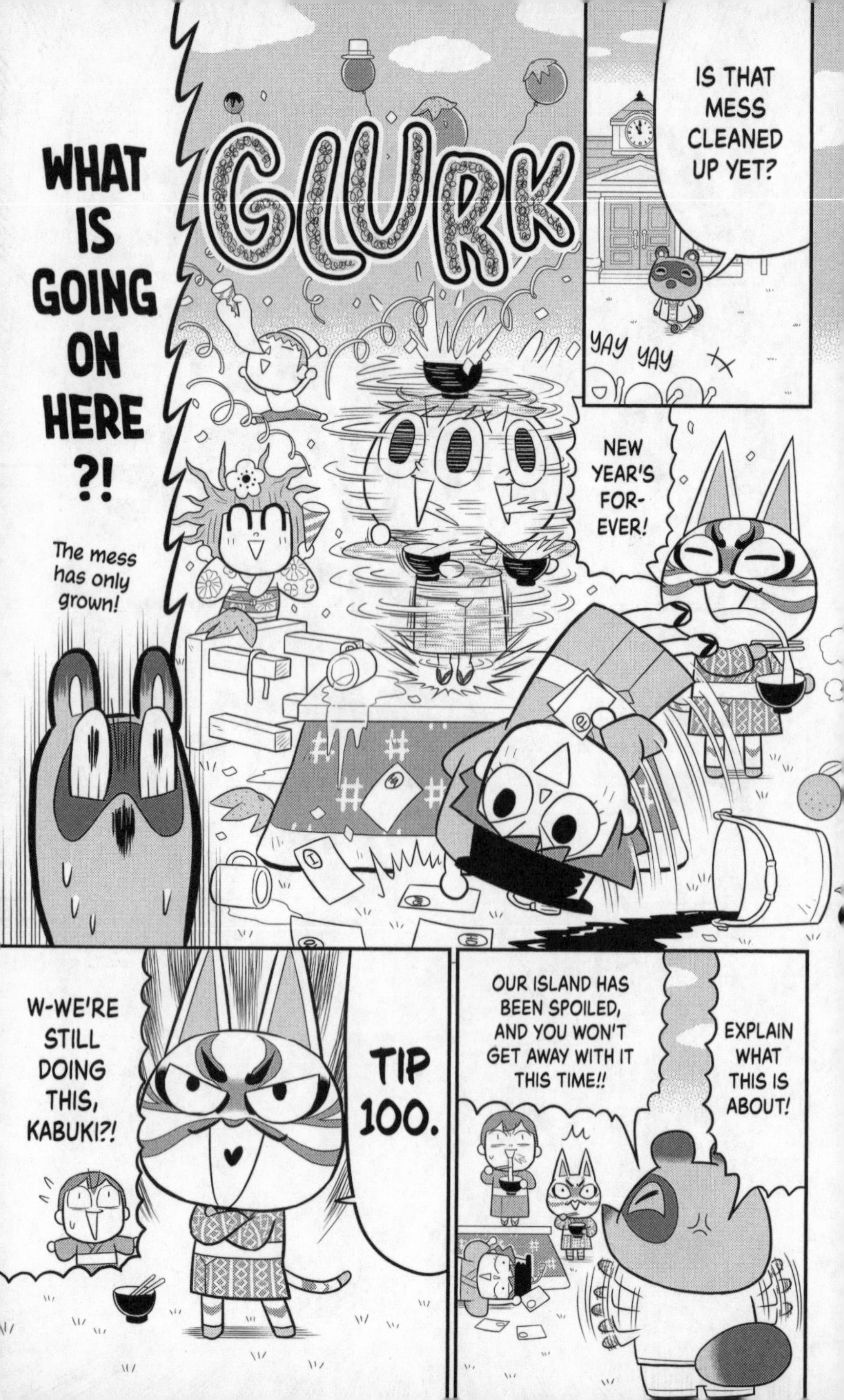
IS THAT MESS CLEANED UP YET?
YAY YAY
GLURK
NEW YEAR'S FOR-EVER!
WHAT IS GOING ON HERE?!
The mess has only grown!
EXPLAIN WHAT THIS IS ABOUT!
OUR ISLAND HAS BEEN SPOILED, AND YOU WON'T GET AWAY WITH IT THIS TIME!!
TIP 100.
W-WE'RE STILL DOING THIS, KABUKI?!

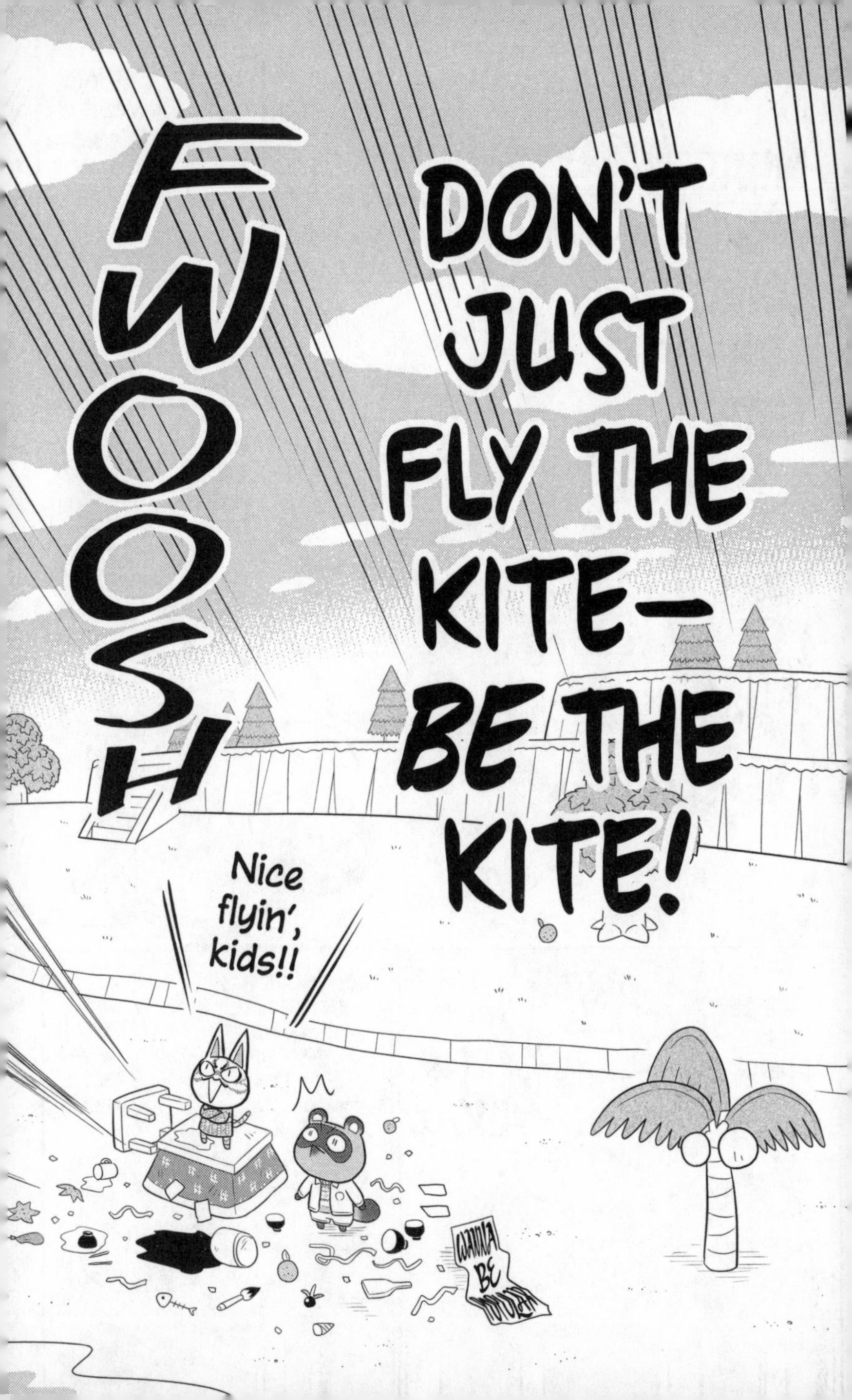
DON'T JUST FLY THE KITE— BE THE KITE!
FWOOSH
Nice flyin', kids!!
WANNA BE

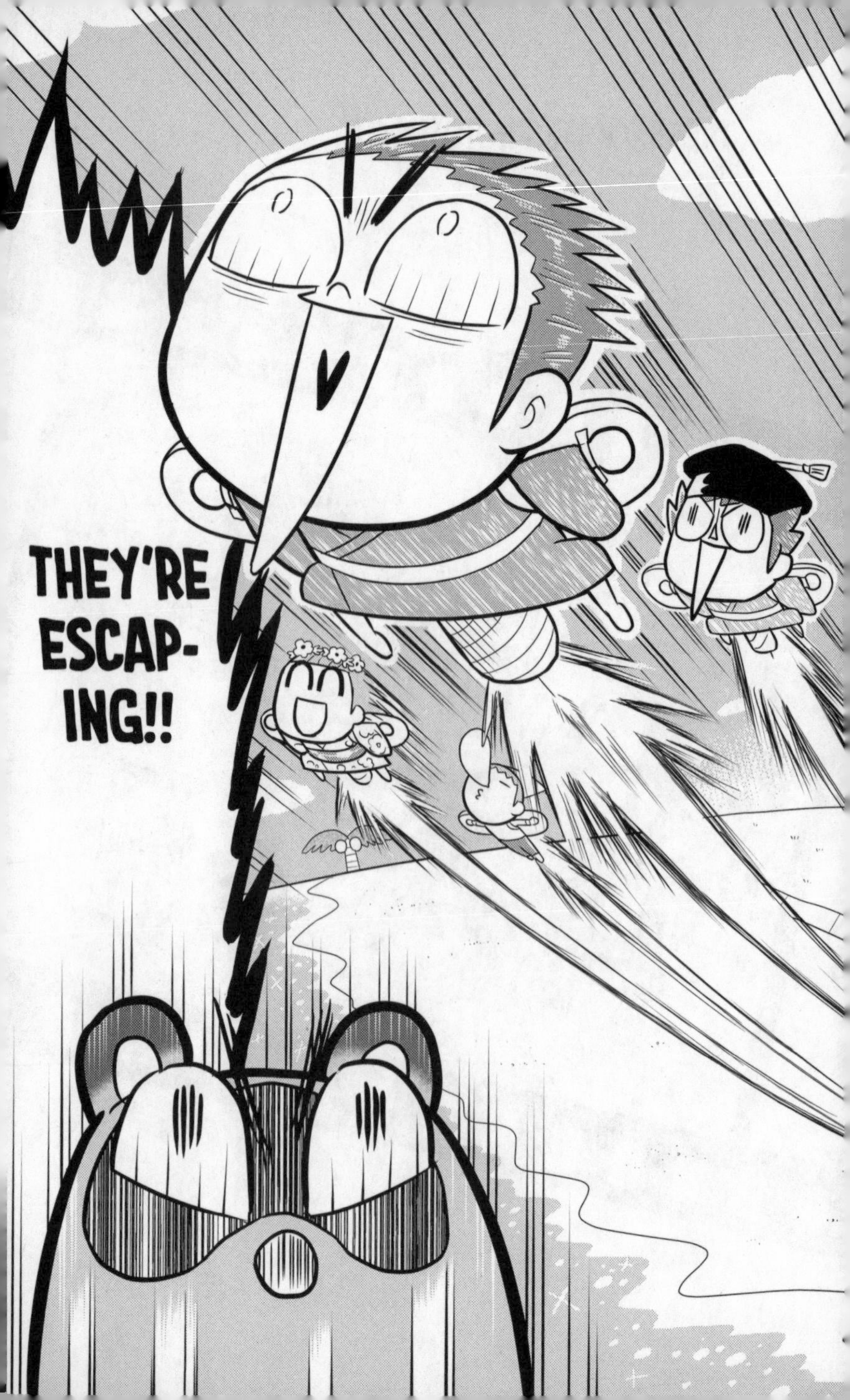
THEY'RE ESCAP-ING!!

THE ULTIMATE PHOTOSHOOT!

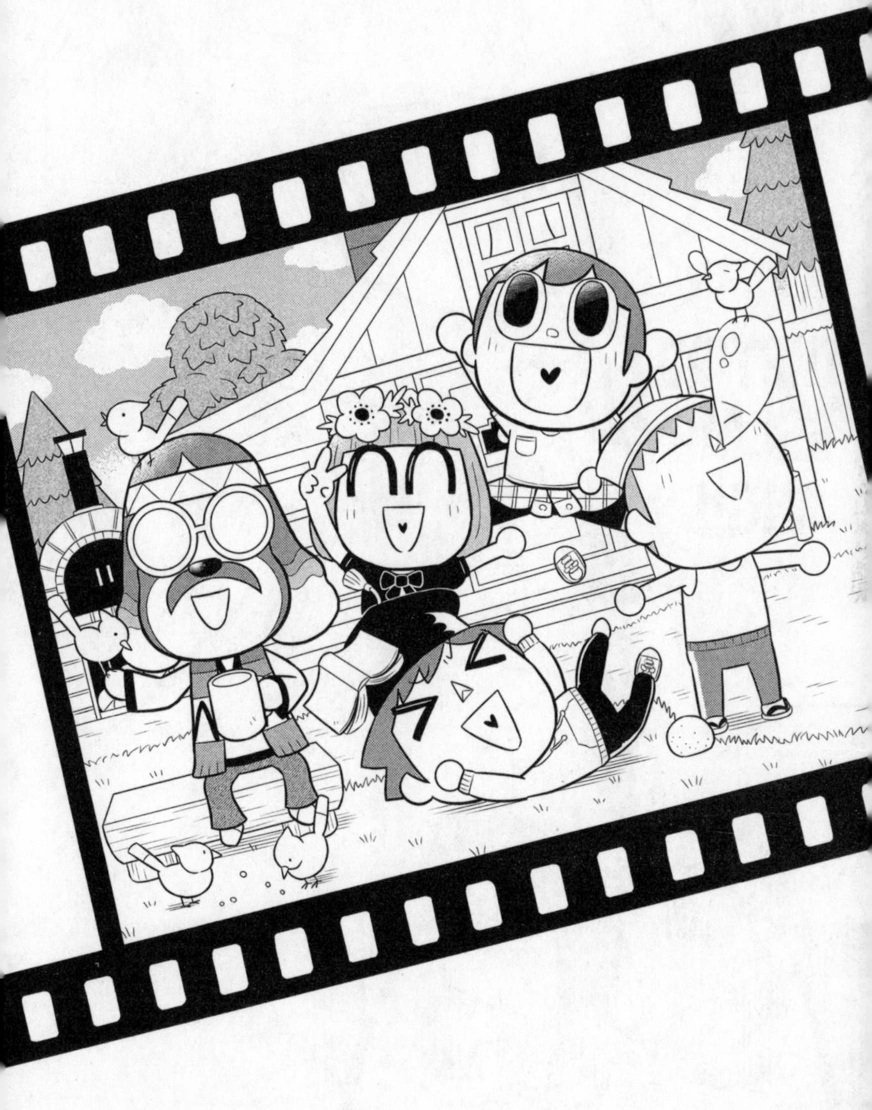

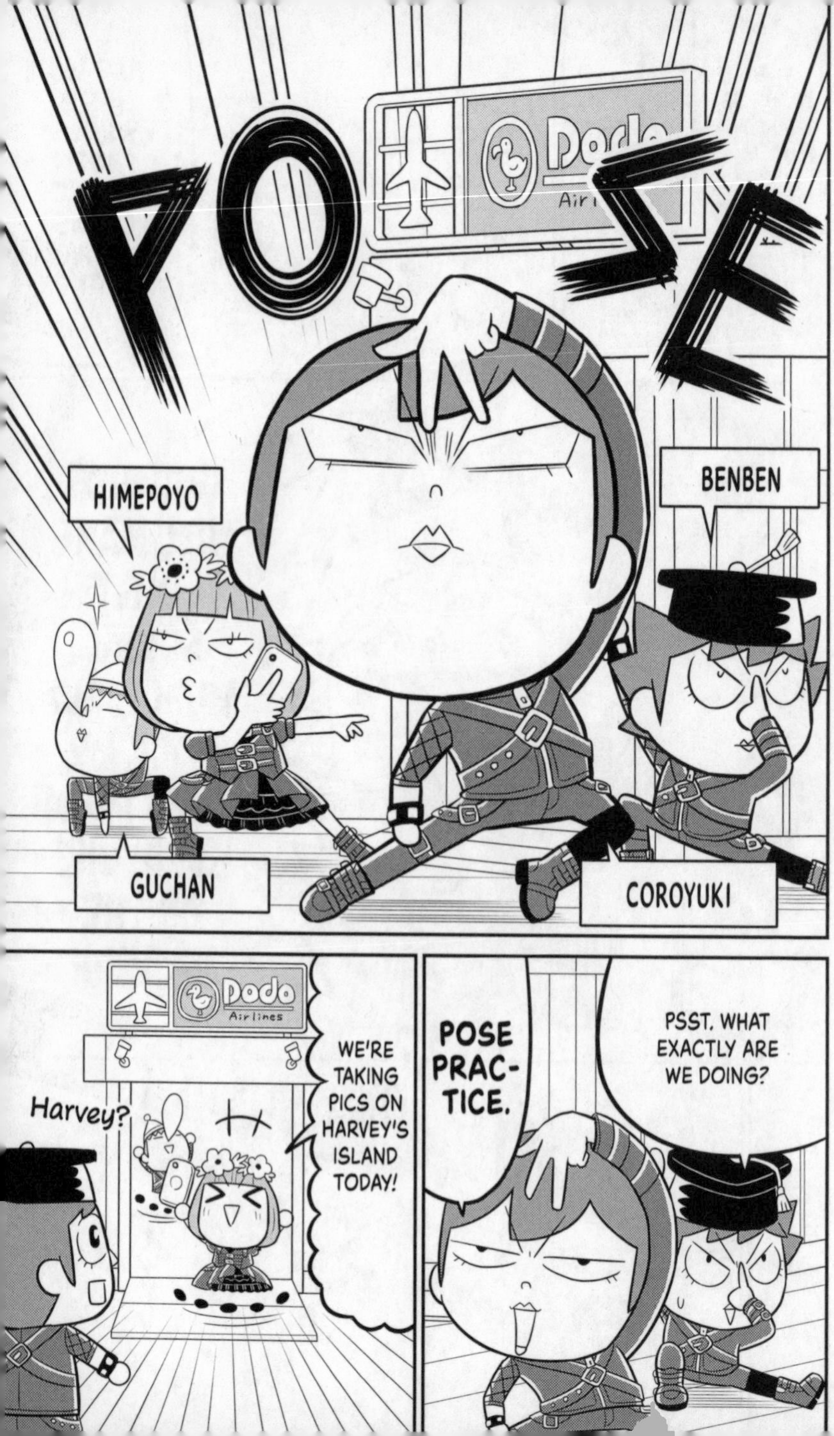
POSE
Dodo
BENBEN
HIMEPOYO
COROYUKI
GUCHAN
PSST. WHAT EXACTLY ARE WE DOING?
POSE PRAC-TICE.
WE'RE TAKING PICS ON HARVEY'S ISLAND TODAY!
Dodo Airlines
Harvey?

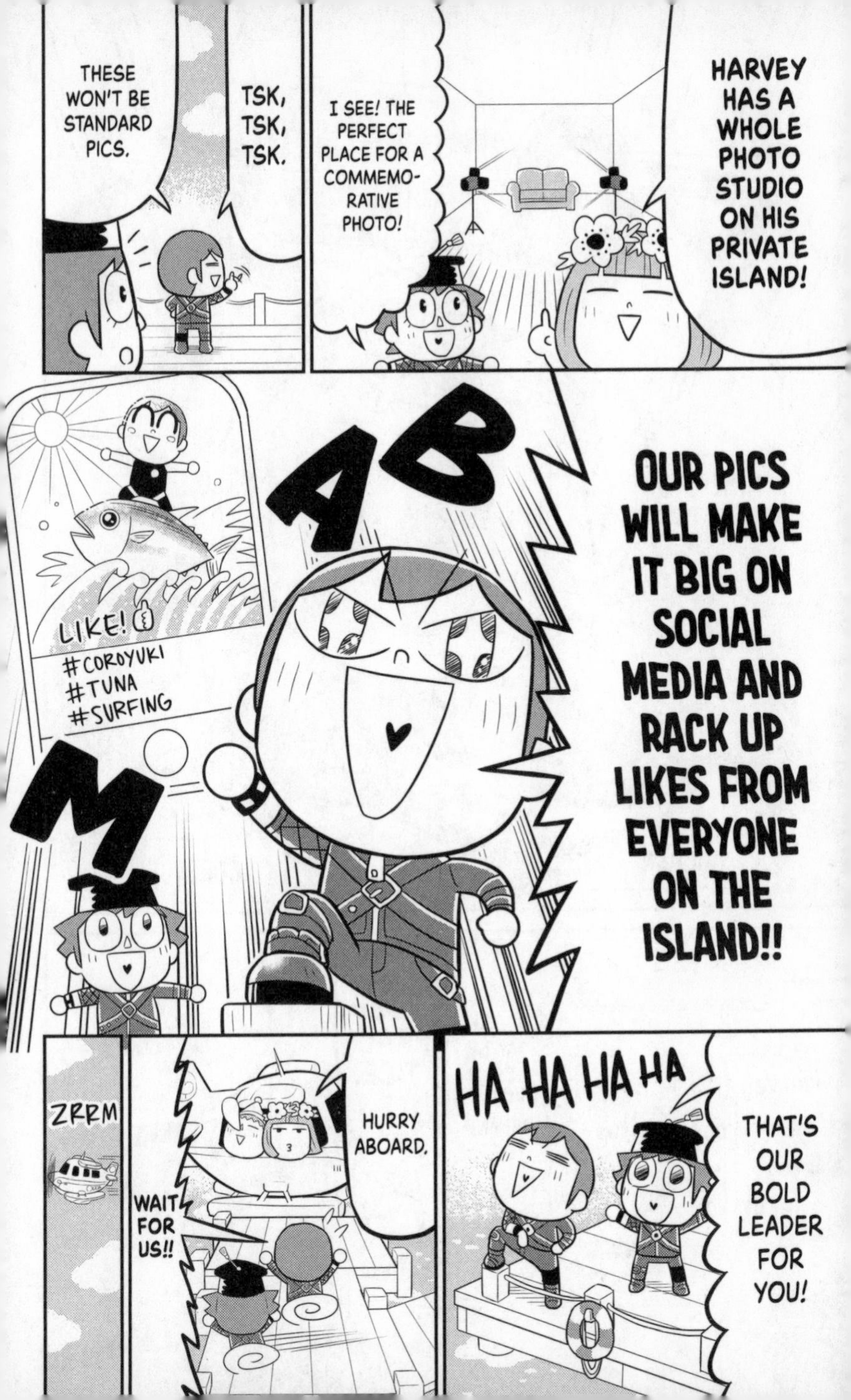
HARVEY HAS A WHOLE PHOTO STUDIO ON HIS PRIVATE ISLAND!
I SEE! THE PERFECT PLACE FOR A COMMEMORATIVE PHOTO!
TSK, TSK, TSK.
THESE WON'T BE STANDARD PICS.
AB
OUR PICS WILL MAKE IT BIG ON SOCIAL MEDIA AND RACK UP LIKES FROM EVERYONE ON THE ISLAND!!
LIKE!
#COROYUKI
#TUNA
#SURFING
M
HA HA HA HA HA
THAT'S OUR BOLD LEADER FOR YOU!
HURRY ABOARD.
WAIT FOR US!!
ZRRM

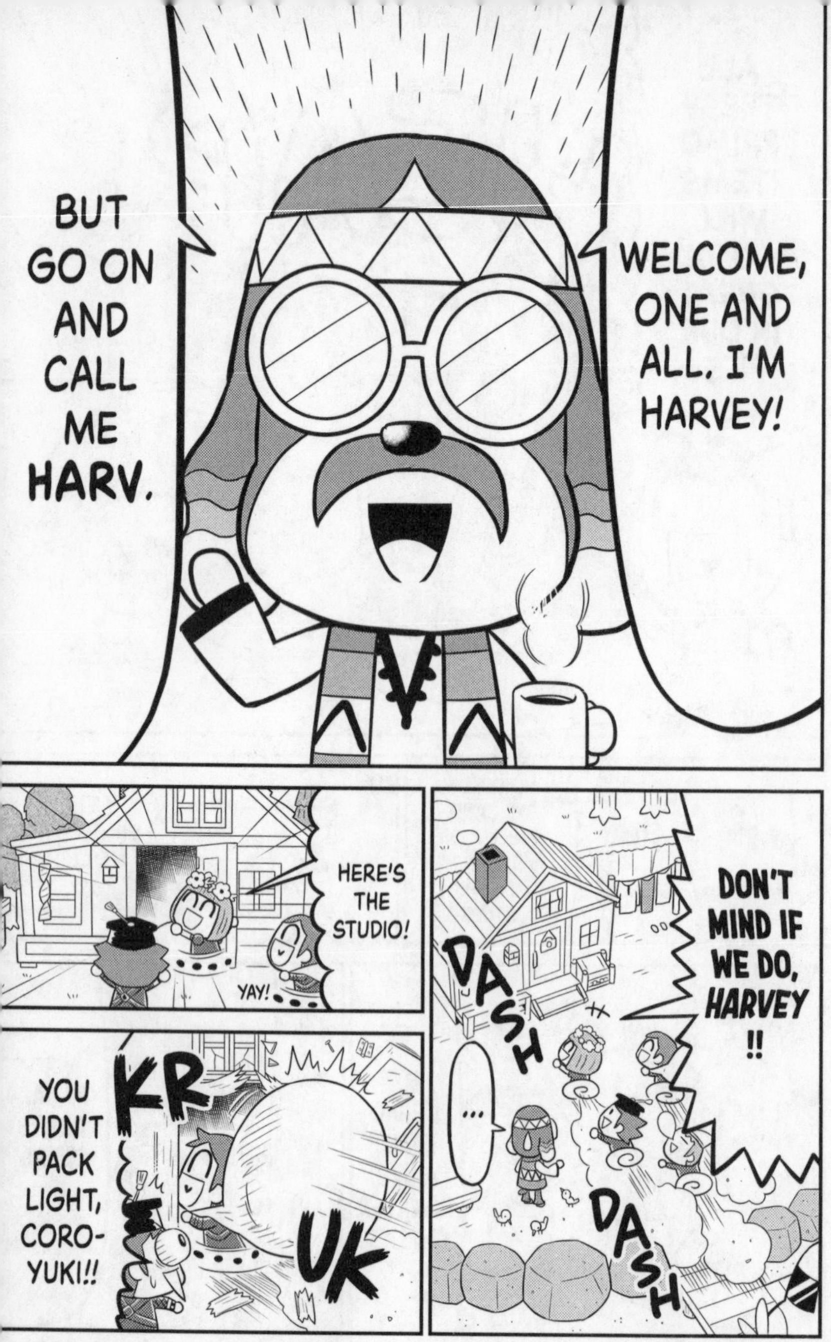

WELCOME, ONE AND ALL. I'M HARVEY!
BUT GO ON AND CALL ME HARV.
DON'T MIND IF WE DO, HARVEY!!
DASH
...
DASH
HERE'S THE STUDIO!
YAY!
KR
UK
YOU DIDN'T PACK LIGHT, CORO-YUKI!!

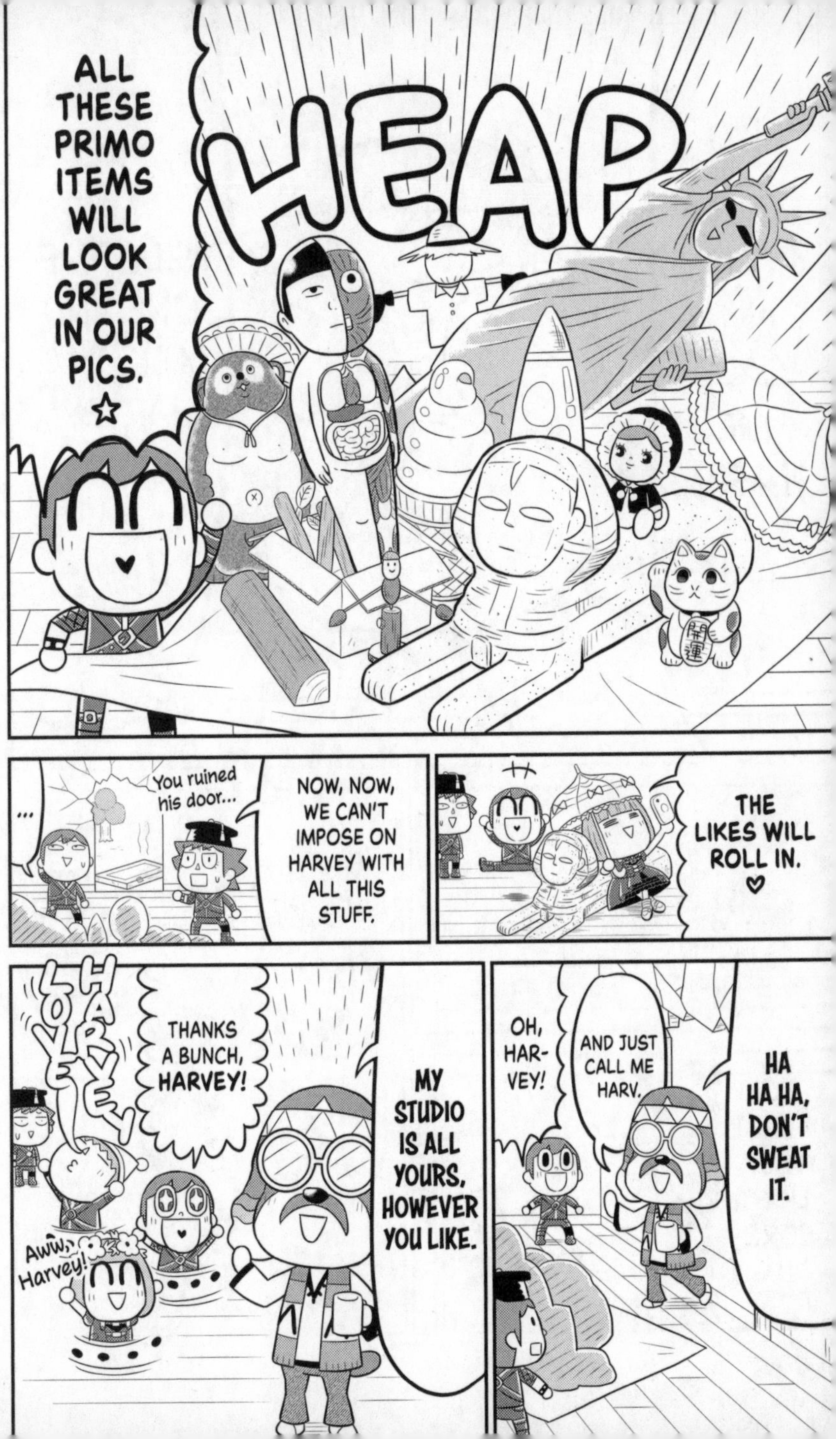
HEAP
ALL THESE PRIMO ITEMS WILL LOOK GREAT IN OUR PICS. ☆
THE LIKES WILL ROLL IN. ♡
NOW, NOW, WE CAN'T IMPOSE ON HARVEY WITH ALL THIS STUFF.
You ruined his door...
...
HA HA HA, DON'T SWEAT IT.
AND JUST CALL ME HARV.
OH, HAR-VEY!
MY STUDIO IS ALL YOURS, HOWEVER YOU LIKE.
THANKS A BUNCH, HARVEY!
HARVEY
LOVE
Aww, Harvey!

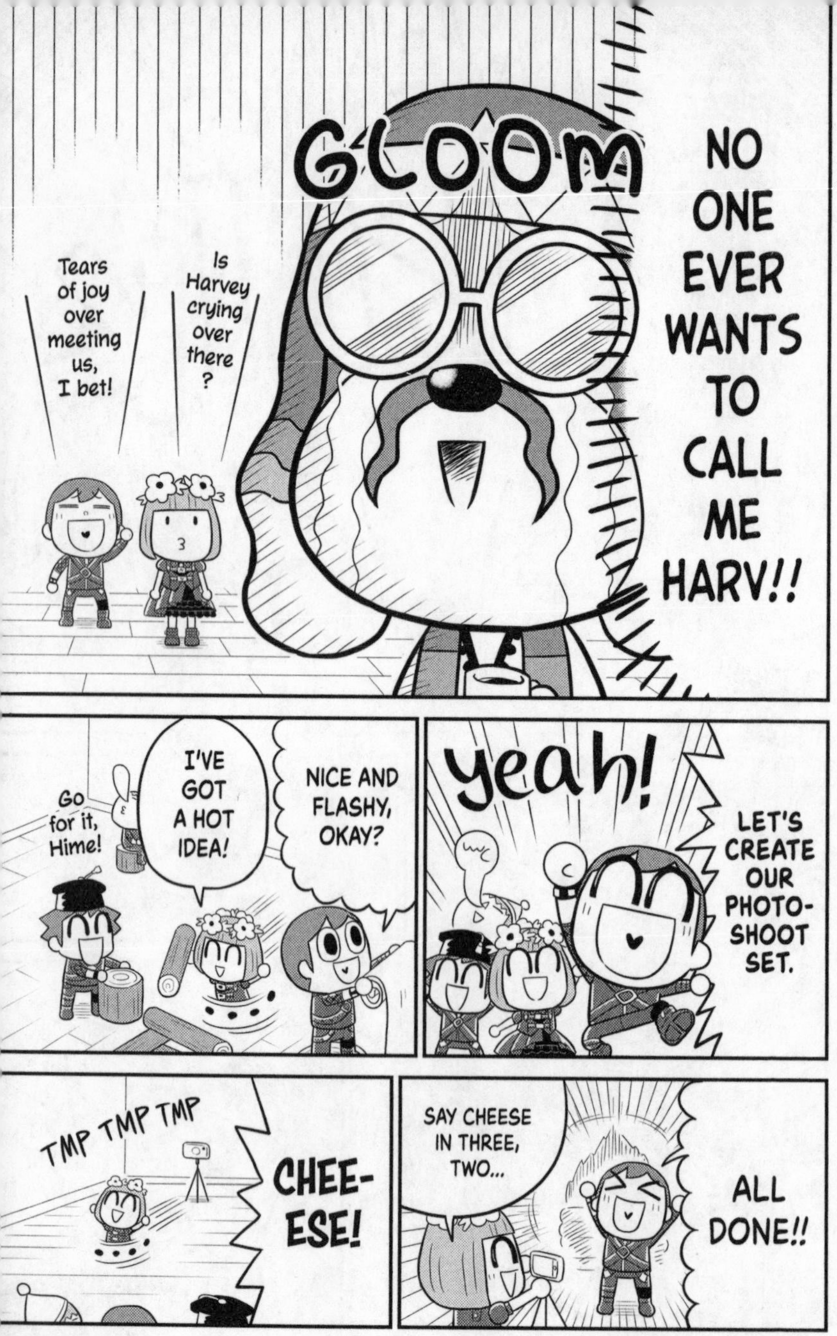
GLOOM
NO ONE EVER WANTS TO CALL ME HARV!!
Is Harvey crying over there?
Tears of joy over meeting us, I bet!
LET'S CREATE OUR PHOTO-SHOOT SET.
yeah!
NICE AND FLASHY, OKAY?
I'VE GOT A HOT IDEA!
Go for it, Hime!
SAY CHEESE IN THREE, TWO...
ALL DONE!!
CHEE-ESE!
TMP TMP TMP

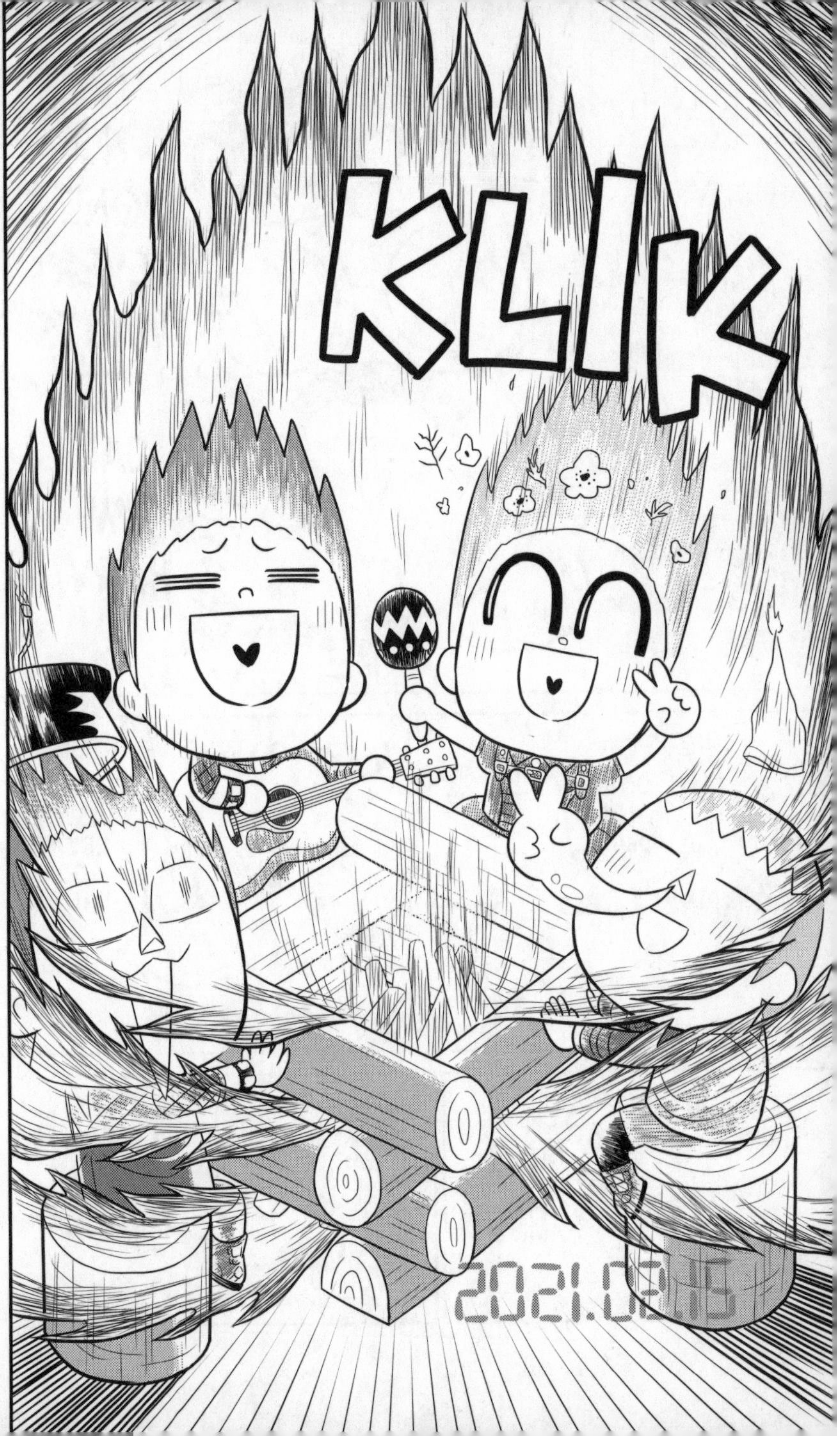
KLIK
2021.03.15

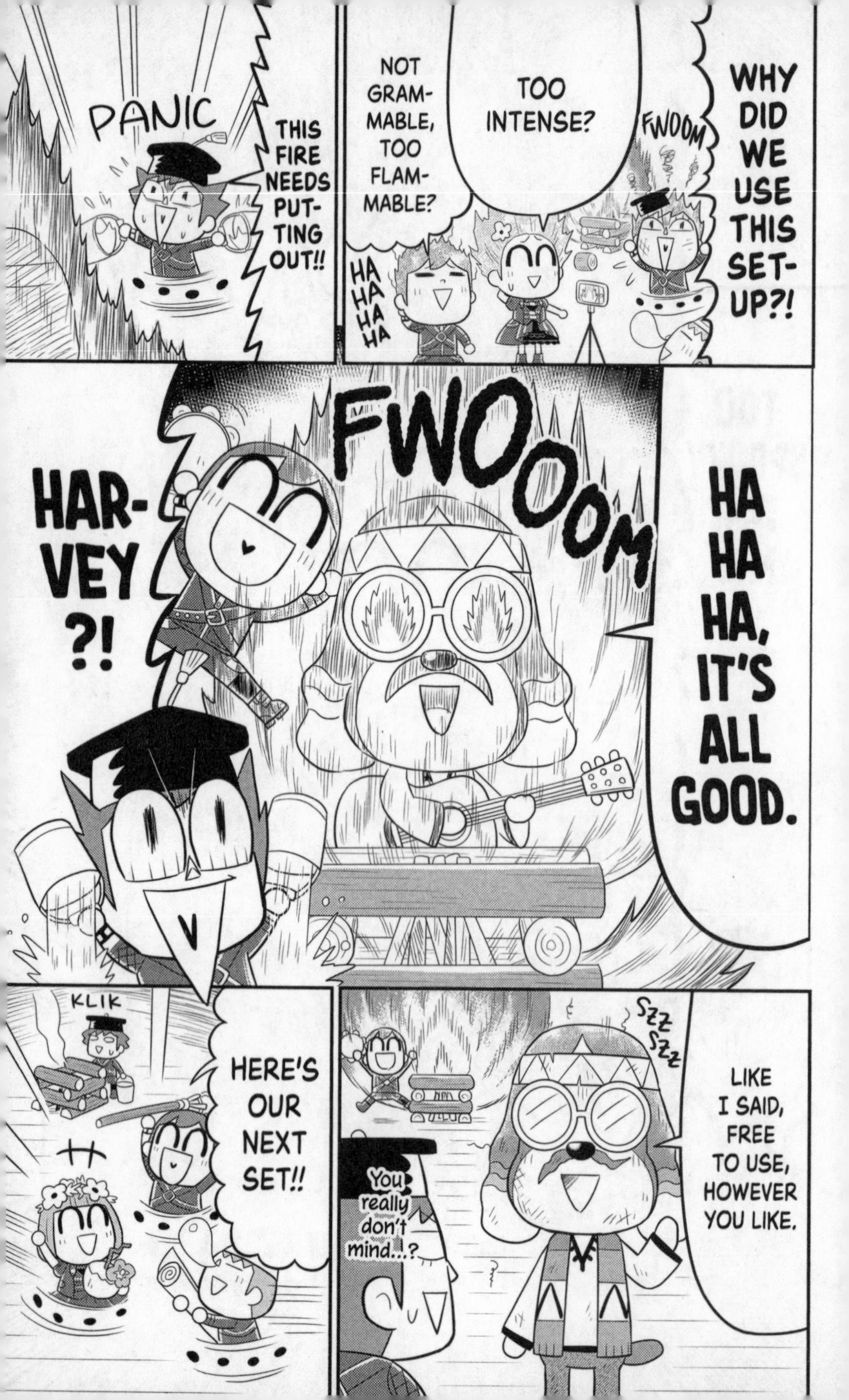
WHY DID WE USE THIS SET-UP?!
FWOOM
TOO INTENSE?
NOT GRAMMABLE, TOO FLAMMABLE?
HA HA HA HA
THIS FIRE NEEDS PUTTING OUT!!
PANIC
HA HA HA, IT'S ALL GOOD.
FWOOOOM
HARVEY?!
SZZ SZZ
LIKE I SAID, FREE TO USE, HOWEVER YOU LIKE.
You really don't mind...?
HERE'S OUR NEXT SET!!
KLIK

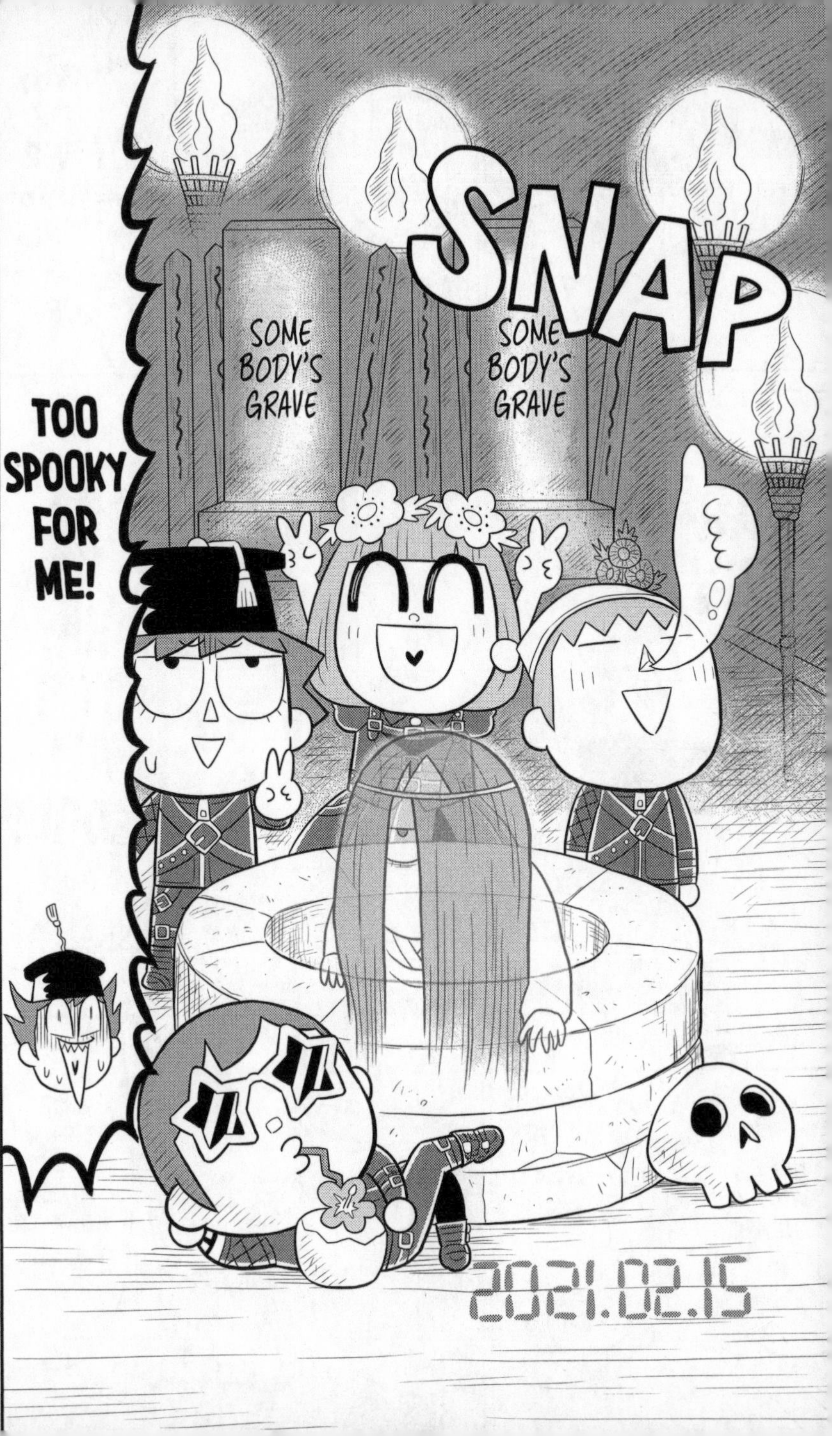
SNAP
SOME BODY'S GRAVE
SOME BODY'S GRAVE
TOO SPOOKY FOR ME!
2021.02.15

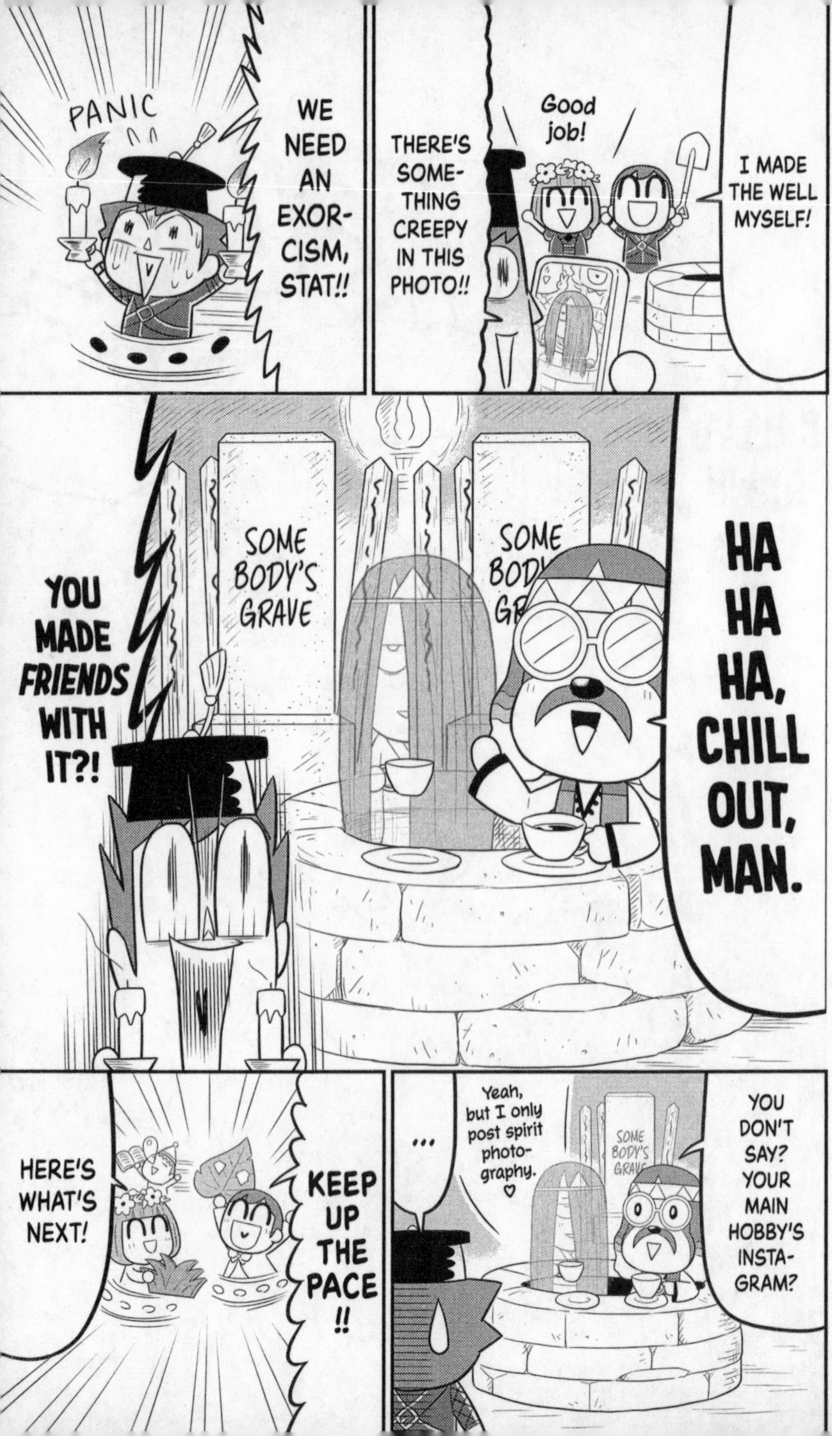
I MADE THE WELL MYSELF!
Good job!
THERE'S SOME-THING CREEPY IN THIS PHOTO!!
WE NEED AN EXOR-CISM, STAT!!
PANIC
HA HA HA, CHILL OUT, MAN.
SOME BODY'S GRAVE
YOU MADE FRIENDS WITH IT?!
YOU DON'T SAY? YOUR MAIN HOBBY'S INSTA-GRAM?
SOME BODY'S GRAVE
Yeah, but I only post spirit photo-graphy. ♡
...
KEEP UP THE PACE!!
HERE'S WHAT'S NEXT!

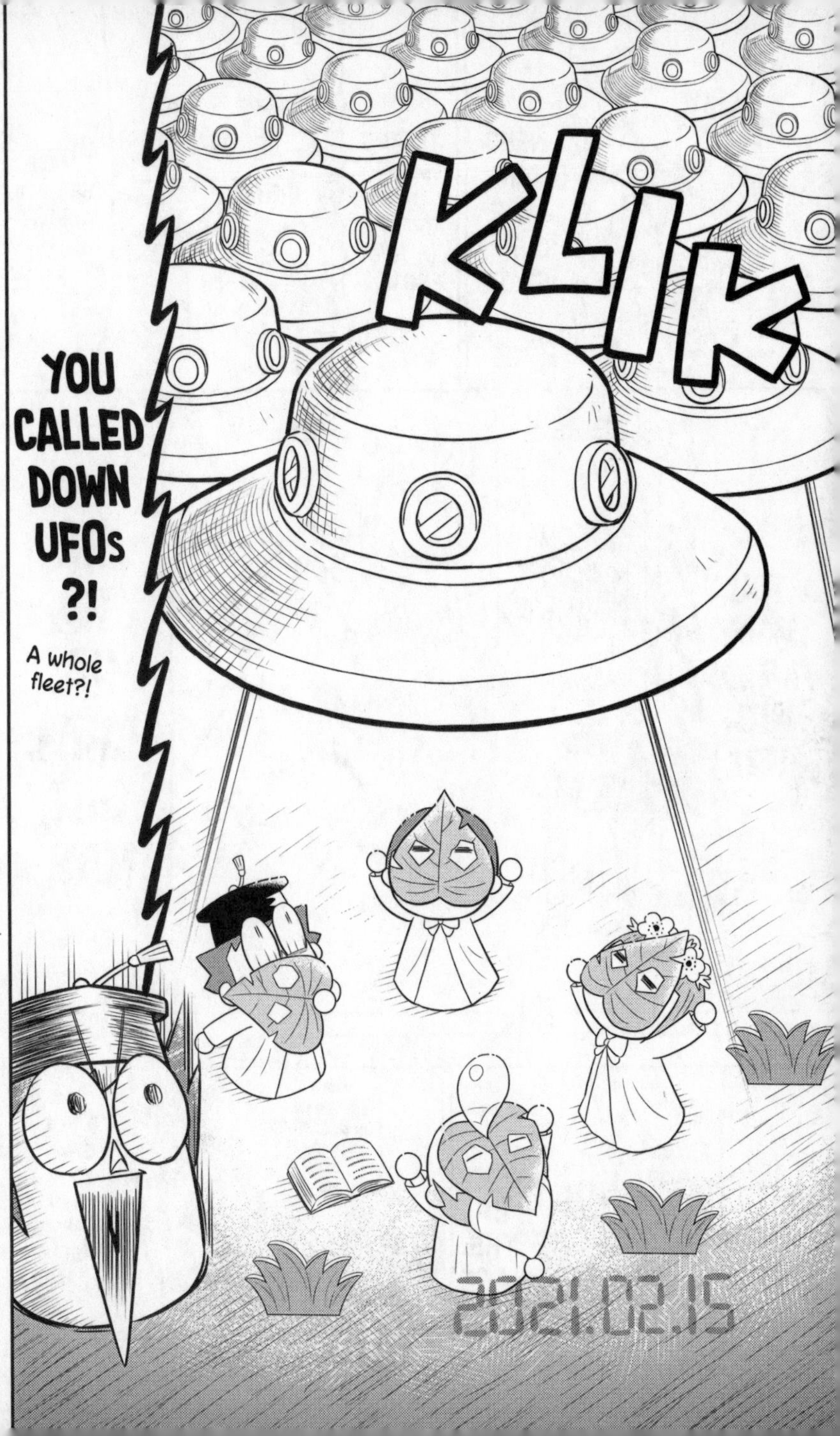
KLIK
YOU CALLED DOWN UFOs ?!
A whole fleet?!

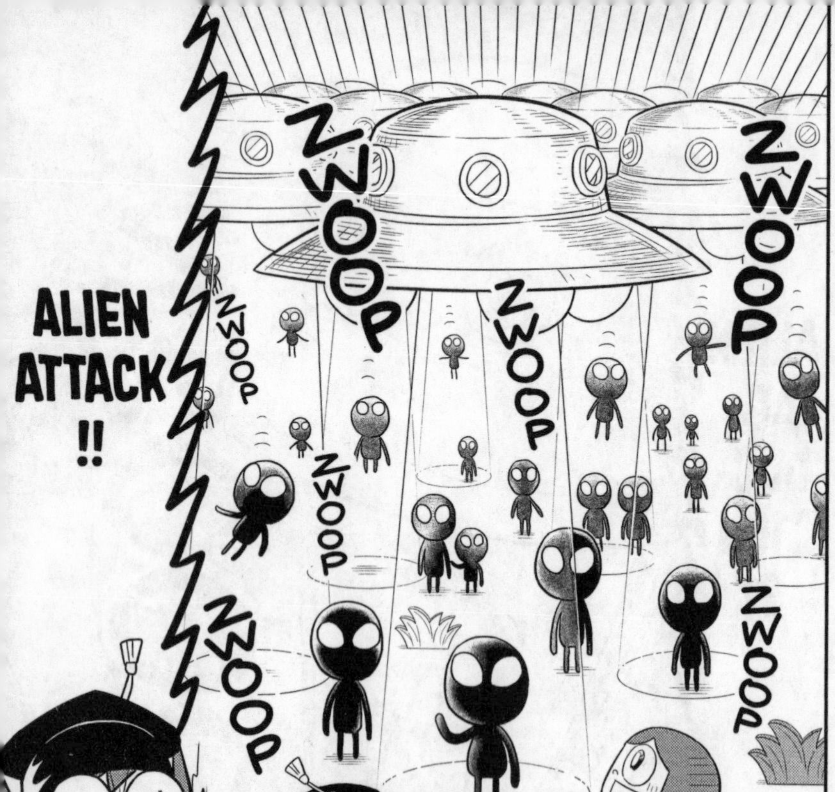
ZWOOP
ZWOOP
ZWOOP
ZWOOP
ZWOOP
ZWOOP
ZWOOP
ALIEN ATTACK!!

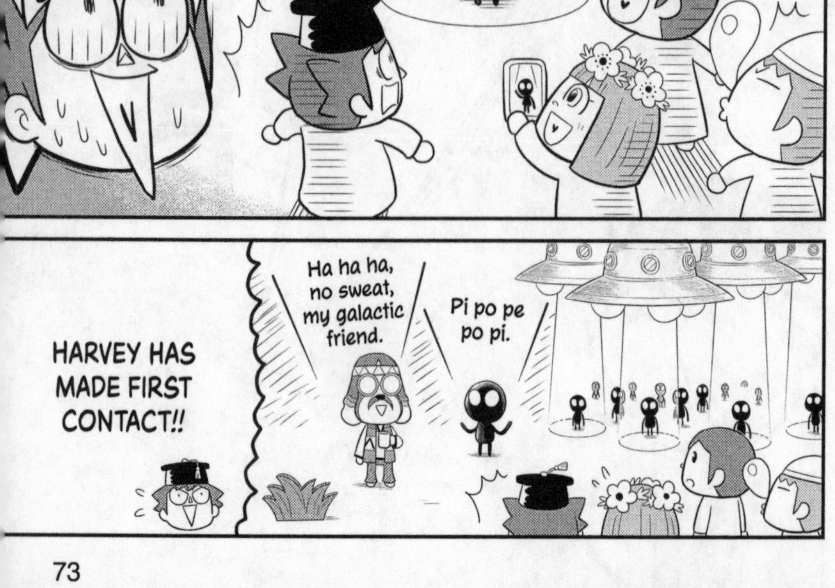
Pi po pe po pi.
Ha ha ha, no sweat, my galactic friend.
HARVEY HAS MADE FIRST CONTACT!!

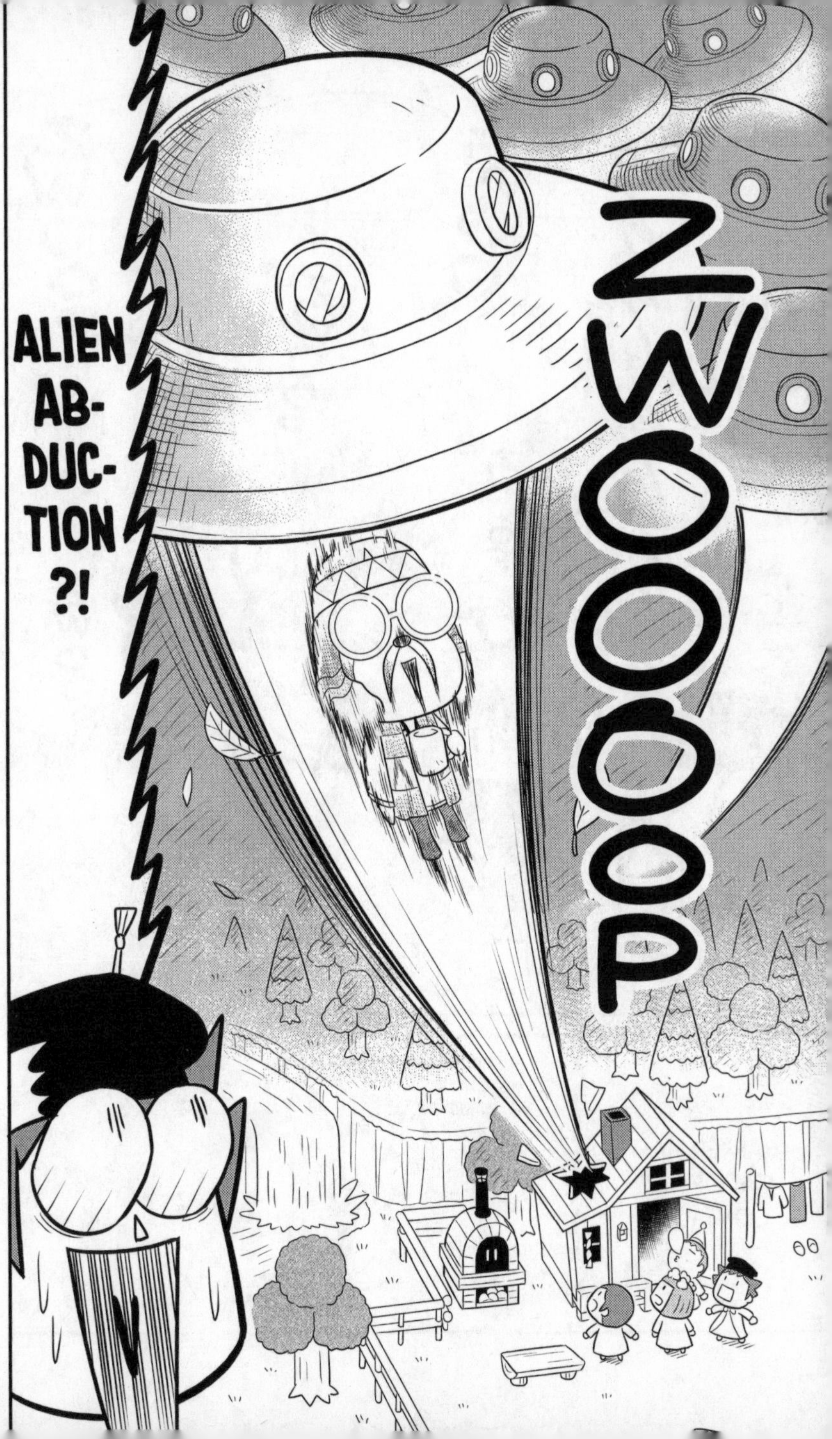
ZWOOOP
ALIEN AB-DUC-TION ?!

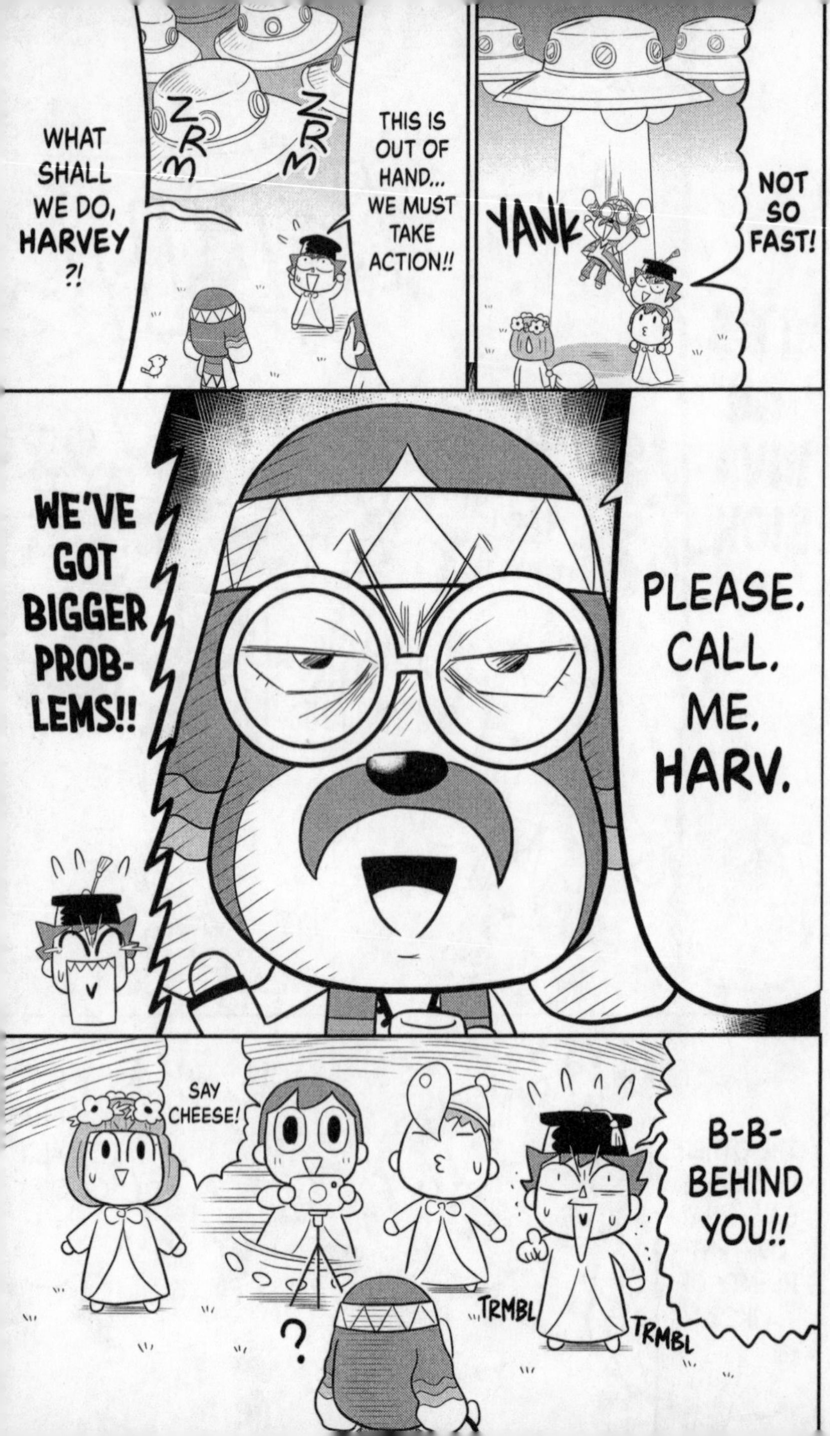
NOT SO FAST!
YANK
ZRM
THIS IS OUT OF HAND... WE MUST TAKE ACTION!!
ZRM
WHAT SHALL WE DO, HARVEY?!
PLEASE. CALL. ME. HARV.
WE'VE GOT BIGGER PROB-LEMS!!
B-B-BEHIND YOU!!
TRMBL
TRMBL
SAY CHEESE!
?

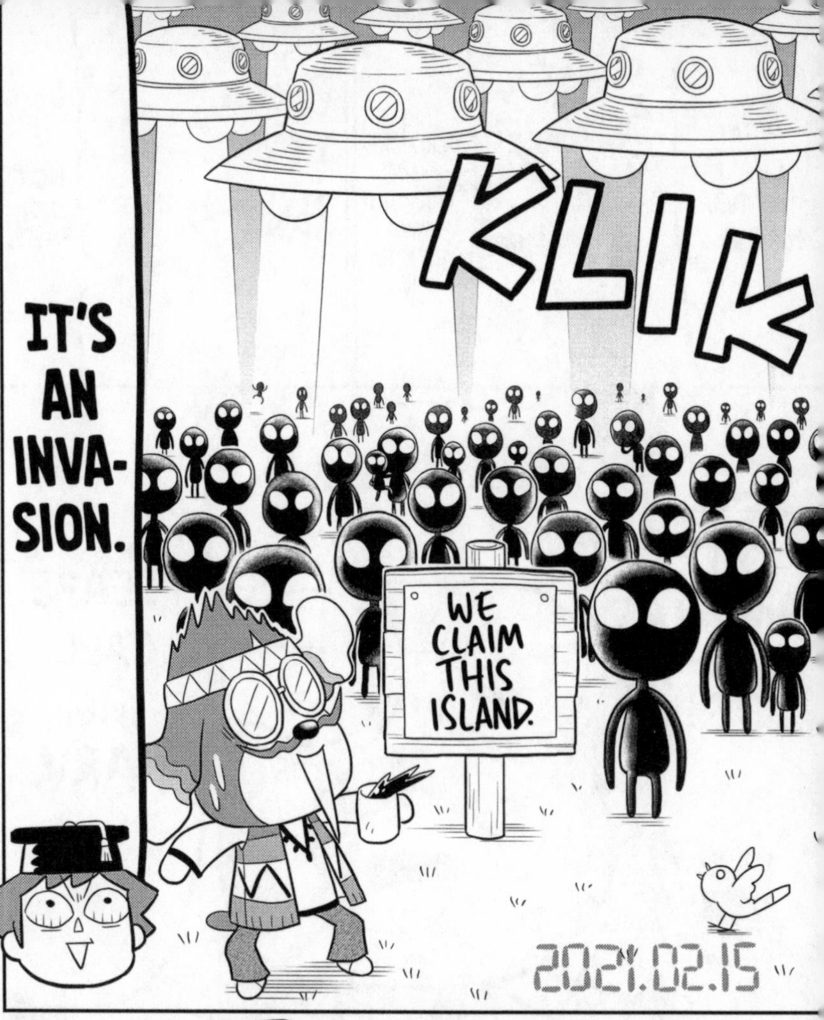
KLIK
WE CLAIM THIS ISLAND.
IT'S AN INVA- SION.
2021.02.15

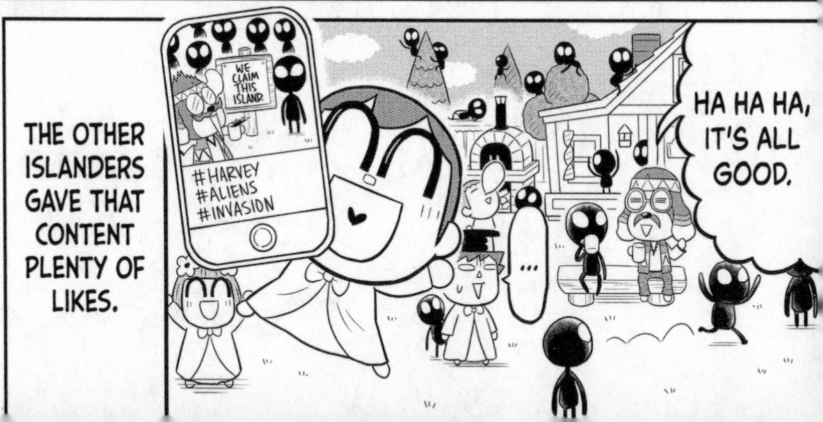
HA HA HA, IT'S ALL GOOD.
...
WE CLAIM THIS ISLAND.
#HARVEY
#ALIENS
#INVASION
THE OTHER ISLANDERS GAVE THAT CONTENT PLENTY OF LIKES.

NEED SOME ACTION? TRY DREAM ISLANDS

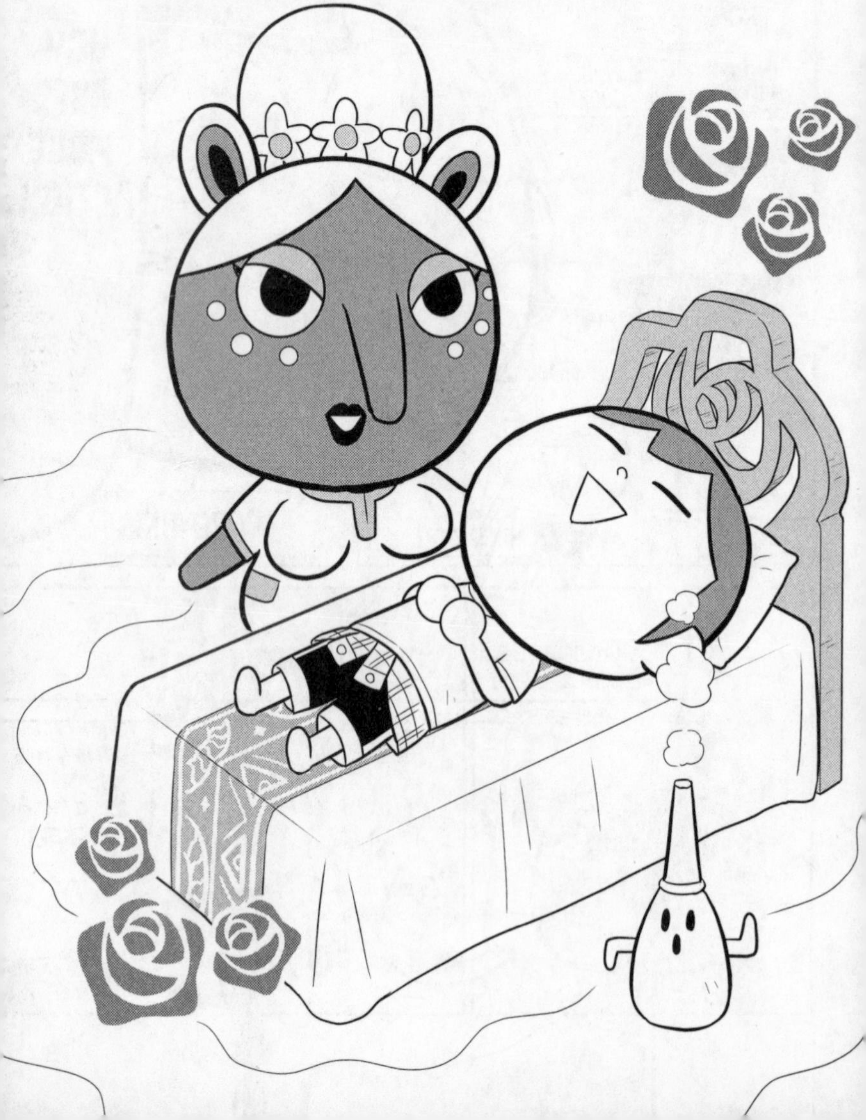

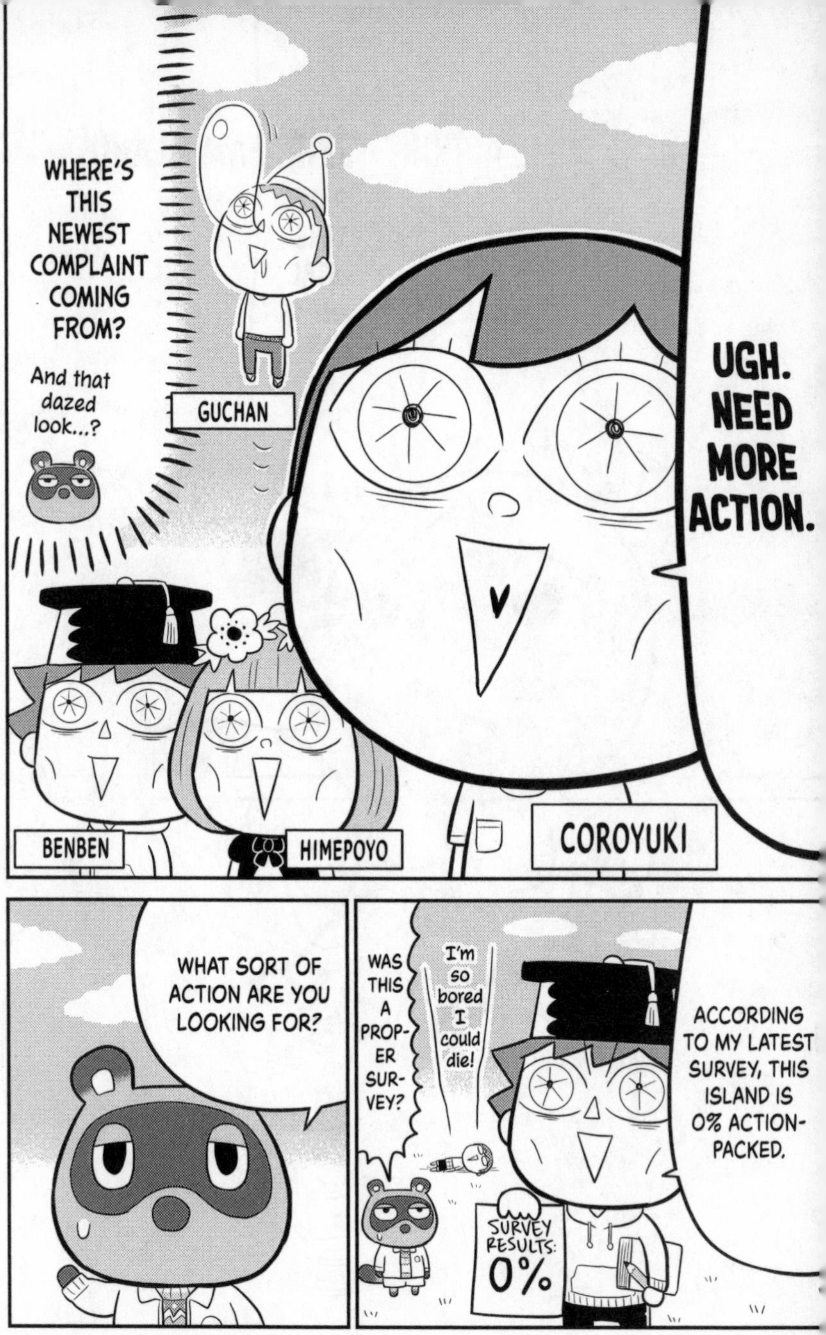
UGH. NEED MORE ACTION.
COROYUKI
WHERE'S THIS NEWEST COMPLAINT COMING FROM?
And that dazed look...?
GUCHAN
HIMEPOYO
BENBEN
ACCORDING TO MY LATEST SURVEY, THIS ISLAND IS 0% ACTION-PACKED.
SURVEY RESULTS: 0%
I'm so bored I could die!
WAS THIS A PROPER SURVEY?
WHAT SORT OF ACTION ARE YOU LOOKING FOR?

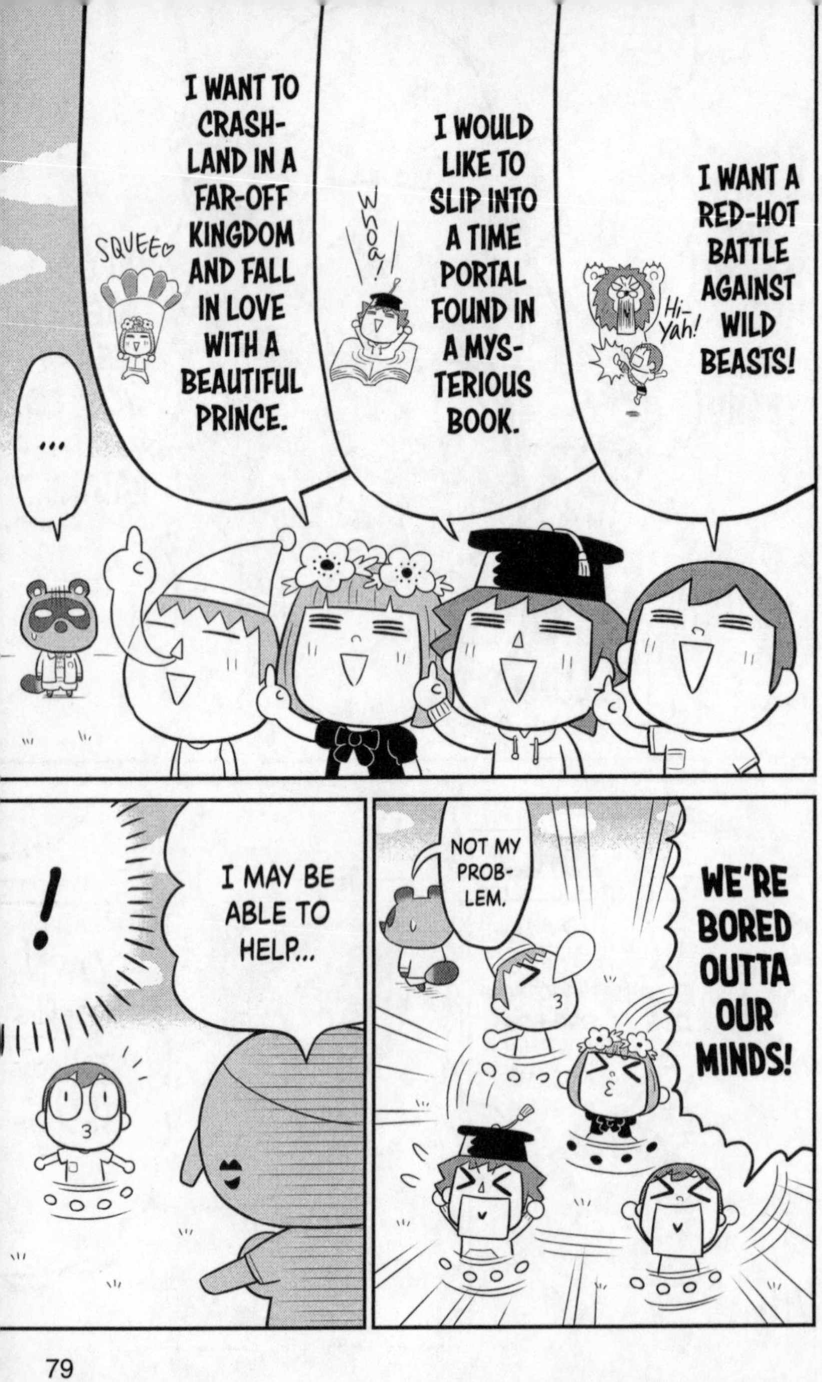
I WANT A RED-HOT BATTLE AGAINST WILD BEASTS!
Hi-Yah!
I WOULD LIKE TO SLIP INTO A TIME PORTAL FOUND IN A MYSTERIOUS BOOK.
Whoa!
I WANT TO CRASH-LAND IN A FAR-OFF KINGDOM AND FALL IN LOVE WITH A BEAUTIFUL PRINCE.
SQUEE♡
...
WE'RE BORED OUTTA OUR MINDS!
NOT MY PROBLEM.
I MAY BE ABLE TO HELP...
!

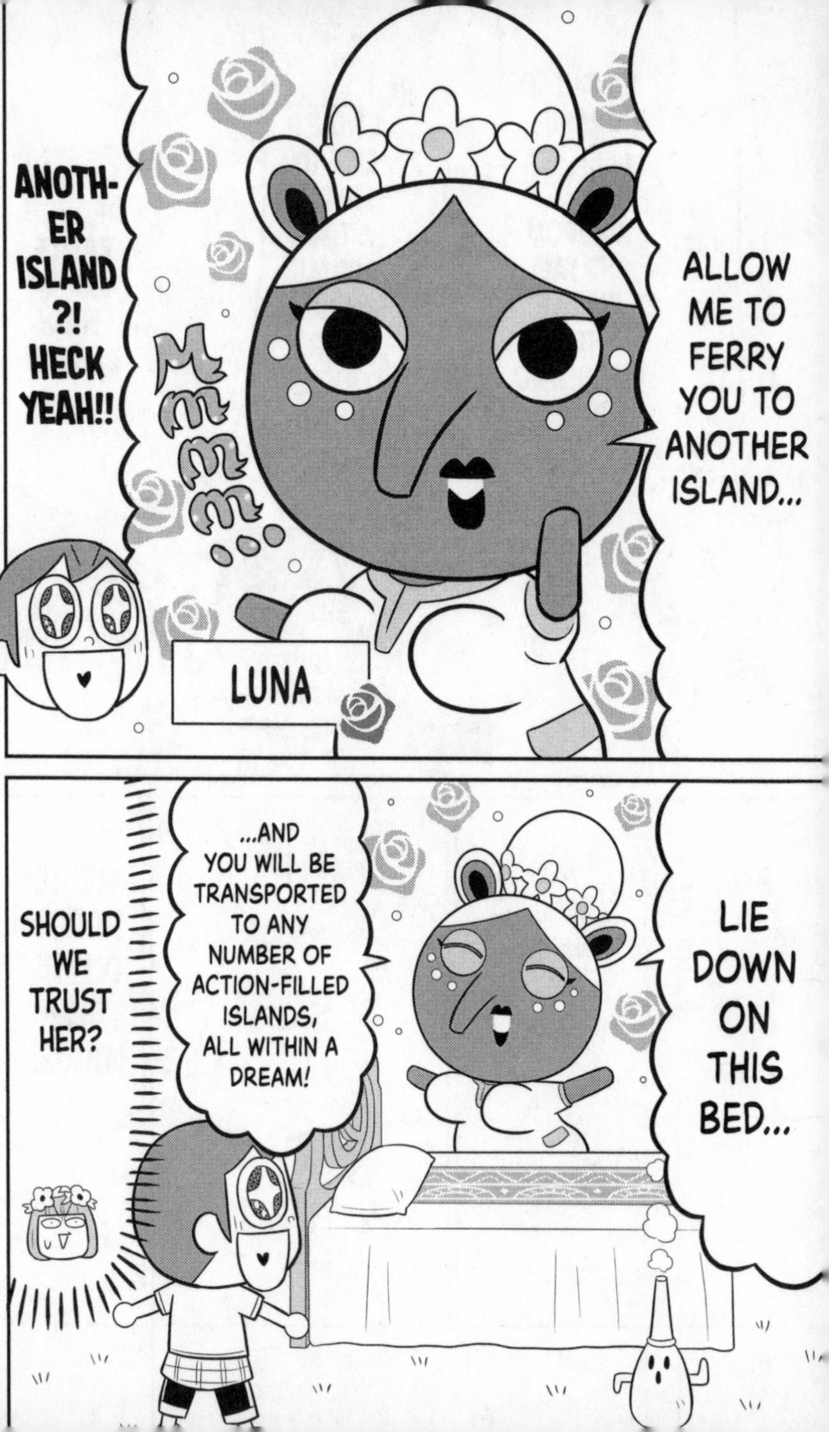
ALLOW ME TO FERRY YOU TO ANOTHER ISLAND...
LUNA
Mmm...
ANOTH-ER ISLAND?! HECK YEAH!!
LIE DOWN ON THIS BED...
...AND YOU WILL BE TRANSPORTED TO ANY NUMBER OF ACTION-FILLED ISLANDS, ALL WITHIN A DREAM!
SHOULD WE TRUST HER?

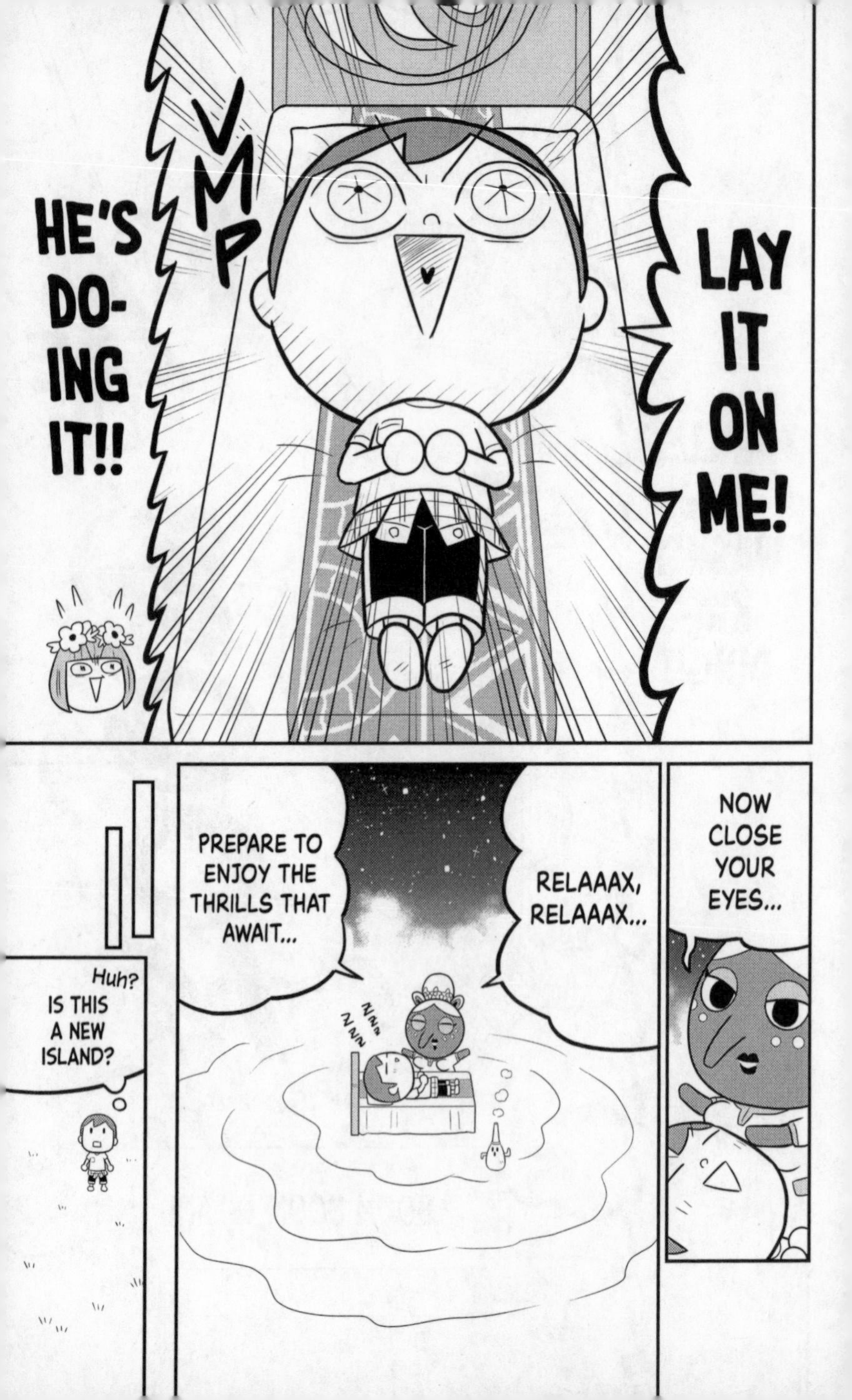
LAY IT ON ME!
JUMP
HE'S DO-ING IT!!
NOW CLOSE YOUR EYES...
RELAAAX, RELAAAX...
PREPARE TO ENJOY THE THRILLS THAT AWAIT...
Huh? IS THIS A NEW ISLAND?

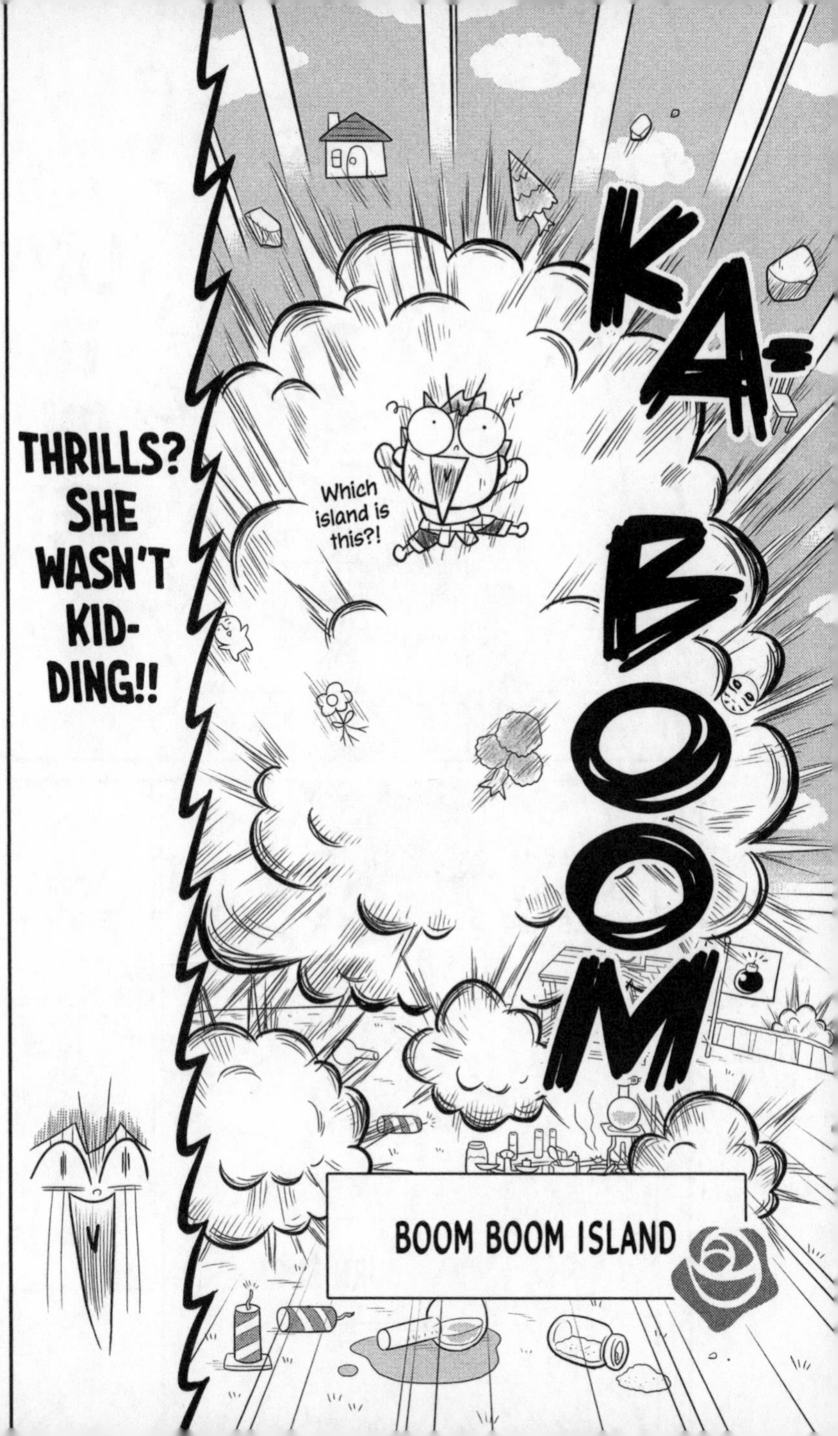
KA-BOOM
Which island is this?!
BOOM BOOM ISLAND
THRILLS? SHE WASN'T KID-DING!!

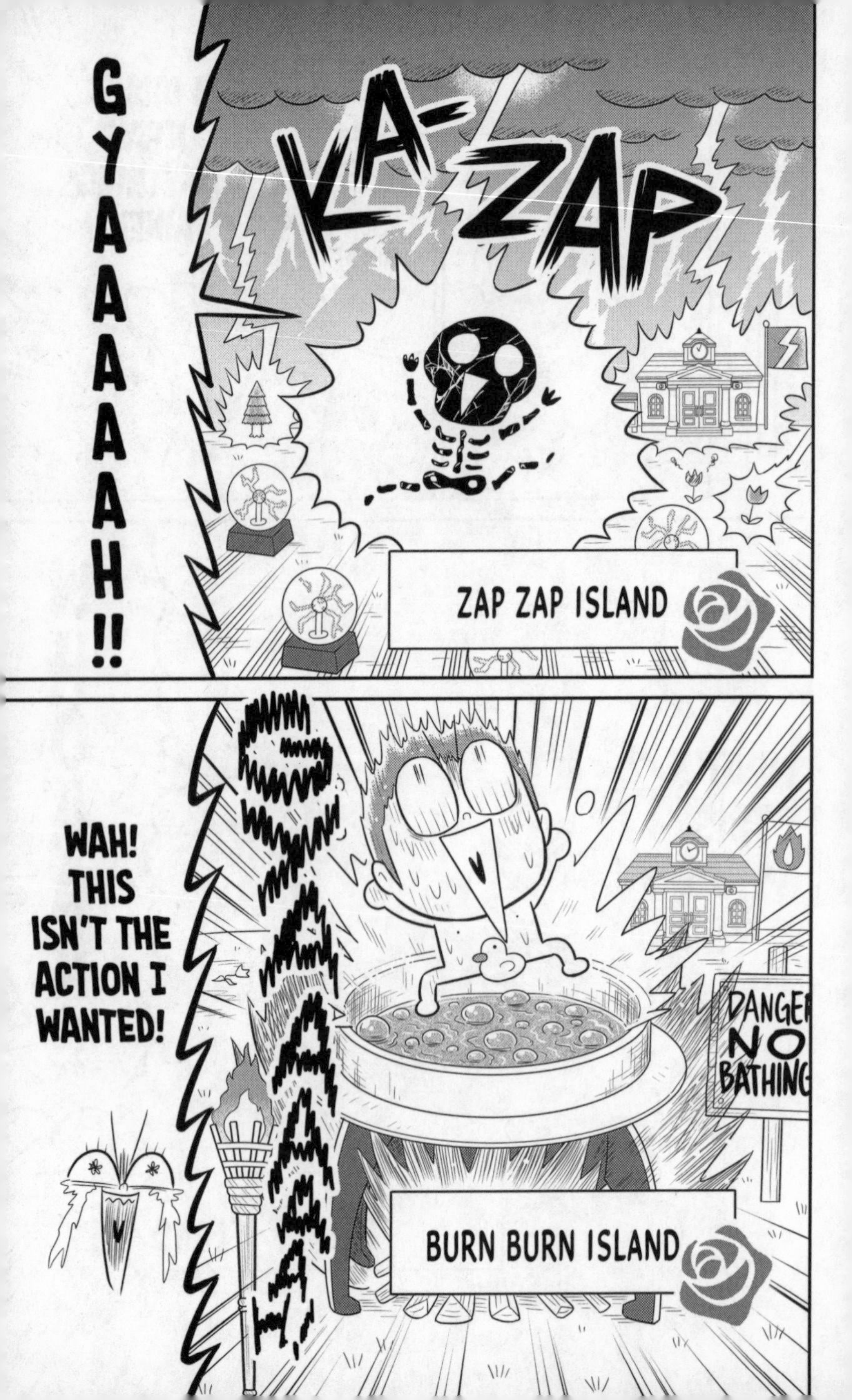
KA-ZAP
GYAAAAAH!!
ZAP ZAP ISLAND
DANGER NO BATHING
WAH! THIS ISN'T THE ACTION I WANTED!
BURN BURN ISLAND

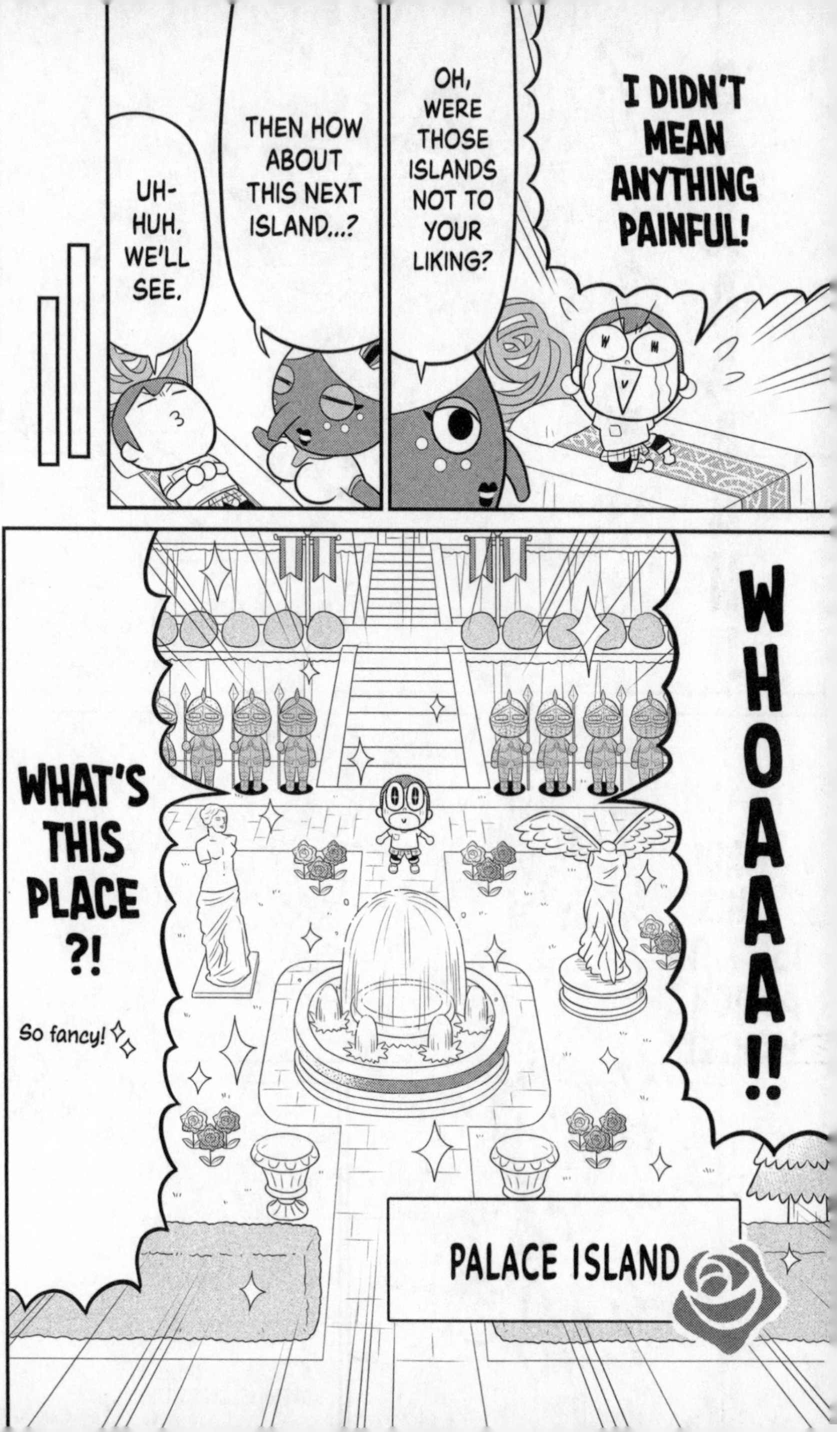
I DIDN'T MEAN ANYTHING PAINFUL!
OH, WERE THOSE ISLANDS NOT TO YOUR LIKING?
THEN HOW ABOUT THIS NEXT ISLAND...?
UH-HUH. WE'LL SEE.
WHOAAA!!
PALACE ISLAND
WHAT'S THIS PLACE?!
So fancy!

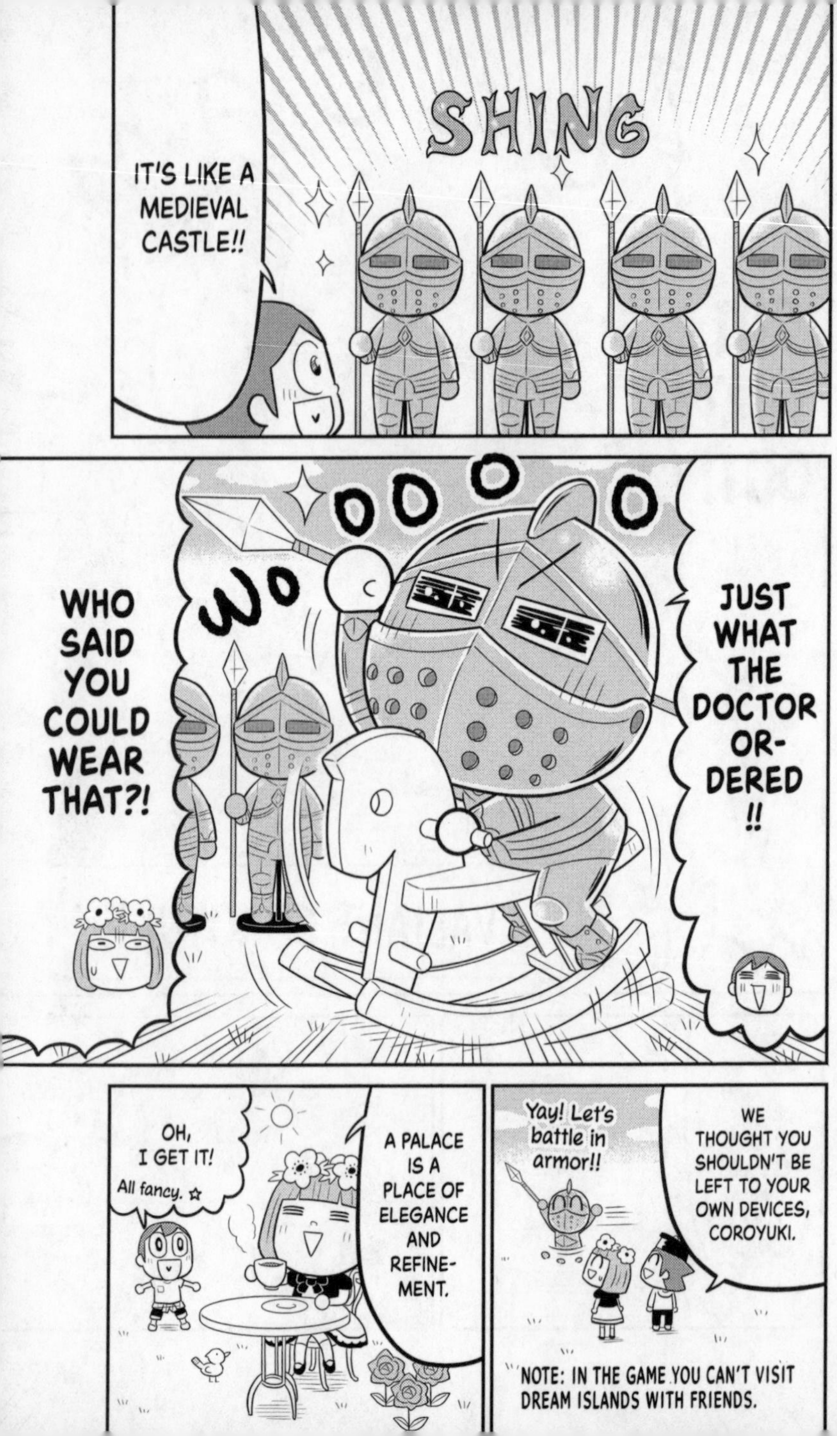
SHING
IT'S LIKE A MEDIEVAL CASTLE!!
JUST WHAT THE DOCTOR OR-DERED!!
WOOOOO
WHO SAID YOU COULD WEAR THAT?!
WE THOUGHT YOU SHOULDN'T BE LEFT TO YOUR OWN DEVICES, COROYUKI.
Yay! Let's battle in armor!!
NOTE: IN THE GAME YOU CAN'T VISIT DREAM ISLANDS WITH FRIENDS.
A PALACE IS A PLACE OF ELEGANCE AND REFINE-MENT.
OH, I GET IT!
All fancy. ☆

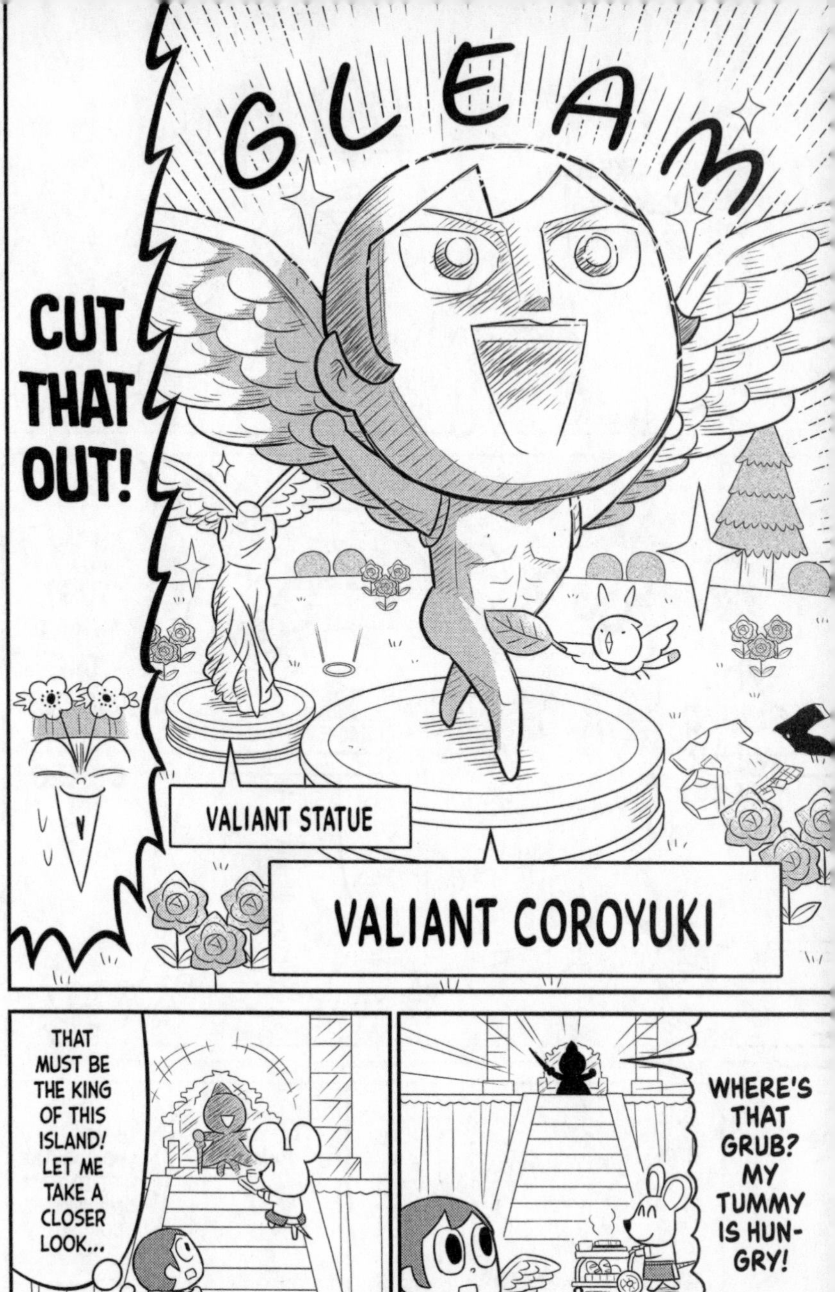
GLEAM
VALIANT STATUE
VALIANT COROYUKI
CUT THAT OUT!
WHERE'S THAT GRUB? MY TUMMY IS HUN-GRY!
THAT MUST BE THE KING OF THIS ISLAND! LET ME TAKE A CLOSER LOOK...

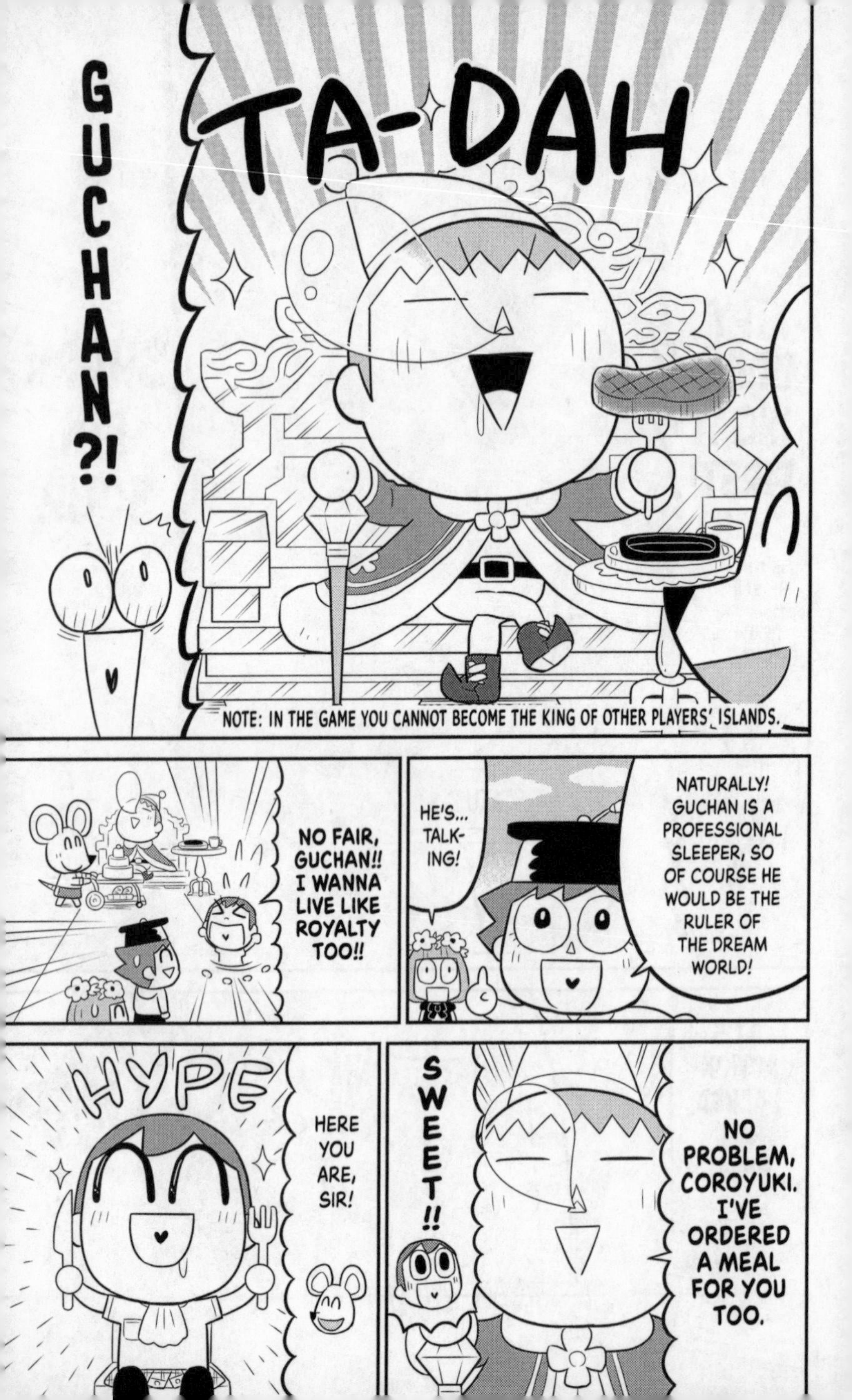
TA-DAH
GUCHAN?!
NOTE: IN THE GAME YOU CANNOT BECOME THE KING OF OTHER PLAYERS' ISLANDS.
NATURALLY! GUCHAN IS A PROFESSIONAL SLEEPER, SO OF COURSE HE WOULD BE THE RULER OF THE DREAM WORLD!
HE'S... TALKING!
NO FAIR, GUCHAN!! I WANNA LIVE LIKE ROYALTY TOO!!
NO PROBLEM, COROYUKI. I'VE ORDERED A MEAL FOR YOU TOO.
SWEET!!
HERE YOU ARE, SIR!
HYPE

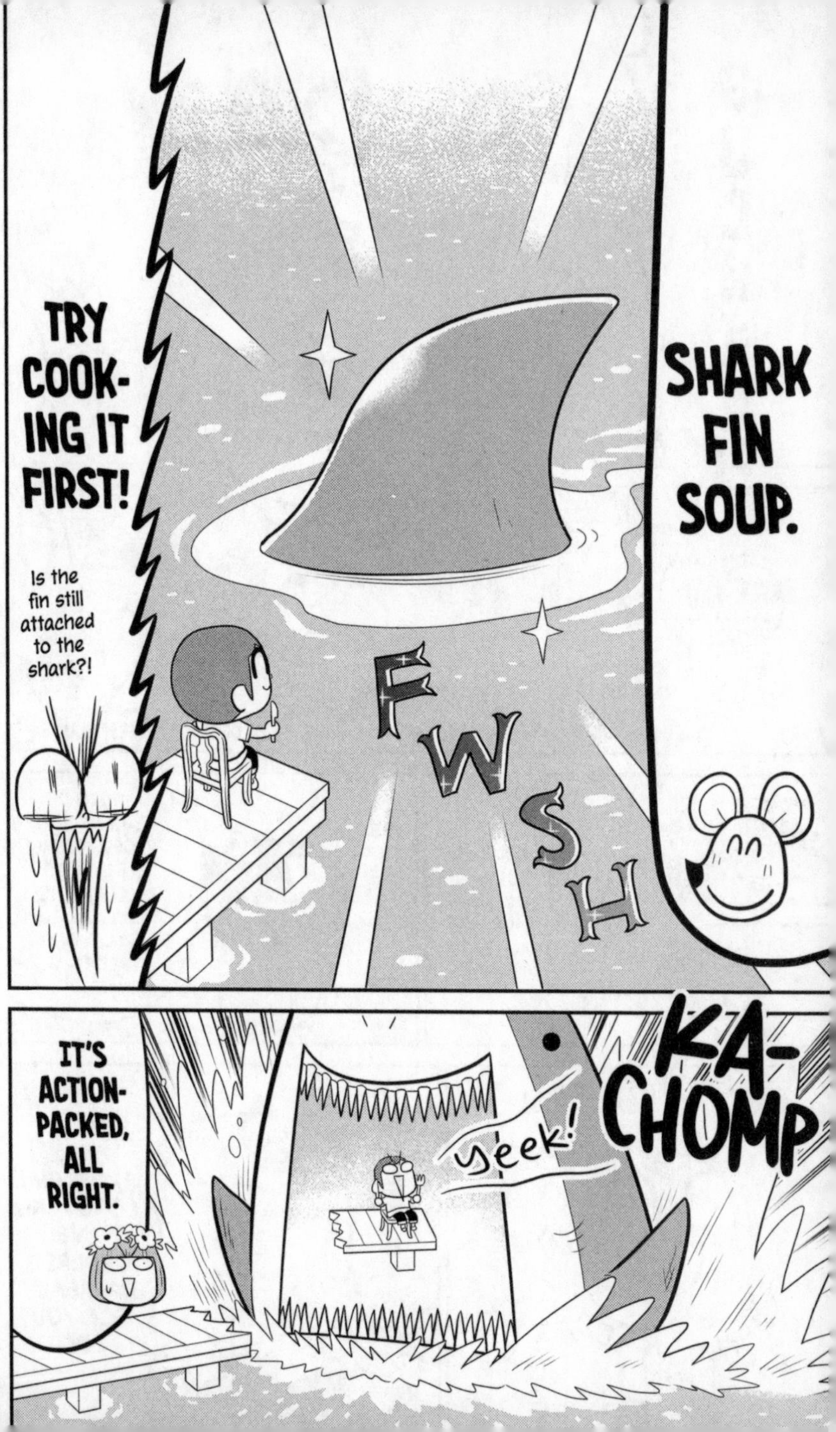
SHARK FIN SOUP.
TRY COOK-ING IT FIRST!
FWSH
Is the fin still attached to the shark?!
KA-CHOMP
Yeek!
IT'S ACTION-PACKED, ALL RIGHT.

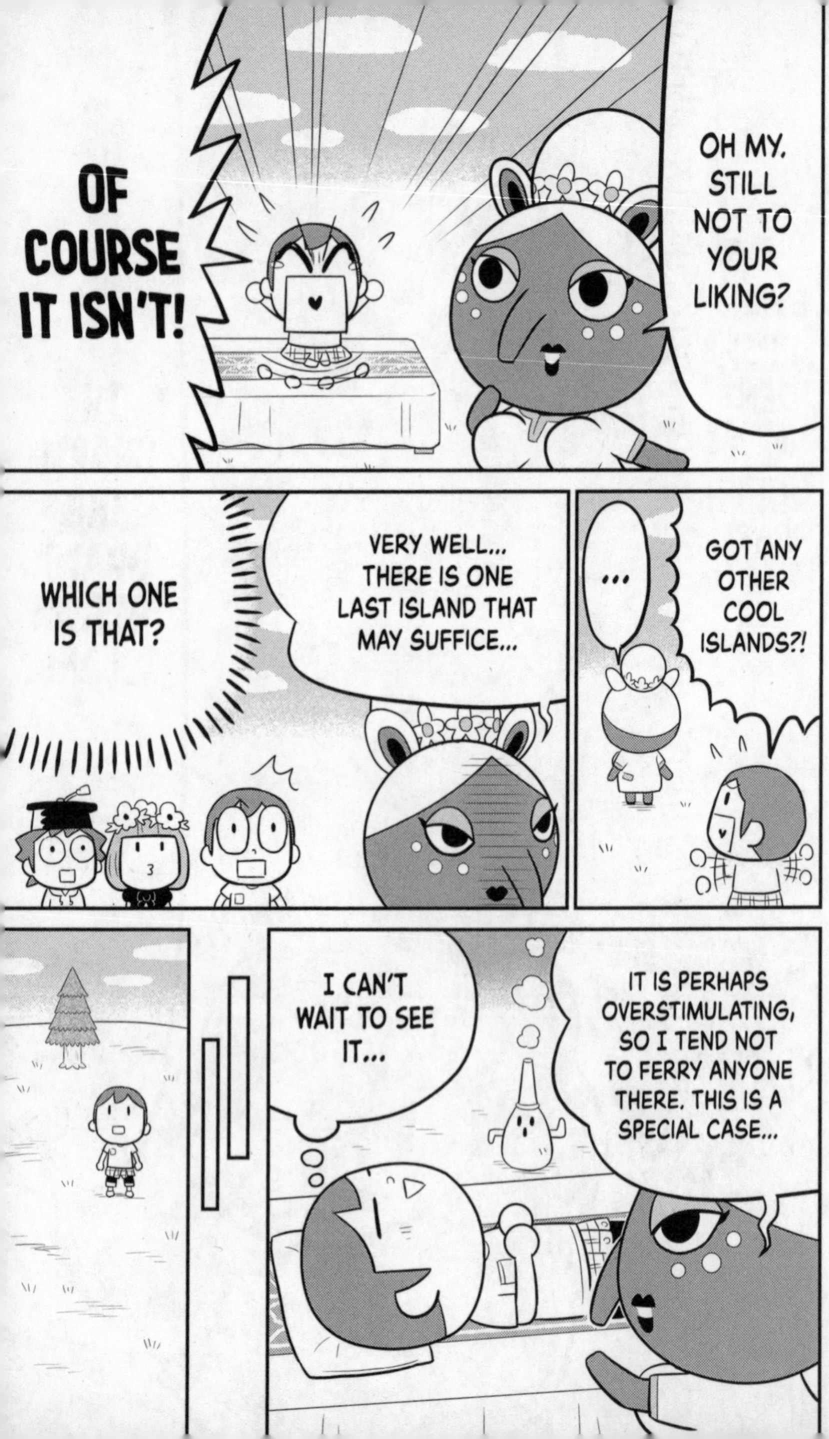
OH MY. STILL NOT TO YOUR LIKING?
OF COURSE IT ISN'T!
GOT ANY OTHER COOL ISLANDS?!
...
VERY WELL... THERE IS ONE LAST ISLAND THAT MAY SUFFICE...
WHICH ONE IS THAT?
IT IS PERHAPS OVERSTIMULATING, SO I TEND NOT TO FERRY ANYONE THERE. THIS IS A SPECIAL CASE...
I CAN'T WAIT TO SEE IT...

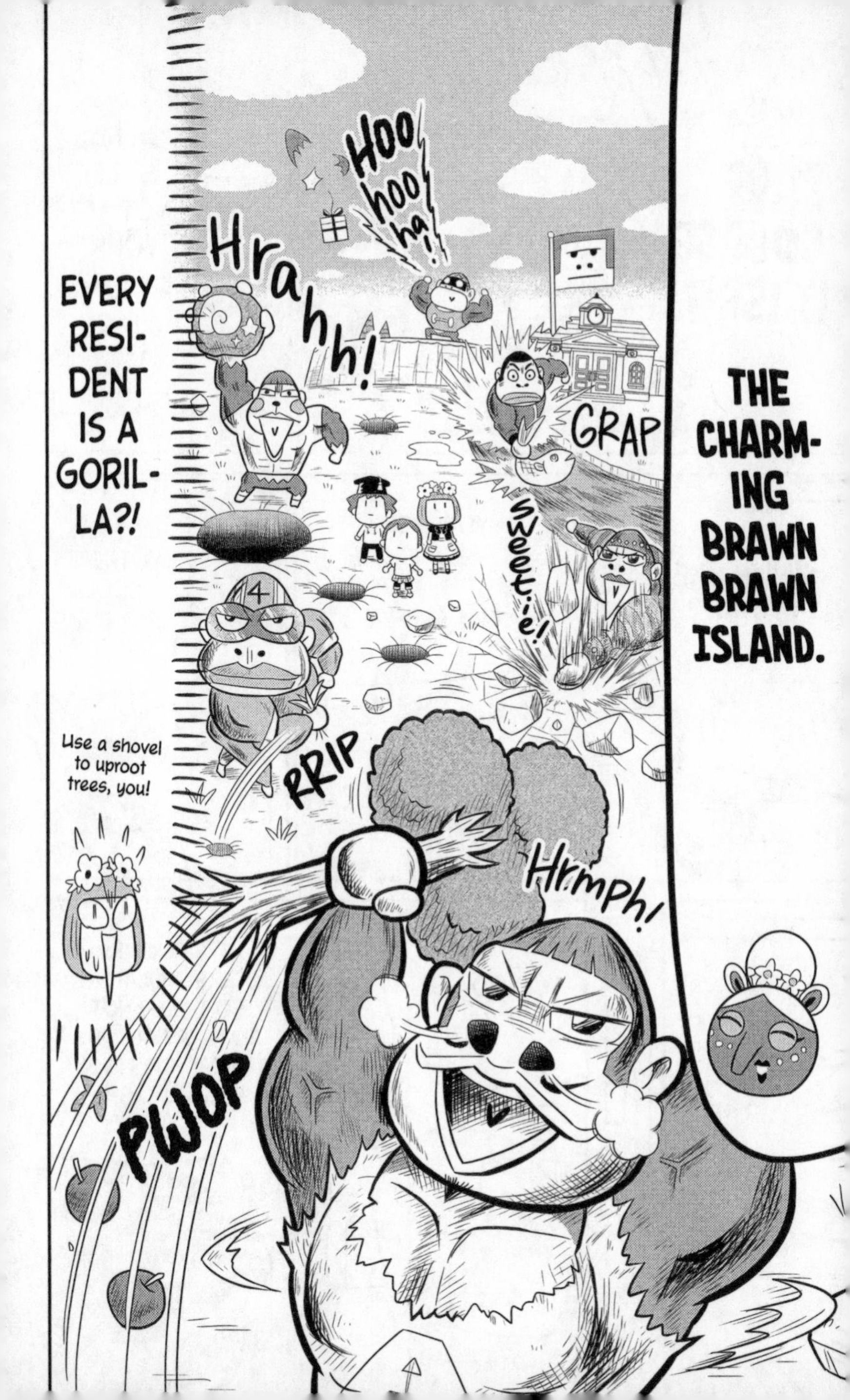
THE CHARMING BRAWN BRAWN ISLAND.
Hoo hoo ha!
Hrahhh!
GRAP
Sweetie!
RRIP
Hrmph!
PWOP
EVERY RESIDENT IS A GORILLA?!
Use a shovel to uproot trees, you!

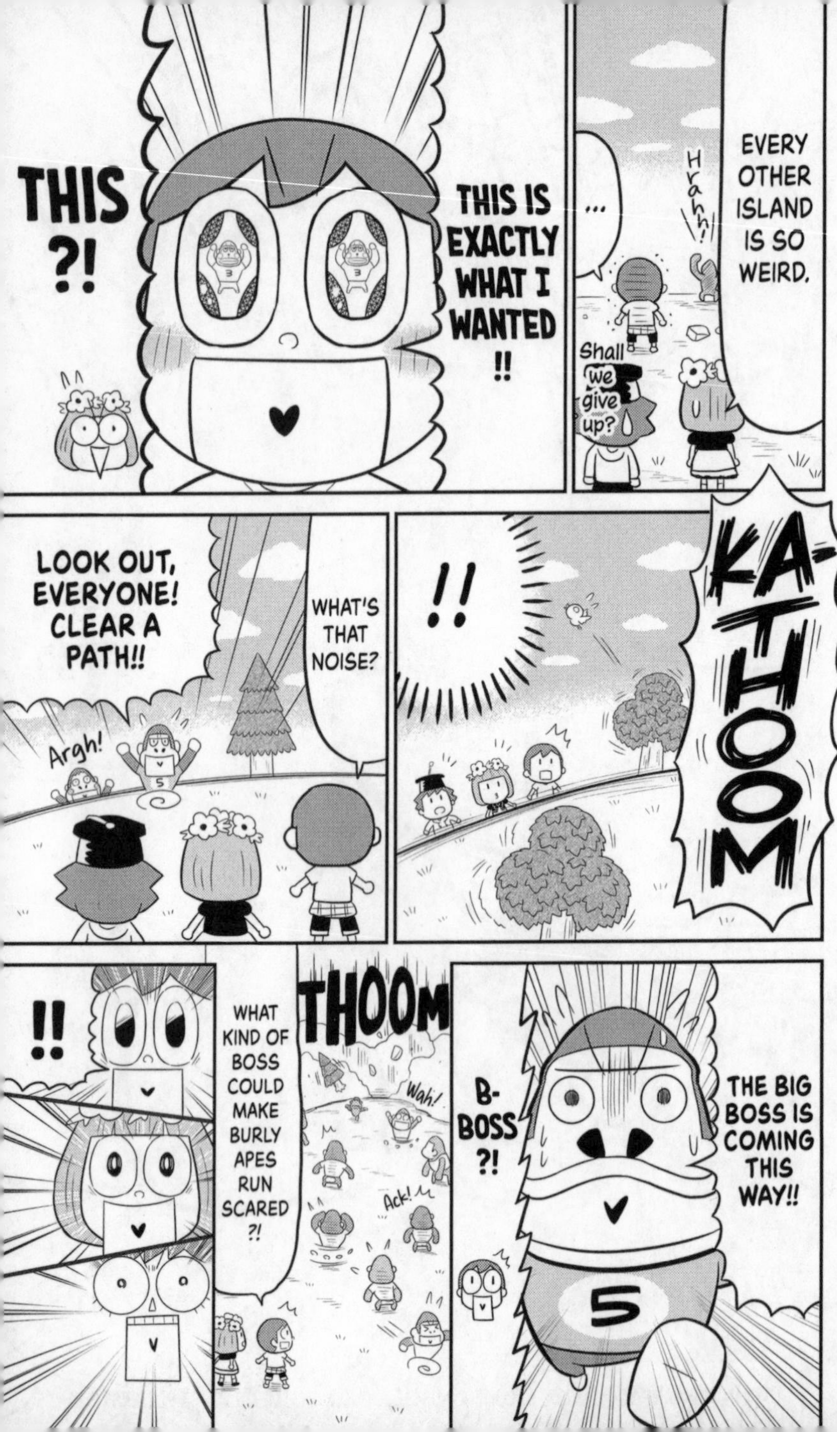
EVERY OTHER ISLAND IS SO WEIRD.
Hrahh!
...
Shall we give up?
THIS IS EXACTLY WHAT I WANTED !!
THIS ?!
KA-THOOM
!!
WHAT'S THAT NOISE?
LOOK OUT, EVERYONE! CLEAR A PATH!!
Argh!
THE BIG BOSS IS COMING THIS WAY!!
B-BOSS ?!
THOOM
Wah!
Ack!
WHAT KIND OF BOSS COULD MAKE BURLY APES RUN SCARED ?!
!!

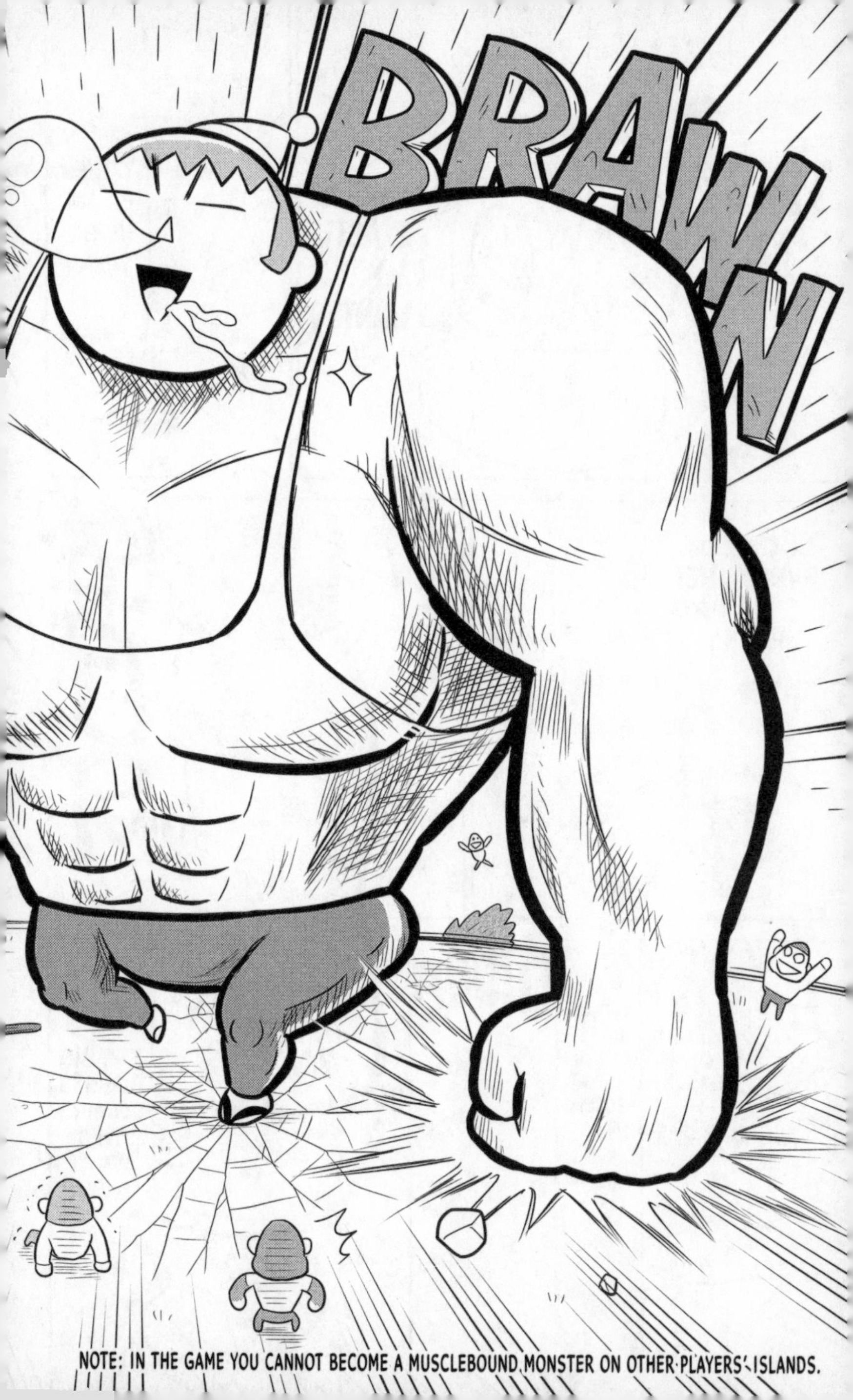
BRAWW
NOTE: IN THE GAME YOU CANNOT BECOME A MUSCLEBOUND MONSTER ON OTHER PLAYERS' ISLANDS.

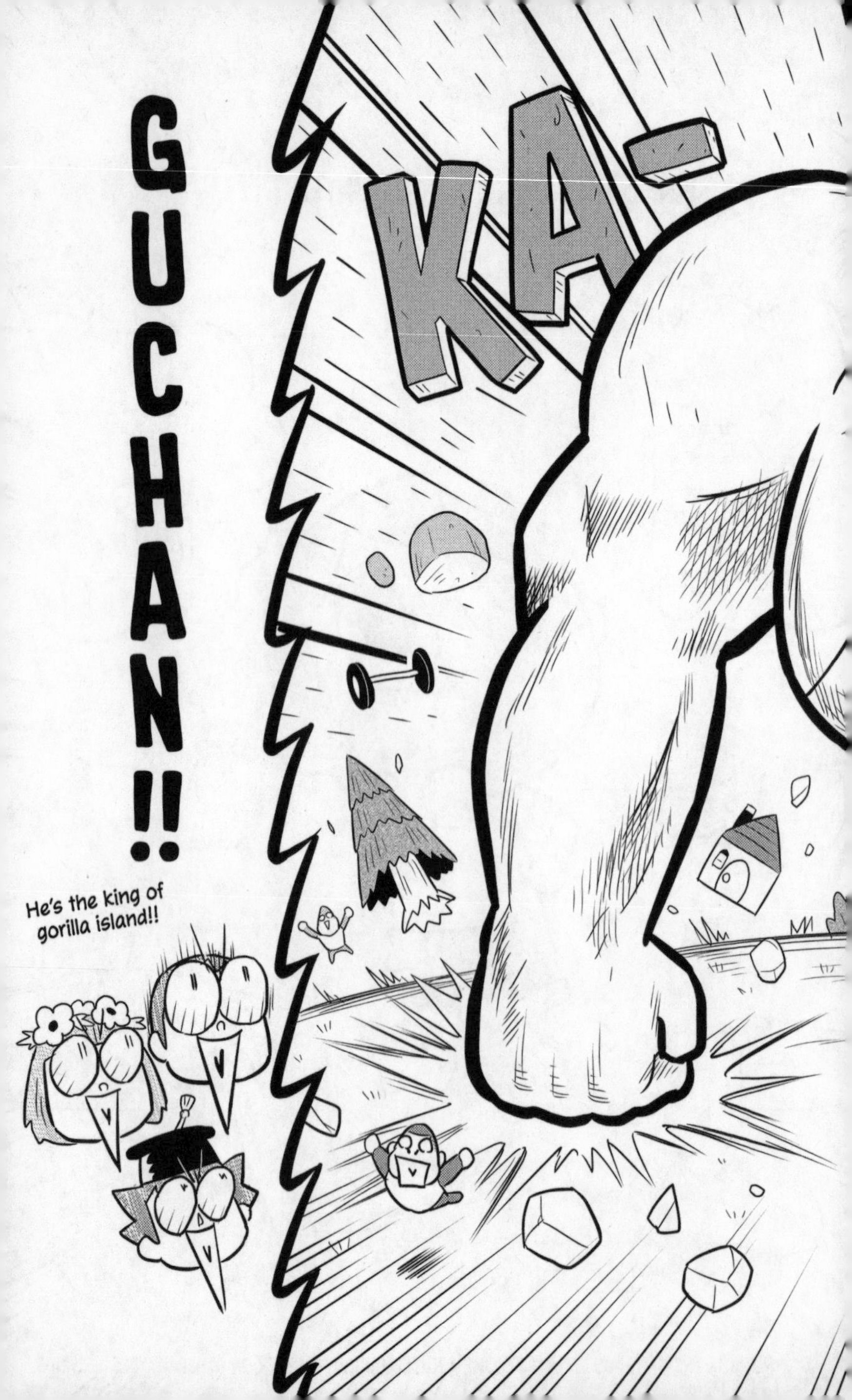
KA-
GUCHAN!!
He's the king of gorilla island!!

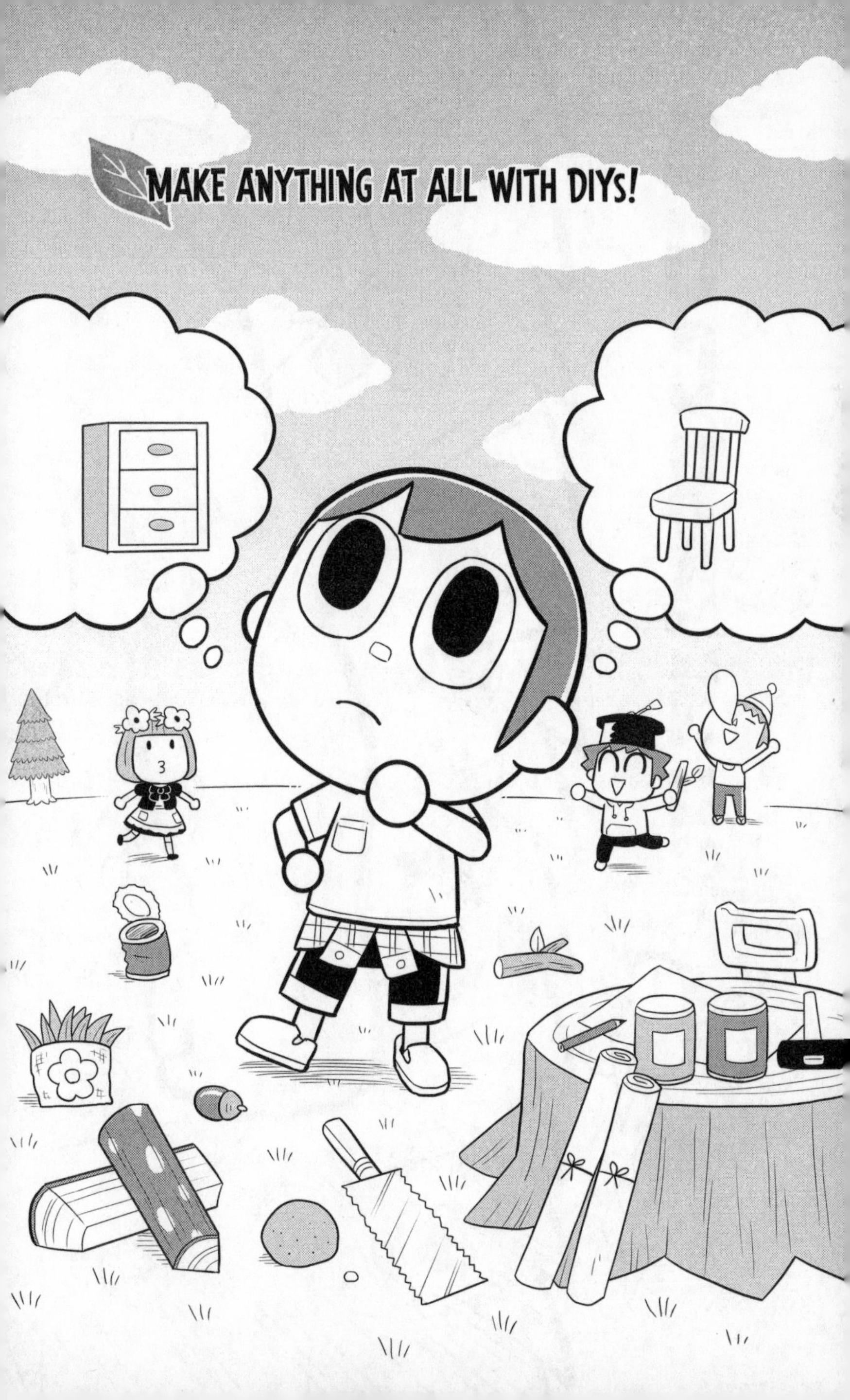
MAKE ANYTHING AT ALL WITH DIYS!

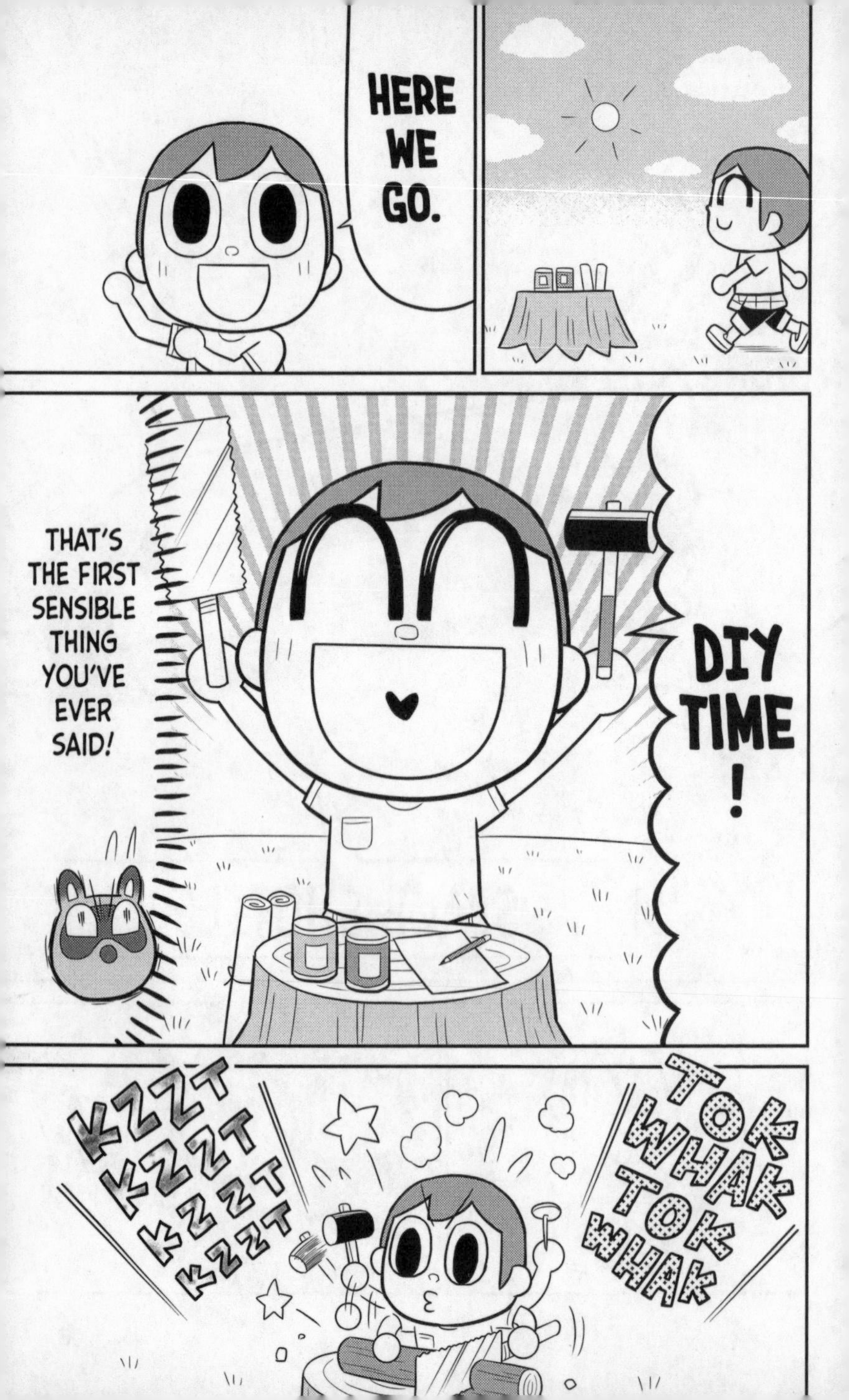
HERE WE GO.
DIY TIME!
THAT'S THE FIRST SENSIBLE THING YOU'VE EVER SAID!
TOK WHAK TOK WHAK
KZZZT KZZZT KZZZT KZZZT

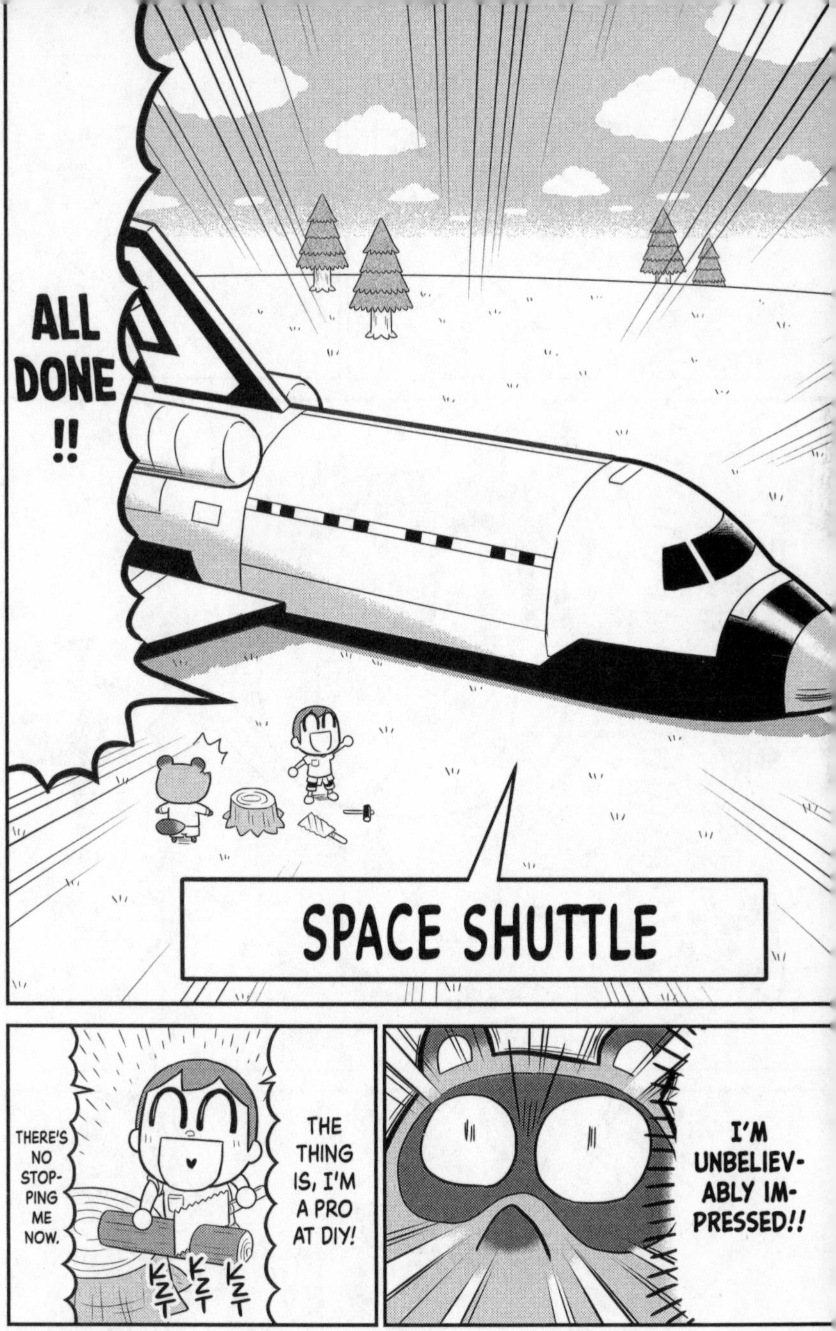
ALL DONE!!
SPACE SHUTTLE
I'M UNBELIEV-ABLY IM-PRESSED!!
THE THING IS, I'M A PRO AT DIY!
THERE'S NO STOP-PING ME NOW.
KZT KZT KZT

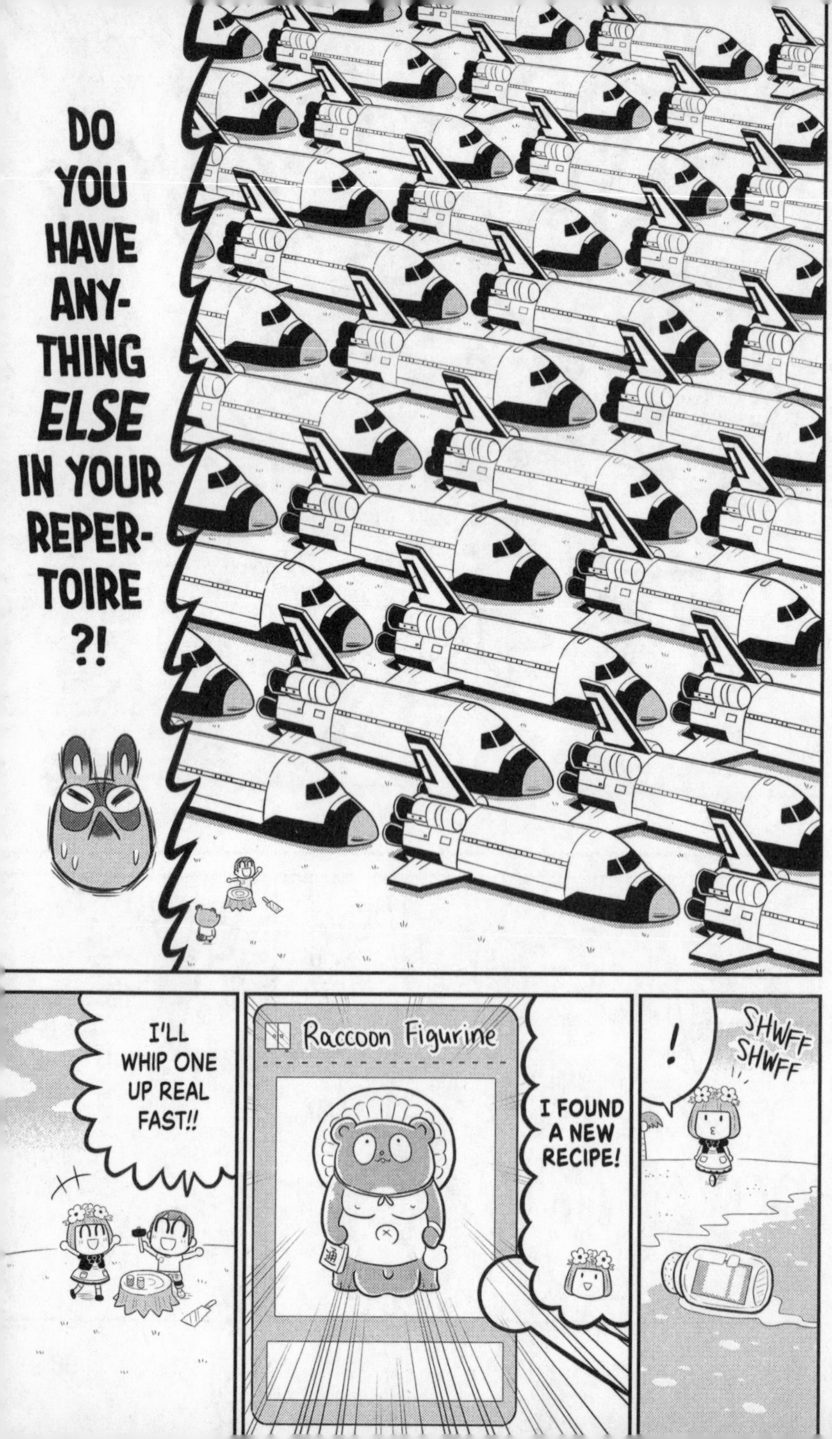
DO YOU HAVE ANYTHING *ELSE* IN YOUR REPERTOIRE?!
!
SHWFF SHWFF
Raccoon Figurine
I FOUND A NEW RECIPE!
I'LL WHIP ONE UP REAL FAST!!

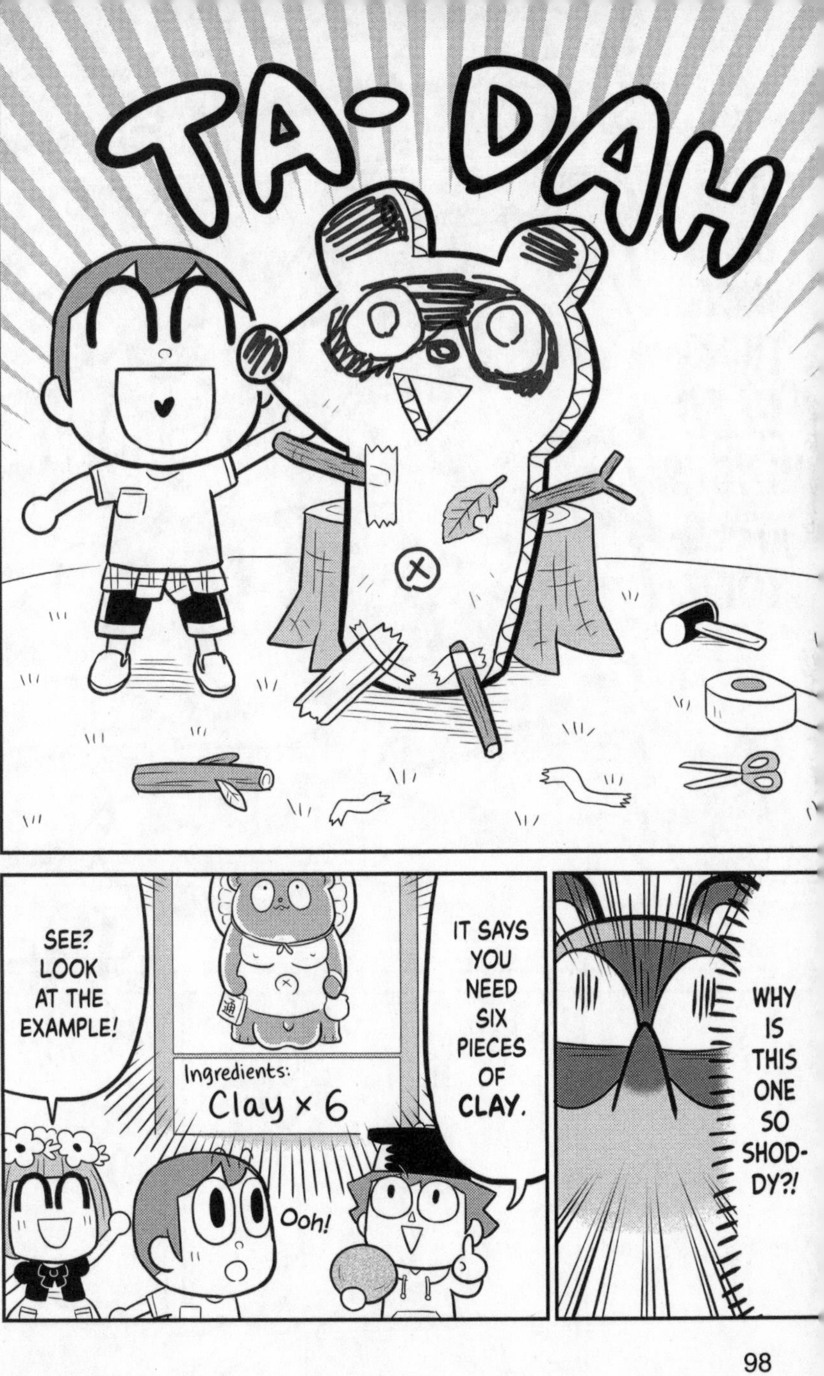
TA-DAH
WHY IS THIS ONE SO SHODDY?!
IT SAYS YOU NEED SIX PIECES OF CLAY.
SEE? LOOK AT THE EXAMPLE!
Ingredients:
Clay × 6
Ooh!

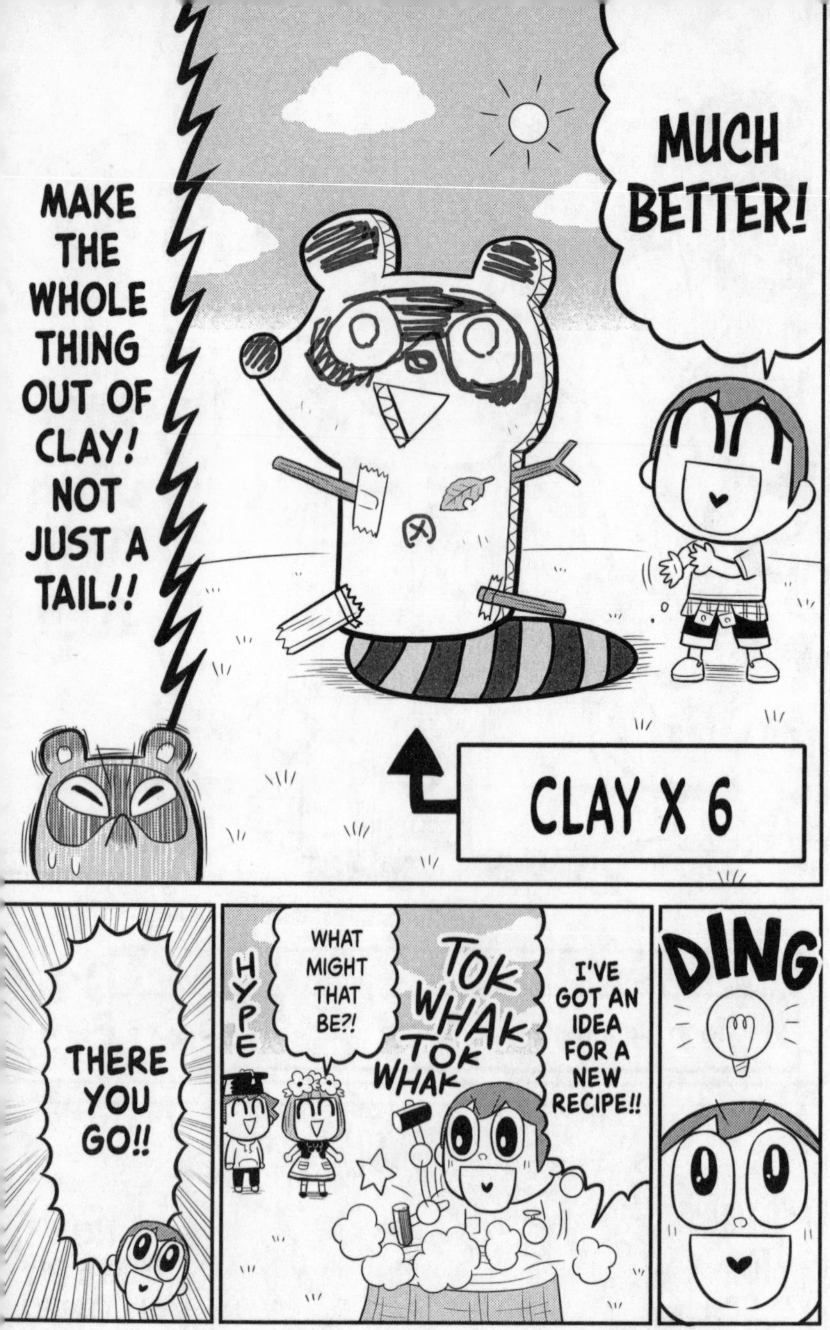
MUCH BETTER!
CLAY X 6
MAKE THE WHOLE THING OUT OF CLAY! NOT JUST A TAIL!!
DING
I'VE GOT AN IDEA FOR A NEW RECIPE!!
TOK WHAK TOK WHAK
WHAT MIGHT THAT BE?!
HYPE
THERE YOU GO!!

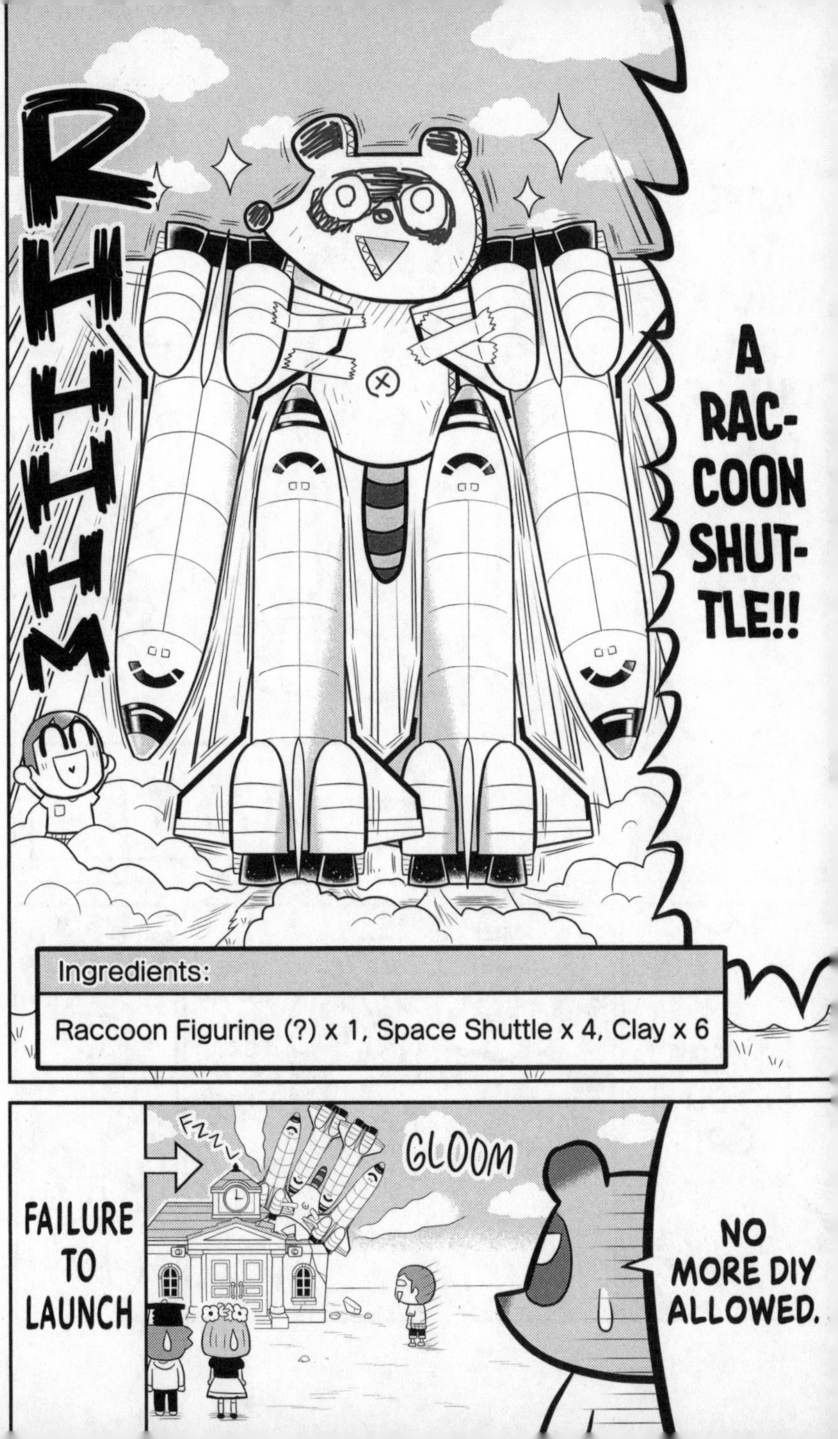
RHHHHM
A RACCOON SHUTTLE!!
Ingredients:
Raccoon Figurine (?) x 1, Space Shuttle x 4, Clay x 6
NO MORE DIY ALLOWED.
GLOOM
FZZZ
FAILURE TO LAUNCH

AT LAST, TIME TO NAME THE ISLAND!

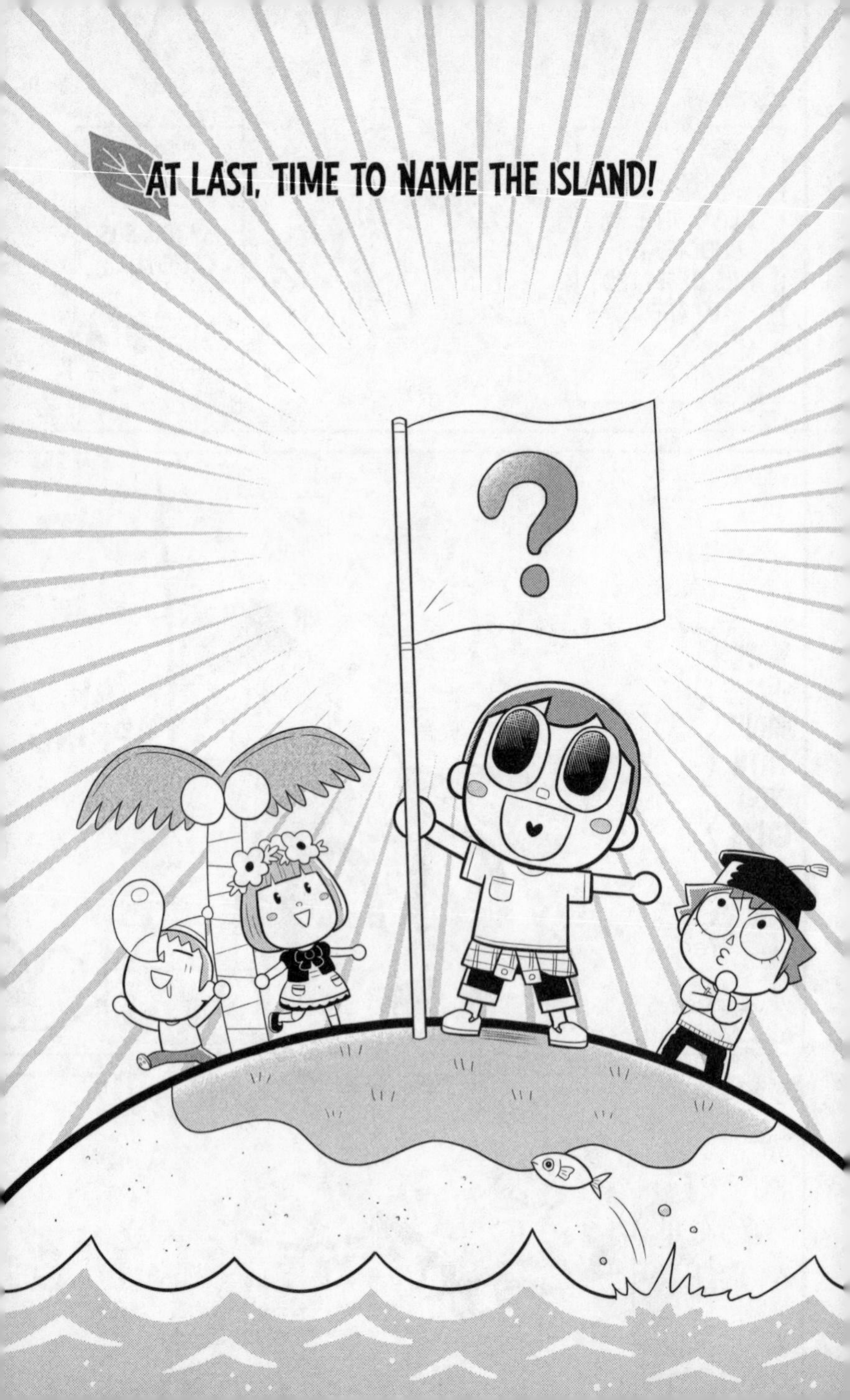

?

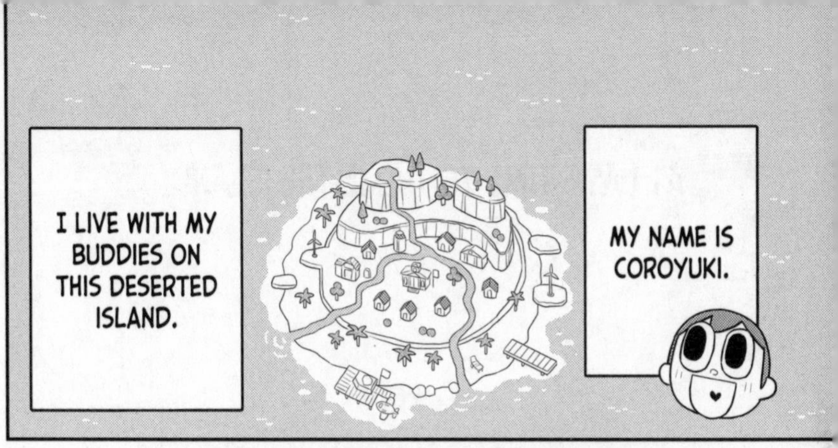
MY NAME IS COROYUKI.
I LIVE WITH MY BUDDIES ON THIS DESERTED ISLAND.

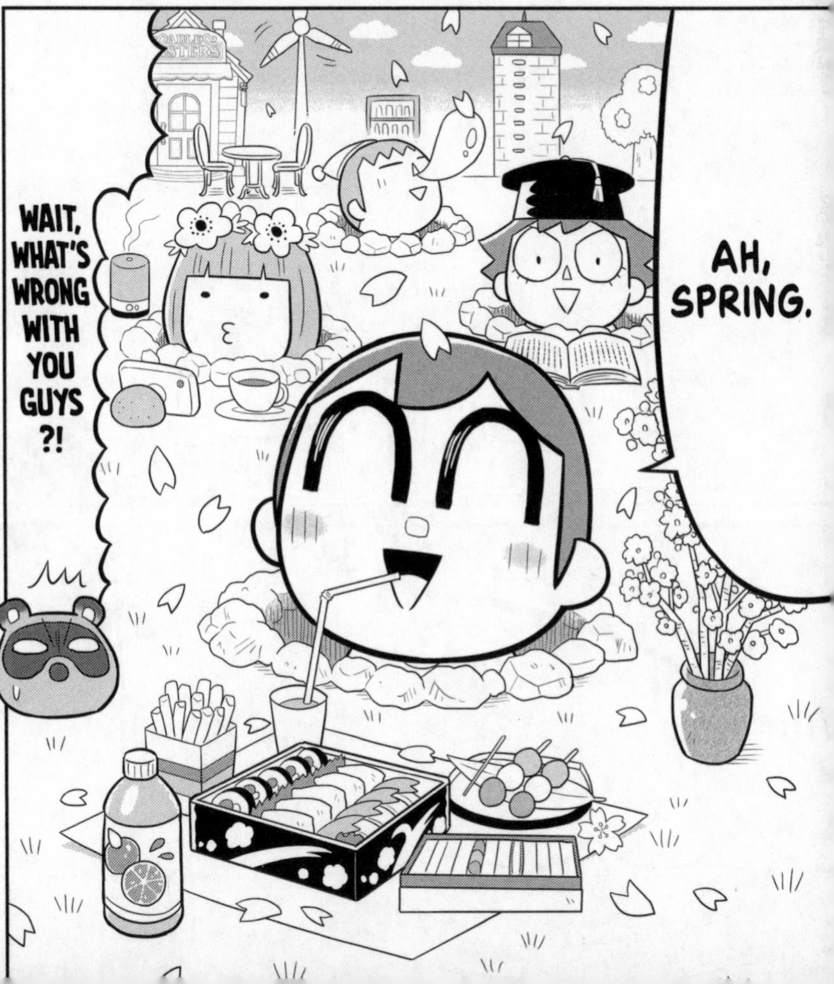
AH, SPRING.
WAIT, WHAT'S WRONG WITH YOU GUYS?!

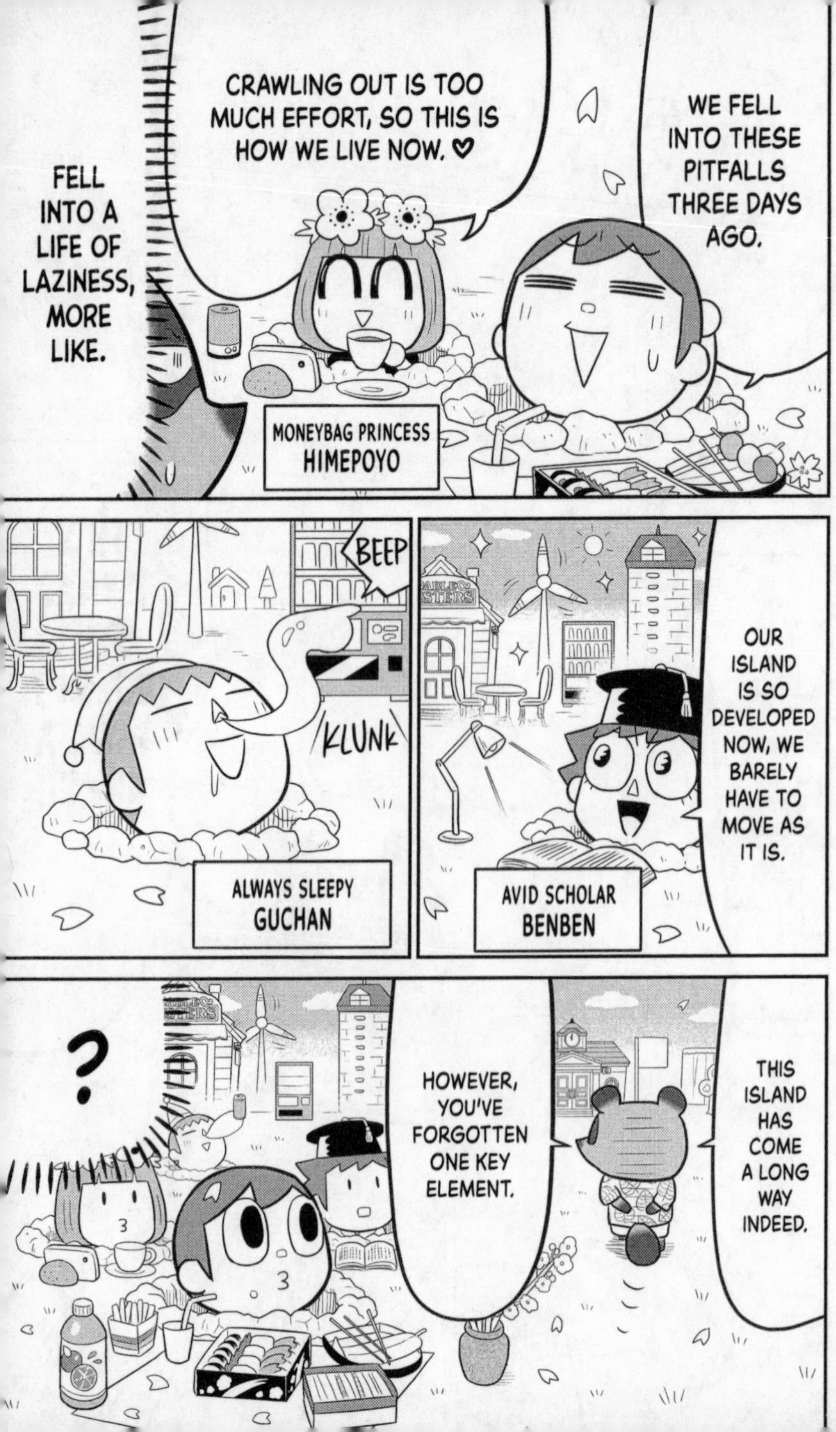
WE FELL INTO THESE PITFALLS THREE DAYS AGO.
CRAWLING OUT IS TOO MUCH EFFORT, SO THIS IS HOW WE LIVE NOW. ♡
FELL INTO A LIFE OF LAZINESS, MORE LIKE.
MONEYBAG PRINCESS HIMEPOYO
OUR ISLAND IS SO DEVELOPED NOW, WE BARELY HAVE TO MOVE AS IT IS.
AVID SCHOLAR BENBEN
BEEP
KLUNK
ALWAYS SLEEPY GUCHAN
THIS ISLAND HAS COME A LONG WAY INDEED.
HOWEVER, YOU'VE FORGOTTEN ONE KEY ELEMENT.
?

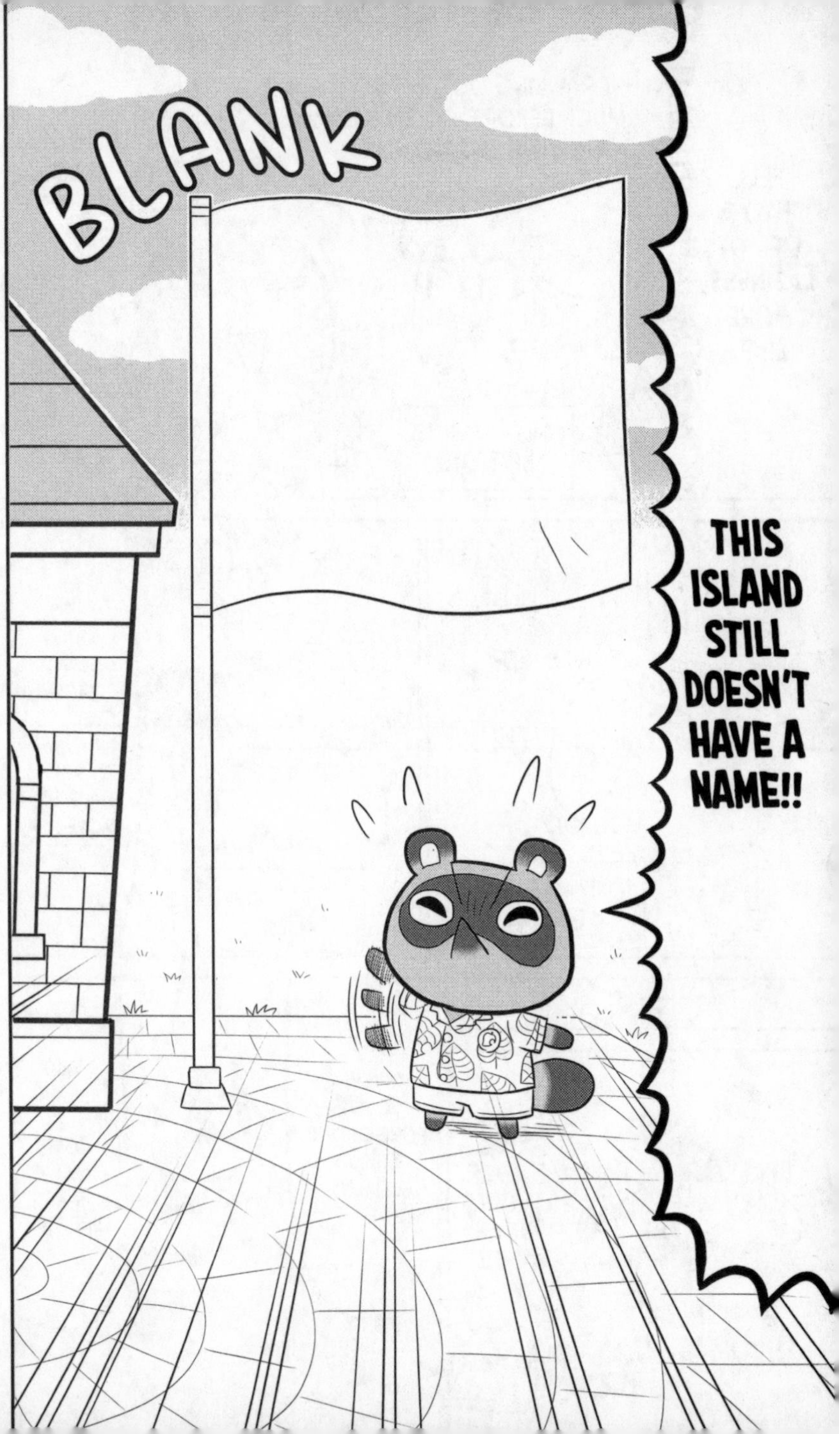
THIS ISLAND STILL DOESN'T HAVE A NAME!!
BLANK

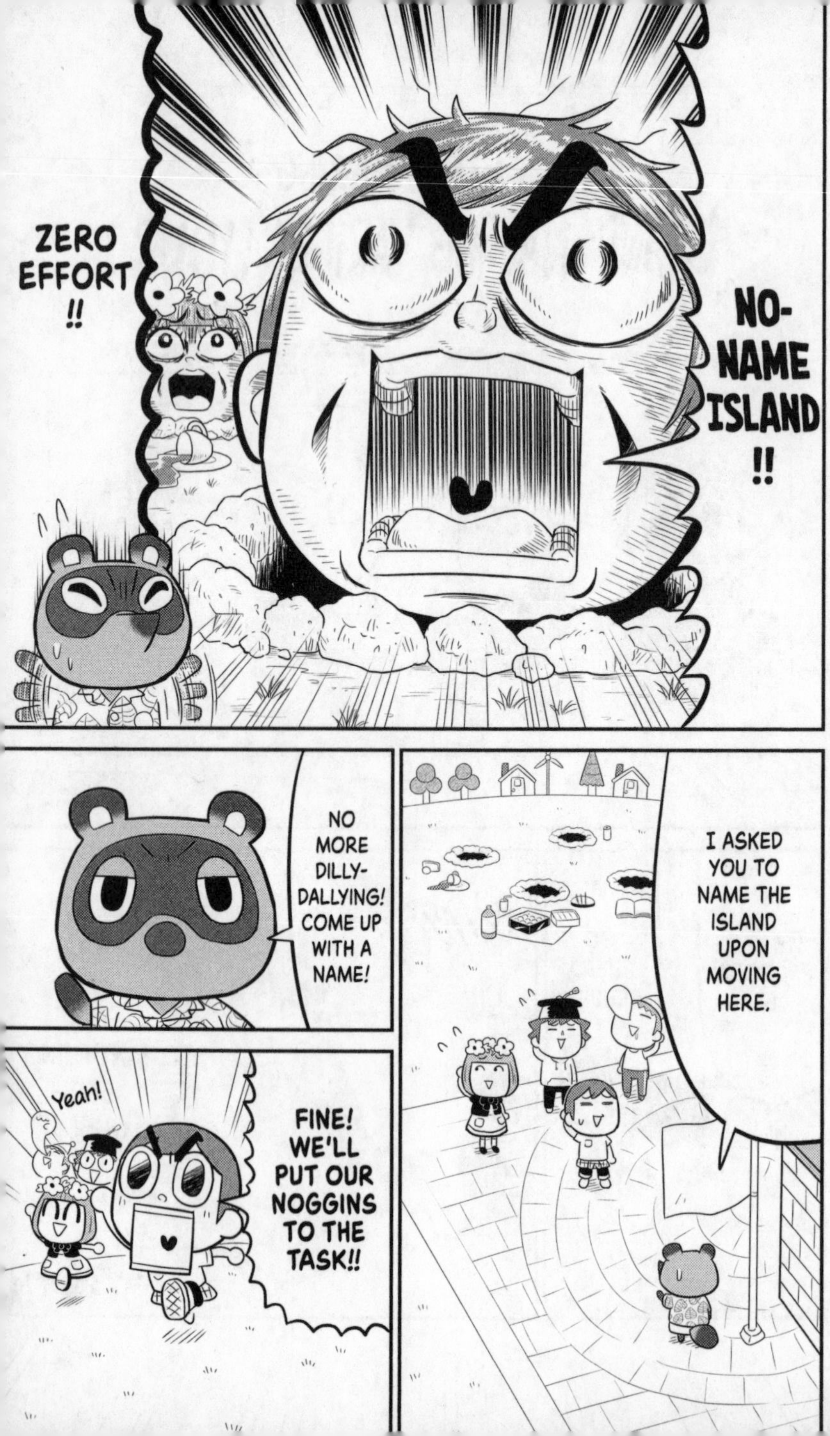
NO-NAME ISLAND!!
ZERO EFFORT!!
I ASKED YOU TO NAME THE ISLAND UPON MOVING HERE.
NO MORE DILLY-DALLYING! COME UP WITH A NAME!
FINE! WE'LL PUT OUR NOGGINS TO THE TASK!!
Yeah!

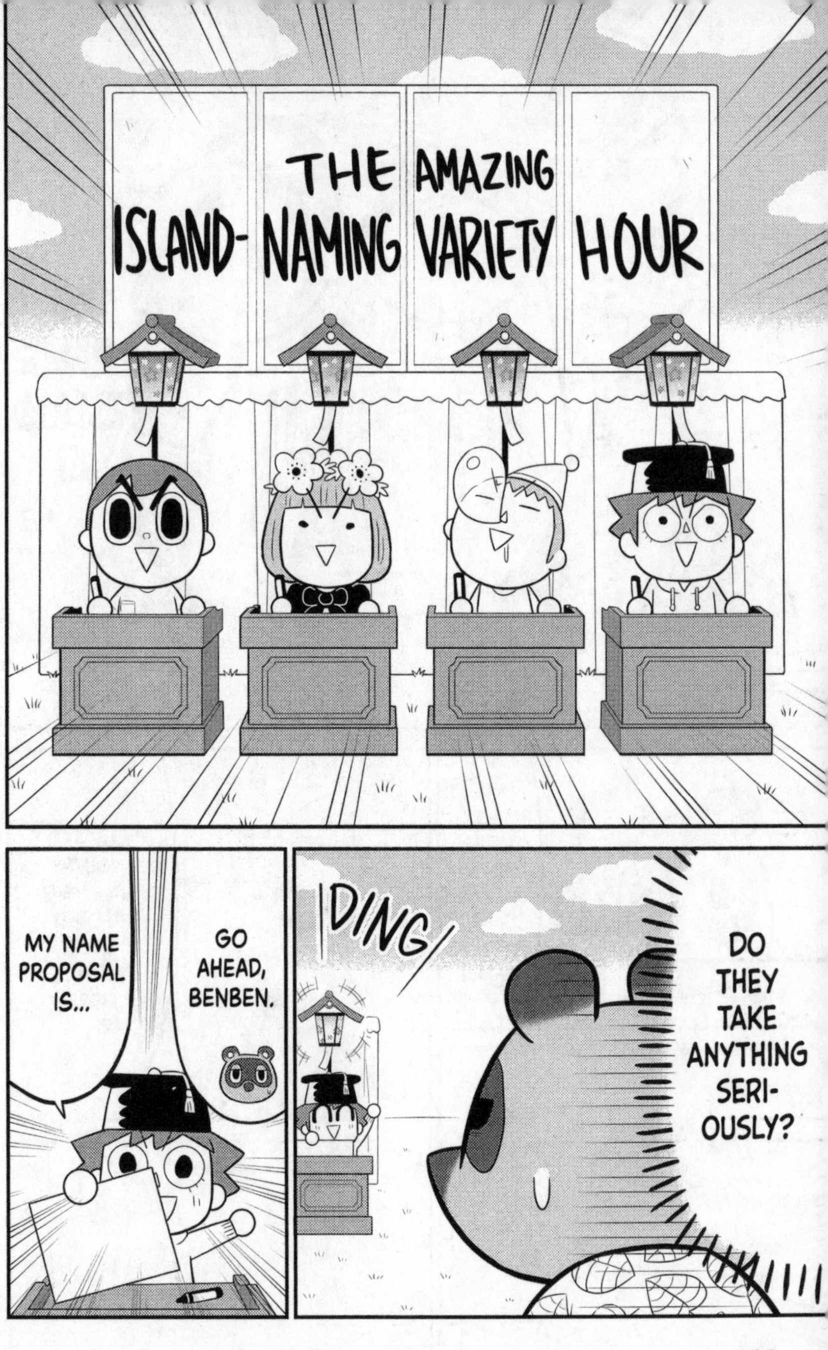
THE AMAZING ISLAND-NAMING VARIETY HOUR
DING
DO THEY TAKE ANYTHING SERI-OUSLY?
GO AHEAD, BENBEN.
MY NAME PROPOSAL IS...

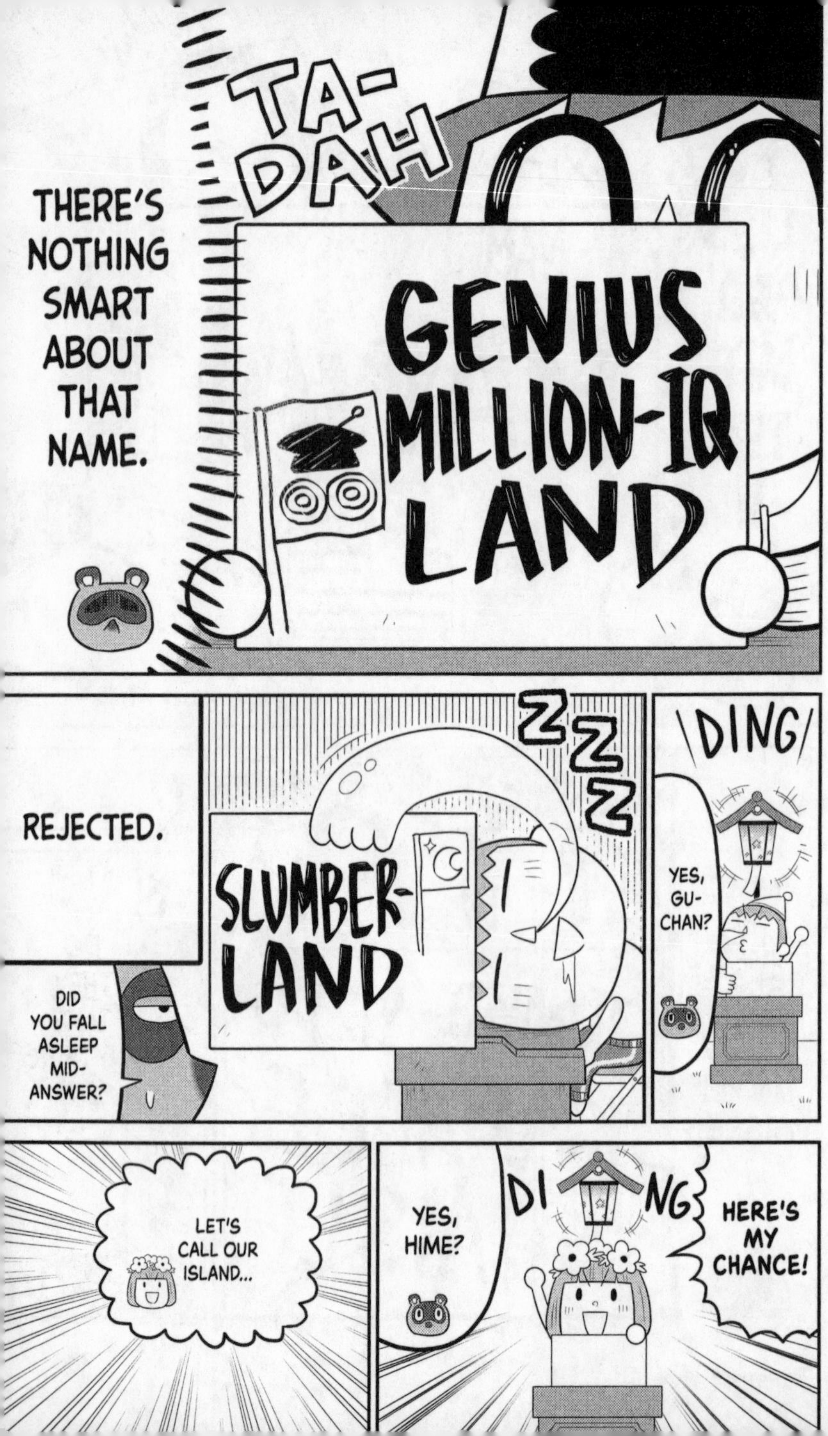
TA-DAH
GENIUS MILLION-IQ LAND
THERE'S NOTHING SMART ABOUT THAT NAME.
DING
YES, GU-CHAN?
ZZZ
SLUMBER-LAND
DID YOU FALL ASLEEP MID-ANSWER?
REJECTED.
HERE'S MY CHANCE!
DING
YES, HIME?
LET'S CALL OUR ISLAND...

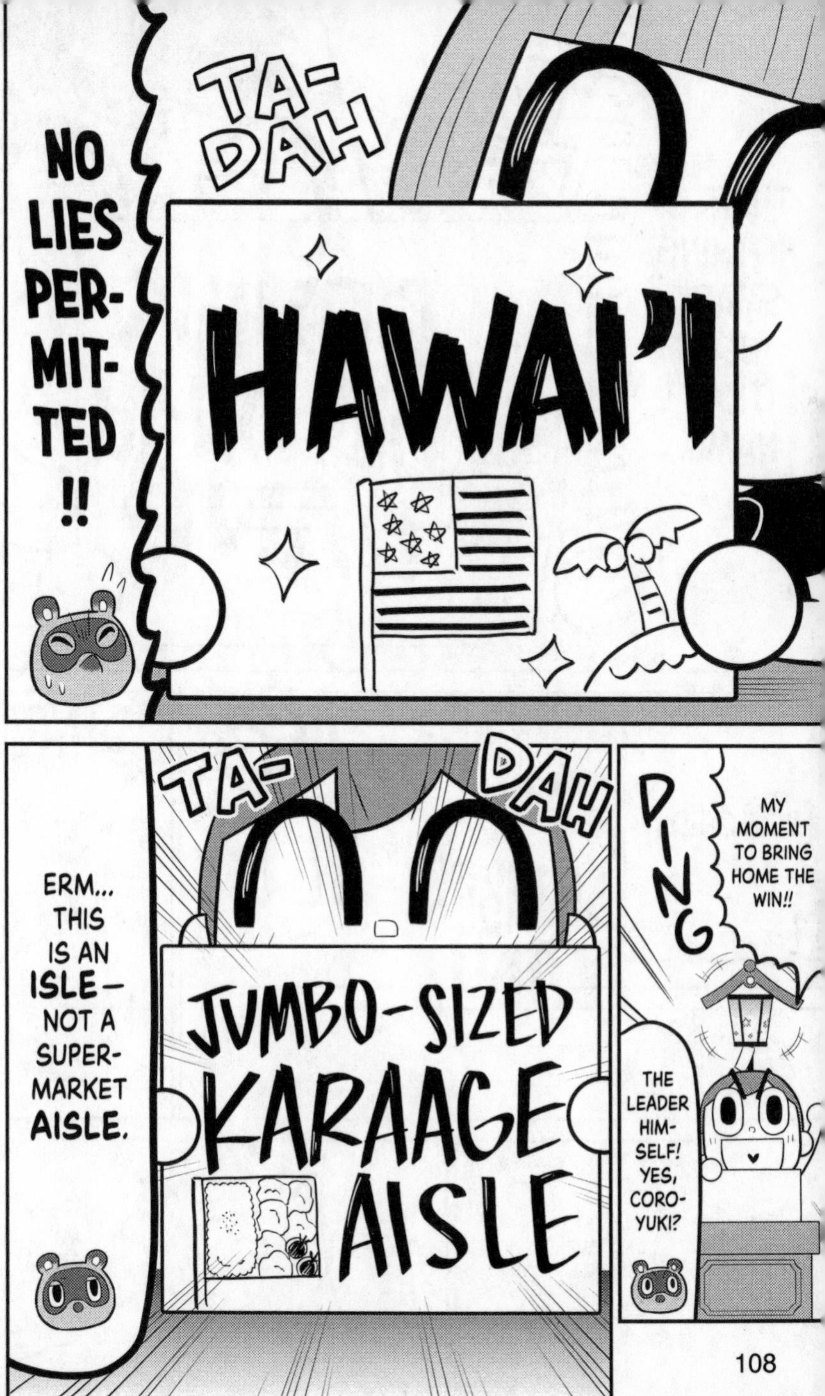
TA-DAH
HAWAI'I
NO LIES PERMITTED!!
DING
MY MOMENT TO BRING HOME THE WIN!!
THE LEADER HIMSELF! YES, COROYUKI?
TA-DAH
JUMBO-SIZED KARAAGE AISLE
ERM... THIS IS AN ISLE—NOT A SUPERMARKET AISLE.

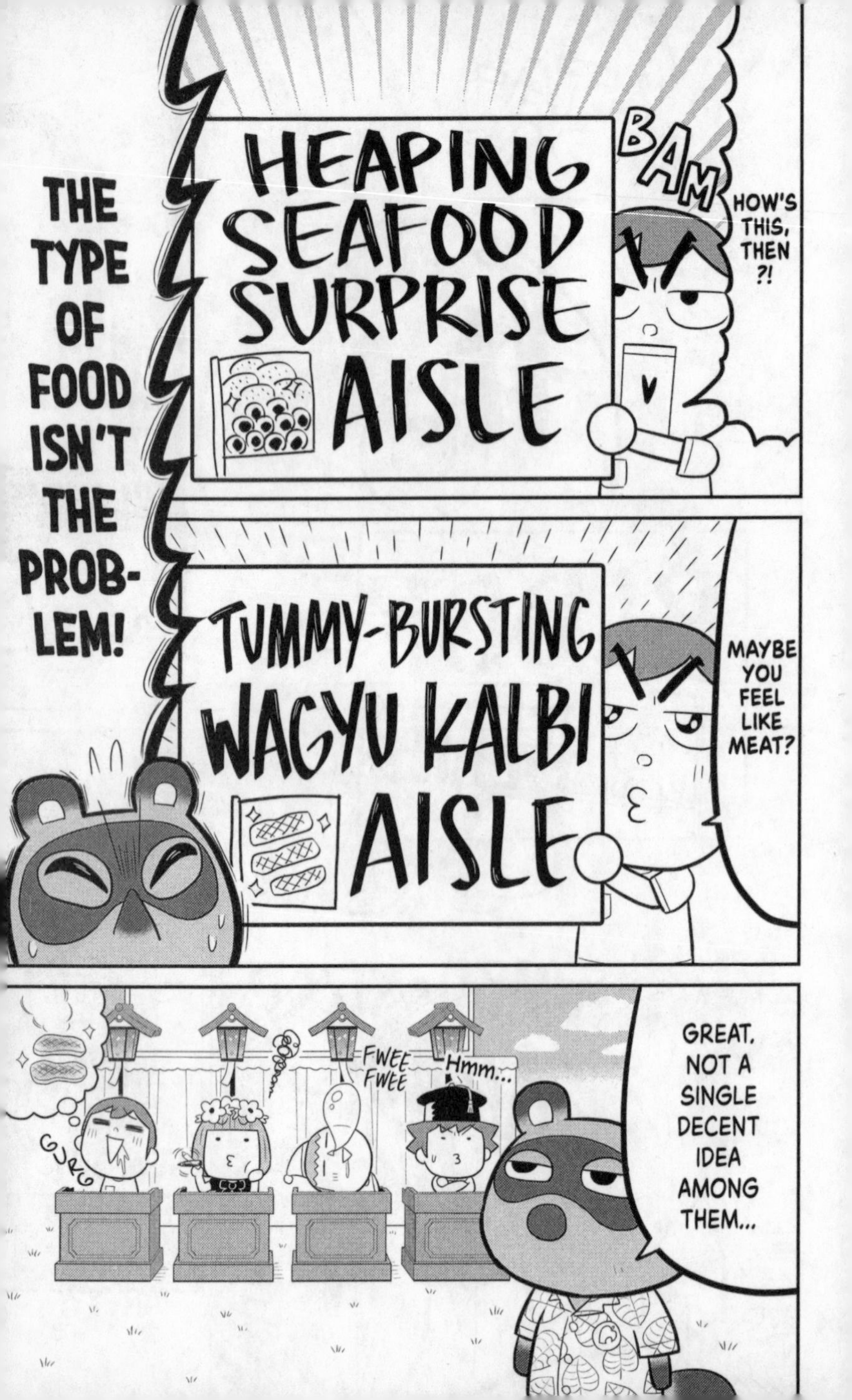
BAM
HOW'S THIS, THEN ?!
HEAPING SEAFOOD SURPRISE AISLE
MAYBE YOU FEEL LIKE MEAT?
TUMMY-BURSTING WAGYU KALBI AISLE
THE TYPE OF FOOD ISN'T THE PROB-LEM!
GREAT. NOT A SINGLE DECENT IDEA AMONG THEM...
Hmm...
FWEE FWEE
GURG

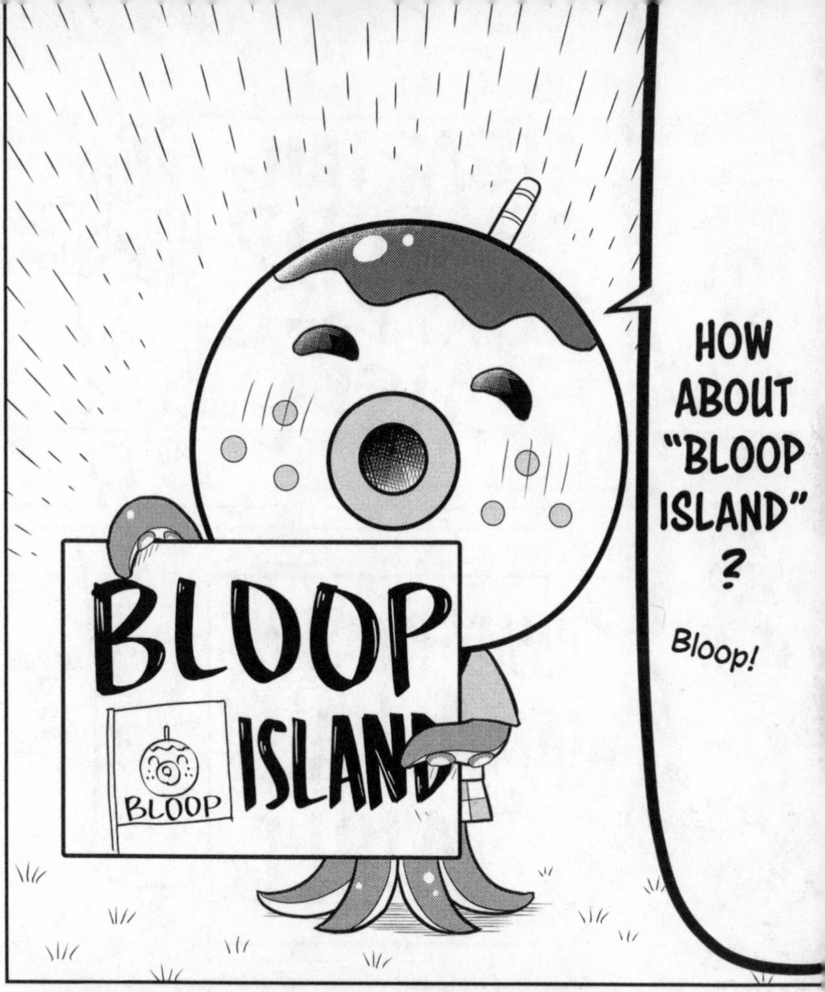
HOW ABOUT "BLOOP ISLAND"?
Bloop!
BLOOP ISLAND
BLOOP

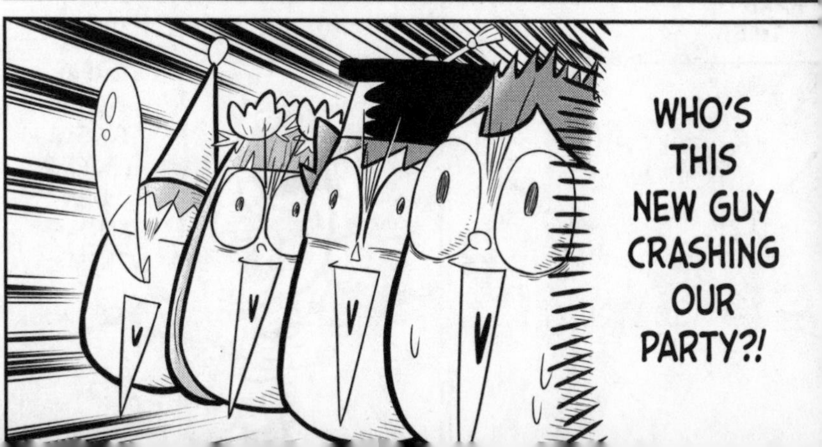
WHO'S THIS NEW GUY CRASHING OUR PARTY?!

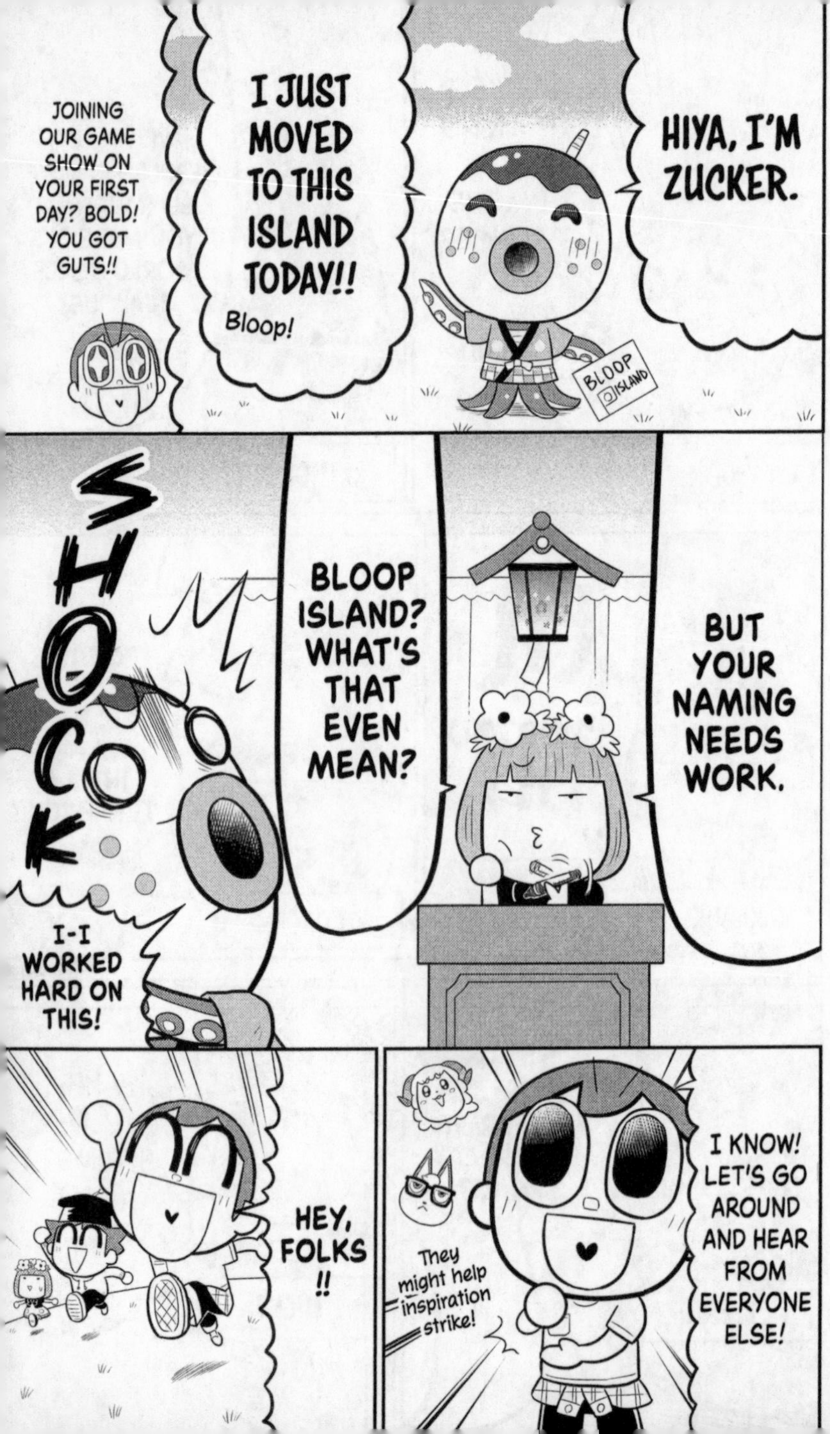
HIYA, I'M ZUCKER.
I JUST MOVED TO THIS ISLAND TODAY!!
Bloop!
BLOOP ISLAND
JOINING OUR GAME SHOW ON YOUR FIRST DAY? BOLD! YOU GOT GUTS!!
BUT YOUR NAMING NEEDS WORK.
BLOOP ISLAND? WHAT'S THAT EVEN MEAN?
SHOCK
I-I WORKED HARD ON THIS!
I KNOW! LET'S GO AROUND AND HEAR FROM EVERYONE ELSE!
They might help inspiration strike!
HEY, FOLKS!!

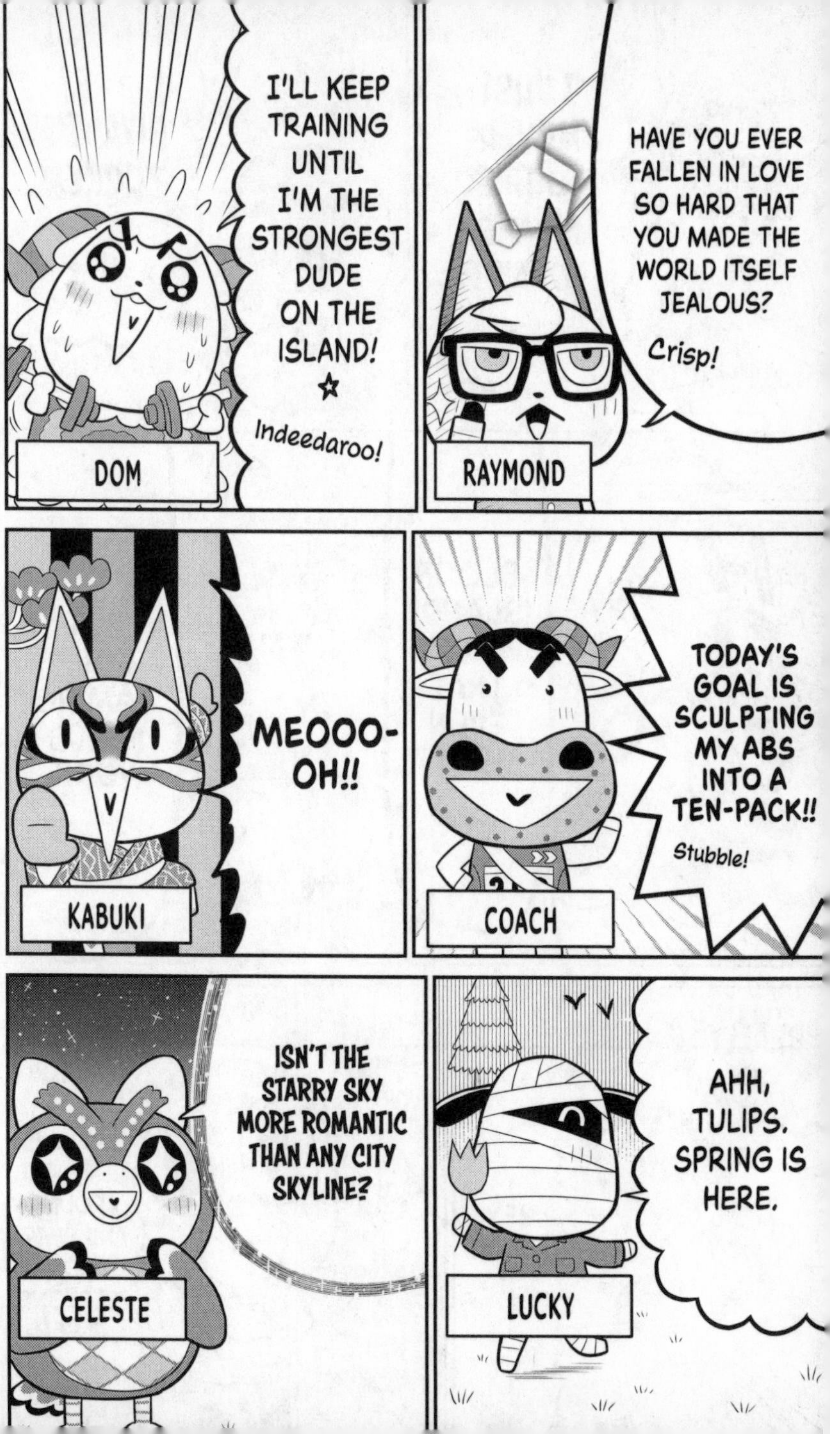
HAVE YOU EVER FALLEN IN LOVE SO HARD THAT YOU MADE THE WORLD ITSELF JEALOUS?
Crisp!
RAYMOND
I'LL KEEP TRAINING UNTIL I'M THE STRONGEST DUDE ON THE ISLAND! ☆
Indeedaroo!
DOM
TODAY'S GOAL IS SCULPTING MY ABS INTO A TEN-PACK!!
Stubble!
COACH
MEOOO-OH!!
KABUKI
AHH, TULIPS. SPRING IS HERE.
LUCKY
ISN'T THE STARRY SKY MORE ROMANTIC THAN ANY CITY SKYLINE?
CELESTE

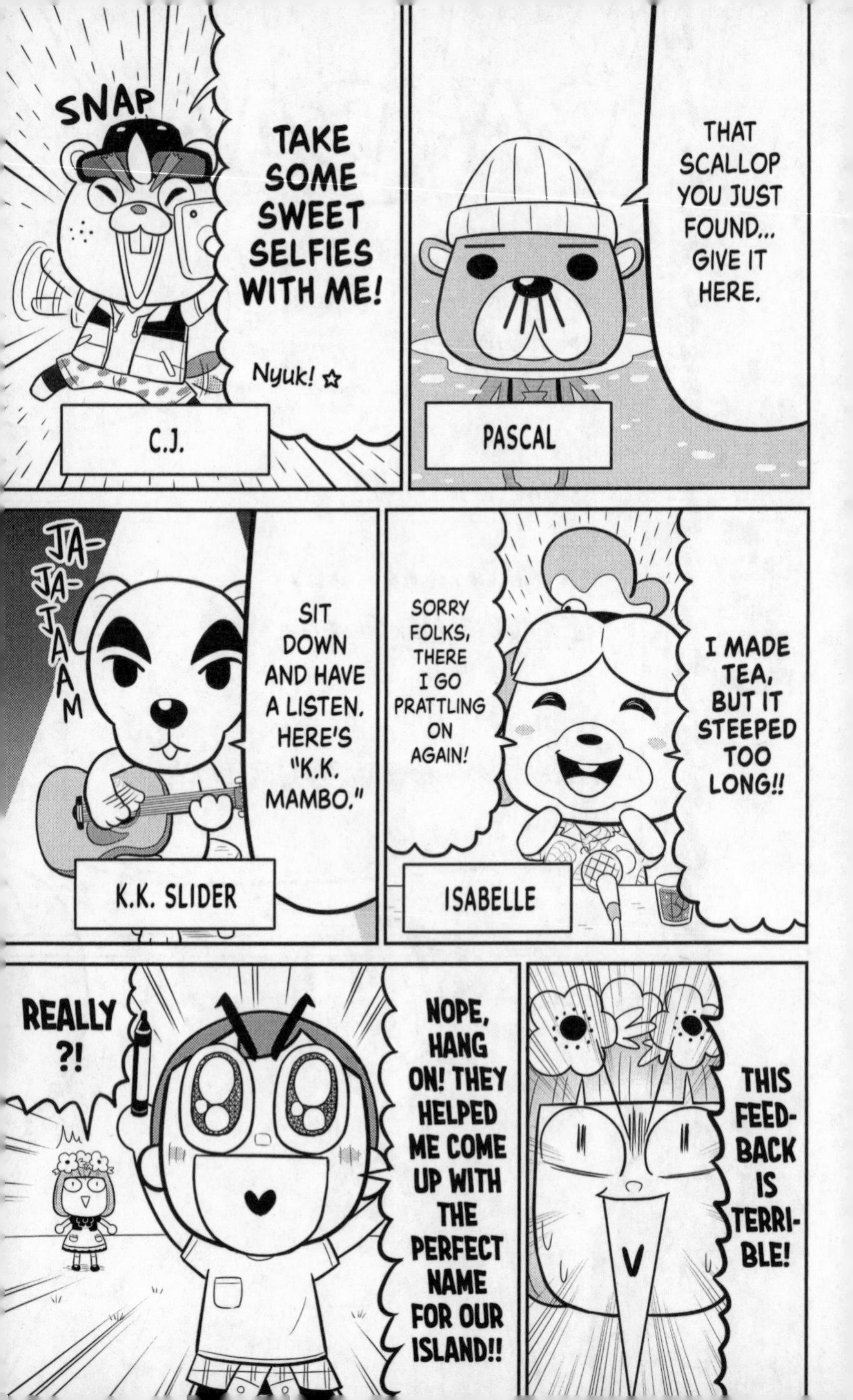
THAT SCALLOP YOU JUST FOUND... GIVE IT HERE.
PASCAL
TAKE SOME SWEET SELFIES WITH ME!
SNAP
Nyuk! ☆
C.J.
I MADE TEA, BUT IT STEEPED TOO LONG!!
SORRY FOLKS, THERE I GO PRATTLING ON AGAIN!
ISABELLE
SIT DOWN AND HAVE A LISTEN. HERE'S "K.K. MAMBO."
JA-JA-JAJAAM
K.K. SLIDER
THIS FEED-BACK IS TERRI-BLE!
NOPE, HANG ON! THEY HELPED ME COME UP WITH THE PERFECT NAME FOR OUR ISLAND!!
REALLY ?!

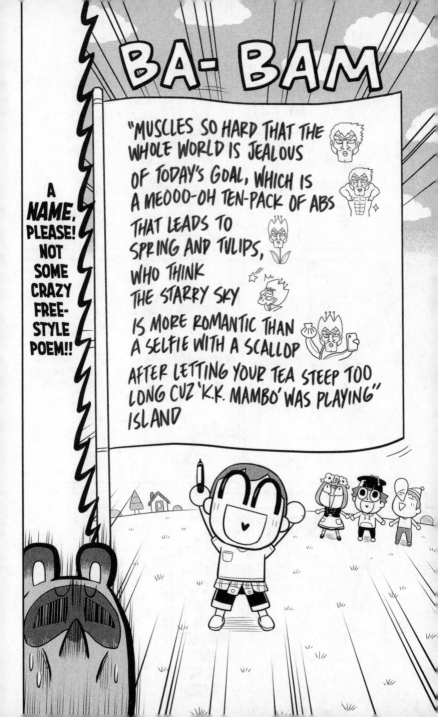

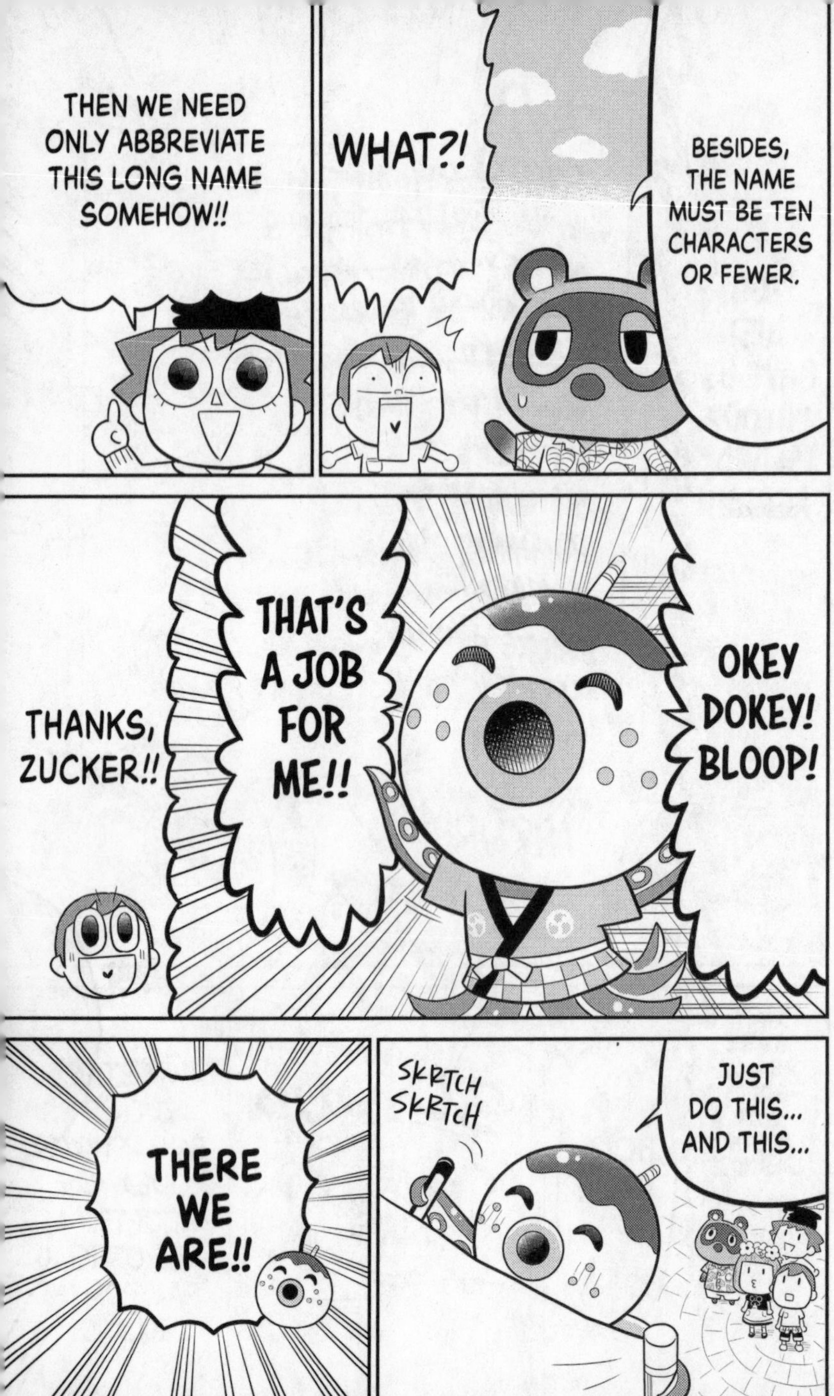
BESIDES, THE NAME MUST BE TEN CHARACTERS OR FEWER.
WHAT?!
THEN WE NEED ONLY ABBREVIATE THIS LONG NAME SOMEHOW!!
OKEY DOKEY! BLOOP!
THAT'S A JOB FOR ME!!
THANKS, ZUCKER!!
JUST DO THIS... AND THIS...
SKRTCH SKRTCH
THERE WE ARE!!

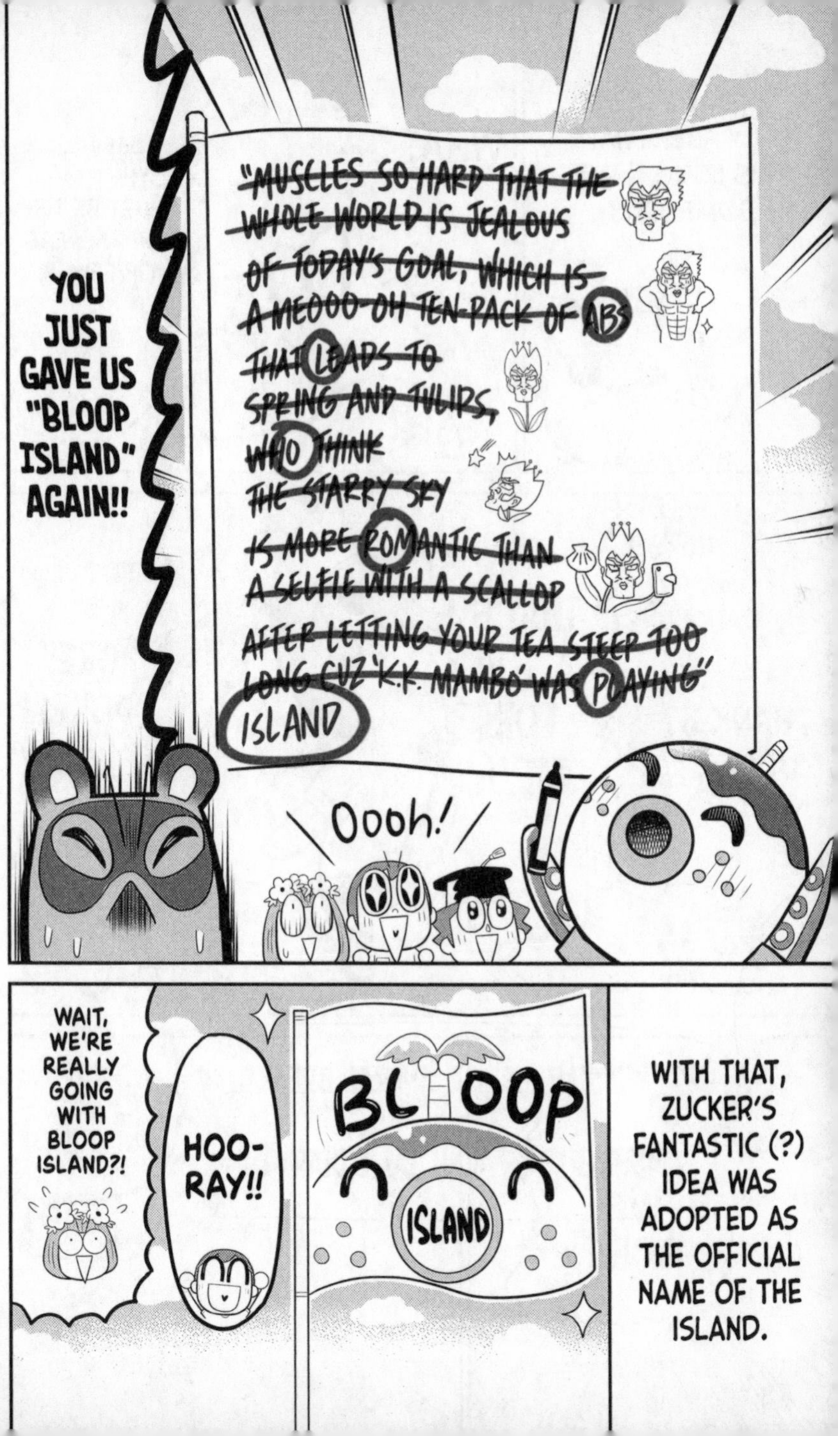
"MUSCLES SO HARD THAT THE WHOLE WORLD IS JEALOUS
OF TODAY'S GOAL, WHICH IS A MEOOO OH TEN-PACK OF ABS
THAT LEADS TO SPRING AND TULIPS,
WHO THINK THE STARRY SKY
IS MORE ROMANTIC THAN A SELFIE WITH A SCALLOP
AFTER LETTING YOUR TEA STEEP TOO LONG CUZ 'K.K. MAMBO' WAS PLAYING"
ISLAND
YOU JUST GAVE US "BLOOP ISLAND" AGAIN!!
Oooh!
WITH THAT, ZUCKER'S FANTASTIC (?) IDEA WAS ADOPTED AS THE OFFICIAL NAME OF THE ISLAND.
BLOOP
ISLAND
HOO-RAY!!
WAIT, WE'RE REALLY GOING WITH BLOOP ISLAND?!

Bonus Diary

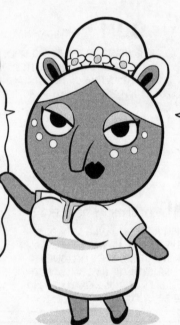

LET THE TENSION LEAVE YOUR BODY AND RELAAAX...
ALLOW YOURSELF TO JOURNEY TO THE CHARMING BONUS PAGES...

- RUMBA-STYLE ANIMAL BREAKDOWN
- RUMBA'S ACNH GAME DIARY

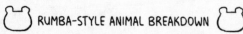

RUMBA-STYLE ANIMAL BREAKDOWN

RESIDENTS OF BLOOP ISLAND EDITION

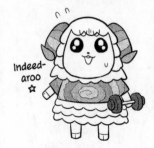

Indeed-aroo ☆

DOM (BIRTHDAY: MARCH 18)

HE MOVED TO THE ISLAND WHEN COROYUKI AND THE GANG DID. DOM'S CUTESY APPEARANCE BELIES A PASSION FOR STRENGTH TRAINING. HE'S A HOT-BLOODED GUY IN BOTH BODY AND SOUL!

RAYMOND (BIRTHDAY: OCTOBER 1)

ANOTHER FOUNDING RESIDENT ALONG WITH DOM, COROYUKI, AND THE OTHERS. HE WAS A FULL-BLOWN NARCISSIST AT FIRST BUT HAS SINCE MELLOWED OUT. BY INTERACTING WITH THE NATURAL WONDERS OF THE ISLAND, PERHAPS RAYMOND FINALLY FOUND SOMETHING MORE BEAUTIFUL THAN HIMSELF...

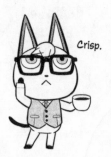

Crisp.

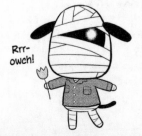

Rrr-owch!

LUCKY (BIRTHDAY: NOVEMBER 4)

DESPITE HIS BONE-CHILLING EXTERIOR, LUCKY IS FOND OF CUTE AND FANCY THINGS. HE'S GOT A GARDEN ON HIS SIDE OF BLOOP ISLAND WHERE HE GROWS FLOWERS AND PUMPKINS. LUCKY GETS ALONG WELL WITH BENBEN AND HOSTS A FANCY TEA PARTY ONCE A WEEK.

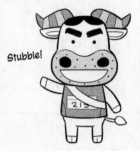

Stubble!

COACH (BIRTHDAY: APRIL 29)

AS A FELLOW MUSCLE MANIAC, COACH STARTED THE "GET SWOLE CLUB" WITH DOM. YOU WOULDN'T EXPECT THAT HE'S BEEN PLAYING PIANO FROM A YOUNG AGE UNTIL YOU HEAR THE LOVELY MUSIC COMING FROM HIS HOUSE... ♪

KABUKI (BIRTHDAY: NOVEMBER 29)

WITH HIS KABUKI-STYLE MAKEUP, THIS FAMOUS CAT PRACTICES HIS DISTINCTIVE MIE POSES AND PRETENDS THAT THE ISLAND'S DOCK IS HIS THEATER STAGE.

IS IT MERE COINCIDENCE THAT KABUKI'S BIRTHDAY IS JUST ONE DAY AFTER THAT OF GOLDEN BOMBER BAND MEMBER, KENJI DARVISH?!

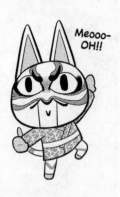

Meooo-OH!!

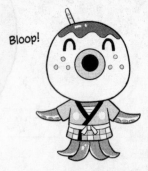

Bloop!

ZUCKER (BIRTHDAY: MARCH 8)

THE OCTOPUS WHO GAVE BLOOP ISLAND ITS NAME. THIS GENTLE FELLOW GOES ABOUT LIFE AT HIS OWN, EASY-BREEZY PACE, BUT HIS ABILITY TO LIGHTEN THE MOOD MAKES HIM A POPULAR RESIDENT.

HIMEPOYO IS THE ONLY ONE WHO REFUSES TO GET ON BOARD WITH ZUCKER'S CHOICE OF ISLAND NAME.

*THESE ARE ALL JUST RUMBA'S PERSONAL OPINIONS.

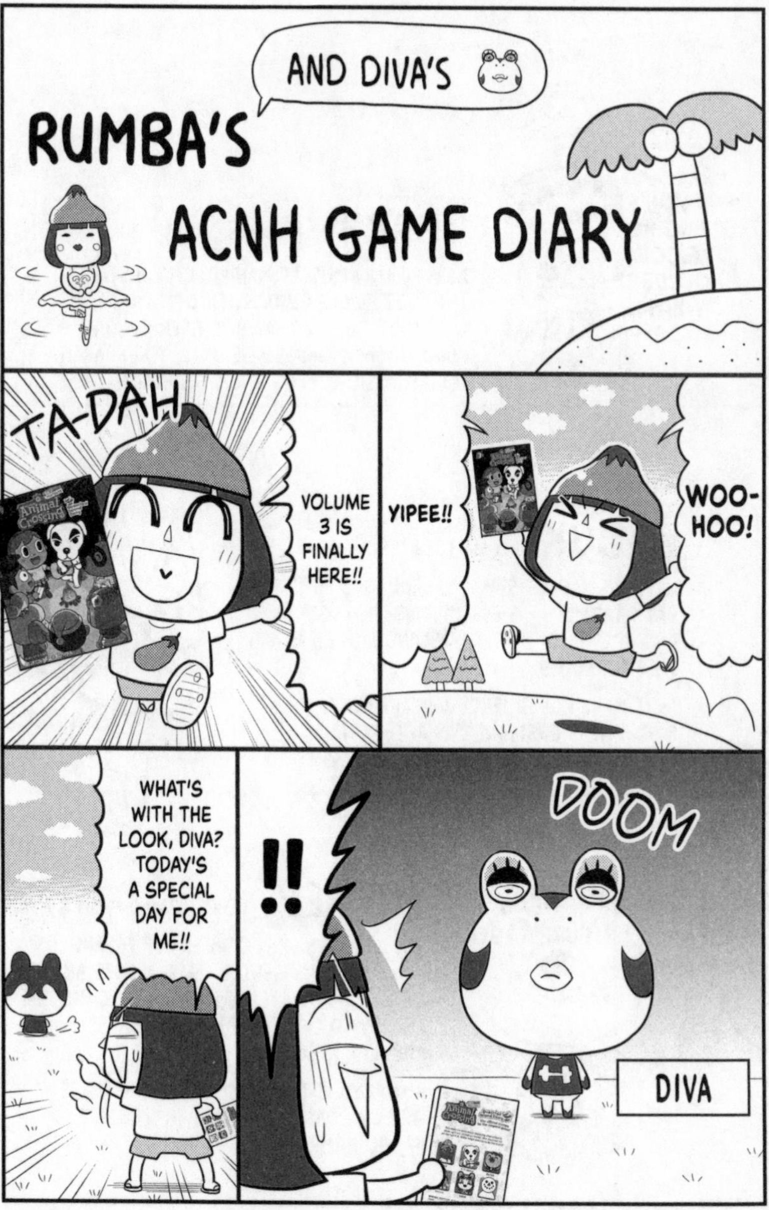
AND DIVA'S
RUMBA'S
ACNH GAME DIARY
WOO-HOO!
YIPEE!!
TA-DAH
VOLUME 3 IS FINALLY HERE!!
DOOM
!!
DIVA
WHAT'S WITH THE LOOK, DIVA? TODAY'S A SPECIAL DAY FOR ME!!

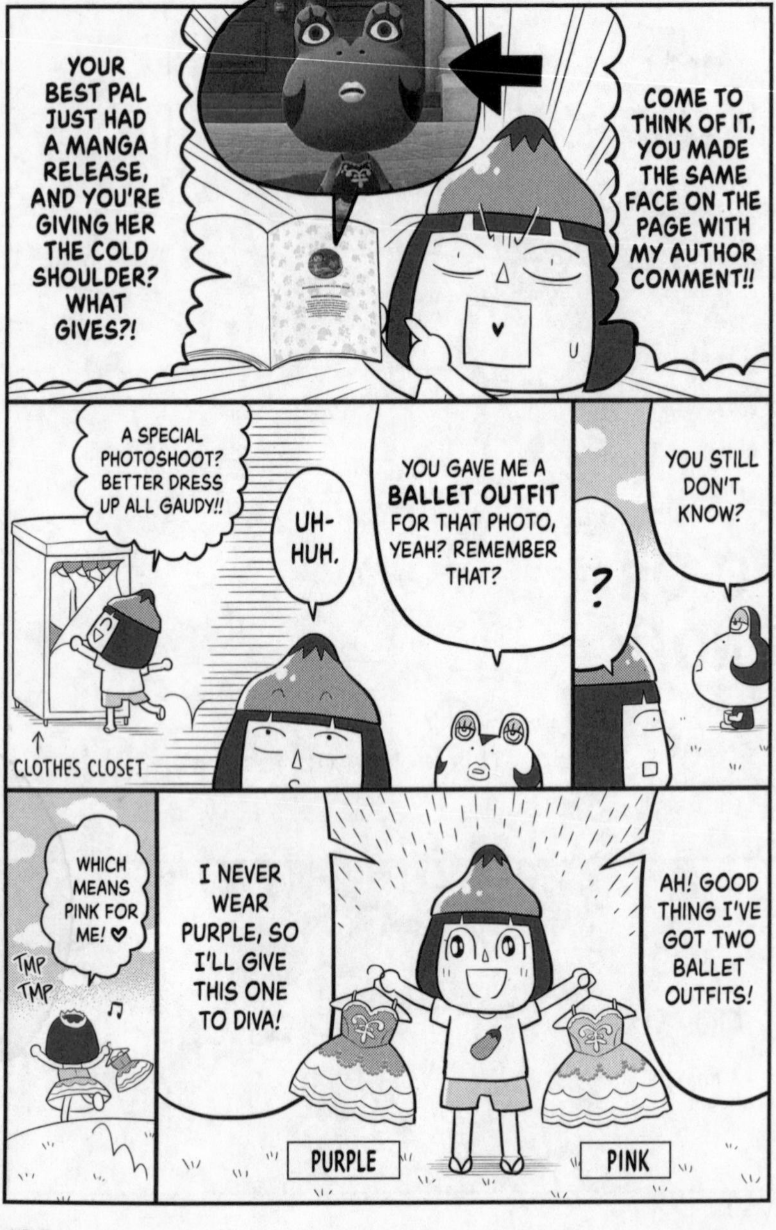
COME TO THINK OF IT, YOU MADE THE SAME FACE ON THE PAGE WITH MY AUTHOR COMMENT!!
YOUR BEST PAL JUST HAD A MANGA RELEASE, AND YOU'RE GIVING HER THE COLD SHOULDER? WHAT GIVES?!
YOU STILL DON'T KNOW?
?
YOU GAVE ME A BALLET OUTFIT FOR THAT PHOTO, YEAH? REMEMBER THAT?
UH-HUH.
A SPECIAL PHOTOSHOOT? BETTER DRESS UP ALL GAUDY!!
CLOTHES CLOSET
AH! GOOD THING I'VE GOT TWO BALLET OUTFITS!
I NEVER WEAR PURPLE, SO I'LL GIVE THIS ONE TO DIVA!
PINK
PURPLE
WHICH MEANS PINK FOR ME! ♡
TMP TMP
♫

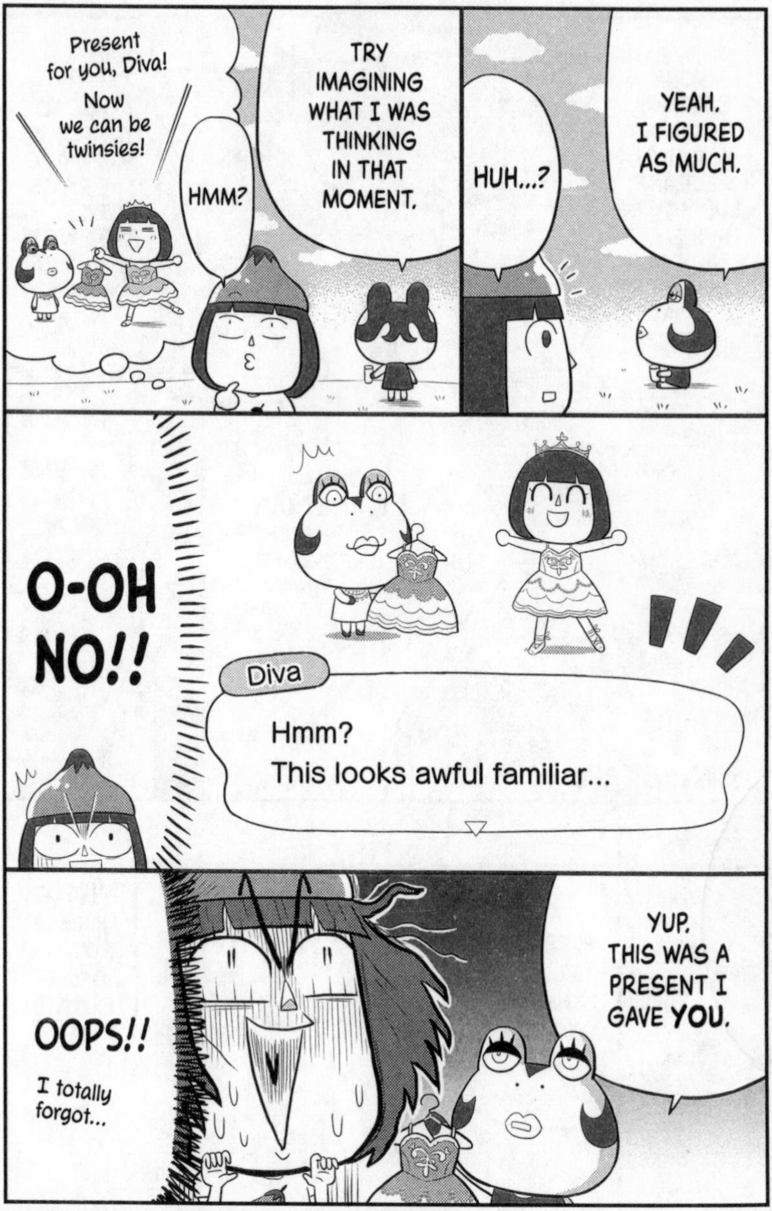
YEAH. I FIGURED AS MUCH.
HUH...?
TRY IMAGINING WHAT I WAS THINKING IN THAT MOMENT.
HMM?
Present for you, Diva!
Now we can be twinsies!
Diva
Hmm? This looks awful familiar...
O-OH NO!!
YUP. THIS WAS A PRESENT I GAVE YOU.
OOPS!!
I totally forgot...

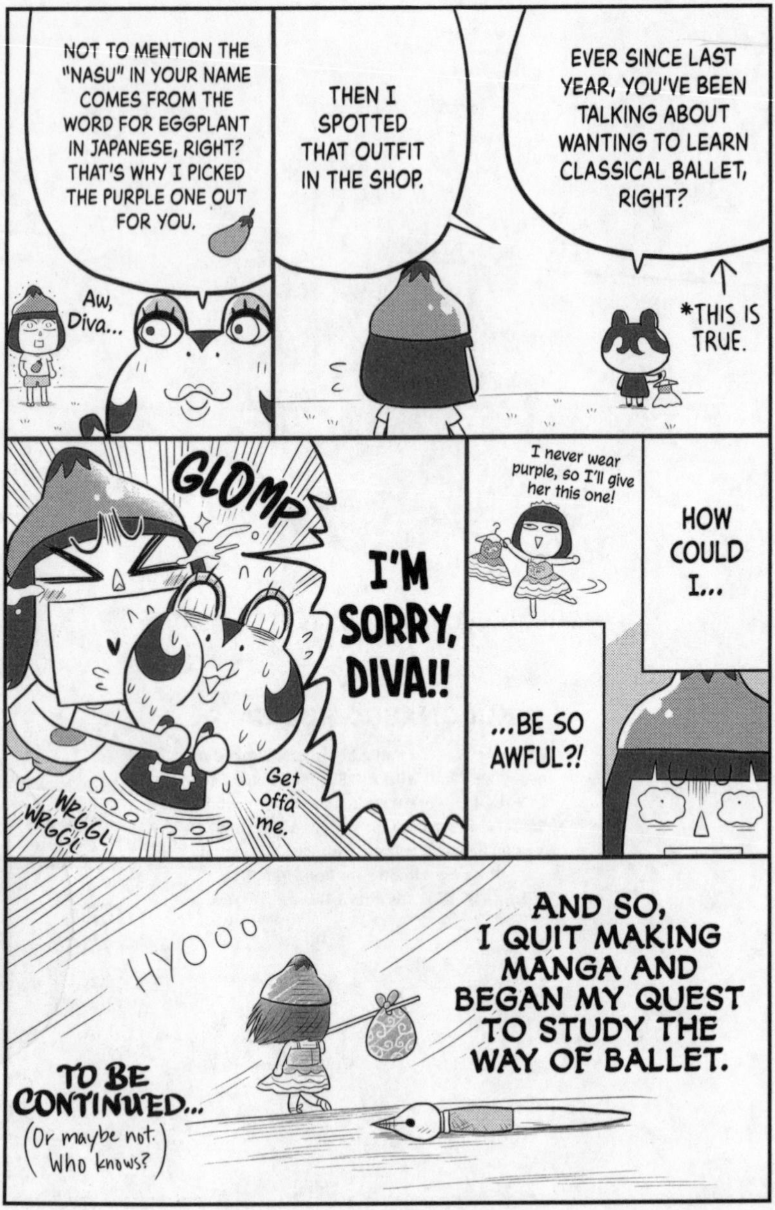
EVER SINCE LAST YEAR, YOU'VE BEEN TALKING ABOUT WANTING TO LEARN CLASSICAL BALLET, RIGHT?
*THIS IS TRUE.
THEN I SPOTTED THAT OUTFIT IN THE SHOP.
NOT TO MENTION THE "NASU" IN YOUR NAME COMES FROM THE WORD FOR EGGPLANT IN JAPANESE, RIGHT? THAT'S WHY I PICKED THE PURPLE ONE OUT FOR YOU.
Aw, Diva...
HOW COULD I...
I never wear purple, so I'll give her this one!
...BE SO AWFUL?!
I'M SORRY, DIVA!!
GLOMP
Get offa me.
WRGGL WRGGL
AND SO, I QUIT MAKING MANGA AND BEGAN MY QUEST TO STUDY THE WAY OF BALLET.
HYOOO
TO BE CONTINUED...
(Or maybe not. Who knows?)

VOL. 3/END

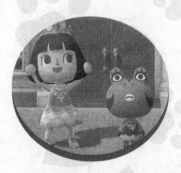

Matching looks with my BFF, Diva!!

KOKONASU☆RUMBA

A Tokyo native, she made her official *CoroCoro*
magazine debut with *Ai♡Burger Bakumaru*.
In 2013, her work *Pokupoku Pokuchin* won
an honorable mention for the 72nd Shogakukan
Newcomer Comics Prize, Children's Division.
She's best known for *Four-Panel
YO-KAI WATCH: Geragera Manga Theater.*

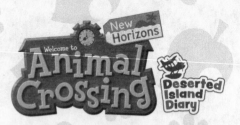

Welcome to
Animal Crossing
New Horizons
Deserted Island Diary

VIZ Media Edition • Volume 3

Story and Art by
KOKONASU☆RUMBA

Translation & Adaptation—Caleb Cook
Touch-Up Art & Lettering—Sara Linsley
Design—Shawn Carrico
Editor—Nancy Thistlethwaite

ATSUMARE DOBUTSU NO MORI -MUJINTO DIARY- Vol. 3
by KOKONASU☆RUMBA
© 2020 KOKONASU☆RUMBA
All rights reserved.
Original Japanese edition published by SHOGAKUKAN.
English translation rights in the United States of America,
Canada, the United Kingdom, Ireland, Australia and
New Zealand arranged with SHOGAKUKAN

Original Cover Design—Takuya KUROSAWA

The stories, characters, and incidents mentioned
in this publication are entirely fictional.

Printed in the U.S.A.

Published by VIZ Media, LLC
P.O. Box 77010
San Francisco, CA 94107

10 9 8 7 6 5 4 3 2 1
First printing, September 2022

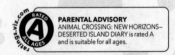

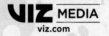

VIZ MEDIA
viz.com

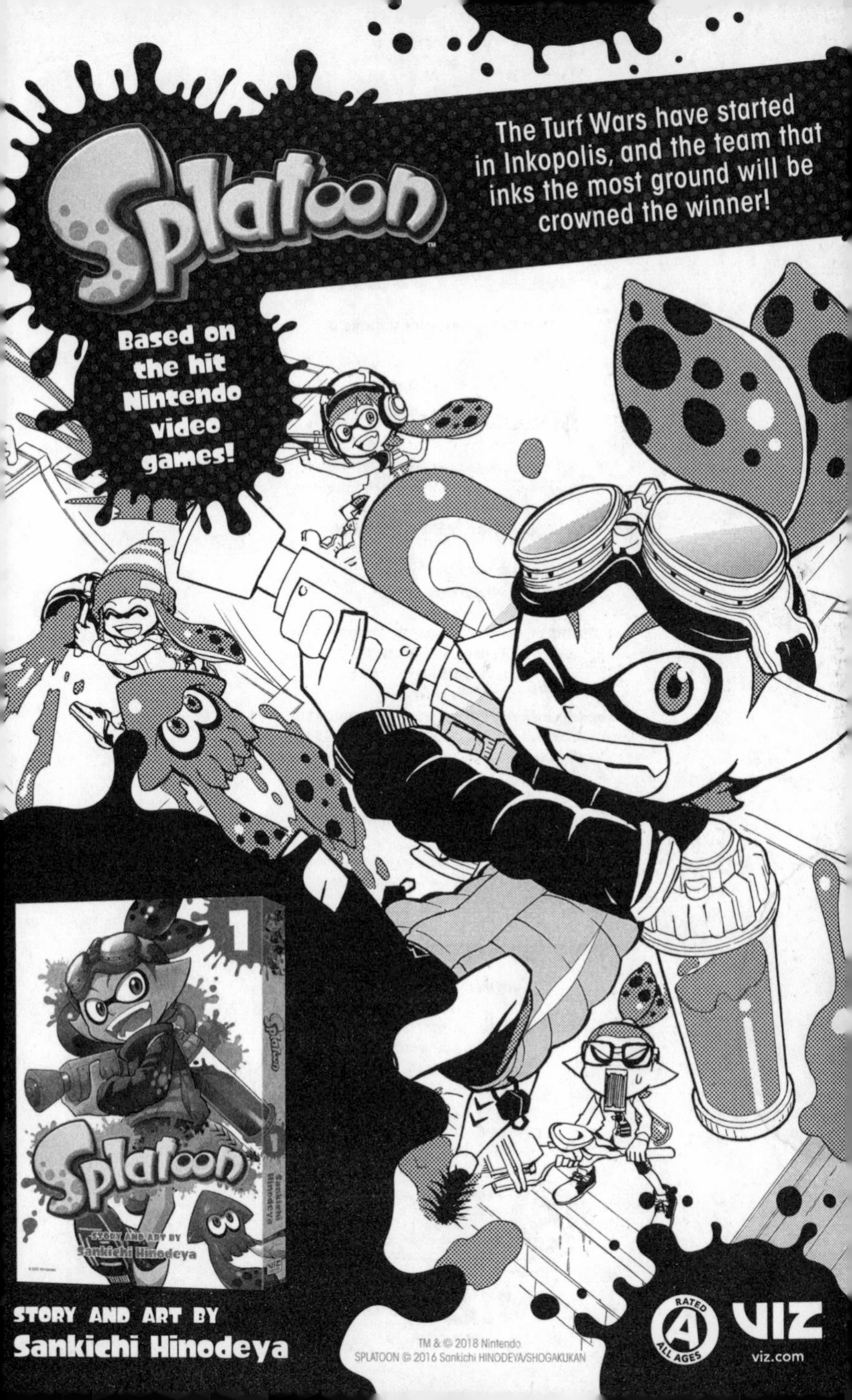

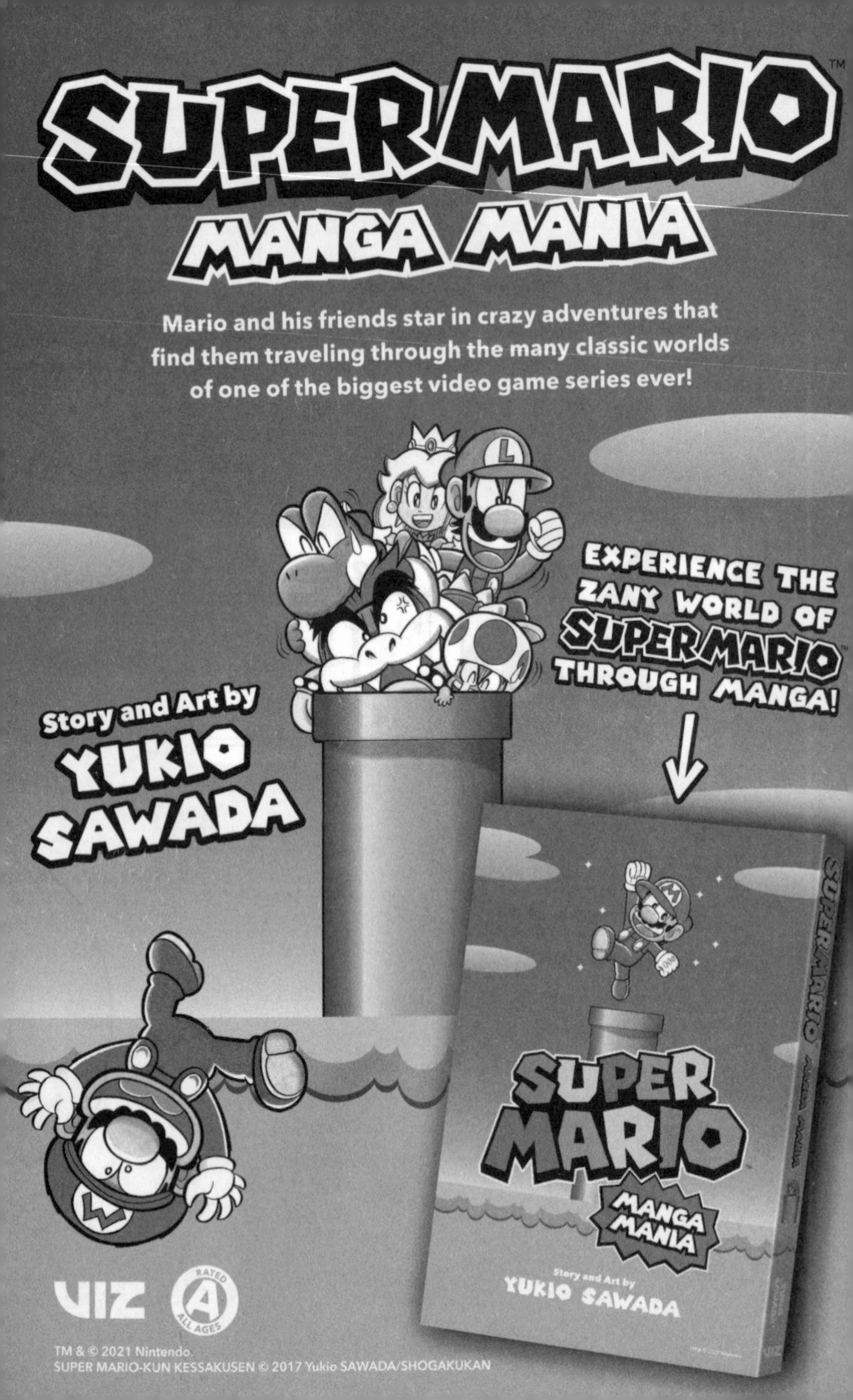
SUPER MARIO™
MANGA MANIA
Mario and his friends star in crazy adventures that find them traveling through the many classic worlds of one of the biggest video game series ever!
EXPERIENCE THE ZANY WORLD OF SUPER MARIO™ THROUGH MANGA!
Story and Art by
YUKIO SAWADA
SUPER MARIO
MANGA MANIA
Story and Art by
YUKIO SAWADA
VIZ
RATED A ALL AGES
TM & © 2021 Nintendo.
SUPER MARIO-KUN KESSAKUSEN © 2017 Yukio SAWADA/SHOGAKUKAN

THIS IS
THE LAST PAGE!

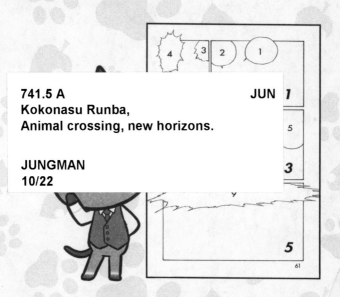

Animal Crossing: New Horizons—Deserted Island Diary
reads from right to left, starting in the upper-right
corner. Japanese is read from right to left, meaning
that action, sound effects, and word-balloon order
are completely reversed from English order.